D0645634

Also by Brad Meltzer

The Tenth Justice
Dead Even
The First Counsel
The Millionaires
The Zero Game
The Book of Fate

About the author

Brad Meltzer is the author of six bestselling thrillers. He is also the author of the graphic novel *Identity Crisis*, and is the co-creator of the critically acclaimed TV series *Jack & Bobby*. A graduate of the University of Michigan and Columbia Law School, he currently lives in Florida. To find out more, visit www.bradmeltzer.com.

THE BOOK
OF LIES

BRAD MELTZER

HODDER

First published in America in 2008 by Grand Central Publishing
First published in Great Britain in 2009 by Hodder & Stoughton
An Hachette UK company

First published in paperback in 2009

2

A CIP catalogue record for this title is available from the British Library

ISBN 978 0 340 84013 9

Typeset in Plantin Light by Palimpsest Book Production Limited,
Grangemouth, Stirlingshire

Printed and bound in the UK by CPI Mackays, Chatham ME5 8TD

Hodder & Stoughton policy is to use papers that are natural, renewable
and recyclable products and made from wood grown in sustainable
forests. The logging and manufacturing processes are expected to
conform to the environmental regulations of the country of origin.

Hodder & Stoughton Ltd
338 Euston Road
London NW1 3BH

www.hodder.co.uk

For my mom,
Teri Meltzer,
who still teaches me how fiercely,
how selflessly,
how beautifully,
a parent can love her child

ACKNOWLEDGMENTS

I believe that what you are now reading is the most important part of this book. And yes, the publisher again asked me to move it to the back, but keeping it right in front is the whole point. So thank you to all – especially you, our incredible readers – whose support is the only reason I get to dream these dreams: First and always, my Wonder Woman, Cori, whose strength and unwavering love convinced me to finally write this book, which is one I've been afraid of for years. I owe her forever for that. And I'll love her for all that time. Jonas, Lila, and Theo, you are the ones I dream for. You are the ones who inspire me. And the love in this father-child story is the love I keep for you. Jill Kneerim, my unwavering anchor, who believes I'm a better writer than I am, even when I fall short; Ike Williams, Hope Denekamp, Cara Shiel, Julie Sayre, and all our friends at the Kneerim & Williams Agency.

In this book about family, I need to thank my parents, who forever let me find my own adventures, especially the creative ones. They gave up so much for me. No one loves me more; my sister, Bari, who continues to lend me strength; Will Norman, for trusting me and reminding me about the real value of family; Dale Flam, whose reach and help knows no bounds; Bobby, Matt, Ami, and Adam, for more than they realize; Noah Kuttler, who is such a vital part of this process. He is a brother and mentor and keeps me intellectually honest about the craft. He also helps me feel cooler than the pathetic, bald little man that adulthood has turned me into. Thanks for pushing me, Calculator. Ethan Kline steers every early draft; Edna Farley, Kim from L.A., Marie Grunbeck, Georgie Brown, Maria Nelson, Michelle Perez-Carroll, and Brad Desnoyer, who do the true hard work; Paul Brennan, Matt Oshinsky, Paulo Pacheco, Joel Rose, Chris Weiss, and Judd Winick, such superfriends, who save me over and over.

As I've always maintained, every novel is a book of lies trying to masquerade as a book of truth. I therefore owe these people huge thank-yous for handing me the truths that are threaded throughout this book. First and without question, Jerry Siegel and Joe Shuster, the creators of Superman, for building something that has meant more to me than any other art form, including novels. For me, the best part of the story has never been the Superman part; it's the Clark Kent part – the idea that any of us, in all our ordinariness, can change the world. I only hope, even in the fictional universe, I did your stories justice. To that end, this is a book about heroes, which is why I was blessed to find so many new ones, so thanks to: Joanne Siegel, Laura Siegel Larson, Marlene Goodman, Rita Hubar, Norma Wolkov, and Jerry and Irving Fine for sharing their memories, their family, and their friendship; Zachary Mann, a dear friend who kept me honest on how crime is really fought in the federal world of ICE investigations; Michael San Giacomo, my master of all things super and all things Cleveland; Courtney at the TaskForce Fore Ending Homelessness, David Abel, and Laura Hansen and Scott Dimarzo at the Coalition to End Homelessness, who fight the good fight every single day; my law enforcement team of Matt Axelrod, Brenda Bauer, Dr John Fox, Steven Klein, Ed Kazarosky, Lisa Monaco, Maria Otero, Wally Perez, and Keith Prager, whose trust means so much; Mark Dimunation, Natalie Firhaber, Georgia Higley, Dianne L. van der Reyden, and Roberta Stevens answered every insane question about ancient book history; Hattie and Jefferson Gray, for sharing the Siegel house; Stan Lee, Paul Levitz, and Jerry Robinson, for so much more than comic book lore; Rabbi Steven Glazer, Rabbi David Golinkin, A. J. Jacobs, James L. Kugel, and Burton Visotzky, who helped steer and guide me through thousands of years of biblical interpretations; Paula Tibbetts and all the stories that came from Covenant House (1-800-999-9999, if you're young and on the street and need help); Brian Fischer, Terry Collins, and Marc C. Houk, for all the prison details; Grant Morrison and Geoff Johns for feeding my Cain fascination, and Mark Lewis and Robert Leighton, artists and puzzle-makers extraordinaire. I also had an incredible group from the Library of Congress who helped with so much of the research: Tema David, Katia Jones, Sara Duke, Martha Kennedy, Peggy Pearlstein, Teri Sierra, and Kathy Woodrell, as well as the librarians at the Western Reserve Historical Society; Gerard Jones's *Men of Tomorrow*, James L. Kugel's *How to Read the Bible*, Louis Ginzberg's *The Legends of the Jews*, Simon Singh's *The Code Book*, and Ruth Mellinkoff's *The Mark of Cain* were all invaluable to this process. Dr Ronald K. Wright and Dr Lee Benjamin yet again aided my medical details; John Ingrassia, Alex Miller, Leslie Collman-Smith, Matt Stringer, Tony Ward, and everyone at Sony BMG for their tremendous vision (check out the companion soundtrack they made for this book at www.BradMeltzer.com); and John Goins, Michael

Orkin, Jacob Booth, Jeff and Emily Camiener, Janet Doniger, and Jessica Gardner trusted me with traits I truly hold dear, especially the ones you see in the characters. Finally, Stewart Berkowitz, Matthew Bogdanos, David Brazil, Sy Frumkin, Jerry Gottlieb, Mike and Laure Heuer, Jay Kislak, Abe Laeser, Brian Lewis, Tony and Jonna Mendez, Ben Powell, Tom Savini, Raquel Suarez, Andy Wright, and Mark Zaid lent their expertise to so many different details; Rob Weisbach for the initial faith; and of course, my family and friends, whose names, as always, inhabit these pages.

I also want to thank everyone at Grand Central Publishing: David Young, Maureen Egen, Emi Battaglia, Jennifer Romanello, Evan Boorstyn, Chris Barba, Martha Otis, Karen Torres, the kindest and hardest-working sales force in show business, Harvey-Jane Kowal, Mari Okuda, Thomas Whatley, Jim Spivey, and all the dear friends who, over the years, have helped build what we're building. I've said this before, but it's still true: They're the real reason this book is in your hands. Also, thanks to Mitch Hoffman, whose insights and editing changed the course of Cal's story. So glad to have you in the family. Finally, let me thank Jamie Raab. When I told her what this book was about, she never hesitated. She forced me to challenge myself, and for that, I am blessed. Thank you, Jamie, for knowing that the best stories are the ones we believe in, and most important, for your faith.

The story of Cain and Abel takes up just sixteen lines
of the Bible.

It is arguably history's most famous murder.

But the story is silent about one key detail: the weapon
Cain used to kill his brother.

It's not a rock. Or a sharpened stone.

And to this day, the world's first murder weapon is still
lost to history.

PROLOGUE

Nineteen years ago
Miami, Florida

When Calvin Harper was five, his petite, four-foot-eleven-inch mom ripped the pillow from his bed at three a.m. and told him that dust mites were feeding off his skin. 'We need to wash it. *Now!*' On that night, his mom seemed to change into someone else, as if she were possessed by some ghost or devil . . . or demon.

His dad told Calvin it was one of Mommy's 'bad days.' The doctors had a name for it, too. Bipolar.

When Calvin was seven, his mom called home with a cheery slur in her voice (the demon loved a good drink) to proudly tell him she had carved Calvin's initials in her arm. When Calvin was eight and she was in a drunken rage, she took the family dog to the pound and 'accidentally' had him put down. The demon liked laughs.

But none of those nights prepared Calvin for this one.

Fresh from his bath, with his white blond hair still soaking wet and dangling over the birthmark near his left eye, nine-year-old Calvin sat in his room, bearing down on his paper with an orange Crayola, while his parents shouted in the kitchen.

Tonight, the demon was back.

'Rosalie, put it *down*!' his father growled.

Crash.

'*Get away from me, Lloyd!*' his mother howled. *Clang.*

His father grunted. '*That's it – you're done!*' he screamed back.

'*You're done!*'

Cling. Clang. Cling.

Calvin twisted the doorknob, ran for the kitchen, and froze as he turned the corner. All the kitchen's lower drawers were open and empty, their contents – pans, pot lids – scattered across the floor. In the corner, the fridge was open, too – and picked just as clean. Jars of ketchup, soda, and spaghetti sauce were still spinning on the floor. In the center of the kitchen, his six-foot-two-inch dad was bent forward in pain as Mom brandished a fat white jar of mayonnaise, ready to smash her husband in the head.

'Mom?' Calvin said in a small voice.

His mother wheeled around, off balance. The jar fell from her grip. Calvin saw it plummet. As it hit the floor and exploded, there was a low, thick *pooomp*, sending a mushroom cloud of mayo spraying across the floor. Calvin's mother never flinched.

'*You always root against me!*' she seethed at her nine-year-old boy with her dark, alligator green eyes.

'Maniac!' his dad erupted, and with one brutal shove pummeled his wife squarely in the chest.

'*Mom!*' Calvin shouted.

The blow hit her like a baseball bat, sending her stumbling backward.

'*Mom, look out for—*'

Her heel hit the mayonnaise at full speed and she flipped backward like a seesaw. If Lloyd hadn't been so big or so enraged . . . if he hadn't blown up with such a fierce physical outburst . . . he might not have shoved her so hard. But he did. And as she fell backward, still looking at Calvin, she had no idea that the back of her neck was headed straight toward the lower kitchen drawer that was still wide open.

Calvin tried to run forward but could scarcely lift his arms and legs.

In mid-air, his mother was turned toward him, her alligator eyes still burning through him. There was no mistaking her final thought. She wasn't scared. Or even in pain. She was angry. At him. The white blond, wet-haired boy who caused her to drop the mayo and . . . from that day forward, in his nine-year-old mind . . . the person who caused her to fall.

'*Mom!*'

She was falling. Falling. Then—

The sound was unforgettable.

'*Rosie!*' his father screamed, leaping forward and scooping her head toward his chest. Her arms rag-dolled across the mayonnaise-smeared floor.

'Calvin, don't you look!' Lloyd cried. The tears were running down his twisted Irish nose. '*Close your eyes! Don't you look!*'

But Calvin looked. He wanted to cry, but nothing came. He wanted to run but couldn't move. As he stood frozen, a stream of urine ran down his right leg.

Most lives crumble over time. Cal Harper's crumbled in one crashing fall. But nineteen years later, thanks to a single call on his radio, he'd begin his quest through history and finally have a chance to put his life together.

1

Nineteen years later
Hong Kong

'Good girl – such a *good girl*,' Ellis said, down on one knee as his dog snatched the beef treat from his open palm. With a bite and a gulp, the treat was gone, and Ellis Belasco, with his sleek copper red hair, smiled proudly and added a strong authoritative pat to the back of his smoky brown pet's neck. As the trainer said, attack dogs had to be rewarded.

'P-Please . . . my leg . . . *he chewed my leg!*' the thin Chinese man whined as he crawled across the worn beige carpet toward the hotel room door.

'To be clear, she chewed your Achilles' tendon,' Ellis said, calmly standing up and brushing back his long European-style haircut – he was always meticulous – to reveal amber eyes framed by striking, lush eyebrows that almost merged on the bridge of his nose. Because of his rosy coloring, his cheeks were always flushed, as were his full lips, which he licked as he stared down at a small tattoo between his thumb and pointer finger.

His birthright was healing nicely.

For the past two months, Ellis had been tracking the ancient book from collector to collector – from the doctor in China whose death gave it away, to Zhao, the shipper, who schemed to deliver it elsewhere. Every culture called it by a different name, but Ellis knew the truth.

'I know you have it,' Ellis said. 'I'd like the Book of Lies now.'

From the corner of the bed, Ellis reached for his small gray pistol.

'*Nonono* . . . you can't— *My fiancée— We just got engaged!*' the young dockworker begged, scrambling on his one good knee as his other leg left a smear of blood across the carpet.

Ellis pressed the barrel of his gun against the man's throat. It was vital he hit the jugular. But he knew he would. That was the advantage of having God on your side. 'I paid what you asked me, Zhao,' Ellis said calmly. 'But it makes me sad that someone else clearly paid you more.'

'I swear – the book – *I told you where it's going!*' Zhao screamed, his eyes rolling toward the pistol as Ellis glanced out the hotel window, into the dim alley. The view was awful – nothing more than a blank brick wall. But that was why Ellis had Zhao meet him here. No view, no witnesses.

With a squeeze, Ellis shot him in the throat.

There was no bang, just a pneumatic hiss. Zhao jerked slightly, and his eyes blinked open. . . . '*Ai! Ai, that—!* What *was* that?' he stuttered as a drop of blood bubbled from his neck.

The military called them 'jet injectors.' Since World War I, they had been used to vaccinate soldiers quickly and easily. There was no needle. The burst of air was so strong, it drilled through the skin with nothing more than a disposable air cartridge and the one-use red nozzle that looked like a thimble with a tiny hole. All you'd feel was the snap of a rubber band, and the vaccine was in your blood. For Ellis, it was a bit overdramatic, but if he was to find the Book that had been taken from him . . . that had been taken from his family . . . He knew every war had rules. His great-grandfather left him this gun – or the plans for this gun, at least – for a reason. It took time and patience to build it from scratch. Ellis had plenty of both.

'Forty . . . thirty-nine . . . thirty-eight . . .' Ellis began to count, peeking under the wrist of his starched shirt and checking his new Ulysse Nardin watch.

'Wait . . . ! The shot—! *What'd you put in me!?*' Zhao screamed, gripping the side of his neck.

'. . . thirty-seven . . . thirty-six . . . thirty-five . . .' Ellis said, his voice as serene as ever. 'My family first encountered it in Belgium. *Conium maculatum.* Hemlock.'

'Are you—? *You put hemlock—!? You put a poison – are you a fool!? Now you get nothing!*' Zhao yelled, fighting hard as he thrashed and crawled toward the door.

In a way, Zhao was right. Shooting him *was* a gamble. But Ellis knew . . . it's not a gamble when you know you'll win. After unscrewing the empty hemlock vial, he replaced it with a vial filled with a cloudy yellow liquid.

'I-Is that the antidote?' Zhao asked. 'It is, isn't it!?'

Ellis stepped back, away from his victim's reach. 'Do you know who Mitchell Siegel is, Zhao?'

'Wh-What're you talking about?'

'Thirty-one . . . thirty . . . twenty-nine . . . In 1932, a man named Mitchell Siegel was shot in the chest and killed. While mourning the death of his father, his young son Jerry came up with the idea of a bulletproof man that he nicknamed Superman.'

Mid-crawl, Zhao's feet stopped moving. 'M-My—! *Wh-What'd you do to my legs!?*'

Ellis nodded and stood still. To this day, scientists didn't know why hemlock poisoning started in the feet and worked up from there.

'Such a dumb idea, right, Zhao – a bulletproof man? But the only reason Superman was born was because a little boy missed his father,' Ellis pointed out. 'And the best part? The murder's still unsolved. In fact, people are still so excited by Superman, they never stop to ask just why Mitchell Siegel was killed – or to even consider that maybe, just maybe, he might've done something that made him the bad guy in this story. . . . Twenty . . . nineteen . . . eighteen . . .'

'*I can't feel my legs!*' Zhao sobbed as tears ran down his face.

'You think I'm the bad guy here, but I'm not,' Ellis said, putting away the empty vial, zipping his leather doctor's case, and smoothing the sheets on the edge of the bed. 'I'm the hero, Zhao. *You're* the bad guy. *You're* the one keeping the Book of Lies from us. Just like Mitchell Siegel kept it from us.'

'P-Please, I don't know who the hell you're talking about!'

Ellis crouched down next to Zhao, who was flat on his belly, barely able to catch his breath. 'I want my Book. Tell me its final destination.'

'I – I – I told you,' Zhao stuttered. 'W-We— It's going to Panama.'

'And *then* where?'

'That's it – *Panama* . . . ' he repeated, his nose pressed to the carpet, his eyes clenched in pain. 'Just . . . the antidote . . .'

'You feel that tightening in your waist?' Ellis asked, looking down and realizing that his shoes could use a new shine. 'Your thighs are dead, Zhao. Then it'll climb to your testicles. Hemlock is what killed Socrates. He narrated his entire death – how it slithered from his waist, to his chest, right up to when his eyes were fixed and dilated.'

'Okay . . . okayokayokay . . . *Miami!* After Panama . . . they're . . . it's going to Miami! *In Florida,*' Zhao insisted. 'The sheet . . . the lading bill . . . it's . . . *I swear* . . . *it's in my pocket! Just make it stop!*'

Ellis reached into Zhao's pocket and extracted the sheet of light pink paper that held all the details of the shipment's arrival.

. . . seven . . . six . . . five . . .

The dog began to growl. She could smell death coming. But Ellis ignored the noise, peacefully reading from the bill of lading: the container's new tracking number, the receiver's name (had to be fake) – everything the Leadership needed.

. . . four . . . three . . . two . . .

Still flat on his stomach and now with his mouth wide open, Zhao gave a final hollow gasp that sounded like the last bits of water being sucked down a drain. Ellis's great-grandfather described the same sound in his diary – right after he mentioned there was no antidote for hemlock poisoning.

. . . one.

Zhao was nice – even kind when they first met at the doctor's funeral – but the mission was bigger than Zhao.

And based on what happened in 1900 with Mitchell Siegel, the mission had enough problems with witnesses.

Zhao's tongue went limp, and his head slumped forward, sending his forehead against the carpet.

Ellis didn't notice. He was already on his phone, dialing Judge Wojtowicz's number.

'I told you not to call me here, Eddie,' answered an older man with a soft, crackly voice.

'Ellis. I'm called *Ellis* now,' he replied, never losing his composure. He spread out his left hand, admiring the tattoo.

'It's five in the morning here, *Ellis*. What do you want?'

Ellis smiled – truly smiled – turning his full attention to the phone. 'What I want is for you to remember just where you were when I found you, *Judge*. Your group – your *Leadership* – your dream was old and dead. Is that how you pictured your final years? Just another discarded, cobwebbed old man sitting in his cramped Michigan apartment and wondering why his glory days weren't more glorious? You're not even a footnote in history, Judge. Not even an asterisk. But if you want, I can put you back there. Maybe one day you'll be a parenthesis.'

'My family has been in the Leadership since—'

'Don't embarrass yourself, Judge. Family names don't get you into Harvard anymore; what makes you think they'll get you in here?'

There was a long pause on the line. 'I appreciate your helping us with this, Ellis,' the Judge finally offered. Clearing his throat, he added, 'You're close to finding the Book, aren't you?'

'And about to get even closer,' Ellis said, glancing at the pink bill of lading and studying the container's new tracking details: when it left the port, when it'd arrive in

Miami, even the truck driver who was responsible for the pickup.

HARPER, LLOYD.

'C'mon, Benoni,' he murmured to the dog.

He knew it was an odd name. Benoni. But according to the diaries, that was the name of Abel's watchdog – the dog that was eventually given to Cain – and the only witness to the world's first murder.

'You're in for a treat, girl,' he said as he stepped over Zhao's dead body and led the dog out into the hallway. 'This time of year, the weather is gorgeous in Florida.'

As the dog ran ahead, Ellis never lost sight of her. He knew his history. Only with Benoni would he find the Book of Lies and solve the true mystery of the world's greatest villain.

2

Two weeks later
Fort Lauderdale, Florida

My name is Cal Harper.

This is the second most important day of my life.

'Remove heem,' the manager of the French bistro calls out behind us.

'S-Sorry, Cal,' my client Alberto apologizes, his body shaking as I hook his arm around my neck and help him hobble back toward our van. From the stench on his breath, Alberto's been drinking hard. From his fresh split lip, plus the tear in his ratty T-shirt, he's been fighting, too. In his left hand, he clutches the dented, rusty RC Cola can that he carries everywhere.

Welcome to Fort Lauderdale beach. Just another day in paradise.

'You planning on helping here?' I call to Roosevelt, who's reclining in the passenger seat of our dumpy white van.

'Ah'm mentoring,' Roosevelt calls back in a thick Tennessee drawl, nodding a hello to Alberto, who offers a gray-toothed smile in return.

'No, you're sitting on your rear while I do all the work,' I point out.

'Whattya think mentoring is?' Roosevelt asks, lumbering out like an old mountain cat and slowly tugging open the side door of the van, a 1991 GMC Safari that another client christened 'the White House.' (Roosevelt and Calvin in the same place? It's downright presidential.)

'You got him?' I ask.

'Isn't that why God put me on this planet?' Roosevelt says, his dyed-black, aging-hippie ponytail flapping in the salty ocean breeze. At forty-two, Roosevelt's old enough to know better than the ponytail, but we all have our weaknesses. 'Man, Alberto, you *reek.*'

To the few passing tourists still walking the beach, we probably look like mobsters. But our job's far more dangerous than that.

'Listen, thanks for calling us instead of the cops,' I tell the restaurant manager, a middle-aged guy who looks like a ferret.

'I'm no schmuck,' he laughs, dropping his French accent. 'Cops would take two hours. You take the trash out *fast.*'

He offers a handshake, and as I reach to take it, I spot a hundred-dollar bill in his palm. I pull back as if he's offering a coiled snake.

'Just our way of saying thanks,' he adds, reaching out again for the handshake.

I don't shake back. '*Listen,*' I insist, stepping toward him. It's clear I'm not the most imposing figure – I slouch and have a shambling walk that's all arms and legs and big hands – but I do have most of my dad's height. Nearly six feet when I stand up straight. And the only time I do that is when I'm pissed. Like now. 'Do you understand what I do?' I ask, my thick Adam's apple pumping with each syllable.

'Aw, jeez, you're gonna give me some self-important speech now, aren't ya?'

'No speech. We take the homeless back to shelters—'

'And what? If you accept a tip it'll make it less of a good deed? I respect that. I do. But c'mon, be fair to yourself,' he says, motioning to my faded black T-shirt, which is barely tucked in. 'What're ya, thirty years old with that baby face? You're wearing secondhand sneakers and sweatpants. To work. When was the last time you got a haircut? And c'mon . . . your van . . .'

I glance back at the van's peeling tinted windows and the swarm of rust along the back fender, then down at my decade-old sweatpants and my checkerboard Vans sneakers.

'Take the money, kid. If you don't use it for yourself, at least help your organization.'

I shake my head. 'You called my client *trash*.'

To my surprise, he doesn't get defensive. Or mad. 'You're right – I'm sorry,' he says, still holding out the money. 'Let this be my apology. Please. Don't make it the end of the world.'

I stare at my sweatpants, calculating all of the underwear and socks I could buy for our clients with an extra hundred dollars.

'C'mon, bro . . . even Bob Dylan did an iPod commercial.'

'And once again, making the world safe for people who eat croque-monsieurs,' I say, yanking open the door of the van and climbing back behind the wheel.

'What the fudge, Cal? You didn't take the money, did you?' Roosevelt asks with a sigh as he reaches into the brown bag on his lap and cracks open a pistachio shell. 'Why you so stubborn?'

'Same reason you say dumb crap like "What the fudge."'

'That's different.'

'It's not different,' I shoot back, looking down at the van's closed ashtray. With a tug, I pull it open, spot the dozens of discarded pistachio shells he's stuffed inside, and dump them in the empty Burger King bag between us. Roosevelt cracks another shell and leans for the ashtray. I shake the Burger King bag in front of him instead. 'You were a minister, so you don't like to curse – I get it, Roosevelt. But it's a choice you make on principle.'

'You were a minister?' Alberto blurts from the back-seat, barely picking his head up from the RC soda can with the plastic wrap on top. It took nearly six different pickups before Alberto told me that's where he keeps his father's ashes. I used to think he was nuts. I still do. But I appreciate the logic. *I'm* what my parents left behind. I understand not wanting to do the same to someone else. 'I thought you were some special agent who got arrested . . .'

Twisting the ignition and hitting the gas, I don't say a word.

'That was Cal,' Roosevelt points out as we take off down A1A, and his ponytail flaps behind him. 'And we've talked about my ministry, Alberto.'

Alberto pauses a moment. 'You're a minister?'

'He *was*,' I offer. 'Ask him why he left.'

'Ask Cal why he got fired,' Roosevelt says in that calm, folksy drawl that filled the church pews every Sunday and immediately has Alberto looking my way. 'Losing his badge . . . y'know that's what turned his hair white?' Roosevelt adds, pointing at my full head of thick silver hair, which is such a scraggly mess it almost covers the birthmark near my left eye.

'Nuh-uh,' Alberto says. 'You didn't get that from your momma or daddy?'

I click my front teeth together, staring out at the closed tourist T-shirt shops that line the beach. The only thing I got from my parents was a light blue government form with the charges against my father.

The prosecutor was smart: He went for manslaughter instead of murder . . . painted a picture of this six-foot-two monster purposely shoving a small, defenseless young mom . . . then for the final spit-shine added in my father yelling, '*That's it – you're done!*' (Testimony courtesy of every neighbor with an adjoining wall.)

My dad got eight years at Glades Correction Institution. The state of Florida gave me six minutes to say good-bye. I remember the room smelled like spearmint gum and hairspray. Life is filled with trapdoors. I happened to swan dive through mine when I was nine years old. That was the last time I ever saw Dad. I don't blame him anymore, even though when he got out, he could've— I don't blame him anymore.

'Gaaah,' Roosevelt shouts, his ruddy features burning bright. 'You shoulda taken that restaurant money.'

'Roosevelt, the only reason he was offering that cash was so when he goes home tonight, he doesn't feel nearly as guilty for sweeping away the homeless guy that he thought was bad for his fake French bistro business. Go pray . . . or send an e-mail to heaven . . . or do whatever you do to let your God weigh in, but I'm telling you: We're here to help those who need it – not to give fudging penance.'

His lips purse at my use of the G-word. Roosevelt'll joke about anything – his long hair, his obsession with early chubby Janet Jackson (so much better than the later thinner model), even his love of 'Yo Momma's So Fat' jokes as a tool for changing the subject during an awkward social situation – but he'll never joke about God.

Staring out the side window, Roosevelt's now the one clicking his teeth. 'Making it a crusade doesn't make it right,' he says, speaking slowly so I feel every word.

'It's not a crusade.'

'Really? Then I suppose when you leave this job every night, your life is filled with a slew of outside interests: like that kindergarten teacher I tried to set you up with. Oh, wait – that's right – you never called her.'

'I called her. She had to run,' I say, gripping the steering wheel and searching the passing side streets for possible clients.

'That's why you set up a date! To make time so you can *talk*, or *eat*, or do something besides riding past mile after mile of gorgeous beach and spending all that time checking every alley for a homeless person!'

I look straight ahead as Roosevelt cracks another pistachio and tosses the shell in the bag. I never had an older brother, but if I did, I bet he'd torture me with the exact same silence.

'I know you can't turn it off, Cal – and I love you for that – but it's unhealthy. You need something . . . a hobby—'

'I have lots of hobbies.'

'Name one.'

'Don't start.' I think a moment. 'Watching cop shows on TV.'

'That's just so you can point out inconsistencies. Name a real form of entertainment. What was the last movie you saw? Or better yet—' He grabs the notebook-size steel case that's wedged between my seat and the center console. My laptop.

'Here we go,' he says, flipping open the computer and clicking the *History* button in my browser. 'Seeing the Web sites someone goes to, it's like looking at the furniture arrangement of their mind.'

On-screen, the list isn't long.

'SmartSunGuide.com?' he asks.

'That's a good site.'

'No, that's where you get Florida traffic reports and the public CCTV cameras – to spot homeless clients who're sleeping under an overpass.'

'So?'

'And this one: ConstructionJournal.com. Lemme guess: up-to-the-minute building permits, so you can find all the new construction sites.'

'That's where our clients tend to sleep.'

'Cal, you not seeing the picture here? No interests, no news, no sports, hell, not even any porn. You're a damn walrus,' Roosevelt insists, cracking another pistachio. 'When it's walking on land, walruses are the most lumbering, awkward creatures God ever gave us. But the moment it enters the water, that sucker is quicksilver. Fwoooo,' he says, slicing his hand through the air like a ski jump. 'Same with you, Cal. When you're working with clients, you're in the water – fwoooo – just quicksilver. The problem is, all you wanna do is stay underwater. And even the walrus knows if it doesn't come up for air, it's gonna die.'

'That's a very inspiring and far too visual analogy. But I know who I am, and I like who I am, and when it comes to ass-face restaurant managers who treat money as some green-colored rosary, well, no offense, but I'm not for sale. And we should never let our clients be, either.'

He rolls his eyes, letting us both calm down. 'Can you be more predictable?' he asks.

'I was trying to be complex.'

'Complex woulda been if you had taken the guy's money, given it to Alberto, and then told him to go back and use it to eat at the restaurant.'

I glance over at him. The pastor in him won't let up. Not until I get the message. As I try to save whoever's out there, he still thinks he needs to save me. I know he misses his parish, but he's wrong about this one. It's not a crusade. Or an obsession. I could leave this job tomorrow. Or the next night. Or the night after that. Tonight, though, isn't that night.

'I'm still not for sale,' I tell him. 'And you of all people shouldn't be, either.'

Roosevelt leans back in his reclined seat and lets out a hearty laugh. 'Yo momma's so fat—'

'Roosevelt, I shouldn't've said that—'

'—the horse on her Polo shirt . . . *is real*!'

'You used that last week.'

'Yo momma's so fat, in elevators, it says: "Maximum Occupancy: Twelve Patrons *OR Yo momma!*"'

'Does that really make you happier?'

'Just take the money next time, Cal,' Roosevelt says as he twists a dial on the old, stolen police scanner we super-glued to the dash. The cops don't care. On homeless calls, they *want* us there first.

'—ave an eighty-six, requesting – *zzzrrr* – nearby units to Victoria Park,' a woman's voice says as the scanner crackles to life. The park is less than a mile away.

Turns out this is the call I'd been waiting nineteen years for.

3

'*Cal . . . I need help!*' Roosevelt screams.

My tenth-grade English teacher once told me that throughout your life, you should use only three exclamation points. That way, when you put one out there, people know it's worth it. I used one of them the day my mom died. But tonight, as I sit in the van and hear the sudden panic in Roosevelt's voice – Across the wide patch of grass known as Victoria Park, he flicks on his flashlight. But all I see is the bright red blood on his hands. No. Please don't let tonight be another.

'Rosey, what the hell's going on?' I yell back, clawing over the passenger seat, sticking my head out the window, and squinting into the darkness. He's kneeling over our newest homeless client – '86' on the radio means 'vagrant' – who's curled at the base of a queen palm tree that stands apart from the rest.

'It's a bad one, Cal. He's a bleeder!'

A ping of rain hits the windshield, and I jump at the impact.

If this were my first day on the job, I'd leap out of the van and rush like a panicked child to Roosevelt's side. But this isn't day one. It's year two.

'You got his Social?' I call out.

Kneeling at the base of the queen palm, Roosevelt tucks his flashlight under his armpit and rolls what looks like a

heavyset man onto his back. As the light shines down –
the lumpy silhouette – even from here, I can see the blood
that soaks the man's stomach.

'His wallet's gone,' Roosevelt shouts, knowing our proto-
cols. 'Sir. . . . *Sir!* Can you hear me? I need your Social
Security number.'

In my left hand, I'm already dialing 911. In my right,
I prop my laptop on the center console. But I never take
my eyes off Roosevelt. Breast cancer took my aunt, the
aunt who raised me, a few years back. I don't have many
friends. I have this job. And I have Roosevelt.

'Cal, I got his Social!' Roosevelt shouts. 'Sir, were you
mugged? You have a gunshot wound.'

'Gimme one sec,' I call out. The computer hums, our
tracking software loads, and I click on the button marked
Find Client. On-screen, a blank form opens, and I tab over
to the section labeled *SSN*.

'Cal, you need to hurry,' Roosevelt adds as the
man whispers something. At least he's conscious. 'He's
starting t—'

'Ready!' I insist, all set to type with one hand. In my
other, I grip my cell and hit *send* as the 911 line starts
ringing.

Years ago, if you wanted to drive around and work with
the homeless, all you needed was a van and some Lysol.
These days, the state of Florida won't let you pick up a
soul unless you're logged on to the statewide computer
network that tracks who's where. The better to see you
with, my dear. And the better to see what diseases, medication, and psychological history you're carrying around
as well.

'Zero seven eight, zero five, one one two zero,' Roosevelt
announces as I key in the man's Social Security number.

In my ear, the 911 line continues to ring.

In the distance, refusing to wait, Roosevelt rips open the man's shirt and starts applying pressure to his wound. And on-screen, I get my first look at his identity.

LLOYD RANDALL HARPER
DANIA BEACH, FLORIDA
DOB: JUNE 19 – 52 YEARS OLD

A swell of heat burns my chest, my throat. I can't breathe. I open my mouth to call Roosevelt's name, but my lips won't move.

LLOYD RANDALL HARPER

My father.

'This is 911,' the operator announces in my ear. 'What's your emergency?'

4

Darting between two oak trees, I race through the black park as the rain collects in little rivers on my face. I ignore it. Just like I ignore my heart kicking from inside my rib cage. All I see is him.

When I was little, I used to have fantasies about finding my dad. That he'd be released early, and my aunt and I would run into him at dinner or while I was getting a haircut. I remember being in church on the plastic kneelers, praying that we'd find each other again in some dumb Disney movie way. But those dreams faded as he missed my tenth birthday. And eleventh. And twelfth. Within a few years, the childhood dreams shifted and hardened – to fantasies of *not* seeing him again. I can still run them in my head: elaborate escape plans for ducking down, running, disappearing. I'd ready myself, checking over my shoulder as I'd pass the bagel place where he used to love to get breakfast. And a few years after that, those dreams settled, too, entering that phase where you think of him only as much as you think of any other dead relative.

For the past nineteen years – for me – that's all he's been. Dead.

And now he's crumpled at the base of a palm tree as a slow, leaky rain drips from above.

'Cal! Med kit!' Roosevelt shouts.

I cut past the white gazebo at the front of the park,

and my foot slips in the grass, sending me flat on my ass, where the damp ground seeps through my pants.

'Cal, where are you?' Roosevelt calls without turning around.

It's a fair question. I close my eyes and tell myself I'm still in the poorly lit park, but all I see is the tarnished doorknob in that spearmint-gum-and-hairspray room where my dad and I said good-bye. I blink once and the doorknob twists, revealing the child psychologist assigned by the state. It's like that Moby song. When you have a damaged kid, you don't ask, 'How you feeling?' You give him a crayon and say, 'Draw something nice.'

I drew lots of nice.

'Med kit!' Roosevelt snaps again.

I scramble to my feet. Years of training rush back. So do decade-old escape plans. I should turn around now. Let Roosevelt handle it. But if I do— No. Not until—

I need to know if it's him.

Ten feet in front of me, Roosevelt still has the flashlight tucked under his armpit. It shines like a spotlight, showcasing the bloody inkblot stained into the man's silk shirt. As I barrel toward them, Roosevelt turns my way and the armpit flashlight follows. There's no missing the terror on my face. 'Cal, what're you—?'

Like a baseball player rounding third, I drop to one knee and slide through the wet grass, slamming the med kit into Roosevelt's chest and almost knocking him over.

'Cal, what's wrong? Do you know this guy?' Roosevelt asks.

Grabbing the flashlight, I don't answer. I'm hunched over the man, shining the light and studying his face. He's got a beard now, tightly trimmed and speckled with gray.

'Shut it off,' the man moans, jerking his head back and

forth. His eyes are clenched from the light and the pain, but his face – the double chin, the extra weight, even the big Adam's apple – it can't be.

'You're blinding him, Cal!' Roosevelt says, snatching the flashlight from my grip and shining it in my face. 'What the hell is wrong with—'

'C-Cal?' the man mumbles, looking at Roosevelt. He heard him say my name. But as the man turns to me, the light hits us both from the side. Our eyes connect. 'N-No. You're not— You're—' He swallows hard. *'Cal?'*

It's an established scientific fact that the sense of smell is the most powerful for triggering memories. But it's wrong. Because the moment I hear that scratchy, stumbly baritone – everyone knows their father's voice.

Our eyes stay locked, and I swear, I see the *old him* under the *new him*, like he's wearing a Halloween mask of his future self. But as I study this middle-aged man with the leathery, sun-beaten skin – God, he looks so old – his terrified pale green eyes, his twisted Irish nose . . . it's more crooked than I remember. Like it's been broken again.

His hand shakes like a Parkinson's patient as he tries to wipe flecks of blood from his mouth. He has to tuck the hand underneath him to stop it from trembling. He spent eight years in prison. It can't be just his nose that's been broken.

'You okay?' Roosevelt asks. I'm not sure who he's talking to, though it's pretty clear it doesn't matter. Down on my knees, I'm once again nine years old, pulling crayons from an old Tupperware bin. To this day, I don't know if it was my greatest fear or deepest desire, but the one thing I drew over and over was my father coming home.

5

'Cal, you need to hurry,' the man with the ponytail called out across the park. 'He's starting t—'

'Ready!' shouted the one called Cal.

From the front seat of his sedan, Ellis stared through his windshield, watching the scene and knowing that co-incidences this perfect were never just coincidences. Next to him, in the passenger seat, his dog rumbled and growled – first at the rain, then at the flashlight, the bobbing and glowing light-stick in the distance.

'Easy, girl. . . . *Good girl*,' Ellis whispered, patting his dog's neck as they spied the two homeless volunteers shouting at the far end of the little park. Cal. One of them was named *Cal*. From this side of the park, it was hard to hear much. But Ellis heard enough.

'Zero seven eight, zero five, one one two zero,' yelled the ponytailed man.

Ellis pulled out the file folder the Judge's office had put together and checked the Social Security number against the one on the pink sheet from Hong Kong. The driver picking up the Book of Lies: Harper, Lloyd.

Ellis's amber eyes narrowed as his thick eyebrows drew together. It wasn't supposed to be like this.

He'd been following Lloyd for barely ten minutes – following the simpleminded courier just to make sure the shipment got through. But what Ellis had seen . . . when the flash of the gun erupted and Lloyd stumbled in the park . . . No, Lloyd wasn't simpleminded at all. Lloyd Harper might not've known exactly what was inside, but he knew the value of what he was carrying. Ellis shouldn't've been so surprised. His own father was a liar, too. And a far worse trickster.

The dog raised her head, always reading Ellis perfectly. 'I'm okay, girl,' he promised.

Across the dark park, there was a burst of light as the door of the van flew open. Ellis saw an older man with white hair— No. He had an open, boyish face and loose-jointed movements. Like a giant marionette out of sync. He was young. Young with white hair.

Ellis flipped through the pages, still rubbing his thumbnail across the corner of the file folder. White hair, twenty-eight years old. There it was. Known relatives. Calvin. Cal.

One of them was named *Cal*. And the way he was running – the shock and fear on his face as he came bursting out into the rainy night – Cal knew exactly whom he'd found.

For a moment, Ellis laughed to himself. Of course. It had to come back to father and son. Just as it began with Adam and Cain. Just as it was with Mitchell and Jerry Siegel.

It was the same when he'd first heard the truth about his own family – the lifelong lie his father had told him. In that instant, Ellis realized how much of his life was a construct. But Ellis wasn't sad. He was thrilled. He *knew* he was meant for something bigger. No question, that's why his mother left him the diary, the softbound journal with the water-stained leather cover.

For over a year he'd been studying the diary's pages, absorbing the theories that his grandfather and great-grandfather – both Leadership officers – spent so many years working on. Throughout the books, his name was spelled differently – Cayin, Kayin, Kenite – depending on the translation and where the story originated. But there was no mistaking the world's first murderer. Or the first man God forgave – and empowered. The man who held the secret of God's true power.

Ellis still remembered – his hands shaking in the estate lawyer's office – the first time he read the words his great-grandfather had written during his time at the Cairo Museum. Ellis had to go find a Bible – check the language himself. Like most, he'd grown up thinking Cain killed Abel with a stone. But as he flipped through the pages, speed-reading through chapter 4 of Genesis: 'And it came to pass, when they were in the field, that Cain rose up against Abel his brother, and slew him.' That was all the Bible said. No mentions of stones or rocks or any sort of weapon.

Time and history added other ideas, filling texts with theories of clubs, sticks, and wooden staffs. The Zohar, the most important work of the Jewish Kabbalah movement, insisted that Cain bit Abel's throat, which led others to proclaim Cain as the world's first vampire. And in ancient Egypt, archaeologists found hieroglyphics depicting a weapon made from an animal's jawbone and sharpened teeth.

It was this theory of the jawbone that filled up half the diary. Shakespeare wrote that Cain's weapon was a jawbone, featuring it in *Hamlet*. Rembrandt depicted the same instrument in one of his portraits, even including Abel's dog barking in the background.

But for Ellis's Cairo-based great-grandfather, the real question was: How did this obscure theory from ancient

Egyptian hieroglyphics suddenly become such a rage in seventeenth-century Europe? For years, there was no logical explanation – until his great-grandfather read the story of a small group of Coptic monks who emigrated from Egypt to the north, where they hoped to hide the small but priceless object they'd stumbled upon. The object from God Himself.

Then the Leadership took interest. The group was new then. Untested. But extremely enthusiastic – like Ellis, especially now that he was so close.

There was only one thing in his way.

Across the park, Cal slid on his knees, his flashlight shining into Lloyd Harper's terrified face.

A trickster, Ellis decided. Every family had a trickster.

In the passenger seat, Benoni cocked her head, which meant Ellis's phone was about to—

The phone vibrated in Ellis's pocket. Somehow the dog always knew.

'Officer Belasco,' Ellis answered as he readjusted the badge on his uniform.

'You still with the driver – what's his name again?' the Judge asked.

'Lloyd,' Ellis replied, watching Cal's father across the park and unable to shake the feeling that the bleeding old man was far more than just a driver.

'He get the Book yet?'

'Soon. He stopped for some help first,' Ellis said as he eyed just Cal.

In 1900, the Book – one writing called it a 'carving,' another an 'emblem' – whatever it was, it was stolen from the Leadership. Ellis's grandfathers hunted it for decades, tracing it to father and son. Always father and son. And tonight, seeing Cal and his dad, Ellis finally understood how near the end was. All he had to do was wipe out these villains. Then Ellis – for himself, for his family – would finally be the hero.

'Is that concern in your voice?' the Judge asked.

'Not at all.' Ellis scratched Benoni's nose, barely even hearing the ambulance siren that approached behind them. 'Lloyd Harper can bring as many dogs as he wants into this fight. It won't take much to put 'em down.'

6

'You're gonna feel a sting,' the nurse says, wheeling my dad into one of the emergency exam rooms. As she's about to pull the curtain shut, she turns back to me and stops. 'Only relatives from here. You related?'

I freeze at the question. She doesn't have time for indecision.

'Waiting room's back there,' she says, whipping the curtain shut like a magician's cape.

Sleepwalking toward the L-shaped hub of pink plastic waiting room chairs, I'm still clutching the mound of my dad's crumpled belongings – his bloody shirt, pants, and shoes – that the EMTs cut off him. A digital clock on the wall tells me it's 1:34 a.m. To Roosevelt's credit, as I slump down in the seat next to him, he doesn't say a word for at least four or five seconds.

'Cal, if he's really your dad—'

'He's my dad.'

'Then you should go back there.'

I start to stand up, then again sit back down.

I've waited nineteen years to see my dad. Nineteen years being mad he's gone. But to hop out of my chair and peek behind that curtain and reenter his life . . . 'What if he doesn't want me back?' I whisper.

Smart enough to not answer, Roosevelt quickly shows me why, after he raised his own hell in high school, he was such a great Methodist minister. Sure, he still had his rebellious side – with a few too many Iron Maiden quotes in his sermons – but the way he breathed life into Scripture and related to people, everyone loved that pastor with the ponytail.

The only problem came when church leaders told Roosevelt they didn't like the fact that he wasn't married. In the wake of all the church pedophile cases, it didn't reflect well that even though he was from one of the wealthiest families in town, at nearly forty years old, he was still single. Roosevelt pleaded, explaining that he hadn't found anyone he loved. His family tried to help by throwing around their financial weight. But in rural Tennessee – where a handsome, unmarried, thirty-eight-year-old man can mean only one thing – his church refused to budge. 'If you want to be queer, don't do it here,' said the message that was spray-painted on the hood of his car. And Roosevelt had his first personal heartbreak.

Which is why he empathizes so well with mine.

'Cal, when you were little, you ever watch *The Ten Commandments*?'

'This gonna be another sermon?'

'Boy, you think you're the only one who likes saving people?' he teases, though I know it's no joke. No matter how happy he is, Roosevelt would kill to have his old parish back. It's not ego; it's just his mission. He'll never say it, but I know that's the reason he took this job. And though I bet his family could easily buy him a new church, well, it's the same reason he won't buy us a new van. Some battles you have to fight by yourself. 'Think about the Moses story, Cal: Little baby gets dropped in a basket, then grows up thinking he's Egyptian royalty – until his past comes kickin' at the door and reveals to him his true purpose.'

'That mean I'm getting the long beard and the sandals?'

'We all hate something about our past, Cal. That's why we run from it, or compensate for it, or even fill our van with homeless people. But when something like this happens – when your dad shows up – maybe there *is* a bigger purpose. "What you intended for evil, God intended for good." Genesis 50:20.'

Staring down at the pointy tips of my dad's shoes in my hand, I don't say a word. When my mom worked in the hospital, she used to lecture us about the importance of good shoes. As a cleaning lady, it was the one personal item she could see in every room. Fancy clothes were replaced by hospital gowns, but under every bed . . . *Show me someone's shoes, and I'll show you their lives.*

Thanks to that ridiculous mantra, my dad used to always have one pair of shiny black lawyer shoes (even though he was a painter) and a pair of tan cordovans (which my mom was convinced meant you were rich).

Today, in my lap, he's got black loafers. And not the cheap kind with the tough leather and the seams coming undone. These are nice – buffed and narrow at the toes; Italian leather soles.

I read the label inside.

'What's wrong?' Roosevelt asks.

'These are Franceschettis.'

He cocks an eyebrow and looks for himself. He's the one from money. He knows what it means.

'Franceschettis are expensive, aren't they?' I ask.

'Four hundred bucks a pair.'

'What about his shirt?' I ask, showing him the label on my dad's bloody silk shirt. Michael Kors. 'Is Michael Kors good?'

'Plenty good. As in three-hundred-bucks-a-pop good.'

'On a guy we found on a homeless call,' I point out.

'Maybe they were donated. We get designer clothes all the time.'

I look at the bottom of the shoes. The leather soles barely have a scuff on them. Brand new. Confused, I once again start to stand up, then quickly sit back down.

When I was little and we had company coming over, my father would buy cheap Scotch at the neighborhood liquor store and pour it into a Johnnie Walker Black Label bottle. He did the same when he first started painting signs at restaurants, pouring discount remainder paint into the Benjamin Moore cans he'd have me fish from the hardware store's trash. My mother used to tease him, calling it his little CIA trick. He never laughed at the joke. For him, appearances mattered.

'Did he say anything in the ambulance?' Roosevelt asks, eyeing the other people in the waiting area. A teenager on crutches stares our way.

'Not much,' I say, lowering my voice. 'He told the medics he was coming out of that dump bar on Third Street when some Hispanic kid with big ears pulled a gun and asked for his wallet. When he refused, the kid took the wallet, pulled the trigger, shoved him into a red Jeep Cherokee, and dumped him in the park where we found him.'

'Okay, so that's a story. He's *not* homeless. He just got robbed.'

I shake my head, still staring at the shirt's snazzy black label. 'People with three-hundred-dollar shirts and four-hundred-dollar shoes don't go into low-life bars on Third.'

'What're you talking about? This is *Florida*. We got stupid rich people *everywhere*. Besides, even if he's out of place, doesn't mean he's out to—' Roosevelt cuts himself off, watching me carefully. 'Oh, you think this is like Miss Deirdre, don't you? No, *no*, boy. This is *not* Miss Deirdre.'

I've known Roosevelt for nearly six years. I first met him back when I was an ICE agent (which is just the cooler-sounding acronym for the U.S. government's Immigration and Customs Enforcement). I guarded the ports, stopped terrorist and drug shipments from coming in, and, at least during my first two years, confiscated shipments of fake Sony TVs and counterfeit Levi's jeans. Until I opened myself up, helped someone I shouldn't have, and in one horrible moment got fired from my job and plummeted through the second trapdoor in my life.

'Cal, what happened with Miss Deirdre—'

'Can we please go back to my father's shoes?'

'That's exactly what I'm doing. I know you, Cal. And I know it's easier to drive around with a van full of strangers where there's no risk of any emotional investment, but just because you got burned once by letting your guard down doesn't mean it'll be the same here. Not everyone you care about will eventually screw you.'

Back during my leap from grace, every newspaper reporter, community leader, and government colleague took me *out* of their Rolodex. Roosevelt, when he heard the story, invited me in. For that alone, I love him like a brother. And while he knows what it's like to be excommunicated from your kingdom, unlike Roosevelt, I'm no longer waiting for someone to bring me back inside.

Within a minute, I've combed through my dad's shirt and pants pockets. All it gives me is some spare change and a few tabs of nicotine gum. No secrets. Nothing revealing. That is, until I toss the shirt and pants into the plastic chair on my left and get my first good look inside his other shoe. I notice a tiny yellow triangle peeking out from inside. It's no bigger than the corner of a stamp, but the way it's tucked in there catches my eye, as if it's hidden under the leather.

I yank the insole. It comes right out, revealing what's tucked underneath—

'What? Is it bad?' Roosevelt asks as I pull out a folded-up yellow sheet of paper. As I go to unfold it, a small laminated card drops and clicks against the floor. He hid this here instead of in his missing wallet. It's got a photo of my dad on it. A commercial driver's license.

'Says here he's a truck driver – double and triple trailers, plus hazardous materials,' I say, reading from the back of the license.

Clumsily, rushing, I unfold the yellow sheet. At first, it looks like an invoice, but when I spot the familiar letter-head up top— Aw, crap.

He's lucky they took away my gun.

7

'I don't get it. He's bringing in a shipment?'

'Not just a shipment. A four-ton metal container – y'know, like those ones you see on the backs of trucks.'

'And that's bad because . . . ?'

'Have you *read* this?' I say to Roosevelt, waving the yellow sheet of paper that—

Roosevelt grabs my wrist and shoots me a look, which is when I notice that half the emergency waiting room is staring our way. A cop in the corner, the teenager on crutches . . . and a creepy older man with a moon chin, who's holding his arm like it's broken but showing no signs of pain.

Roosevelt quickly stands up, and I follow him outside, under the overhang of the emergency room's main entrance. The sky's still black, and the December wind whips under the overhang, sending the yellow sheet fluttering back and forth in my hand like a dragonfly's wings.

'We call them *hold notices*,' I explain, reading from the first paragraph. '". . . wish to inform you that your shipment may experience a short delay. This doesn't indicate there are any problems with your shipment . . ."'

'Doesn't sound so bad – they're just saying it's delayed.'

'That's only because if they say the word *hold*, all the drug dealers will run away. That's also why they say *there are no problems*.'

'But there are problems?'

'Look at the letterhead on top – U.S. Customs and Border Protection.'

'That's where you used to work, right?'

'Roosevelt, I'm trying hard to not be paranoid. I really am. But now my long-lost father just *happens* to be bleeding in the one park that just *happens* to be on the homeless route of his long abandoned son, who just *happens* to've worked at the one place that just *happens* to be holding on to the one package that he just *happens* to be trying to pick up? Forget the designer shoes – that's a helluva lotta happenstance, with an extra-large order of coincidence.'

'I don't know. Separated all those years, then bringing you together – sometimes the clichés get it right: The Lord works in mysterious ways.'

'Not for me. And not with my—'

'Cal?' a deep voice calls out behind me as the emergency room's glass doors slide open.

I turn around just as Dr Paulo Pollack joins us outside. Like most doctors, he's got the God swagger. I just happen to know this one, which made it easier to call him from the ambulance.

'How's he doing, Paulo?' I ask.

'He's fine. Luckily, the bullet didn't hit anything organwise. Looks like it went in on an angle and got trapped under the skin, right above his liver. In this case, it's good he had a little bit of chub on him.'

'But you got the bullet out?'

Two years ago, Roosevelt and I picked up a homeless girl who had done so much cocaine, the cartilage between her nostrils deteriorated, and the bridge of her nose collapsed. The girl was Dr Paulo Pollack's seventeen-year-old niece. From then on, he's waited to return the favor.

'One cleaned-off slug at your service,' Paulo says, handing me a small plastic bag with an old copper-jacketed bullet. 'You know the rules, Cal – it's your dad's property, but if the cops come asking . . .'

'Send 'em my way,' I say, squinting hard at the contents of the bag. The single bullet is squatty, with shallow grooves that twist left along the bottom half. I don't recognize the make and model, but it's definitely got a unique shape. Won't be hard to find out.

'When he came in, I could touch his stomach and feel the bullet right under his skin,' Paulo points out. 'But when I made the incision – and this is with no pain medication, just some anesthetic by the wound – but even as I tweezed it out, your dad grunted once, but never cried in pain.'

'All those years in prison. He's lived through worse,' I say.

Roosevelt stares me down. So does the doctor. It's so damn easy to judge. But as Paulo knows from his niece, no matter how much you want someone back in your life, sometimes it's the letting-them-back-in part that hurts the most.

'So how long you keeping him for?' I ask.

'*Keeping* him?' Paulo asks. 'You watch too many cop shows. I sliced it out, gave him his grand total of five stitches, and let him borrow some hospital scrubs so he wouldn't have to wear his own blood home. You should be careful, though – he's overweight, high blood pressure, and although he won't admit to any chest pains, he's got the beginnings of myocardial ischemia. Wherever he's going next, he needs to watch his heart. Otherwise, he's yours.'

Just behind the doctor's shoulder, there's a hushed electric *whoosh*. But it's not until he steps aside that I spot the tall man with the grassy green eyes and the twisted Irish nose. Dressed in a fresh pair of blue hospital scrubs, my father climbs out of his required wheelchair ride. And shuffles directly toward us.

8

Roosevelt cuts in front of me and motions back to the yellow sheet in my hand. I stuff it back in my dad's shoe and cover it up with his bloody silk shirt and pants.

Like kids watching fireworks, Roosevelt and I crane our necks up. My dad's six foot two. In all the carrying and rushing from the ambulance, this is the first moment he looks it. He's got a face that reminds me of an egg, made wider at the bottom by his gray-speckled beard, which is trimmed and neat. For a second, it looks like the pain in his side is too much. But when he sees us watching, he takes a deep breath, brushes his fine gray hair from his forehead, and squares his shoulders into a near perfect stance. No question, appearances still matter.

'Cal, I'm inside if you need anything,' Paulo says, and quickly excuses himself.

Roosevelt stays right where he is. By my side.

My father clears his throat, taking a long look at Roosevelt, but Roosevelt doesn't take the hint. I expect my dad to get annoyed . . . maybe even lose his temper the way he used to. But all he does is glance back toward the emergency room and scratch his knuckles against his beard. By his side, his left hand is clenched in a tight fist. Whatever he's holding in, he's fighting hard with it.

'I'll be fine,' I whisper to Roosevelt, motioning him inside. There's no mentoring with this one.

'I . . . uh . . . I'll be inside pretending to get coffee,' Roosevelt announces as he heads back through the sliding doors.

We stand silently outside the emergency room entrance. On both sides of the overhang, the rain continues its prickly tap dance. My father lowers himself onto a metal bench and looks my way. I've practiced this moment for years. How, depending on the mood I was in, I'd tell him off, or ask him questions, or even embrace him in the inevitable swell of tears and regret that would follow my ruthless verbal assault. But as I sit down next to him, the only thing I notice is the gold U.S. Navy military ring on his right hand. As far as I know, he was never in the military. And as much as I try to make eye contact, he won't stop staring at the pile of designer clothes and shoes I'm still holding.

'Calvin—'

'Cal,' I correct him. 'I go by Cal now.'

'Yeah . . . no . . . I . . . Here's the thing, Cal—' He cuts himself off. 'I'm glad you're the one who found me.'

It's a perfect line, delivered with as much polish and determination as my own preplanned speech. The only problem is, it doesn't answer the only question that matters.

'Where the hell have you been?' I blurt.

'Y'mean with the park? I told you: I was at the bar, then got jumped . . .' He studies me, reading my anger all too well. 'Ah. You mean for the past few years.'

'Yes, Lloyd. For the past *nineteen* years. You left me, remember? And when you went to prison—' My voice cracks, and I curse myself for the weakness. But I've earned this answer. 'Why didn't you come back for me?'

Staring over my shoulder, my dad anxiously studies both ends of the U-shaped driveway, then scans the empty sidewalk that runs in front of the hospital. Like he's worried someone's watching. 'Calvin, is there anything I can possibly say to satisfy that question?'

'That's not the point. Y-You missed everything in my—' I shake my head. 'You missed Aunt Rosey's funeral.'

I wait for his excuse. He's too smart to make one. He knows there's no changing the past. And the way he keeps checking the area, he's far more worried about the future.

'The doctor told me you drive around and pick up homeless people,' he offers, eyeing the parking garage on our right. 'Good for you.'

'Why's that *good for me*?' I challenge.

'This isn't a fight, Calvin—'

'Cal.'

'—I just think it's nice that you help people,' he adds, rechecking the street.

'Oh, so now you like helping people?'

'I'm just saying . . . it's good to help people.'

'Are you asking me for help, Lloyd?'

For the first time, my father looks directly at me. I know he's a truck driver. I know about the delivery slip. And I know that whatever it is he's picking up at the port, he's not getting that shipment unless he has someone remove the hold notice, a favor that wouldn't take me more than a single phone call.

'Thank you, but I'm fine,' he tells me, standing slowly from his seat. He's clearly aching. But as he grips the armrest, I can't help but stare at his fingers, which are marked by hairy knuckles and crooked pinkies. Just like mine. 'Calvin, can we please have the rest of this argument later? With all this pain medication, it's like everyone's talking in slow motion.'

I just stare as he limps away. Paulo said he hadn't given

him any pain medication. Just a shot of anesthetic by the wound.

'Hey, Lloyd – you never told me what you do these days. You still painting restaurants?'

'For sure. Lots of painting,' he says, his back still to me.

'That's great. And you can do it full-time? No odd jobs or anything else to make the rent?'

My father stands up straight and looks back. But in his eyes . . . all I see is panic. Real panic. My father spent eight years in prison. If he's scared, it's for something that's worth being scared about. 'Business is really great,' he insists.

'I'm sure it is if you can afford this nice shirt and shoes,' I say, still holding his belongings.

His mouth is open, like he's ready to say something. It's as if I have a grip on his scab and I'm slowly pulling it off. That's it, Lloyd. Tell me what you're really here for. But instead, he shakes his head slightly, like he's begging, pleading for me to stay away.

'I – I can handle my own problems, Calvin. Please. . . .'

On our left, an old rumbling car turns into the corner of the hospital's driveway. The rain glows like a tiny meteor shower in the car's headlights. 'I gotta go,' he says, heading for the car but still scanning the area. Whoever this is, he knows them.

In front of us, a dark green Pontiac Grand Prix pulls up to the emergency room entrance and bucks to a stop right next to me.

'*¡Ay, Dios mio!*' a young, fair-skinned black woman with short hair shouts from the driver's seat. '*¿¡Que paso!?*'

'*Estoy bien, Serena,*' my dad replies. Serena. When'd my dad learn Spanish? '*Callate,*' he adds. '*No digas nada,* okay?'

Serena's voice is rushed. She's scared. *'Pero el carga-mento . . . ¿Por favor, yo espero que el cargamento ha sido protegido?'*

'¡Escúchame!' he insists, struggling to stay calm as he turns back to me. 'I promise, Calvin,' he tells me as he scoops his clothes and Franceschetti shoes from my arms and slides into the passenger seat of the car. The woman touches my dad's forearm with the kind of tender-ness and affection that comes with a wedding band. She looks about twenty-seven or so. Almost my age.

'I swear, Calvin. I swear I'll call you,' my dad promises.

The door slams shut, tires howl, and the car disappears – its red taillights zigzagging like twin laser beams into the darkness, and I scream after it, 'You don't have my phone number!'

'What'd he say?' Roosevelt calls out as the emergency doors *whoosh* open and he rushes outside. 'He ask for your help with his shipment?'

I shake my head, feeling the knots of rage and pain and sadness tighten in my chest. I don't know who the girl is, or where they're going, or why they're in such a rush at two in the morning. But I do know one thing: My father isn't the only one who learned how to speak Spanish in Miami.

Por favor, yo espero que el cargamento ha sido protegido, the woman had said. Please tell me you protected the shipment.

My father said he was robbed and shot by some kid with big ears. But I saw the terror in his eyes when I started sniffing around his shipment – like he's hiding the devil himself in that delivery. For that alone, I should walk away now and leave him to his mess. I should. That's all he deserves. The problem is, the last time I stood around and did nothing, I lost my mom. I could've helped . . . could've run forward . . . But I didn't.

I don't care how much I hate him. I don't care how much I'm already kicking myself. I just found my father – please – don't let me lose him again.

When my father disappeared, I was nine years old and couldn't do anything about it. Nineteen years make a hell of a difference.

I flick open my cell phone as my brain searches for the number. Fortunately, I've got a good memory. So does he. And like Paulo, he knows what he owes me.

'Cal, it's two-fourteen in the morning,' Special Agent Timothy Balfanz answers on the other line, not even pretending to hide his exhaustion. 'Whattya need?'

'Personal favor.'

'Mm I gonna get in trouble?'

'Only if we're caught. There's a container at the port I need to get a look at.'

There's another two-second pause. 'When?' Timothy asks.

'How's right now?'

9

'You should've stayed with the father,' the Judge said through Ellis's phone.

'You're wrong,' Ellis replied, staring from inside the hospital waiting room and studying Cal, who, through the wide panel of glass, was barely twenty feet away. There were plenty of reasons for Ellis to stay in full police uniform. But none was better than simply hiding in plain sight.

There was a soft *whoosh* as the automatic doors slid open and Roosevelt rushed outside to join Cal. As the doors again slid shut, Ellis could hear Roosevelt's first question: *'He ask for your help with his shipment?'*

The shipment. Now Cal knew about the shipment.

'If Cal starts chasing it . . . ' the Judge began.

'He's now talking on his phone,' Ellis said without the least bit of panic. 'You told me you were tracking his calls.'

'Hold on, it usually takes a minute.' The Judge paused a moment. 'Here we go – and people say the courts have no power anymore – pen register is picking up an outgoing call to a Timothy Balfanz. I'll wager it's an old fellow agent.'

Ellis didn't say a word. He knew Cal was smart. Smart enough to know that Lloyd Harper was a liar. And that the only real truth would come from ripping open Lloyd's shipment. It was no different a century ago with Mitchell

Siegel. No different than with Ellis's own dad. No different than with Adam and Cain. It was the first truth in the Book of Lies: In the chosen families, the son was always far more dangerous than the father.

'Ellis, if Cal grabs it first—'

'If Cal grabs the Book, it'll be our greatest day,' Ellis said, never losing sight of his new target and following fearlessly as Cal ran toward his beat-up white van.

Even with his badge, Ellis knew better than to risk being spotted on federal property. That's the reason he'd followed Lloyd to begin with. But with Cal now making calls – with the shipment and the Siegels' fabled prize about to be returned – it was going to be a great day indeed.

10

'You're not being smart,' Roosevelt says through my cell phone.

'It's not a question of smart,' I tell him as I pull the van into the empty parking lot that sits in front of the Port of Miami's main administration building, a stumpy glass mess stolen straight from 1972. There're a few cars in front – one . . . two . . . all three of them Ford Crown Vics. Nothing changes. Unmarked feds.

'It's not safe, either, Cal,' Roosevelt insists.

He's right. That's why I left him at home.

With a twist of the wheel, I weave through the dark lot and the dozens of spots marked OFFICIAL USE ONLY. I got fired from official use over four years ago. But that doesn't mean I don't still have a way in.

'Cal, if you get in trouble—'

'You're the first person I'll call from jail,' I say, heading to the back of the lot, where I steer good ol' White House into a corner spot underneath a crooked palmetto tree.

I hear him seething on the other end. 'Lemme just say one last thing, and then I promise I'll stop.'

'You won't stop.'

'You're right. I won't,' he admits. 'But before you trash your professional career for the *second* time, just think for a moment: If your father *is* setting you up – if this *is* all one big production number – then you're doing exactly what he wants you to do.'

'Roosevelt, why didn't you marry Christine? Or Wendy? Or that woman you went to visit in Chicago? You tie the knot and you *know* they'll take you off whatever blackball list your name is on. But you don't, right? And why? Because some fights are too important.'

'That's fine – and a beautiful change of subject – but if you keep letting your nine-year-old, little hurt self make all your decisions in this situation, you're not just gonna get yourself in trouble – you're gonna get yourself *killed.*'

A burst of light ricochets off my rearview mirror. I look back as a white Crown Vic closes in from behind. There's a slight screech, then a muted *thunk* as his front bumper kisses the back of mine and adds yet another scratch to the rear of the White House. Same jackass trick we used to do when we were rookies.

I wait for him to get out of the car, but he stays put. I get the message. This is *his* hometown. Forget my few years here. Tonight I'm just a guest.

'Roosevelt, I'll call you back.'

Hopping out of the van, I put on a Homeland Security baseball cap, squint through the light rain, and then walk over to the passenger side of his car. It's nearly three in the morning, when everyone in the world looks like crap – except Timothy, who, as I open the door, has a crisp white button-down and a perfect side part in his just trimmed brown hair.

'You're sweating,' Timothy says, reading me perfectly as always.

I've known him since my very first days on the job – before we got promoted to agent (him first, of course, then me) – when we were both lower-level Customs inspectors who spent every day X-raying containers filled with everything from bananas to buzz saws to belt buckles. Even back then, when I'd be dripping in the Miami sun, his shirt didn't have a wrinkle, which is probably why, when all the bad went down and I tipped off Miss Deirdre, even though he was right there next to me, Timothy never tumbled. He should've – he was always the bigger outlaw, and that night he had his own Miss Deirdre as well. But I don't resent him for it. I told him I'd never tattle. And tonight, that's the only reason he's risking his job for me.

'Cal, if anyone finds out I'm bringing you inside—' He holsters the threat and reaches for a new one. 'Is this really that important?'

'Would I ask if it wasn't?'

He stays silent. He knows it isn't just about finding some shipment. I'm searching for something far bigger than that.

Timothy's blue lights – the movable siren that sits on his dash – remind me of the consequences. I expect him to give me the weary glare. Instead, he tosses me an expired copy of his own ICE agent credentials. After 9/11, security at our nation's ports got better. But it didn't get that much better.

'We all set?' I ask.

'The hold is gone, if that's what you're asking.' Reading the panic in my reaction, he adds, 'What? You said you wanted it cleared so you could check it outside.'

'I also said I wanted to get a look first,' I tell him, ripping open his car door. 'I bet he's already on his way.'

I look up at the tall light poles that peek out above the port's nearby container storage yard. On top of each pole, there's a small videocamera, along with chemical sniffers and shotgun microphones. Those are new.

'Don't panic just yet,' he says.

I hop in, he hits the gas, and we head straight for my latest federal crime.

11

It was nearly four in the morning as Lloyd Harper flashed his ID and pulled the tractor truck with the long empty trailer through the main gate at the Port of Miami. Sure, he was tired – his side ached as the anesthetic wore off – but he knew what was at stake. When he got the e-mail notification that the hold was off, well, some rewards were better than cash.

He'd been at this long enough to know that juicy worms usually had a hidden hook. And he'd lived in Miami long enough to know that if he got caught, the payback would be unforgiving. But what the doctor said tonight: the pains he'd been having in his shoulders and chest, plus the way his hands started shaking over the past few years . . . He'd lost his wife, lost his family, in prison they took his dignity – life had already taken so much from him. Was it really so bad to try to get something back?

With a tap of the gas and a sharp right turn, Lloyd headed for the open metal fence of the shipping yard, where dozens of forty-foot metal containers were piled up on top of one another – rusted rectangular monoliths, each one as long as a train car.

But as Lloyd tugged the wide steering wheel, a light-ning bolt of pain knifed his side. He told himself it was the bullet wound, but he knew the truth: just seeing Cal tonight – seeing the white hair and the heartbroken eyes

– just like the ones that burned through him nineteen years ago. Tonight's bullet wound was nothing. The sharpest pains in life come from our own swords. Lloyd had spent the past two decades building his shield, but this was one blade he couldn't stop.

'I'm here for GATH 601174-7,' Lloyd called out his window as he read the container number from the yellow sheet.

Across the open lot, an older black man was sitting on a pyramid of three boxes as he read yesterday's newspaper. He didn't bother looking up.

'Excuse me . . . sir . . .' Lloyd began.

'I ain't deaf. My shift don't start till four.'

Lloyd glanced at the digital clock on his dash: 3:58. Typical union.

'Okay, whatcha need?' the black man called out two minutes later, approaching Lloyd's truck and reaching up for the paperwork. 'Lemme guess: Startin' this early – y'r trynna make Virginia by nightfall.'

'Something like that,' Lloyd replied.

From there, it didn't take long for the man to find the rust-colored forty-foot container with *601174-7* painted on the outside or to climb on his forklift and load it onto the back of Lloyd's tractor trailer. To be safe, Lloyd came out to check the numbers for himself. And the seal they put on the back to make sure the container hadn't been opened during transit.

As he was about to climb back in his cab, he took a quick glance around the metal towers of the container yard. No one in sight. Back in the driver's seat, he checked again, peering in his rearview as he shifted the truck through the first few gears and headed for the exit. And he checked again as he drove toward the final security checkpoint – a three-story-tall radiation portal monitor that looked like an enormous upside-down letter U. The detector was new, designed to catch smuggled nuclear devices. Everyone who left the port had to drive through it. For a moment, Lloyd edged his foot toward the brakes.

He held his breath as he approached the detector. The truck bounced slightly. Slowly rolling forward, he kept his eye on the red and green bulbs that were embedded in the roof of the detector. Once again, a bolt of pain burned at his side. But when the green light blinked, he smiled, slammed the gas, and never looked back.

And that's why, as the eighteen-wheeler climbed and lumbered over the bridge toward Miami . . . and as he stared into the darkness, searching for the coming sunrise . . . Lloyd Harper didn't notice the white, unmarked Crown Vic that was trailing a few hundred feet behind him.

'Think he knows what he's hauling in back?' Timothy asked.

'I don't really care,' Cal replied from the passenger seat, never taking his eyes off his father's truck. 'But we're about to find out.'

12

'Guns or drugs – *gotta be*,' Timothy says as my dad's eighteen-wheeler makes a slow, sharp left toward the entrance for I-95. We're at least three football fields behind him, with our lights still off. But at four-thirty in the morning, with only a few cars between us, he's impossible to miss.

'Maybe your dad's container—'

'Maybe it's not my dad's. For all I know, he's just another feeb doing a pickup.'

'But if you thought that, would you really have shown up at three in the morning? Or would he have shown up at four, fresh from his new bullet wound? I know you can't bring yourself to say it – and I know it was just a random hold – but you *should* be worried about him,' Timothy says. 'Don't apologize, Cal. I got twin teenage girls – and no matter how much they hate me, only monsters would let their father take a beating. In fact, it's not that different from Deirdre—'

'Can we just focus on what's in the shipment? Please.'

To his credit, Timothy lets it go. And I try my best to ignore my crooked pinkies.

According to the bill of lading, GATH 601174-7 is a refrigerated container that's (supposedly) carrying 3,850 pounds of frozen shrimp coming (supposedly) from Panama. My dad definitely gets credit for that. In the world of smuggling – drugs or anything else – you never know when you'll be inspected. But if you want to improve your odds, pick a quiet, seafood-producing country (like Panama), fill the container with one of its top exports (like shrimp), and make sure it's refrigerated (because once it's listed as 'perishable,' it'll move twice as fast through inspection).

This isn't just about some really good shrimp.

'Turn for the worse,' Timothy says, motioning to the truck.

The shipment was scheduled to be delivered to a warehouse in Coral Gables. That's south of here. Which is why I'm surprised to see him heading for the on-ramp of I-95 North.

'Maybe he's smuggling people,' Timothy says.

'It's not people,' I tell him, surprised by my own defensiveness. 'You said the shipment checked out fine. No buzzers ringing; no dogs barking. If he were smuggling people, audio would've picked up the heartbeats.'

'Then what? Plastic nuclear triggers? F-14 parts? Stolen Picassos? What can you possibly hide amidst four thousand pounds of frozen shrimp?'

I don't bother answering. During our first year as agents, Timothy and I ripped open a suspicious crate and found two hundred snakes with their anuses sewed shut, their stomachs filled with diamonds they'd been forced to swallow. There's no end to what people will try to hide.

Next to us on the highway, an orange taxi blows by us, then races past my dad and disappears in the horizon of night. 'So you never looked him up?' Timothy asks.

'Pardon?'

'Your dad. All those years at ICE – you had access to computers that could find the addresses, phone numbers, and birthmarks of every known felon in the country. You never took a glance to see where your missing dad was living or what he was up to?'

I stare at the outline of my father's truck in the distance and can't help but picture our client Alberto whispering to his father's ashes in that rusted old RC Cola can. 'No,' I say. 'Never did.'

Timothy turns my way and studies me as I fidget with the stray wires that run down from the blue lights on his dash. There's no end to what people will try to hide.

Twenty minutes later, the sky's still black, my dad's still ahead, and the highway – as we blow past the exits of Fort Lauderdale – is dotted with the first batch of early risers.

'You think he sees us?' Timothy asks as my dad veers toward the exit that sends us west on I-595.

'If he saw us, he'd try to lose us. Or at least slow down to get a better look.'

It's a fair point. But as my dad once again clicks his blinker, I realize we've got a brand-new problem. The exit and highway signs say I-75, but every local knows the thin stretch of road known as Alligator Alley.

'Why am I not surprised?' Timothy asks as we follow the exit and no other cars follow behind us. 'Cal, I need to call for backup.'

'And where do you plan on hiding me?' I ask as the grass and trees on the side of the road give way to miles of muddy swampland.

Connecting Florida's east and west coasts, the narrow and mostly abandoned lanes of Alligator Alley plow straight through the mosquito marshes known as the Everglades. To protect the land, the road has no gas stations, though it *is* lined with metal fences to keep the ample alligator population from getting hit by cars and . . . well . . . eating people.

'There's no way you're leaving me out here,' I tell Timothy.

He doesn't argue. He's too busy realizing that at barely five a.m., with the December sky as black as the road in front of us, there's no one on Alligator Alley but us. It's like driving full speed through a cave.

'Cal, I have to put the lights on.'

'Don't!' I shout as he reaches for the switch. My dad's truck is still a good half mile in front of us – two faint red dragon's eyes staring back from the depths of the cave. But with no other cars to hide behind . . . 'He'll see us.'

'Then he'll see us. But I can't drive like this. I wouldn't worry, though – we're so far, he'll never make us out.'

With a twist, Timothy flicks on the lights, and the gray road appears in front of us. I wait for the dragon's eyes to glow brighter . . . for my dad to panic and hit the brakes . . . but he just keeps moving. It doesn't make me feel any better. I pull out my cell phone to check the time. The bars for my signal fade from four . . . three . . . two . . . just a tiny X. No signal.

'If you want, we can turn back,' Timothy offers. 'Have them call in the helicopters and—'

'No,' I insist. I lost my father once. Now that he's back, I need to know why. 'I'm fine,' I tell him.

'I didn't ask that, Cal.'

'Just stay with him,' I add, squinting into the night and never losing sight of the dragon's eyes.

For the next few miles, we chase him deeper down the desolate road, which I swear narrows with each mile marker. By the time we hit mile marker twenty-two, we're so deep in the Everglades, the black sky presses down like a circus tent after they've yanked the main pole.

'This was stupid of us,' Timothy says. 'What if this was the whole point: to lead us out where there're no witnesses, no one to protect us, and only one way to get in or out?'

I've known Timothy a long time. He rarely lets a hair get out of place. But as he grips the steering wheel, I see a clump of them matted by sweat on his forehead. 'Listen, Timothy, if this were an ambush—'

Out in the darkness, halfway between us and my dad, two other red dragon's eyes pop open.

'Cal—'

'I see it.'

We both lean forward, tightening our squints. It's another car. Parked on the side of the road from the looks of it.

Without a word, Timothy pumps the brakes and shuts the lights. I assume he's trying to use the darkness to hide us – but in the distance, the new dragon's eyes shake and rumble . . . then shrink away from us. This new car – it's got no interest in us. It takes off, chasing my dad.

'Maybe that's his buyer. Or his girlfriend.'

A burst of blue light explodes from the new car. I blink once, then again, making sure I see it right. Damn.

'Cops,' Timothy agrees. 'State troopers, I bet. They love Alligator Alley as a speed trap.'

Sure enough, the new car zips forward, a blazing blue firefly zigzagging toward my dad's truck. The dragon's eyes on the eighteen-wheeler go bright red as my dad hits the brakes. But it's not until they both slow down and pull off onto the shoulder of the road that we finally get our first good look.

'You sure that's a cop car?' Timothy asks.

I lean forward in the passenger seat, my fingertips touching the dash and my forehead almost touching the front windshield. That's not a car. It's a van. And not a police van. No, the siren's not on top. The blue light pulses from within, lighting up the two back windows where the tint is peeling.

I lean in closer. My forehead taps the windshield.

There's a swarm of rust along the back.

My tongue swells in my mouth, and I can barely breathe. What the hell's my van doing out here?

13

Timothy rides the brakes, keeping his distance. 'Cal, maybe we should wait back and—'

'That's my— Someone stole my van from the parking lot. *Get us up there!'*

We're barely a few hundred feet away as a uniformed cop approaches the driver's-side door of my father's truck. My dad rolls down his window . . . a few words go back and forth . . .

'Looks like he's giving him a ticket,' Timothy says as we slow down and veer toward the shoulder of the road. The cop looks our way, shielding his eyes as we flick on our headlights. I'm too busy rechecking the license plate: M34 DZP. That's ours.

'How'd he even get it?' Timothy asks.

Thankful that Roosevelt's safe at home, I open Timothy's glove box. 'You still have your—? Ah.' Toward the back of the glove box, his metal telescoping baton sits among the mess of maps and fast-food napkins.

'What're you doing?' Timothy asks as I pull it out and slide it up my sleeve.

'Being smart for once,' I say, kicking open the car door even though we're still moving.

'Cal . . . don't—!'

It's not until my door smashes into a concrete barrier that I realize what he's warning me about. The car jerks to the left and rumbles over what feels like a speed bump. I was so busy looking at the van, I didn't even see that we were passing over a small canal, one of the hundreds that run underneath Alligator Alley.

Just beyond the short overpass, Timothy pulls back onto the shoulder of the road, flicks on his own blue lights, and stops nearly fifty feet behind the van. He knows what happens when you surprise a cop.

'Hands!' the cop yells, pulling his gun as we both get out of the car.

'Federal agent! ICE!' Timothy shouts, flashing his credentials and sounding plenty annoyed.

He's not the only one. 'What the hell're you doing with my van!?' I shout, racing forward without even thinking.

'W-Was I speeding?' my dad asks, panicking through his open window and not seeing us yet.

The cop smiles to himself and raises his gun toward my father. 'Please step out of the truck, Mr Harper.'

'I – I don't—'

'I'm not counting to three,' the cop warns as the hammer cocks on his gun.

My father opens his door and climbs down from the cab, his face lit by the pulsing blue lights. '*Cal?* What're you doing here?' he stutters.

Behind me, Timothy freezes.

On my right, just as I pass the open door of my van, there's a low roar that rumbles like thunder. I turn just in time to see a snarling brown dog with pointy black ears and pale yellow teeth.

'Stay, Benoni,' the cop warns, never lowering his gun. With his free hand, he shoves my dad toward me. The movement's too much for my father, who bends forward, holding his side.

As the cop finally turns and points his gun at all of us, we get our first good look at him. The headlights of the van ricochet off his grown-out copper red hair and thick eyebrows. But what lights up most is the prominent tattoo between his thumb and pointer finger. 'Nice to finally meet you, Cal. You should call me Ellis.'

14

'Wait— Okay, *wait*— Why would—?' I look around at my dad and Timothy, at this guy Ellis and his gun, and at the attack dog that's perched in the front seat of my van. 'What the crap is going on here?'

'Ask your father,' Ellis says. 'Though good luck in getting the truth.'

'*Me?*' my dad asks, fighting to stand up straight but still holding his side. 'I don't even know who you—'

'My father was a liar, too,' Ellis says, pointing his gun at my dad. 'He lied like you, Lloyd. Easily. Without even a thought.'

'Cal, I swear on my life, I've never seen this man.'

'That part's true. You can tell the way his left hand's shaking,' Ellis agrees as my dad grips his own left wrist. 'But I saw you tonight, Mr Harper. The way your son came to your aid, taking you to the hospital: He needs to rescue, doesn't he? That was pretty fortunate for—'

'Hold on,' I interrupt. 'You saw us in the park?'

A chorus of crickets squeals from the Everglades, and my father draws himself up straight, blocking the head-lights and casting a shadow across both Ellis's badge and his face.

'Calvin had no hand in this,' my dad says.

'Really? Then why was he so quick to get rid of that hold notice on your shipment?' Ellis challenges, motioning with his gun. He has handsome, chiseled features and the ramrod posture of an officer, but from the perfect Windsor knot of his uniform's tie to the shine on that expensive belt he's wearing, he's got his eye on something bigger. 'It's pretty convenient having a son who used to be an agent, isn't it, Lloyd?'

As they continue to argue, my brain swirls, struggling to— It's like trying to fill in a crossword without any clues. For Ellis to know we got rid of the hold notice . . . For him to steal my van from the port and bring it out here . . . That's the part I keep playing over and over. When I pulled up to the port, I checked half a dozen times – whoever this guy Ellis is, no matter how good a cop he is – there's no way he was trailing me. But if that's the case, for him to get my van— Once again, I run through the mental reel. Roosevelt's at home, which means there's only one other person who knew where it was parked. The one person who picked me up there. And the only other member of law enforcement who hasn't said a single word since I got out of his car.

There's a metallic click behind me. The swirling blue lights stab at my senses, and my stomach sags like a hammock holding a bowling ball.

'Sorry, Cal,' Timothy says as he cocks his gun behind my ear. 'Once the twins were born . . . Those braces aren't gonna pay for themselves.'

15

Hundreds of People's Choice Award–winning movies tell me this is when I'm supposed to shake a fist at the sky and yell, 'Nooo! Timothy, how could you!?' But I know exactly how he could. His ethical apathy is why I approached him in the first place. And why I didn't bat twice when he offered to sneak me inside the port instead of signing me in and getting a proper pass. I thought he was doing me a favor. All he was really doing was making sure nothing linked the two of us together. My heart constricts, like it's being gripped by a fist. Dammit, when'd I get so blind? I glance at my dad and know the answer. The only good news is, I apparently wasn't the only one Timothy was trying to keep hidden.

'Cal's already seen it – you, me, *all of it!*' Timothy shouts at Ellis. 'And what about *the van*!? What was your grand thinking there? Bring it out on the road and hope no one notices?'

'Watch your tone,' Ellis warns.

To my surprise, Timothy does, his shoulders shrinking just slightly.

'You said you just wanted the shipment,' Timothy adds through gritted teeth, fighting hard to stay calm. 'Now you have far more than that.'

The pulsing blue lights pump like heartbeats from both sides. I'm tempted to run, but that won't tell me what's going on. On my right, in the front seat of the van, Ellis's dog, protective of its master, growls at Timothy, whose gun is still trained on me. On my left, my father stares at Ellis, then Timothy, then back to Ellis.

Then he looks at me.

I see desperation every day. For the homeless, it overrides despair, depression, even fear. But when my dad's wide eyes beg for help . . . I've seen that look before – all those years ago when the cops came and arrested him.

'I didn't do anything wrong,' he blurts.

Across from us, Ellis pulls the cuff of his shirt out from the wrist of his uniform's jacket, then flicks the safety on his gun. 'I don't care. We've waited over a century. I want my Book.'

Just behind me, my father puts a hand on my shoulder. There's nothing tender about it. For the second time, I tell myself to run, but the way he's gripping me – he needs the handhold to help him stand.

'All you had to do was leave the van downtown!' Timothy says to Ellis. 'But with this— You know how much harder you just made this?' Timothy explodes, barely looking at us. This isn't about me. Timothy is the same old Timothy. Just protecting his share. 'Don't you see? Now that he knows I'm working with— *Sonuva*—! You just wrecked my damn life!'

'He's right,' I interrupt, knowing this isn't a ride Timothy can afford to let me walk away from. Time to work the weak spots. 'But if I disappear, they'll go talk to all my friends, co-workers . . . even former co-workers,' I add, raising an eyebrow at Timothy. 'You'll get a call tomorrow morning.'

Timothy knows what I'm up to – he had the same hostage training with the same dumb tricks for getting the bad guys to fight among themselves – but that doesn't mean it won't work.

'You don't even see it, do you?' Ellis asks, sounding far more comfortable than he should be. 'I've already won.'

'Not if there's a manhunt for Cal's killer!' Timothy shoots back as the blue lights continue their assault. 'You promised me no risk at all!'

'No, I promised you an easy reward.'

While they argue, I work the telescoping baton hidden in my sleeve toward the inside of my forearm. I've heard enough. Time to let actions speak louder than—

'Be very careful about your next move,' Ellis warns as he points his gun at my face. I freeze. He's clearly planning to pull the trigger, but he's not quite ready to do it yet. 'I can see the baton, Calvin.'

Next to him, Timothy shakes his head, his anger now exploding. 'This was so stupidly easy and— *Dammit!* How could you be so *stupid*!?'

The dog barks. But Ellis, who's now close enough that I spot the odd red thimble-shaped nozzle on his gun, is calmer than ever. 'It'll work out fine,' he says.

'For who?' Timothy challenges. 'For you?'

Ellis nods, raising his eyebrows. 'You were right about the manhunt. But there's no manhunt if I give them Cal's killer.' Without another word, he points his gun at Timothy's neck. I want to jump forward, but my body steps back.

'I have twins! For God's sake!' Timothy says in horror.

Ellis grins. 'It *is* for God's sake.'

Fttt.

The dog barks again. A tiny fleck of blood hits my cheek. And Timothy falls to the ground.

Behind us, at least a mile or two up the road, a set of faint white eyes blink open. There's a car back there. Coming right at us.

16

'Ohnonono!' my father stutters, still clutching my shoulder as he stumbles and pulls us back.

Ellis stares over our shoulders at the car that's coming our way.

'Hand me his gun,' Ellis says to us as he motions to Timothy, who's flat on his back with what looks like a pinprick at his jugular. There's no stream of blood as his body convulses like a snake and he continues to threaten and scream. First, Timothy's left knee freezes awkwardly, cocked out to the side, then his torso stops moving. In less than a minute, he's motionless on the pavement. He looks dead, his gun still clutched in his hand.

'I'm waiting,' Ellis adds, and for the first time, I see the new reality he's building. If he shoots us with Timothy's gun, then leaves my van here along with Timothy's unmarked car – now the picture shifts: It'll look like Timothy and I were having a late night get-together . . . two dirty feds arguing over a deal. My father was with me because, of course, we're in on it together. Maybe a few words got exchanged, and both sides wound up dead. Best of all, with no one searching for the real killer, Ellis rides off in my father's truck and whatever prize – he called it a book – he thinks is inside.

'I'd like that gun now,' Ellis says, his pistol now aimed at my dad's face.

Panicking, my dad picks up the gun and tosses it to—
'*Don't!*' I call out.

Ellis catches it with his free hand – a hand that I realize is covered by a plastic glove – but never takes his eyes off me. 'You're smarter than Timothy,' he says. 'You understand why I'm here, Cal.'

Behind me, the car on the road is about a half mile away. But the way Ellis keeps staring at me – his amber eyes barely blinking even as the headlights grow brighter – it's like he doesn't even care the car's coming. His uniform tells me he's a cop, but that burning obsessed look . . . that odd tattoo on his hand and how he rubs it over and over . . . and especially the way he keeps glancing at his dog like it's the Messiah. I don't know what he meant when he said he's been searching for a century. But I know a zealot when I see one.

'Easy, Benoni,' he murmurs as he finally notices the approaching car, about a city block away.

For a moment, I'm worried it's someone he knows. But as Ellis lowers his chin at the arriving lights and hides both guns behind his back, it's clear this is a stranger. And potential witness. For at least the next thirty seconds, Ellis knows better than to pull the trigger, which means I still have a chance to—

'Don't be this stupid,' Ellis tells me in a condescending tone.

But I've always been stupid. And stubborn. And lots of other things that look bad on a report card. Right now, that's the only thing to keep me alive. Behind me, I hear my dad breathing heavily. *Us* alive. That'll keep *us* alive.

The car's fifty yards away. In this darkness, its lights barrel at my back like a freight train and mix with the swirling blue lights that I swear are pulsing at the exact same speed as my pulse.

'If you flag them down, their deaths will forever be on your conscience,' Ellis says, already starting to squint.

I believe him. But if I let them pass, 'forever' is going to last about twenty more seconds.

'Calvin,' my dad pleads, tugging on my sleeve. As I turn around, I figure he'll be pleading for help. He's not. His brow furrows, and his eyebrows knit into an angry glare. He's pissed. *This is my fault,* he says with a glance. *Go. Leave.* I consider it for a moment. But I'm not listening to him, either. Ellis has two guns. We have none. Once this car passes, those bullets are going in both our heads.

I take a step toward Ellis, who's still too smart to raise his guns. But that doesn't mean he's out of options.

'Benoni, *ready!*' Ellis commands as the dog prepares to pounce.

I squat slightly, preparing to spring. The crickets squeal in every direction. The car's so close, Ellis's pupils shrink. This is it. On three . . .

One . . . two . . .

I leap as fast as I can. But not at Ellis. At his dog.

'Benoni, *attack!*' Ellis shouts just as the car blows past us, pelting us with an air pocket full of dust and gravel.

From the front seat, Benoni leaps like a wolf, all muscle and sharp teeth.

Finally, something goes my way.

I raise my right forearm like Dracula hiding behind his cape. The dog sees it as a giant bone and opens its jaw. I did six months of K-9 duty. This is the part that hurts.

Like a metal trap, the dog's jaw clamps down with all its strength. Its top teeth sink into my forearm, but its bottom teeth get a mouthful of metal pole courtesy of the telescoping baton that's still hidden in place. I see the pain in the dog's eyes, but that's nothing compared with the pain felt by its owner.

'*Benoni!*' Ellis screams as the dog cries with a high-pitched yelp. Letting go of my arm, Benoni collapses on its back, whining and bleeding from the mouth.

'*Go . . . move!*' I say to my dad, ignoring my own pain, grabbing the shoulder of his shirt, and darting back toward Timothy's car. For a moment, Ellis freezes. It's a choice between us and checking on his dog. When I was twelve, I had a beagle named Snoopy 2. It's no choice at all.

'Benoni, you okay, girl? . . . *Y'okay?*' Ellis asks, dropping to his knees.

It's all the distraction we need. I try the door to Timothy's car (locked, no luck), then keep running along the shoulder of the road. My dad's panting, holding his side. We won't be able to outrun Ellis and the dog for long.

On our left is the short chain-link fence that separates us from the Everglades and its alligator population. Directly below us is one of the dozens of canals that run underneath Alligator Alley. As I said, it's no choice at all.

'I can't run,' my father insists.

'That's fine,' I tell him as I grab the back of his arm and drag him up onto the ledge of the overpass. 'Can you swim?'

17

'Y'think they see us?'

'*Shhh . . .*' I hiss. For the past fifteen minutes, we've been waist-high in black water, ducking and hiding behind a thick, thorny bush that sits like a hairy beach ball on the edge of the canal. My shoes and pockets are filled with mud, and the tall sea grass is so thick, it's like plowing through a giant soaked carpet.

We had only a few minutes' lead time, enough to follow the canal underneath Alligator Alley, where it forked and split into the wider canals that run parallel to the road. If we'd gone left, we would've gone farther from Ellis. That's the only reason I went right.

No question, we were fast. But that doesn't mean we're fast enough. Except for the pulsing blue lights, the night is dark as a coffin. Ellis can't see us. But as I crane my neck to peer out, we can't see him, either.

There's a hushed splash on our far right. We both turn just in time to hear the *krkk krkk krkk* – someone walking through the dried saw grass on the edge of the canal. The sound gets louder the closer they get. I squint and peer between the branches, up toward the road. There's a fast scratching sound – someone running – then the un-mistakable pant – *hhh hhh hhh* – that's the dog. Benoni. The dog's right above us. By the road. I see her.

My father and I both duck deeper into the water. It's

freezing cold and my shirt sucks like a jellyfish to my chest. The dog bite didn't break skin, but my arm still stings. Behind me, my father's still holding the wound at his side. We both know how filthy this water is. But as the panting gets closer, we lower ourselves without a word.

Up on the embankment, the dog stands there, her pointy ears at full attention. I squat even lower until the muddy black water reaches my neck, my chin, my ears. I've got my head tilted back, trying to keep everything submerged. My father does the same – as far underwater as he can get. A few feet in front of us, there's a squiggle in the water as a thin indigo snake skates across the surface. I hold my breath, pretending it's not there.

'Benoni! *Come!*' Ellis calls as the dog darts to the right, back the way she came.

My father doesn't move. I don't move. Nothing moves until the *krkk krkk krkk* fades in the distance. For a moment, I worry they're coming back – until, from the opposite side of the road, I hear the hiccup of an engine, followed by a huge diesel belch, followed by a final piercing hiss that slashes the night. My father's truck – Ellis wants the prize inside even more than he wants us. I lift my head as the muddy water streams down my neck and face.

'They're leaving,' I whisper.

Behind me, my dad doesn't say a word, even as the engine rumbles and fades. I assume it's because he's still terrified . . . still in shock . . . and most likely way pissed if Ellis drove off with his truck.

'You saved me,' my dad blurts. As I turn around to face him, he's got tears in his eyes.

'You did—You saved my life.' He shakes his head over and over. 'I thought you hated me.' He starts sniffling.

I raise my hands from the water and pull him toward

the bank. 'Listen, erm . . . *Lloyd* . . . I appreciate that – I do. But can we please have this talk later?'

He nods, but the tears are still there. 'I just— What you did— You didn't have to do that for me.'

Sometimes a speech can make things better. This isn't one of those times.

'Can we just go back to that cop? Ellis. Who the hell is he?' I ask as we slosh through the canal, climbing back up toward the road and eyeing the fence that separates us from the alligators.

'I have no idea.'

'Don't lie,' I challenge, waiting to see his reaction.

'Cal, I swear to you, I've never seen him until tonight. When he pulled me over, I thought he was giving me a ticket.' His voice is flying – he means it – but as he says the words, the consequences finally hit. Reaching the top of the embankment, he looks across the road at my van and Timothy's car, where the blue lights are still spinning.

'Motherf—! He stole my *truck*!' my dad shouts.

'What was in it, anyway? He mentioned a book.'

'D'you know what this—? I'm dead.'

'What book was in the truck, Lloyd?'

'Mary, mother of— *I'm dead*!' he explodes at full detonation, spit flying through the air. 'We should've killed his fu—' He catches himself.

During my short career in law enforcement, I sent eleven people to prison. To real prison. And when you go to prison – no matter how straitlaced and Dr Jekyll you are going *in*, the monsters within those walls always bring a little bit more of your own monster *out*.

My father swallows hard, clearly regretting the outburst. Whatever tears he had are long gone. 'I'm sorry, Cal. I'm not— It's been a tough few years.'

'Just tell me what's in the truck, and who you're so scared of.'

'It's not that simple.'

'Sure it is. Give me the name and we'll at least know who we're dealing with – or at least who Ellis is working against.'

'That's the thing: When they got in contact, they didn't give me a name.'

'How could you not—?'

'Last year, I got my second DUI, which got me fired from my company. Since then, business is more word of mouth these days, y'know? I get a phone call. They send the paperwork and tell me where to drop it off – in this case, I was supposed to leave Alligator Alley at Naples and wait for a call. I know they have a 216 area code. From Cleveland. But that's it.'

'That's it? You sure?'

'Why wouldn't I be sure?'

'A minute ago, you were saying, "I'm dead! I'm dead!" Why be afraid of someone you don't know?'

My father studies me. I look for his U.S. Navy ring and realize he's no longer wearing it.

'Calvin, I may not be the best father . . .'

'Don't sell yourself short, Great Santini. Though I have to admit, I *cannot wait* to see how you finish this sentence.'

'. . . but I'm not a liar.'

'No, Lloyd, you're just an innocent truck driver. Nothing more than that, right?'

He tugs his soaking silk shirt away from his chest. From what I can tell, it's another Michael Kors.

'You're giving me too much credit,' my dad says. 'I never heard of no books, and got no idea what could take centuries to find, except for maybe some old art or something. Ease up, okay?'

'Oh, I'm sorry – usually when I get attacked, potentially framed for murder, and almost killed, I'm much more cheery and fun.'

'What do you want from me, Calvin?'

'I wanna know what the hell is really going on! You're fresh out of the hospital and still got up at four in the morning for this! You're telling me you thought it was for three thousand pounds of frozen shrimp!?'

'It's Miami, Calvin. If they're calling *me* instead of a real company – I figured it was guns or . . . or . . . or something like that.' He shakes his head before I can argue. 'I'm not *proud* of it, y'know? But once you have that excon label on your neck— You don't know what it's like to be judged like that.'

I think back to the days after they took my gun and badge. Even the secretaries from the office were instructed to hang up when I called.

'Okay, first we need to get out of here,' I say. As we run across the road and back to my van, I scan the ground, the road, even under the van itself. Timothy. His body's gone.

'Y'think he's still alive?' my dad asks.

I pause a moment. Then I picture that bubble of blood in Timothy's neck. 'I don't think so.'

'Maybe Ellis took the body with him.'

'Maybe,' I say. But to set all this up – to bring my van out here just to make us look like the killers . . . to leave no witnesses . . . I cross around to the passenger side of the White House. Down the tall grass of the embankment, there's another canal that runs parallel to the road. When we were hiding on the other side . . . There was another splash.

'Gator food,' my father says, pointing over the fence.

'That's what I would do.'

I wait for him to ask why, but to've abandoned me this long, my dad's got plenty of heartless in him. He doesn't need help developing the picture: Ellis is a cop. He did his homework. My dad's a convicted murderer . . . I'm a disgraced agent . . . There's no question who's the easiest to blame for this. And why he asked my dad to hand him Timothy's gun.

'He's got my prints on one of the weapons,' my father says.

'You think he didn't drive my van all around the port, making sure the eyes-in-the-sky got a good look? Ten seconds' worth of homework before ICE realizes I'm the one who snuck into the port with Timothy. . . .'

'On behalf of a shipment that's tied to your father,' my dad adds.

Which brings us right back to the gun. We're both silent as it all seeps in. Forget what happened with Mom. Ellis just has to point his cop finger our way. Once they hear we killed a federal agent – we're repeat offenders. They don't make bags small enough that'll carry our remains.

'We should follow the truck,' my dad suggests, looking out toward the dark road. 'He didn't have that much of a lead.'

'Yeah, maybe,' I reply.

'*Maybe?* The only way to prove what actually happened is by finding what's really in that—'

I turn away. That's all he needs.

'You know what's in that truck, don't you, Calvin?'

18

'Stay, girl. . . . That's my girl,' Ellis said to Benoni, adding a quick scratch between the dog's ears. In the passenger seat of the truck, Benoni was breathing calmly now – but with her ears pinned back and her eyes narrow and intently fixed out the window, it was clear she was just simmering.

After setting the odometer back to zero, Ellis grabbed an old pair of bolt cutters from the toolbox behind his seat, shoved open the driver's door, and climbed down from the cab of the truck. He was still annoyed that he'd let Cal get away, but when he'd heard Benoni cry like that – the way she was shaking on the ground – family had to come first.

Most important, as he glanced around the empty rest stop and walked around to the back of the truck, he had what he wanted. And thanks to his police uniform, surprise was most definitely on his side. Especially with Timothy. But that was the benefit of taking on a partner – there was always someone else to blame things on. As his grandfather wrote, the mission was bigger than a single man. Finally, after the headache in China and Hong Kong and Panama and here – finally – mission accomplished.

He dialed quickly on his cell, then pinched the phone between his chin and shoulder and lifted the bolt cutters to the metal seal that looked like a silver bolt at the back of the rust-colored container. The phone rang in his ear . . . once . . . twice . . . He knew the time – it was six a.m. in Michigan – but this was victory.

There was a loud *cunk* as the bolt cutters bit down and snapped the seal.

'Judge Wojtowicz's line,' a female voice answered. 'You need him to sign a warrant?'

'No warrants. This is a personal call. For Felix,' Ellis said, knowing that using the Judge's first name would speed things up. With a twist of the thin metal bars on the back of the container, Ellis unlocked the double doors.

He knew how he got to this moment. His grandfathers – in their commitment to the Leadership – began the quest. For all Ellis knew, his mother had searched, too. But the research had survived only because of the water-stained diary.

The word *Schetsboek* was embossed in faded gold on the front. Dutch for 'Sketchbook.' Flipping through it that first time, Ellis had stopped on a page dated February 16, 1922, on a passage about the covenants between God and man. In the story of Noah, God made a rainbow as a sign of His covenant. With Abraham, God's sign was a circumcision. And with Moses, the sign was the engraving on the tablets. But covenants could also be between people. That's what the diary was, Ellis realized. He'd been so focused on the Cain part – on the tattoo and the dog – he'd nearly missed it. The diary was his true sign. *His* covenant. The promise from his mother. And the way, over a century later, surrounded by cricket songs, he finally found the Book that was more powerful than death itself.

'Who may I say is calling?' the woman asked through Ellis's phone.

'He'll know,' Ellis said as he tugged on the back doors of the truck. There was a rusty howl as the metal doors swung wide open, clanging against their respective sides of the truck. Surprised by his own excitement, Ellis was up on his tiptoes, peering through the mist of—

It was supposed to be cold. And smell like shrimp. Why didn't it smell like—?

Reaching up and pulling frantically, Ellis yanked the nearest box to the ground. His breathing started to quicken as he ripped it open. Pineapples. Plastic pineapples. He pulled out another box. Fake. They were all fake. Like the government uses when they—

Damn.

They switched it. Switched the bloody trucks.

'I'm paging him now, sir,' the secretary announced.

'Paging?' Ellis asked. He looked at the phone. 'Don't page him. Leave him be.' Shutting his cell phone, Ellis stood there a second. Just stood there, eyes closed. A *rat-tt-tat* drumbeat – *rat-tt-tat, rat-tt-tat* – hammered at the back of his neck at the top of his spine. He clenched his jaw so hard, he heard a high-pitched scream rushing in his ears. Anger. All he had was anger now. People didn't understand what a life's worth of holding back and hiding could do.

He wouldn't hold back anymore.

He knew who'd done this. Timothy. Timothy and the other one. The one who hurt Benoni. Cal.

Cal caused this. Cal and his damn father. But Ellis had it wrong before. Lloyd wasn't the only trickster. Cal was one, too. To switch the trucks – to steal what was inside – Cal hadn't just stumbled into this. He'd planned it. Stolen it. And now Cal had the Book of Lies. He had what Ellis had waited a lifetime to find.

But the one thing Cal didn't have? A good enough head start.

Ellis looked down at his tattoo. With the Book, Cain unleashed murder into the world. That was nothing compared to what Ellis would unleash on Cal Harper.

19

'Do you know what's in the truck or don't you?' my dad asks.

I stomp my feet to shake off the excess water, then open the door to my van, hop inside, and flick off the blue lights. 'Not yet.'

'Whoa, whoa – hold on,' my dad says, climbing into the passenger seat. 'I saw him take the truck and drive off with—'

'He didn't take anything.'

Landing with a squish in the passenger seat, my father looks at me, then out at the empty road, then back at me. 'No, I saw it – container number 601174-7. I checked the numbers myself. There's no way you could've unloaded it that fast. And when I drove it out, you were following right behi—'

I close my eyes and picture the black numbers on the side of the forty-foot rust-colored container: 601174-7. At three in the morning, in the dark, it's amazing what you can do with some black electrical tape.

'The numbers. You switched them, didn't you?' my dad blurts. 'That container Ellis just drove off with—'

'Is filled with three thousand pounds of plastic pineapples, courtesy of the controlled delivery sting operations that Customs keeps prepared for just such an occasion.'

Starting the van and noticing the exposed wires that

Ellis used to hot-wire underneath, I swing the steering wheel into a U-turn and do my best to ignore the blue pulsing swirls as Timothy's unmarked car fades behind us. Up above, the purple-and-orange sunrise cracks a hairline fissure through the black sky. The water from my clothes soaks my seat and puddles at my crotch. But as I look in the rearview mirror, it still hasn't washed off the flecks of Timothy's blood that're sprayed across my cheek.

'You think this book – whatever it is – you think maybe there could be something good in it? Y'know, like, maybe we're finally getting some good luck?' my father asks.

I turn to my dad, who's eyeing the steering wheel and— Is he studying my hands? He turns away fast, but there's no mistaking that gleam in his eyes. He's anxious, but also . . . it's almost like he's enjoying himself.

'Lloyd, let me be clear here. There's nothing *good* about this. The shipment . . . the shooting . . . *everything*. It's rotten, okay? And once something's rotten, it can never be good again.'

Surprised by my own outburst, I sit there silently, my chest rising and falling far too rapidly. I'm not stupid. I know all the emotional reasons I went chasing after my dad instead of just writing him off after the hospital. I still believe in those reasons. But that doesn't mean I believe *him*.

'Cal, I promise you, I have no idea what book Ellis is after, or what's inside that container.'

'Doesn't matter,' I shoot back. 'We're about to get our answer.'

20

'*Here?*' my father asks, looking inside the dark doorway. Our clothes were soaked from the water, but he's still fidgeting with the spare dry T-shirt and jeans I always keep stored in the van. 'Y'sure?'

I nod, holding open the door with no doorknob and thankful that the punch-code lock is still so easy to jimmy. Inside the old warehouse, the walls are bare and peeling, while each corner hosts a small hill of crumpled newspapers and garbage. Up high, the few horizontal windows are shattered. And the sign out front carries the spray-painted love note 'LO' (a gang-inspired tag that means 'Latinos Only' just in case anyone misses the welcome mat).

But as I flick a switch and the fluorescent lights blink to life, they reveal what we're really after: the navy blue container with black tracking number 601174-7 painted across its back. Beached like a metal whale, it rests its tail against the narrow loading dock that runs along the back of the room.

'You sure it's safe?' my father asks, racing for the container.

He's missing the point. The warehouse may be decorated in modern dungeon, but that's the goal. Hidden under layers of fake corporate names, this place is owned by the U.S. government.

We— They. They own them all around the city: fake warehouses that ICE, Customs, and the FBI can use for whatever sting operations they happen to be running. When Timothy offered to have the container delivered here, I thought he was doing me a favor. All he was really doing – once he presumably got rid of me and my dad – was swiping it for himself.

'So you don't think Ellis knows this's here?' my father asks.

'If he did, you really think he'd've driven off with a truck full of plastic pineapples? Now c'mon – I figure we've got an hour on him. Time to see what's behind door number two.'

'Y'sure there's no door number three?' my father moans forty-five minutes later, up to his knees in the rancid smell of slowly melting frozen shrimp.

Back in the day, I'd have half a dozen agents burrow to the center of a four-thousand-pound container, send in the dogs, and empty whatever looked suspicious, all within twenty minutes. I don't have half a dozen agents. Or dogs. I have my dad, and all my dad has is a gunshot wound and a bad back.

'Y'okay?' I ask, walking backward and dragging yet another fifty-pound carton of shrimp out the back doors of the truck, onto the ledge of the loading dock.

My father nods, nudging the carton with his foot so he doesn't have to bend over. But the sun is up – it's nearly seven a.m., and the warm air is baking us in the seafood stench – I can see it reflecting off the sweat on his face.

'Halfway through,' I tell him.

With a sharp kick, he sends the newest box toward the maze of cartons that crowd the left half of the loading area.

On a small radio in the corner, he put on the local *Paul and Young Ron* morning show. Still, my dad's not laughing. From the hospital to being up all night, he's had it. But as he turns my way, he suddenly looks oddly . . . proud.

'When'd you start wearing it facing in?' he asks.

'Excuse me?'

'Your watch,' he says, pointing to the inside of my wrist. 'You wear it facing in.' He then lifts his arm so his palm and the face of his own watch are aimed at me. 'Me, too,' he says. 'Funny, huh?'

I look down at my watch, then over at his. Both are cheap. Both are digital. Both have nearly identical thick black bands.

'It doesn't mean anything,' I insist.

'N-No, I know – I just meant—'

'It's a stupid coincidence, okay, Lloyd? Now can we drop it and finish unloading the rest of this?'

I squat down and tug another wet box full of shrimp toward my dad. Using his foot like a broom, he sweeps it along and adds it to the pile.

'You're right,' he says. 'We need to focus on what's important.'

'Okay, now what?'

'Just gimme a sec,' I say, shoving aside the last box and staring into the now completely empty container.

'I don't think we have a sec,' my dad replies as he turns his wrist and stares down at his watch.

I glance down at my own, ignoring the slight throb of my dog bite. He may be right. Outside, there's a siren in the distance. This neighborhood hears them all the time. But I can still picture Ellis's blue lights pulsing in the dark. We don't have much time.

Of the seventy-six cartons we pulled from the container, all are the same size, same shape, and, from what we can tell, same weight. And as they melt in the Florida heat, each one has a slowly growing puddle beneath it.

'You were hoping one of them wouldn't be packed with ice?' my dad asks.

'Something like that. Anything to save us from opening and digging through each one.'

'Maybe one of them has a tattooed frozen head in it. Or someone's brain.'

'A tattooed head?'

'Okay, not a tattooed head. But y'know what I mean – maybe it's a different kinda book. Either way – it's almost nine – time to get out of here, Calvin.'

'And where you plan on going? To your apartment? To mine? You think those aren't the first places Ellis is gonna look? He shot a federal agent, Lloyd! Trust me, the only way to bargain with this nutbag is if we have his favorite chip.'

My father steps back at the outburst – not at the words, but at who it came from.

'And stop giving me that my-boy's-become-a-man look!' I quickly add. 'It's fifty times past annoying already!'

'I wasn't looking at *you*,' he admits. 'I was . . . *There* . . .' he says, motioning over my shoulder.

I turn around, following his finger to the open doors of the yawning, empty container.

'Where's that water go to?' my father asks. Reading my confusion, he points again. 'There. Right along . . .'

I crane my head and finally see it: on the floor of the container, in the very back. To the untrained eye, it's another of the many thin puddles from the now melted ice. Something you'd never look twice at. Unless you happen to notice that the puddle is somehow running and disappearing underneath the container's back wall.

I've seen this magic trick before: bad guys adding fake floors and ceilings in the hopes of smuggling something in.

My father kicks one of the shrimp boxes and sends it slamming into the back wall. There's a hollow echo. No question, there's something behind there.

Within thirty seconds, my dad's got the handle from the jack in my van. He rams it like a shovel at the bottom right corner of the back wall, where there's a small gap at the floor. After wedging it in place, he grabs the handle, pushes down with all his weight, and tries to pry it open. 'It's screwed into the—'

'Lemme try,' I say.

He pushes again. It doesn't budge.

Outside, the siren keeps getting louder. As if it's coming right at us.

'Lloyd!'

'I'm trying, it's just— I *can't . . .*' he blurts, clearly upset as he lets go, and I take over. The computer said he's fifty-two years old. At this moment, the way he looks away and scratches his beard . . . he looks north of sixty.

With both hands gripping the handle, I wedge one foot against the wall, lean backward, and pull down as hard as I can. The wood is cheap, but it barely gives.

I reset my foot and pull harder. The siren howls toward us.

Krrrk.

The wood gives way and there's a loud snap, sending me falling backward. As I crash on my ass, two screws tumble and ping along the metal floor, freeing the bottom right corner of the wall.

'Now *here!*' my dad blurts, pointing to the next set of screws on the far right side of the wall. They're at waist height and, with the makeshift crowbar, easy to get at, but all I'm focused on is the unnerving excitement in my dad's voice.

'C'mon, Cal – we got it!' he says as I put my weight into it and another hunk of wood is pulled away from the screws. Years ago during my father's trial, his lawyer argued that the true cause of my mother's death was her mental instability – he said she had an alter ego, like a second face: one that was good, one that was evil. Naturally, the prosecutor pounced on it, saying my dad was the one with the alter ego: Lloyd the Saintly Defendant and Lloyd the Reckless Killer.

Three minutes ago, my dad was winded and hobbling. Suddenly, he's gripping the right side of the thin wooden wall, prying and bending it open and thrilled to find his treasure. One man. Two faces.

'This is it! Grab it here!' he says, tugging the right side of the thin wall, which has now lost enough screws that the harder we pull, the more it curves toward us. I try to see what's behind it – some kind of box with its long side running against the true back wall – but with the shadow of the wood, it's too dark to see. 'Keep pulling!' my father says, still cheerleading as the wood finally begins to crack. '*Uno . . . dos . .* ?'

With a final awkward semi-karate move, my father kicks the wood panel, which snaps on impact and sends us both stumbling back. As the last splinters of particleboard somersault through the morning sun, we both stare at what my dad was really transporting – the true object of Ellis's desire.

That's not just a box.

It's a coffin.

21

'It's a casket,' my father stutters.

'I know what it is. Is it—? Is someone *in* it?'

He doesn't move, still staring at the dark wood box as another siren begins to scream in the distance. It's only a matter of time till one's headed here.

In front of us, it's definitely a coffin, though it's oddly rounded at the edges. Along the top, yellow and white papers are pasted randomly in place, while a thin band of copper piping runs along the bottom. To be honest, I thought my dad was bullshitting when he said he didn't know what was in the truck, but from the confusion on his face, this is news to him.

'Help me get it out,' my dad says, rushing forward and grabbing one of the wooden handles at the head of the casket. 'Yuuuh!' he yells, leaping back and frantically wiping his hand on his pants.

'What? Something's on there?'

He holds up his open palm, which is dotted with small black flecks of dirt. Fresh soil. I look back at the coffin. Most of it's wiped clean, but you can still see chunks of soil caked in the edges of the trim.

'Someone dug this out of the ground,' I say.

'Before Panama, the sheet said it was in Hong Kong,' my dad says. 'Do they have rounded coffins there?'

'You think there's a body inside?'

There's a loud chirp as my phone shrieks through the warehouse. It's nearly ten a.m. and we still haven't slept. Caller ID tells me who it is. If it were anyone else, I wouldn't pick up.

'Cal here,' I answer.

'Good time, bad time?' a fast-talking man with a deep baritone asks through my cell as yet another siren yet again gets louder.

I watch my father wrap a page of old newspaper around the pull bar on the coffin, which is only half sticking out through the hole in the fake wall. My dad tugs hard, but he can't do it alone. Pinching the phone with my shoulder, I race next to him, grip the other pull bar along the side, and pull as hard as I can.

'No . . . *ruhhhh* . . . perfect time,' I say into the phone, feeling every hour of my exhaustion.

No surprise, Benny laughs.

Two years ago, Benny Ocala came tearing out of the local Seminole Indian reservation, searching for his Alzheimer's-afflicted grandfather, who had wandered, literally, off the reservation. Roosevelt and I found the old man in a Pembroke Pines front yard, sitting in a kid-die pool with his socks on. Today, Benny's the Seminole tribe's very own chief of police. His own sovereign nation. Which explains why, when I left the hospital earlier tonight, I drove the extra six miles to give Benny the bullet that the doctor pulled outta my dad.

'Please tell me you were able to trace it,' I say with another tug. The casket rolls to the right, shedding bits of dirt along the floor as we angle it through the open hole.

'We're Indians, Cal. My ancestors traced deer farts.'

I'm tempted to point out he went to Tulane and drives a Camry, but I'm far too focused on the yellow and white papers pasted to the coffin. I can't read the writing – it's either Chinese or Japanese – but there's no mistaking the small crosses at the bottom of each page. Across the top of one of the pages it says, in English, 'Ecclesiastes.' These are Bible pages. Is that what Ellis meant by a *book*?

'This is a bad one, isn't it?' Benny asks, suddenly serious.

I stand up straight, letting go of the coffin. 'What'd the trace say?' I ask.

'That's the thing, Cal – bullets aren't like fingerprints. If I only have the bullet, unless it's a rare gun, which'll leave signature grooves on th—'

'Benny, I hate *CSI*. I don't wanna learn.'

'Yeah, well, I didn't wanna call up that woman with the fangy teeth who runs the computer room at the Broward Sheriff's Office, and then pretend to flirt with her just so she'll do me a favor and run a bullet through the ATF database and their experts there.'

'But you did, didn't you?'

'Can't help it – I'm a sucker for a girl with a snaggle-tooth,' Benny teases as my dad continues his tug-of-war with the coffin. 'The point is,' he adds, 'your bullet was fired by a rare gun. Really rare: a Walther from 1930. Apparently, it was made as a prototype for the military – Russian army in this case – then discarded. Only something like twenty ever existed.'

He stops for a moment.

'Benny, why're you giving me the dramatic pause?'

'It's just odd, Cal. Guns like this – they don't show up a lot. Out of the grillions of guns out there, well . . . that gun's only been used once – *one time* – apparently during some unsolved murder in Cleveland, Ohio.'

Cleveland. That was the area code from my dad's phone call. I look at my father, who's now shimmying the coffin back and forth, trying to angle it through the open hole. As I pace through the empty container, he gives it one final pull, which frees the casket from its hiding spot.

'When was the murder in Cleveland?' I ask.

'Now you're seeing the problem, Cal. The last time we know that gun was fired was back in 1932,' Benny explains. 'In fact, if this is right, it's the same gun that killed some guy named Mitchell Siegel.'

'Who's Mitchell Siegel?'

My dad turns to me as I say the name, but not for long. He turns back to the coffin and starts circling it, trying to figure out how to get it open.

'You didn't look him up?' I ask.

'Of course I looked him up. Deer farts, remember? So according to this, Mitchell Siegel is just a normal 1930s average Joe. Lived in Cleveland for years . . . ran a tailor shop . . . had a nice family.'

'Why'd he get killed?'

'No one knows. Death certificate says two men came in and stole some clothes.'

'He was killed for clothes?'

'It was the Depression – I have no idea. Like I said, the case is unsolved. Just a bullet in this guy from this gun. Just like your dad.'

'Yeah,' I say as my father grips the lid at the top corner of the coffin and tries to lift it open. It doesn't budge. He tries the bottom corner. Same thing. I went to my first funeral when I was nine years old. With our clientele, Roosevelt and I went to lots more. Even I know coffins are locked with a key.

'Oh, and in case you needed even more news of the odd: This guy Mitchell? He's the father of Jerry Siegel.'

'Am I supposed to know that name?'

'Jerry Siegel. The writer who created Superman.'

'Like *Clark Kent* Superman? As in "faster than a speeding bullet"?'

'Apparently his dad wasn't. Bullet hit Mitchell square in the chest,' Benny says. 'Kinda kooky, though, huh? The gun that shoots your dad is the same one that shot the dad of Superman's creator?' He lowers his voice, doing a bad Vincent Price. '*Two mysteries, nearly eighty years apart.* You not hearing that *Twilight Zone* music?'

'Yeah, that's very—' Across from me, my dad reaches into his pocket, pulls out what looks like a small L-wrench, and slides it into a small hole at the upper half of the casket. Is that—? Son of a bitch. He's got a key.

'Benny, I gotta go,' I say, and slap my phone shut.

I rush toward my dad, whose back is still to me. Outside, the multiple sirens in the distance go suddenly silent, which is even worse. 'Where'd you get that?' I shout.

He doesn't turn around.

'Lloyd, I'm talking to you! Where'd you get that key!?'

Still no response.

There's a loud *thunk* as he twists the metal key. The bolt in the coffin slides and unlocks.

When my dad first saw the coffin, he was definitely scared. But the way his hands crawl like tarantulas across the side – as fast as they're moving – now he's excited. Digging his fingers into the lip of the casket, he lets out the smallest of grunts.

With that, the coffin opens.

22

'Hold on . . . I'm booting up now,' Special Agent Naomi Molina said, reaching down to turn on her home computer while working hard not to spill her oatmeal across her keyboard. It was harder than it looked. But like any Jewban (Jewish mom, Cuban dad), finding balance was everything for her.

It started when Naomi was eleven years old, which was when she discovered her first calling, sports (over Dad's screaming, 'Cuban girls should only wear dresses!'). Taller than all the prepubescent boys, young Naomi was an all-star catcher two years in a row.

'Jeez, Nomi, whatcha on, a Speak and Spell there?' Scotty teased through the phone, laughing his snorty laugh.

'Scotty . . .'

'Yeah?'

'Shut up,' Naomi said through a mouthful of oatmeal as she flipped through the files she'd been faxed this morning. She had known something was wrong when Timothy didn't report in last night. She'd been working with him at ICE for nearly two years now. Timothy always reported in.

When Naomi was sixteen and fully hugging her wild side, she started working at her dad's repo shop, translating insurance documents from Spanish to English. And when her father died a few years later, that's when she found her second calling.

'What kinda oatmeal?' Scotty asked. 'No . . . lemme guess: cinnamon, brown sugar.'

Naomi stayed silent and swallowed another spoonful, hating that at thirty-four years old, she'd become that predictable.

She was eighteen when she went out on her first repo job, breaking into an old orange Camaro with an ease that would've made her dad proud. That was the next five years of her life: cars, boats, motorcycles, Jet Skis, even a plane once – she could find and break into anything. It was dangerous, though. And that was always the problem with the repo business: lots of headache, no stability, and it always attracted the worst employees – sleeping all day and working all night makes for a tough crew to manage. But Naomi managed it – even loved it – until the parties went too late and the drinking was too much.

She saw it in her boyfriend first, when he started with the heavier drugs. Then with her friend Denise, who called her up one morning and in a heroin rush said, 'Nomi, I can't handle Lucas. My head's not on straight and – and – and – I'm thinking of— I don't wanna hurt my boy!' she'd sobbed about her son. 'Please, Nomi – I'm dropping him off now – I need you to take him! Just for— I need to get better!' Lucas was two at the time. Today he was eight. He'd been with Naomi every day in between.

Every life has forks in its road. And sometimes, the tines of that fork stab deep. A year later, her repo business was sold, her boyfriend was long gone, and Naomi Molina was back to translating documents for a local insurance company. It took three months for the itch of excitement to hit, which was when she applied for a job at Customs, eventually getting promoted to her third calling: as a special agent at ICE.

For nearly two years, she'd been working with Timothy, which is why she got the report about his abandoned car being found on Alligator Alley this morning. But in total, all it took was four short years for an impatient, plus-size, single girl with a splash of purple hair to be magically transformed into an impatient plus-fluffy-size single mom with a L'Oréal medium-maple dye job and an eight-year-old son who refused to learn how to tie his shoes.

'Mom,' young Lucas asked as he entered the living room, 'can you—?'

'You wanted basketball shoes, tie them yourself,' Naomi threatened, still poring over the reports as her computer finally began to boot up. 'Otherwise, wear the Velcro ones.'

'Didja try teaching him using two bows?' Scotty asked through the phone in his heavy Bronx accent.

'Scotty . . .' Naomi shot back.

'Yeah?'

'You have kids?'

'Nope.'

'It shows. Two bows is harder. And the more frustrating it gets, the more he'll cry, and the more I'll be forced to consider abandoning this life with nothing more than the clothes on my back and a bag of mint Milanos.'

'That's funny, Naomi – but I seen your office and the way you taped all those photos around the edge of your monitor. Whattya got, forty, fifty pics there? Everyone knows whatcha think about that boy.'

Again, she stayed silent. At least once a year, Naomi's mother would call and not-so-subtly hint about how her daughter's life – how everything from the repo business, to the adopted son, to the filthy law enforcement job – how everything somehow *found* her. But Naomi knew that when it came to this life, she was the one who *found* it.

That was always Naomi's specialty. Finding things.
That's what her dad taught her – from repossessed cars,
to bad guys on the job . . . to finding what happened to
her partner, Timothy, when he left the Port of Miami at
four a.m. and drove out to Alligator Alley. Where the hell
could he be?

On-screen, she opened the e-mail from Scotty and
clicked on the embedded link. The video footage started
playing in front of her.

'Okay, I got it – this's from last night?' she asked as
she looked at a shot of the roof of the H-shaped warehouse. 'Those pole cameras still don't do color?'

'Just watch.'

Sure enough, a white Crown Vic pulled up into the
corner of the screen. But for a full two minutes, no one
got out. Timothy must've been talking to someone. 'How's
the audio?' Naomi asked.

'Poor. Keep watching. . . .'

The passenger door flew open, and a man with a baseball hat jumped out, then got back in the car. A minute
later, Baseball Hat stepped out again, followed by Timothy,
who got out on the driver's side and quickly checked over
his own shoulder. No question, they were worried about
something.

'And that's the best we got?' Naomi asked. 'Sixty-million
dollars' worth of increased surveillance, and we're outdone
by a . . .' She hit the pause button and squinted at the
screen. 'Is that a Homeland Security baseball cap?'

'There's lots of cameras. We're collecting all the footage
now.'

'What about Timothy's cell phone?'

'Nothing to trace, which means it's either smashed,
underground, or underwater. I'm telling you, it's ugly,

Naomi. They're combing the canals, but it's been five hours since—'

'Mom, can I wear flip-flops?' Lucas asked, walking into the living room with them already on his feet.

Naomi turned, her eyes filled with fire. 'You are *not* wearing flip-flops, y'hear me!?' But even as the words left her lips, she caught her breath, cursed the existence of winter break, and brushed her medium-maple brown hair back behind her ear. 'That's— It's fine. Flip-flops are fine.'

'Naomi, you okay?' Scotty asked through the phone.

'Yeah, I'm – I'm just doing the preliminaries for my son's future therapy.' With a deep breath, she added, 'Tell me you at least have Timothy's phone records.'

'Sending them right now. Apparently, he didn't place a call all night – but at two-fourteen a.m., he did get one from a guy named Calvin Harper.'

Gazing at the computer screen, Naomi studied the frozen black-and-white image of the blurry man with the baseball cap.

Cal.

One of their own. Smart enough to know about the cameras. Of course it was Cal.

'Don't worry. I can definitely find him,' Naomi called out as she tossed her cell phone to her son. 'Lucas, call Nana. Tell her I need her to come over earlier.'

23

'Don't touch it!' I call out. 'It's evidence!'

'Evidence?' my dad asks, shaking his head. 'You're not a cop anymore, Cal. Screw *evidence*. From here on in, we need to figure out how to stay alive – and near as I can tell, it's by finding out what's really going on and nabbing whatever's in *here*.'

He motions down at the open, white-velvet-lined casket, where a dead Asian man with black hair and surprisingly dark skin lies, arms crossed over his chest. He's slightly off center, a result of all the shaking and tugging we did to get the coffin out.

Best of all, he has firm skin, lots of makeup, and not a bit of smell. He's been embalmed. But it's his fine pinstriped suit, Yale tie, and pristine manicure that tells me he's from money.

'Okay, enough already,' I growl at my dad. '*What the eff is going on?*'

Down on his knees and ignoring the question, he squints into the coffin like he's searching for a lost contact lens.

'Lloyd . . .'

'Help me open the other side,' he says, his voice racing. With a shove, he flips open the lower lid, revealing the interior at the foot end of the casket. It's cluttered like the back of an old junk drawer: a silver key ring, some dead flowers, a dark wooden rosary, half a dozen family photos, a broken comb (which I think is a tradition in China), a bottle of perfume, a stethoscope (maybe a doctor), and even a full set of clothes wrapped and tied neatly in a blue bow. Accompaniments for the afterlife.

I go for the photos, trying to figure out who this dead guy is. My father goes for the clutter. He pushes aside the flowers and digs underneath the pile of perfectly folded clothes. He's searching for something, and as fast as he's moving – he already knows it's there.

At the bottom of the interior chamber of the coffin, there's a flat white package the size of a FedEx delivery envelope wrapped in what looks like an oversize Ziploc bag.

My father yanks it out. There's a zigzagging smile on his face.

'Is it easy for you to lie like that?' I ask. 'You're not just some truck driver. You knew all along this coffin was in here – and what was in it.'

'Cal, stop talking. I think I just saved our lives.'

With a pop, he rips open the Ziploc and— At first it looks like two sheets of paper stuck together, but as he touches it – it's sticky. Like . . .

'Wax paper,' my father says, running his fingers along the edges, which have been ironed or melted together. In the bottom right corner, there's faint lettering.

My father pulls it closer, and we both read the typed note:

If found, please return to:
10622 Kimberly Ave. Cleveland

But what's far more important is what the wax paper holds hidden inside. You can almost see through it – tons of bright colors.

'Oh, man – if this is a Renoir,' my dad blurts. Like a child with a bag of candy, he tugs the two sides and pulls it open. A hiccup of dust and stale air floats upward, revealing an old yellowed magazine that's trapped within. But as my dad takes out the magazine and thumbs through it . . . No. Not a magazine. The hand-drawn pictures . . . the childish art . . . He flips to the front, and the bright red font on the cover says: *Action Comics*. In the corner, it says: 'No 1. June 1938.' But there's no mistaking the drawing of the hero with the bright red cape and the big red *S* on his chest. Superman.

'Oh, we got 'em, Cal. We *got* 'em!' my father says, his zigzag smile spreading wider.

For a moment, it feels as if someone's punctured my lungs with a metal hook and is tugging them up through my throat. Ellis said he wanted a book. Benny's words echo in my head. That murder eighty years ago . . . Mitchell Siegel . . . and his son created—

No way this comic book is just a comic book.

24

'You knew, didn't you? You knew what was in there,' I say, reaching for the old Superman comic and snatching it from my dad's hands.

'Be careful with that!'

'*Why'd you lie!?*' I explode, my voice rebounding through the metal container.

He takes a half-step back, surprised by my anger. 'Cal, if you think I knew anything—'

'Enough bullshit, Lloyd! That's why they shot you, didn't they!? That's what they wanted: that key and what was in that coffin! And you've been lying about it the whole time!'

'No, that's fair. You're right – I lied. I'm sorry for that. But that was it. I swear to you, Cal – I had no idea the key went to a coffin. They sent it to me with the paperwork.'

'So they sent you a key and said, "You'll know what to do with this"?'

'They said, here's the key and when I got to Naples, I was supposed to unload the truck, find the book – they didn't say what kind – and wait for further directions. Look, does it sound a little suspicious? Of course – that's why they hired me. But that's the way it happened. To be honest—'

'Oooh, *honest*. What would that be like?'

He stops, but not for long. Outside, the sirens are still silent. 'Whoever hired me, they're not stupid, Cal. When you ship something that you think is important, you don't tell anyone what's inside. *"Oh, yes – please go pick up my metal case with twenty million dollars tucked in there. I trust that you won't steal it, Mr Cheap-hired-hand-who-I-don't-know."* You send it and you give as little info as possible.'

'Then why even send the whole coffin? Why not just take the comic and FedEx it?'

'I have no idea. I'm assuming this comic was this guy's prized possession, right? That's why he's buried with it. That's the book Ellis wanted. So maybe they were worried the guys who dug up the casket would pick it clean if they opened it . . . or maybe they just told the grave diggers that they were some crazy relative who wanted the body, so that way, no one asked questions. The point is, the trouble they went through to get this – one side hiring me, then Timothy and Ellis trying to steal it away – if this baby's worth dying for, can you imagine what it's worth paying for?'

'For a comic?'

'C'mon, you know this isn't just a comic. I don't care how popular Superman is, people don't get shot just for some old funny-book,' he says, snatching the comic back, his voice once again racing. 'Now I don't care if it's got some secret treasure map or some superhero Da Vinci Code that needs a Captain Midnight decoder ring, we have what they want! We won the lottery, Cal – now we just gotta find out how to cash it in!'

'You're right,' I say, snatching the comic right back and storming out of the metal container, back through the warehouse. 'And the way to do that is by going to ICE, taking it to the authorities, and telling the truth.'

I cut through the stacked maze of shrimp boxes, trying my best to ignore the smell. I'd rather be out with the non-sirens.

'You'll be dead by tomorrow,' my father calls out.

'I'm done being manipulated, Lloyd. Especially by someone who thinks it's okay to dig up someone's dead body and use their coffin as a shipping envelope. That man was someone's family – not that you know the definition of that.'

For once, he's silent.

I step over the last box of shrimp, hop off the loading platform, and head straight for the door. My father stays where he is.

'Calvin, you don't have to believe this – but if I'd known they had dug up someone's father – even *I* wouldn't've taken the job.'

'Yet another wonderful speech. Good-bye, Lloyd. Time to be smart.'

'You think turning yourself in is *smart*? You think you'll get a medal and a big thank-you? No, Calvin. They're gonna lock you in a room and grill you about Timothy, giving Ellis plenty of time to flash his badge, come inside, and put that final bullet in your brain.'

'ICE would never let that happen.'

'*Timothy was ICE!* And for all you know, he wasn't working alone!'

I stop right there. I know my dad's just in it for the cash.

'This isn't just about the money, Cal. Look at the logic: It's just a matter of time until Timothy's body shows up. If we turn ourselves in, guess who the murder suspects are? No one's believing the two convicts.'

'I'm not a convict.'

'No, you're just Timothy and Ellis and everyone else's target practice. They're not stopping till you're convicted or dead. But if we figure out what's really going on, then we'll have the steering wheel.'

I know what my father's doing. I saw the way he went straight for that comic, how his eyes went wide, and the greedy thrill when he realized that whatever's really going on is now solely in his hands. I know this isn't about just keeping me safe. But that doesn't mean he's not right.

I turn around and finally face my dad, who hasn't taken a step from the open container. From here, his face is hidden by the shadows. Outside, the brand-new siren screams from less than a block away. 'I thought you didn't know who hired you,' I call out.

'So?'

'So how you plan on tracking him down?'

Stepping out into the morning light, he holds up the wax-paper sleeve with the faint typed message in the bottom corner.

If found, please return to:
10622 Kimberly Ave. Cleveland

'You kidding?' he calls back with his zigzag smile. 'We got the address right here.'

'That's fine,' I say. 'I just need to check something at home first.'

25

In his black rental car, Ellis circled the block slowly, studying the protective metal fence that surrounded the two-story brown building that looked like a 1970s Howard Johnson's. He noted the delivery entrance at the rear of the building. No sense going in the front if the trickster could just sneak out the back.

733 Breakers Avenue. Cal's home. The small sign in front had a dove flying from an open palm:

Covenant House

Ellis knew Covenant House from the force. There was one in Michigan, too. Local homeless shelter. Cal clearly had his own penance he was paying. But as Ellis turned the corner, all he really cared about was that the white van with the three dents – Cal's van – was parked in front.

To come back here, either Cal needed something or he was just being cocky. But that's what happens when you think you've won. No question, Cal and his dad had found the coffin. They opened it – and grabbed what Mitchell Siegel stole in the name of—

A low rumble coughed through the beach air as a convertible Chevy Cavalier turned the corner of the block. From its speed alone, Ellis knew something was wrong. He stayed where he was, didn't even duck down as the forest green car skidded to a stop right behind the white van. Blocking Cal in.

A tall woman with a creased tan suit and brown hair got out. The way her worn shoes attacked the pavement – *tunk tunk tunk* – there was no slowing her down. Even from here, Ellis could see the outline of a gun strap under her cheap suit jacket. Cops were the same everywhere.

'Naomi here,' she said, pulling out her cell phone. 'No, Ma . . . why would you—? I don't care what he says, don't buy him any more Hot Wheels cars, okay? He's lying. Treat him like a little junkie stripper on blow: He'll say anything to get more.'

Clipping the phone back on her belt, the woman pounded past the privacy wall and disappeared inside the building.

Across the street, Ellis reached over to the passenger seat and unzipped a small leather case. If cops were here, they were already searching for Timothy. Searching for Cal. To be honest, Ellis didn't care. Let them fight it out. He'd take what he wanted from the winner.

26

'He's still here?' Naomi asked, running through the shelter's open courtyard.

'I'm looking at a tracking screen right now,' Scotty replied through her earpiece. 'According to his cell signal, Cal's definitely in the building.'

'And you can't get me closer than that? I thought they improved all this nonsense after 9/11 – y'know, so they could find trapped people within a few feet.'

'And that's true – especially in the *Bourne Identity* trilogy. But back in *reality*, where we all still use our *old* phones, we pinpoint based on cell towers – and that gets us a few dozen feet at the closest. Listen, I gotta run. I'm a tech guy, not a sidekick.'

Racing up the outdoor stairs two at a time, Naomi reached for her gun.

On the second floor, she darted across the outdoor breezeway as she traced the room numbers – 210 . . . 208 . . . 206. Cal's apartment was 202. As she passed each metal door, she saw a blue sign on each one:

SINGLE RESIDENTS BEDTIME IS 9:45 P.M.

She finally stopped at the last door on her right:

202
RESIDENT ADVISER

From what she could tell, the door was slightly open. As if someone were still there. Or about to leave. She lowered her shoulder and plowed forward. As the door swung open and crashed into the wall, Naomi burst into the room.

A gang of six clearly pissed-off black kids looked up from the video game they were crowded around. The second-biggest kid, in his twenties, with braids, an over-size Knicks jersey, and a panther tattoo across his neck, dropped his game controller and strode directly at her.

'Whatsamatta, lady?' he asked, flashing a bottom row of bright gold teeth as Naomi hid her gun behind her back. 'Dontcha like black people?'

27

'His *whut*?' asked the kid with the panther tattoo.

'She's thumpin' ya, she is, Desi,' added one of his friends, a fat black kid with a British accent and a blue bandanna on his head. He stepped forward with Panther Tattoo, hoping to scare Naomi. She didn't step back.

'Listen . . . Desi, right?' Naomi asked, knowing better than to pull her badge in a group like this. 'Desi, I promise you – I'm not *thumpin'*, or *lying*, or whatever you're suggesting that verb means. I'm Cal's girlfriend. Naomi. We've been dating three weeks. Naomi. Ask him. Call him.'

It was the simplest way to find out if they knew something. But the way these guys were watching her . . . the cold doubt in their eyes. Covenant House was a shelter for homeless kids. Kids who got lit on fire when they left their gang. Or got sold by their dad as a sex toy for quick drug money. These kids . . . weren't kids.

'Cal don't date no giant girls,' Panther Tattoo challenged.

'Well, he dates me,' Naomi insisted.

'Yah? When wuz ya last date?'

Naomi didn't even hesitate. 'Two nights ago.'

'Tha's funny – cuz he wuz here playin' Xbox with us two nights back.'

The chubby kid with the accent leaned in and pointed a finger at Naomi's face. 'You got a problem now, luv.

And don't think we didn't spot that bloody little pistol you got hidin' behind your—'

In a blur, Naomi gripped the kid's stubby finger and bent it back, then twirled him around, pinned his arm behind his back, and rammed his chest and chin against the nearby wall. A dozen different plaques and commendations shook at the impact.

'*ICE agent*, which means *federal*, which means *be really* bloody *careful* what you do next,' Naomi growled, using her free hand to slide open her jacket and show off the badge on her belt.

To her surprise, none of the gang rushed forward or mouthed off. In fact, since the moment she came in, they'd all been standing almost entirely in the same—

Crap.

'Outta the way! *Now!*' Naomi ordered, waving them toward the corner of the sparse old motel room and heading for the bathroom at the back.

'Lady, you can't just—'

'Giant people can do anything,' Naomi shot back, shoving British Boy aside and finally getting her first good look at the bathroom's closed door . . . and the light that was on underneath. A shadow flitted, then disappeared. Someone was definitely in there.

'Get back to your rooms!' she yelled at the kids, who scattered onto the breezeway as she pulled her gun. 'And Cal, I checked when I was outside. I know there's no window in there!'

She kicked the door and tried the handle. Locked.

'Cal, I'm counting to one!' Naomi shouted. 'After that, you're paying for whatever it costs to get a bullet out of your—'

Click.

The door opened, revealing a man with a thick nose, an even thicker waist, and thinning black hair that was tied back in a ponytail.

'If you need to use the can, all you gotta do is ask,' Roosevelt said with a grin as he rolled Cal's phone in his palm.

28

Stepping out from the bathroom, Roosevelt studied the tall woman carefully. Cal warned him they'd send someone – and she clearly wasn't a novice. But that didn't mean their stalling hadn't worked.

'You switched phones with him,' Naomi said, annoyed.

'Me? I'm a man of God. I'd never—' Roosevelt glanced down at the phone in his hand and forced a look of surprise. 'This isn't my phone! Sweet mother of Shirley Hemphill, how'd this happen?'

Naomi's hand jumped out, snatching the phone from Roosevelt's palm.

'Hey! You can't—'

Naomi aimed her gun at Roosevelt's chest. 'I can.' Without another word, she started clicking through the menu on Cal's phone: Call Log, Placed Calls . . . 'Here we go,' she announced. 'Last number dialed: Roosevelt (Mobile).' Naomi pushed the *call* button and waited.

But as the phone rang in her ear, there was another ring in Roosevelt's front pocket.

Roosevelt reached down and pulled out a second ringing phone, flipped it open, and held it to his ear.

'Hello,' he sang, watching Naomi's face as his words echoed in her ear. 'I musta had both phones all along. What're the oddsa that?'

For a moment, Naomi just stood there, her light blue

eyes narrowing. Roosevelt knew she could lock him up and sling questions at him for the next few hours. But by then, Cal would be long gone.

'You really a former priest?' Naomi asked.

'Former pastor.'

'My partner's missing. I'm praying not dead,' she said of Timothy. 'Did Cal tell you that?'

Roosevelt stayed silent. She was smart – going right for his preacher's guilt. Years ago, Roosevelt's superiors in the church did the same when they told him he was hurting his parish by not being married. Back then, he refused to fight and lost everything he loved. Not a single day went by where he didn't wish he could have that life back. When he didn't think of ways to reclaim that pulpit. So an hour ago, when Cal and his father had come scrambling in here, searching for help – he could see the way that Cal, even through his fear, kept glancing over and over at his dad. At nine years old, Cal had had his life taken from him, too. This was his chance to have *that* life back, somehow, in some form. And as Roosevelt knew, that was well worth fighting for.

'You work your side of the street, and I'll work mine,' Roosevelt said.

Naomi just stood there. Then she turned to open the door, and with a slam, she was gone.

After giving it a minute, Roosevelt flipped open his phone and started dialing. It rang twice before—

'Roosevelt?' Cal answered. 'I told you not to call unless—'

'They sent someone, Cal. From ICE, just like you said.'

The door burst open, and Naomi stormed back into the room. 'Couldn't even wait two minutes, could you!?'

she yelled, snatching the phone from Roosevelt's hand. He tried to grab it back.

She pulled her gun and aimed it directly at his neck.

As Roosevelt raised his hands, Naomi put the phone to her ear. 'Hey, Cal,' she said. 'Naomi. Remember me?'

29

Ten minutes ago
Fort Lauderdale Airport

We enter the terminal separately. We get in line separately. We pick up our tickets separately. My father's calm. I'm not. I spent years covering every port, including this airport. I know where all the security cameras are hidden. I know which taxicabs out front have undercover agents in them (the ones lingering in the limo line), ready at any moment to pick up an arriving suspect who thinks he's home free. But what's got me scanning the crowd is whether Ellis saw us leaving as we snuck out of my building.

'Here you go, Mr Frenzel,' says the woman at the airline counter, handing me my ticket and calling me by the name of one of the dozens of fake IDs that had been left in the van over the years.

'Have a nice day, Mr Sanone,' another agent says to my dad, who for once is following my directions and keeping his head down as he leaves the counter. By flying under fake names, we're untraceable. But if Ellis is half the cop I think he is – the way he got to Timothy right after I did – all he has to do is pull airport video to be right back on our trail. That's what I would do. But that doesn't mean I'm making it easy for him.

Readjusting the green backpack that holds the Superman comic in its wax-paper protector, I keep my chin down but am surprised to see a spy cam – flat and thin like a calculator – mounted in a fake palm tree at the end of the airline counter. Dammit. I duck under the velvet check-in rope, wishing I could blame it on my lack of sleep. But I'm clearly rusty. I've been off the job for over four years. Of course there's gonna be new cameras.

Trying to be smarter as I head toward security, I glance back at my father, but he's barely moving. Worst of all, he's no longer staring down, hiding his face. In fact, the way he's looking around . . . like he sees something. Or someone.

On our left, by the airport gift shop, a dolly stacked with old magazines and newspapers is wheeled out of the way, revealing a young, light-skinned black woman in a rhinestoned Bob Marley T-shirt, dark jeans, and 80s *Top Gun* sunglasses. I've seen her before. At the hospital.

'Serena,' my dad blurts just as I reach the front of the security line.

'I'm sorry, I forgot something,' I tell the lady checking tickets at security. Swimming upstream and squeezing past the other passengers, I fight toward the back of the line and grab my dad by the biceps.

'What're you *doing*?' I hiss.

'Cal, this isn't my fault.'

'We were supposed to tell no one. As in *no one*.'

'I swear to you, I didn't say a word,' my dad insists.

'He *didn't* say a word,' Serena adds. *'Quisiera estar aquí para ti,'* she whispers to my dad in Spanish. I just wanted to be here for you.

From the shock on my dad's face – as I tug his arm and steer us away from security – he's just as surprised as I am. 'Cal . . . son . . .'

'Don't call me *son*!' I explode as every nearby TSA employee turns our way. I don't care.

My dad forces a smile and puts a hand on my shoulder like all is well. I jerk back until he takes it off.

'Please don't blame your father. Every soul needs its own flow,' Serena says, carefully pronouncing each syllable. She has a tender voice that's as calming as wind chimes, and as she speaks, her yellow blue eyes make peaceful contact. First with me, then my dad. Like she's seeing something within.

'That's the mushiest, new-agey-ist manure I've ever heard,' I tell her, finally stopping all three of us in front of a set of floral sofas, where there are no cameras in sight. 'Now tell me why you're really here!'

She steps back slightly, almost as if she's confused. 'When we were on the phone – when I heard the terror in his voice – how could I not help him? He needed me.'

'*Needed* you? What're you, his muse?'

She shakes her head, but I've been around enough addicts to know what's really going on.

'She's your sponsor, isn't she?' I ask my dad.

'No. That's not—'

The phone I traded with one of the kids vibrates in my front pocket. Only one other person knows I have it.

'Roosevelt?' I answer. 'I told you not to call unless—'

'They sent someone, Cal. From ICE, just like you sa—'

There's a loud noise, like a door slamming. I hear some arguing, but nothing I can make out.

'Hey, Cal,' a female voice says. 'Naomi. Remember me?'

30

Silent on the phone, I leave my father and Serena by the floral sofas as I keep scanning the area for cameras. The only good news is, it takes a solid six minutes to track my cell. Plenty of time to find out who I'm up against.

'Sorry, not ringing my bells,' I tell the woman, hoping she'll give me her last name.

'Naomi Molina.'

Naomi Molina . . . Naomi . . . Naomi . . . If I knew her, it wasn't well. Still, the name . . . 'Oh, wait – you're the one who adopted that kid – the lesbian, right?' It's an old cop trick: riling her to see what she blurts.

'C'mon, Cal. The big-boned female agent who's also a lesbo? Isn't that a bit overdone?' she flings back. 'No thanks, but I like mine straight up, no twist. But yes, I came aboard right as you were fired.'

'I wasn't fired,' I shoot back, already regretting it. I should've seen it: riling me to see what I blurt.

'Oh, that's right – you took the far more honorable resign-on-your-own-and-avoid-the-indictment. Let me ask: Were you really in love with Miss Deirdre or was that just the story you saved for Internal Affairs?'

Once again, I stay silent. Across from me, Serena motions for my dad to join her on one of the floral sofas. He doesn't hesitate. And as they face each other – their knees almost touching – she whispers something to him and he smiles with a strange, newfound calm. From the body language alone, she knows him well.

'Aw, that bump old bruises, Cal?' Naomi asks in my ear. 'Now you know how *we* felt when we heard you were kissing one of your CIs and putting your fellow agents at risk.'

'You don't know what you're talking about.'

'Deirdre was your informant, Cal! You were supposed to pay her a few hundred bucks for tips on shipments! Instead, you were sleeping with her and buying her sappy poetry books for her birthday!'

'I never slept with her.'

'No, you did something far more ridiculous: You fell in love, didn't you? And then when you heard we were raiding a South Beach steakhouse that she was gonna be at, you whispered in her ear and told her to stay away.'

'I had a right to protect my informant!'

'Then you should've done it like everyone else: let her get swept up and then pull strings from the inside!' Naomi shouts at full blast. 'But to tip her in advance in some pathetic come-on: You have any idea how many of our guys could've gotten killed, racing into a raid where everyone knew they were coming?'

'No one got killed.'

'Only because she ratted you out for the scumbag you are! But that's the true justice, isn't it? Here you are fighting to keep this dear, defenseless woman safe, and she runs back to headquarters, says she got tipped off by an agent, and offers you up as long as she gets citizenship for the rest of her family. Man, that must've stung, huh, Cal? Almost as bad as doing a favor for ... I don't know, your own father, and then realizing you're suddenly the one holding the smoking gun.'

On the sofa, Serena scratches my dad's back as I stand

there, silent. I remember my mom scratching his back when he had a tough day at work.

'I thought for sure you'd nibble at that one,' Naomi tells me.

'Then you remember me as stupid.'

'Actually, I remember you as a stubborn idealist. But I got your psych profile right here, Cal. Every few years, we get a new candidate who takes the job to right some wrong in his past – and then becomes so obsessed with saving people, he starts letting the job substitute for his entire life. That's your problem, Cal. You're Sisyphus. You just don't know it,' she says. 'But if I'm reading that wrong . . . yee-haw . . . life must be going pretty beautifully for you these days, huh?'

In front of me, Serena continues her back-scratch, doing her best to calm my dad down. Maybe she is here just to help him. But the way my dad watches her and stares at her – even the way he laughs extra hard at whatever she's saying – I don't know what Serena thinks of him, but he clearly would love to have his hands on her.

'Things are just stunning here, thanks.'

'Wonderful. Then let's do the rest of this face-to-face. You wouldn't mind coming over for a quick chat, would you?'

Another cop trick: Offer something easy – if I run, she knows I'm guilty. Still, I need to know whether she's working on hunches or facts. 'Happy to, Naomi. Just tell me what we'd be chatting about.'

'Oh, you know – silly little details like why we haven't heard from Timothy since last night, and what his abandoned car was doing on Alligator Alley. . . . Or to really put a pin in your balloon: how yours was the last call on his cell, and how your van is on every camera in the port at three in the morning, and how the one shipment Timothy was fiddling with just happens to be the one that was picked up by your ex-con dad. Not the prettiest picture that's being painted here, Cal. Now you wanna tell me what's really going on, or would you rather fast-forward eight months and tell it to a jury? I'm sure they'll take your side – I mean, who wouldn't trust a disgraced agent and his convict father?'

On the floral couch, my dad and Serena both look up at me. I stay where I am, trying to keep my own calm. Between Ellis the killer cop and Naomi the overdetermined agent, I feel another trapdoor ready to open beneath my feet. The only thing keeping it shut is, from what I can tell, they still haven't found Timothy's body. As long as that's true, I may be suspicious, but I'm not a murder suspect.

'Cal, y'know that part in *The Fugitive* where Harrison Ford says he didn't kill his wife?' Naomi asks.

'Y'mean when Tommy Lee Jones tells him, "I don't care"?'

'Exactly. But here's the thing: Despite what you think, I *do* care. Especially about my partner. Now I know you've gotta be exhausted – that's the only reason you made the mistake of getting on the phone with me, right? So if you tell me what you and Timothy were really up to out there, you know I can save you so many kinds of headache.'

It's a perfect offer, delivered with perfect pitch. But every story needs a bad guy, and once Ellis comes racing in, pointing his cop finger at me—

'This is a TSA security announcement,' the PA system blares from above. I snap the phone shut, praying she didn't— *Oh, my crap!* Of course she did! Her whole maudlin speech – just a stall so she could figure out where I— *Dammit, that was rookie of me!*

'We need to get out of here,' I shout to my dad. 'Feds are on their way!'

31

'He's in an airport!' Naomi barked into her earpiece, darting from Cal's room and weaving through the small mob of black kids who were eavesdropping from outside. 'Scotty, I need all local flights leaving from Miami and Fort Lauderdale in the next two hours. I'm going to Lauderdale now.'

Flying down the stairs, she could hear the clicking of Scotty's keyboard in her ear. If she was fast, she'd make the airport in no time.

'Okay, here we go,' Scotty said. 'There're over sixty flights, not including international. But when I put in "Cal Harper" . . . He has reservations on three different flights, all of them to Texas: Austin, Dallas . . .'

'He's not going to Texas.'

'How d'you—?'

'Cal Harper was one of us. He's not flying under his real name. Those are fake reservations to slow us down. Check the flights again, but this time, make a list of every ticket that was bought today and/or paid in cash.'

'That's gonna take some time. Oh, and by the by, when I traced Cal's phone – assuming he didn't switch it until this morning: Last call went to Benny Ocala. Seminole Police.'

'That's fine. Send me his number,' Naomi said, jumping down the last three steps. Above her, all the homeless kids had flooded back into Cal's room. Glancing back as she ran, Naomi couldn't help but stare.

'Why you so quiet?' Scotty asked.

'Dunno,' Naomi said as she cut through the courtyard, past a skinny girl with greasy hair. 'If you saw this place – even Cal's room – this guy doesn't just *work* at the shelter – he lives here. With kids.'

'Maybe they give him free rent.'

'Maybe. But the way they were all crowded and playing video games in his room, he's the one they all hang out with.'

'Oh, c'mon – so now he's the disgraced cop who's also a hero to the sad, pathetic homeless kids? How many more clichés you wanna add? Lemme guess: He's gonna coach their debate team all the way to the state championships.'

'You're missing the point, Scotty. From what I can tell, Cal sleeps and works and eats his meals surrounded by lost teenagers. So do it like this: Is Cal taking care of these kids – or are these kids taking care of him?'

'Nomi, don't dream Cal into a wounded hero. If he were an angel, he wouldn't be running. And neither would you.'

Nodding to herself, Naomi plowed through the lobby and shoved her way through the set of doors that led outside. A blast of Florida heat embraced her, and as she darted toward her car, the repo girl inside her couldn't help but scan the area: Cal's van still parked out front, the beat-up Fords, Pontiacs, and Hyundais that sat in a neat row and lined the south side of the building, and even the single black sedan that was parked at one of the meters across the street. There was a man inside that one. She still had time. If she was lucky, maybe he'd seen Cal leave.

As she cut toward him, she realized the man was a cop – and from the looks of it, there was a dog in back. Nothing really odd in that.

Except for the fact that Cal clearly just snuck out of here, and that his last call was to Seminole law enforcement, and that there's not a single good reason for anyone to sit in a car – with their dog – in this kind of heat.

Rolling her tongue inside her cheek, Naomi crossed the street, headed for the black sedan, and did her best to keep it friendly.

'Hey there,' she called out, flashing her badge as the cop rolled down his window. 'What's your doggie's name?'

32

'Benoni,' Ellis replied, squinting up at the round-faced female agent who stared down through his open window. She was pretty under the bad haircut and cheap suit – her blue eyes were as pale as tears – but the dark circles that were under them . . . the wear that they betrayed . . . hers was a tired life. And from the way she was breathing, she was already in a rush. 'Her name's Benoni,' Ellis added. 'She's a real good girl.'

'She looks it,' Naomi said, peering into the backseat at Benoni, who jumped toward the front, clawed across Ellis's lap, and stuck her head out the window. 'Naomi Molina,' she added as Ellis spotted the ICE ID on her belt.

If ICE was out here, Cal was long gone. Ellis knew he had to keep this quick.

'Oh, she's gorgeous,' Naomi added, giving the dog a brisk scratch under the chin. No question, Naomi was playing nice, but Ellis could see her studying the Michigan State Police shoulder patch on his uniform.

'Pretty long commute from home, no?' she asked.

'Yeah, I'm down for a trial. Some dealer we gripped in Detroit. Supposed to testify this morning, but they ran out of time, which means I'm wearing this again tomorrow,' he said, pointing at, but never touching, the well-polished badge on his uniform. 'Officer Ellis Belasco, Michigan State Police,' he added, offering his long, bony fingers for a handshake. He shook her hand with perfect ease. 'Only good part was I got to let Benoni enjoy the beach. You loved it, didn't you, girl?'

Benoni barked. That should be more than enough.

'Mind showing me your B and C's?' Naomi asked.

Ellis lowered his chin and stared at Naomi. Something happened inside with Cal. Something that pissed her off and made her suspicious. Hence her testing him: making sure he knew cop lingo as a way of checking if he was real or just wearing the suit. B and C's. Badge and creds. Ellis reached for his French Berluti wallet.

'Here,' he said, handing her his creds. When she didn't notice the handcraft of the wallet, Ellis knew she didn't have taste. But that didn't mean she couldn't be a problem.

Naomi smiled when she saw the ID and the polished badge.

'So what kinda dog is she?' she asked, handing Ellis his wallet back as she patted Benoni, whose head was still out the window. Test passed. No problem at all.

'They call 'em Canaan dogs,' Ellis replied, eyeing a passing silver car. If Cal was already gone, he needed to go, too. 'They're bred from the ancient pariah dogs from Palestine,' he added as he started his car.

'I've heard of those,' Naomi said, too dense to take the hint. 'They're one of the oldest breeds in the world, right?'

'Some say *the* oldest.' Ellis tugged the dog's dark leather collar and sent her to the back. 'I'm going now.'

'No, of course – enjoy the rest of your trip,' she said. 'Bye, Benoni,' she added, stepping back with a friendly wave. 'And sorry you gotta wear your clothes twice.'

Ellis forced a half-smile, grabbed the steering wheel

with his left hand . . . and just then noticed Naomi staring at his tattoo.

'They give you hell about that?' Naomi asked far too slowly. This was bad.

'I have an understanding supervisor. He knows we all make mistakes when we're young.'

'Yeah, I make that same excuse for that Tweety Bird tattoo I got on my butt. Though blaming a twelve-pack of wine coolers and a kinda fruity twelfth-grade boyfriend does the trick, too.'

Ellis nodded. He was wrong. Naomi was no threat at all.

With a hard shift, he put the car in gear and hit the gas. As he watched Naomi disappear in his rearview, his phone started ringing. Caller ID said *000-000-000 Unknown*. No one but the Judge had this number.

'Who's this?' Ellis answered.

'That's the key question, isn't it, Ellis?' a voice said on the other line.

'Tell me who this is, or I'm hanging up now.'

'I'm here to help you, Ellis. I know what you're searching for. I want it, too. But you need to know: Calvin doesn't have the Book yet. He has the Map.'

'You're the shipper of the package, aren't you?' Jerking the steering wheel to the left, Ellis turned onto A1A. 'The one who hired Calvin's father.'

'All that matters is that neither of us is getting what we want if Calvin grabs it first.'

'I'm already taking care of Calvin,' Ellis insisted.

'No. You're not. If you were, you'd already be here by now.'

'Be where?'

'You know the history, Ellis. Where do you think he's

going? We're in the airport, waiting to leave for Cleveland. If you hurry, you can still make the flight.'

'You're sure about this?' Ellis asked.

'Of course. That's why they call me the Prophet.'

And with a click, the voice was gone.

33

'Who were you talking to?' Scotty asked through Naomi's earpiece.

'Run this badge for me,' Naomi insisted, her voice flying as she raced for her car.

'Just text it and I'll—'

'Write this! *Edward Belasco*,' she said, repeating the name she'd memorized from his credentials. 'Though he called himself *Ellis*. Michigan State Police. Badge 1519.' As she heard the clicks on Scotty's keyboard, she added, 'Sorry, Scotty – once old age hits, memory fades quick.'

'Naomi, you're thirty-four.'

'Actually, I'm thirty-three. No . . . wait . . . you're right – I'm thirty-four.' She stopped for a moment as she slid into her car. 'Why do you know my age?'

'I was at your office party.'

'No, you weren't.'

'I was. After everyone left. And by not shutting off your phone – which I admire and appreciate – you've now let me know you have a Tweety Bird on your tush. I have a GoBot on my ankle.'

'What's a GoBot?'

'Like a Transformer. But . . . more pathetic.'

Naomi grinned as she tugged the car door shut. 'Was that you sharing a moment with me?'

All she heard was the furious clicking of his keyboard.

'Scotty, you're gonna make a helluva sidekick yet.' She stuffed the key in the ignition and took what looked like a calculator from her purse. Flicking a switch on top, she pulled out of the parking spot and waited for the screen to come online.

> *GPS link . . . searching . . .*
> *. . . searching . . .*
> *Link activated.*

'He's headed toward the airport. He knows Cal's there,' Naomi said, making a left on US-1 as a small crimson triangle inched across the digital map on-screen.

'Who's headed toward—? Wait,' Scotty said. 'You put a tracking device on Roosevelt?'

'I planned to. But then when I went in there— Cal knows our magic tricks. They're too smart for our James Bond nonsense.'

'So who're you tracking?'

'I told you: Ellis/Edward Belasco. Badge 1519.'

'Naomi, to GPS someone's car, you need a warrant, as in *court order*, as in *probable cause*. You didn't even ask him if he *saw* Cal.'

'First, he's a liar. Said he walked his dog on the beach, but there wasn't a grain of sand in his backseat. Second, the fancy wallet and the manicured hands? He's treating himself far too well. Third, his eyebrows are the devil's. Fourth, back to his wallet – all his dollar bills were right side up and facing out. Again . . . *devil's*. And finally, who says I GPSed his car?'

Scotty stopped. 'You didn't GPS his car?'

'Couldn't get close enough – but then that durn dog of his was sniffing my hand so hard – and *whoof* – ate that GPS device right outta my poor defenseless finger-tips. Bad dog. Very bad.'

'You fed the dog the device.'

'No . . . I fed the dog one of my son's old gummy worms, that just happened to be in my pocket, and just happened to have a miniature GPS device shoved inside it. What luck, eh? Couldn't believe it myself.'

'If you hurt that dog—'

'Me?' she asked, pointing to herself as she slammed the gas and raced toward the airport. 'Dog lover. *Big* dog lover. Believe me, Benoni's fine – it's the same technology they put in pets in case they get lost or—'

'Uh-oh.'

'What's *uh-oh*?' Naomi put her hand to her earpiece. 'They find Timothy?'

'I put in your Michigan cop with the GPS dog. And from what it says here . . . well . . . looks like *liar* isn't the only thing on Ellis's résumé.'

34

'Whattya mean, *the feds are on their way?*' my dad asks, sitting straight up on the floral sofa.

'She. Naomi. She knows we're in an airport,' I tell him.

'But all those fake reservations—'

'Will hold her off for ten minutes. She's smart. She knows Lauderdale is closest. We need to go,' I insist. 'And *you* need to leave,' I bark at Serena.

'Th-That's not possible. I *know* I'm meant to help him,' she says, standing from her seat.

'And I *know* I'm meant to escort you outside and save your loopy life,' I shoot back, gripping her by the elbow.

'Please . . . your father needs to settle his spirit,' Serena begs, trying to pull away.

'Cal, let go of her!' my dad growls.

Once again, a nearby TSA employee turns toward us. But it's not half as bad as the flat black box that I spot over his shoulder, hanging in the corner. Another camera I missed. Staring directly at us.

Following my eyeline, my father freezes when he sees it. He knows what it means. He knows Naomi's on her way. And he knows what Ellis will do to Serena when he finds out she's been seen with us.

'Calvin, how much cash do we have left?' my father asks.

'That's smart – no, good thought,' I tell him. 'If we hide her in a motel, she'll be safe until—'

'I'm not getting her a motel. I'm getting her a plane ticket.' He turns to Serena. 'You're coming with us.'

'Wait . . . *what*?' I ask.

'Don't argue with me, Calvin. Not about this. I know what I'm doing.'

'Oh, that's right – I forgot how good you were at saving the women you love.'

My father stops right there, burning me with the kind of glare that should come with medical attention. Serena starts to scratch his back. It doesn't help at all.

'Enough with the subtext, Calvin. Where's all the anger *really* coming from: that I'm looking out for Serena, or that I didn't look out for your mother?'

'*Didn't look out for?* Lloyd, you *killed* her. You pushed her and killed her.'

'That's not what happened!'

'You kidding? I *saw* it!'

My father falls silent, like he's surprised I remember.

We're both breathing hard, but he's the one to break the quiet. 'Why'd you follow me after the hospital, Calvin? Was it to help me, or just to remind me of my life's greatest regret?'

I shake my head. 'You have no idea how much you don't know me.'

He studies me carefully, unsure of whether to fight. But he also knows that if we don't move quick, we're not going anywhere.

'Lloyd, if this is the journey – between you and Cal . . .' Serena begins behind him, 'maybe I was wrong. Maybe I'm not meant to be on this trip.'

'She's right,' I shoot back.

'She's *not*,' my father insists. 'We can't just leave her here.'

'We're not leaving her. If we get her someplace safe . . .'

'Where? In what time?' my dad challenges. 'You said they're already on their way. And then when they pull the video from those cameras – you saw what happened to Timothy. Once Ellis shows his badge and sees that Serena was with us, he's gonna track her down, leap for her throat, and . . .' He looks over at Serena, refusing to say the words. 'Tell me you think I'm wrong, Calvin. She knows what *flight we're on.* Tell me if we leave her here you really believe Ellis will walk away peacefully and leave her untouched?'

I stare at Serena, knowing the answer. The last thing I need is another death on my conscience. Besides, I heard her ask about the package last night. At least this way, I've got my eyes right on her.

'The moment we get to Cleveland, we're checking her into the first hotel we see,' I say.

'That's fine,' my dad says, rushing back to the airline counter.

Behind him, Serena makes a quick pit stop in the restroom.

And I'm left alone by the floral sofas, staring through the tall plateglass windows, studying the arriving cars and taxis, and praying Naomi and Ellis aren't as close as I think they are.

35

'First of all, his name's not *Ellis*.'

'Yeah, I kinda figured that from his ID saying *Edward*,' Naomi replied as her blue lights swirled and her car whipped across the bridge on Sunrise Boulevard. Glancing down at her GPS device, she eyed the small crimson triangle, which was almost at Griffin Road. Ellis was definitely going for the airport. Now it was making sense. That explained him spying at the building. He was working with Cal. 'How's he check out otherwise? He really a cop?'

'*Was* a cop. Stepped down about a year ago.'

'Like Cal.'

'No. Very much *not* like Cal. First of all—'

'You already did *first of all*.'

'Excuse me?' Scotty asked.

'You can't say *first of all* more than once. You already said it.'

Scotty paused, stewing in silence. '*Second* of all . . . this guy Edward Belasco,' he said through her earpiece. 'He's bad news – and worst of all, he knows the system. Never been arrested, never been caught.'

'Just tell me what he did,' Naomi said with yet another glance at the GPS's glowing crimson triangle. Still on target.

'See, that's the problem, no one can *prove* he did anything,' Scotty explained. 'It goes back to when he was seven years old and he and his mom got into this mess of a car wreck in some schmancy neighborhood in Michigan.'

'You're joking, right? Another broken bird with parent issues? I thought you said he wasn't like Cal.'

'Trust me, this is far from Cal. Anyway, Mom gets slammed in the car wreck, young Edward is untouched, and as a result, he gets sent to live with his recently divorced dad for two weeks while the mom recovers. Two weeks. Instead, a few days into the visit, his father tells him that his mom has suddenly died. Young Edward never went back home again.'

'Oh, boy. And Edward believed him?'

'Dad said it, didn't he? Of course he believed him. Until one rainy day when now fully grown *Officer* Edward, who's moved back to Michigan, opens up the morning newspaper and sees his mom's obituary staring back at him. With a few phone calls, he tracks down the lawyer for his mom's estate, who tells him his mom had spent decades, and most of her money, searching for him. And that's the first time in twenty years that he hears his real name: Ellis.'

'Real candidate for Thorazine, huh?'

'Candidate? We're talking *spokesmodel*,' Scotty said.

'How'd you even get all this info?'

'It's in his file.'

'His personnel file has this?'

'Personnel? No, no, no. This is his *case* file. That's what happens when there's a *murder* investigation,' Scotty explained. 'A few days later, the estate lawyer reports a break-in at his office, with Mom's books and papers suddenly gone, including an old Missing Child flyer that was in the files. Two weeks after that, Edward's dad is found floating facedown in a lake behind his house. With no one to blame, it gets labeled as a boating accident.'

'Until . . .'

'Until six months later, when Edward's suspicious squad leader opens Edward's locker at work and finds the old Missing Child poster from when Edward was young. But instead of the picture of him as a little boy, your man Officer Edward had taken photos of his father and glued the head shots onto the head of his own old childhood body. Now they revisit Dad's so-called *accidental* death. Anything seem a little fishy to you?'

'Who knew that collage skills could be used for evil?' Naomi asked as she made another left and veered toward the entrance for the highway. No question, traffic was murder, but with her blue lights, it wouldn't slow her down. 'So they fired Ellis right there?' she asked, pulling around the pack and riding along the shoulder of the road.

'Fired? Please. First they put him on leave, then they tried to prove he committed the murder, and then they let him resign, pension and all. You know the game: If they fire him, he'll slap back with a lawsuit, then all this home-made Missing Child stuff hits the cable shows, and then the Michigan cops will have one of those public headaches that even the public doesn't want. Better to just – poof – wave your wand and make it disappear.'

'But the way he's calling himself Ellis again . . . going all Mr Ripley with himself . . .'

'No doubt. He clearly found something he loved in his old life,' Scotty said. 'Anyway, where's Officer Nutbag now?'

As Naomi plowed along the shoulder of the road, she again eyed the crimson triangle on the digital screen.

'Approaching the rental car center. I'm betting he's meeting Cal at the airport.'

'You think they're in it together?'

But before Naomi could answer, her phone beeped and *Seminole Police* appeared on caller ID. 'Scotty, I gotta take this.'

With a click, she flipped to the other line. 'Agent Molina,' she answered.

'Benny Ocala,' replied a man with a creaky low voice.

Benny Ocala, Naomi nodded to herself. Chief of the Seminole Police. And the last person Cal called from his cell phone last night.

'Thanks for getting back to me, Benny,' she said, pumping the gas, nearly at the airport. 'I think we have a good friend in common.'

36

My dad heads to the gate alone. Serena follows by herself. By the time I get there, the plane's already boarding. But my father's waiting, tucked in the corner by the wide, sun-filled windows. I'd like to think he's concerned about me, but I can see what he's really looking at. He's not going anywhere without my backpack.

Wasting no time, he heads toward me, limping slightly and tender from the stitches. It's amazing how much slower he moves when he needs something. Especially sympathy. As he steps next to me, he just stands there, waiting for his moment, and I can feel him teeing up his apology for what he said about Mom.

'Calvin, I just want you to know . . .' He clears his throat. 'I really appreciate you looking out for Serena like this.'

'Any families with small children or requiring special assistance are invited to board at this time,' the gate agent announces.

'Anyway, I think having her here – it'll be good for us,' he adds, though when I see who he's looking at, I don't think *us* means him and me.

Tracing his glance, I spot Serena in the corner. She's staring up at the sky as she marvels at one of the departing planes while talking on her cell. Her skin's splotchy, and a bit of tummy chub rolls over the front of her jeans.

But the way the sun hits her – it's like she's made of bronze. She's gotta be my age. Maybe a year or two younger.

'See that?' my dad adds, turning his crooked face back at me. 'I don't never get women like that. So the fact she even came here – for me—'

'Who's she talking to on the phone?'

'She does nutritional consulting for people on chemo. She's just canceling appointments.'

'You willing to bet your life on that?' I ask, searching the crowd for Naomi and Ellis.

'Calvin, listen: For that agent to even catch you on the phone – feds are already at your house, aren't they? They're racing here. What other proof do you need? We're fighting for our lives now. And Serena's part of mine. So if you wanna back out – if you don't wanna come, I understand. But Serena and me—' He breathes hard through his nose. From his front pocket, he pulls out the scrap of paper where he copied the Cleveland address. I make a mental note. He thinks it's about the address and not the comic. 'Anyhow, I hope you come with us.'

My dad walks slowly to the boarding gate. I keep waiting for him to look back to see my decision. But he just keeps watching Serena.

I still don't move. I know it's pathetic, but— *C'mon, just look back.*

He doesn't.

I still wait.

And he still walks. Part of me can't blame him. I've been out of his life for—

He glances over his shoulder. Our eyes lock.

It's small and silly and far too precious to actually matter . . .

But it matters.

Everything with your father matters.

Ten feet in front of me, Serena slides next to my dad, and they quickly lock pinkies. She's not even a bit scared. He's walking fine now. No limp at all. Boy, was that easy for them.

I don't know *her*. I barely know *him*. And they're headed to Cleveland based on a delivery address my father pulled out of a dead man's coffin.

I can stay here. I can. But I heard Naomi's threats. I saw Ellis's gun. My father was right about one thing: If I don't get on this plane, I'll be arrested today and dead by tomorrow.

My father and Serena disappear down the jetway.

I follow right behind them.

Up, up, and away.

37

'Benoni, what's wrong? What happened?' Ellis asked his dog, who was down on her stomach, barely moving in the backseat.

Ellis pulled into an open spot at the rental car return center, then hopped out, ripped open the back door, and leaned down toward Benoni. 'What? What do you see?' he asked, following the dog's eyeline and looking over his own shoulder. Behind him, up in the corner of the garage, a security camera in a black globe peered directly at him.

Craning his neck up, Ellis stared directly into the camera for a full thirty seconds. Let 'em try. His life of hiding was over.

He knew it with each turned page when he first found the diary. He could see his family's – his *real* family's – legacy. All their work. They were scholars.

Back then, Ellis thought the Mark of Cain was a cross or a horn or something on Cain's forehead. But his family knew the true story of the Book of Lies.

From there . . . with the names . . . it wasn't hard for him to track the Leadership. So much of their rank and strength had been decimated over the years. But a few remained. Judge Wojtowicz remained. And therefore, so did the dream. The dream guided him. It still did. His mother's dream for him.

That's what it took to be Ellis.

It was a simple goal – the birthright – the Book – would help him reclaim his life – but it wouldn't be easy. The Judge said as much . . . tried to turn him away. Even threatened him. But as he learned at the lake with his father, fear makes the wolf bigger than he is.

And that was where he began: with the wolf.

'Hey, bud,' a rental car employee with a handheld computer called out, 'what's wrong with your dog? She carsick?'

'She's fine,' Ellis insisted, still staring at the security camera.

'You sure?'

Ellis leaned down into the back of the car. Benoni twisted her head slightly. Her eyes were glazed. Something was definitely wrong.

It had taken Ellis less than three weeks to find Benoni. That path was clear. The first pariah dog was Abel's . . . and then . . . then eventually Cain's. Cain's first true mark. His first gift from God. But not his most vital one. That was the one still hidden – hidden and buried for centuries – then uncovered by the Coptic monks, redeemed by the Leadership, and stolen by the soldier – young Mitchell Siegel – so long ago. Stolen, then hidden again by Siegel's own child. Parent and child. Always parent and child. Just like with his mom.

Patting Benoni's head with both hands, Ellis glanced at his tattoo – at the dog, the thorns . . . and the man embraced by the moon. . . .

Parent and child. God's perfect symmetry. It made even more sense when the Prophet told him what Cal had found. The Map. The address. Of course. Siegel's son never hid the Book of Lies. He kept it. And now . . . that original address . . . Of course they were going to Cleveland.

'Hjjjkkkk . . . hjjkkkk . . .' At first, Ellis thought it was a sneeze. Then, still leaning in the back door, he saw Benoni's head jerk down, then up, then down again. A slobbering waterfall of drool poured from the dog's mouth. Her legs shook.

'Benoni!' he screamed, fighting to pull the dog out.

'Hjjkkk . . . hjjjkkkkk . . . !' The convulsing quickened, and the dog's legs buckled as she collapsed in the back-seat. She was having a seizure.

'Benoni!' Frantically gripping her legs, her body . . . he lifted her out through the back door.

'Hggggguuh . . .' There was a loud splash as a clear, mucousy liquid erupted from Benoni's mouth, spraying the concrete and pooling on the garage floor. Benoni hacked and coughed a few times, jerking her head as though she were trying to twist it off. Ellis held Benoni close, embracing her as the acidic smell hit. Vomit. Not a seizure. For her to throw up like that, she was choking on something.

There. On the floor of the garage: A small, bright orange gob peeked out of the shallow puddle like a chewed piece of gum. But as Ellis reached down for it—

He pinched the dripping, mangled gummy worm with two fingers . . . and saw the gray, flat oval disk that was stuck in its half-chewed web.

A transmitter. She put a—

Ellis's phone beeped, and a text message appeared on-screen:

Too late.
We're off.
Next flight is 1 hr.
    —The Prophet

In his lap, the dog sneezed, then whimpered slightly as she finally caught her breath.

'Yeah, I know, girl – Cal's gone,' Ellis said, patting Benoni's stomach and squinting hard at the oval transmitter. 'Don't worry, we'll use the time. The Judge should be able to find her easily.'

Benoni again coughed a wet cough.

'Exactly, girl,' he said as he tweezed two fingers toward the transmitter's battery. 'I don't want to hurt her, either.'

But that's what it took to be Ellis.

38

There was a high-pitched *bloop* as the red triangle blinked and disappeared.

'Craparoo,' Naomi whispered to herself as she looked down at the GPS screen.

'You need to grab that?' Chief Benny Ocala asked through the phone as Naomi's car zipped toward the rental car building.

Naomi stared outside, where a dozen passengers – most of them tourists – buzzed like bees from the rental car bus and flooded the front doors of the modern white building, making it far too hard to see. Based on Ellis's last signal, he was close, but . . . No, there's no way he knew Naomi was following. And to track her that fast? No way. But that didn't stop her from staring at each and every passenger.

'Agent Molina?' Ocala asked.

'Sorry . . . I was—' She tucked the GPS back in her jacket and followed the signs for *Departures*. If she was lucky, Scotty would be calling in soon with the right terminal. 'So you were telling me about Cal.'

'No, you were asking me *questions* about Cal. I was simply being courteous and trying hard not to embarrass you. Agent Molina—'

'Naomi.'

'Naomi, even when you dial our phone number, it's

like you're entering sovereign land, as in *sovereign nation*, as in the most utilitarian use for your badge right now is as a Halloween costume, though to be honest, we Native Americans don't much like Halloween.'

'See, I hate Halloween, too – my son dressed up as a Thug Life rapper this year, whatever that is. But I got a potential homicide I need to ask your pal Cal about.'

'Homicide's a state crime. You're a federal employee. Wanna try again?'

'The victim is a guy I partner with – Timothy Balfanz – he's a friend,' Naomi explained, hitting the brakes at the crosswalk and carefully watching the small group of passengers that were now passing in front of her, on their way to Terminal 2. 'So no offense, Chief, but if someone went up to one of *your* people – say, that sweet girl with the lisp that I left my message with – if someone nabbed her on a dark road and chopped her into hors d'oeuvres . . . I'd like to think, if it was someone *you* cared about and you needed *my* help, I'd do more than tell you off and bad-mouth Halloween.'

Ocala was silent as Naomi noticed a sudden blur in her rearview, where a tall man in a windbreaker stepped out of the crosswalk and cut behind her car.

'I just wanna know what Cal called about,' Naomi pleaded, glancing over her shoulder and out the back window. The man was already gone. And being out here, exposed to every passing airport stranger, she knew she wasn't being safe.

'Y'know what the Seminole word for *guilt* is?' Ocala finally asked. '*You.*' She heard a sudden *thunk* through the phone. Like a file cabinet being opened and shut. 'I got the bullet here that they pulled from his dad last night.'

'His dad?'

'Cal asked me to run it through the ATF folks, who traced it back to Cleveland and some obscure gun that was used to kill a man named Mitchell Siegel—'

'Mitchell Siegel,' Naomi said, jotting down the name as she heard a beep through her earpiece. Caller ID told her it was Scotty. 'I'll run him ASAP.'

'Think what you want, Naomi,' Ocala added, 'but I'm telling you right now, Cal Harper isn't the demon in this.'

'A dirty badge is a dirty badge – you know that. Besides, if he's such an angel, why doesn't he at least come in and talk with us?'

'Maybe he's worried that instead of listening to reason, you'll just spout silly catchphrases like "A dirty badge is a dirty badge."'

'I appreciate your help,' Naomi said to Ocala as she clicked to the other line.

'Nomi, I think I found Cal,' Scotty blurted. 'I need to double-check, but on that airport list of who paid in cash, there were a few tickets bought this morning – at least three headed to Cleveland.'

Naomi was about to re-enter the loop for departures when a high-pitched *bloop* whistled from her GPS device. Ellis's tracer – the bright crimson triangle – was back in place and once again moving.

It took a moment to read the streets and orient herself, but as the crimson triangle turned onto NE 23rd Court . . .

Naomi's eyes went wide. *No. That can't—*

Oh, God.

'Nomi, you okay?'

'He's there, Scotty.'

'Where? What're you talking about?'

'Twenty-third Court. Ellis . . . he's . . . I think Ellis is at my house.'

39

'Ladies and gentlemen, the captain has turned off the *Fasten Seat Belt* sign – you may now move freely about the cabin,' the flight attendant announces as I stare through the egg-shaped window and watch Florida disappear beneath the cotton candy clouds.

All around me, seats are empty. Still, all three of us sit separately, just to keep it safe.

Checking over my shoulder, I peer ten rows back at my dad, who's fast asleep with his head sagging forward. After everything we've been through, he needs some rest. So do I. Across from him, I look for Serena, but her seat's empty. I glance back at my dad. Don't tell me she snuck over to—

'Calvin,' a female voice interrupts, 'would you mind if I joined you?'

In the aisle, Serena stands over me, her back leaning on the edge of the seat behind her, as if she's trying to steer clear of my personal space. I'm tempted to keep her there, but I can't risk letting anyone overhear.

She slides into the aisle seat, with the empty middle seat between us, then crosses her legs Indian style. It's then that I see she's barefoot. 'I appreciate the kindness,' she says.

'I didn't offer any.'

'You were about to, Calvin. Your eyes said so.'

I'm ready to vomit right there. 'Listen, Serena – I don't know you very well, and I don't know Lloyd much better. But when I look at his expensive silk shirts . . . or his unscuffed shoes – I know my dad has a big need to impress. And as I know from my clients, desperate men are the most easily mesmerized by new-agey, yoga-filled nonsense – especially when it comes from younger, sexed-up women who lock pinkies with them in hopes of getting whatever it is they think those men can get for them. Now I realize this isn't a complex analogy, so to stay with that theme: Go flap your lashes somewhere else.'

She looks at me in silence for what seems like a full minute. 'I'm sorry I made you angry.'

'No, *angry*'s what you get when someone dings your car. This is the cold bitter rage that comes when someone kicks around in your personal crisis.'

'Calvin—'

'Cal,' I growl at her.

She's still unfazed. 'Cal, I'm not sleeping with your father.'

'Then what's with the pinkies and the hand-holding?'

'He was shaking, Cal. In all your anger, did you not see that? I was trying to calm him – refocus his energy.'

'His *energy*? Oh, Lord. Listen, even as a stranger, I can tell he's clearly in love with you.'

'And I love him, but as I've told him, it's solely as a teacher. When we first started doing meditation—'

'Whoa ho ho – my father couldn't meditate if—'

'He's doing it right now,' she says, calm as ever.

I turn back to my dad, whose head is still down. His eyes are closed. I thought he was sleeping, but the way he's swaying forward and back . . .

'The key is breathing through your nose,' Serena adds. 'Each breath needs to reach down to your diaphragm.'

I stare at her across the empty middle seat. She nods and smiles.

'Serena, why're you really here? And please don't insult me by saying you came all the way to the airport and potentially risked your life just to wave good-bye and teach my dad how to breathe and realign his energy.'

Most people turn away when you ask them a hard question. Serena continues to look straight at me, and her yellow blue eyes . . . I hate to say it . . . there's a real depth to her stare.

'He helped my brother. Andrew,' she finally says.

'Who? My dad?'

'You almost had it right before, Cal. Your dad – he's *Andrew's* sponsor,' she explains. 'And my brother – been in AA for years – always relapsing. A few months ago, the judge sent him back, and your dad – it wasn't anything heroic – but your dad was nice to him. They connected. Really connected. Whatever they had in common, Andrew was Andrew again.'

'So all this – coming to help my dad – it's just a thank-you?'

'Oh, no. I'm not just helping your dad. I'm helping myself,' she says as easily as if she's telling me her shoe size. Reading my confusion, she adds, 'Two weeks ago, they found Andrew's body in the sea grapes grove – near Holiday Park. But it was your dad who helped us locate him – he knew Andrew's old hiding spots. He knew my brother. And even though I think you have a hard time with things like this – being near your dad . . . somehow I'm still connected with Andrew.'

'Can I offer you a snack?' a flight attendant interrupts,

approaching just behind Serena and holding out a tiny bag of pretzels.

'No peanuts?' Serena asks.

'Sorry, just pretzels,' the attendant says.

'Then I'm meant to have pretzels,' Serena decides, smiling as she pops open the little bag and turns back to me. 'Your dad tried to save my brother, Cal. And by helping Andrew – with that strength your dad shows, like in the airport – your father helped *me*. He's *still* helping me. And I'm helping him. Do you not see that? That's what being family is – that's the best part – it's not tit for tat or who owes more, it's simply – when one hurts, so does the other; when one finds good, you share in that, too. *That's* family.' But as Serena continues to stare my way . . . 'This is making you uncomfortable, isn't it?' she asks.

I shake my head, trying to convince her she's wrong.

She goes silent, her stare digging even deeper. She's not upset. She's excited. 'I was wrong before. This is why I'm here, isn't it?' she blurts, not the least bit concerned that we brought her on this plane to save her life. 'Not just for what your father and I share . . . the lessons are for you, too, for all three of us. Oh, I didn't see it before. I mean, until you showed up, I didn't even think he had family.'

'He *did* have family! He just—' I catch myself, clenching the fuse that's lit in my chest and digging my feet into the airplane's thin carpet. 'He has a family,' I say quietly. 'He just chose to ignore me.'

'You sure about that?' She tugs on her ankles, tightening her Indian-style position and reaching for a pretzel.

'What're you talking about?'

'You were, what, sixteen years old when he was released? Just taking the SATs, starting to wonder about going to college. You really think having a convicted murderer enter your life was the best thing for you?'

'You don't know that. You met him, what, four months ago?'

'Six months,' she says. 'How'd you know that, anyway?'

'I was bluffing. But that's my point: You barely know him. I heard you at the hospital, asking if he got the shipment. So answer my question, Serena: Why'd you really come to the airport?'

I wait for her yellow blue eyes to narrow, but they just get wider. She's not insulted. She's hurt. 'I came for the same reason you did,' she tells me.

'Let me guarantee right now that's not true.'

'Do you really think you're the only one whose life didn't turn out the way they dreamed, Cal? When I was eleven years old, my mother remarried a man who . . . well, shouldn't've been living around eleven-year-old girls. Or their younger brothers. I still pay for those years. But when I was seventeen – when I finally *told* my mom, and she threw me out because she couldn't handle that it might actually be true – I remember sitting in this filthy McDonald's. It was pouring, one of those thick Florida rains, and I had this feeling to go outside. When I did, I saw this puddle – shaped like a mitten – that reminded me of this great puddle we used to jump in back when we could afford camp. And reliving that moment . . . that was blissful. Real bliss. All because I listened to that feeling to go outside.'

'Okay – so to find true meaning in life, I need to go stand out in some sentient downpour. Very *Shawshank Redemption*.'

'Let me ask you something, Cal: Why'd *you* come on this trip?'

'I almost got killed this morning.'

'Before that. When you saw your dad lying there in the rain . . . You had your own feeling, right? You listened to something inside yourself and suddenly your life was reignited. Like in *Don Juan*, where he says that sometimes you need to lace your belt the opposite way. We get so comfortable in our lives, things get so mundane, we spiritually fall asleep. But you don't have to go to an ashram in India to reignite your life. If we just follow those feelings, like my feeling to go talk to your dad at the airport—'

'Serena, the only reason I got on this plane was to save my own rear.'

She undoes her Indian-style position, stands up from her seat, and never abandons the soft, knowing smile that lifts her cheeks. 'Your father told me where you work, Cal. If you really were as tough as you think, you wouldn't be there. And if you really didn't want to connect with him, you wouldn't be *here*. It's no different than taking me along with you. In that act, you did one of the most beautiful things anyone can do. You said *yes* to me. And with your father, just getting on this plane, you did the same. You buckled your belt the other way.'

As she walks back to her seat, I look down at my unfastened seat belt. 'Airline buckles only go one way,' I call out.

'Not when you share them with the person next to you,' she calls back.

40

The blue lights swirled, the siren howled, and Naomi held her breath.

Three minutes. She'd be there in three minutes, Naomi told herself, clenching the wheel as her car slowly elbowed through the lunchtime traffic on Miami Gardens Drive.

In her ear, Scotty was gone. She needed her cell to make sure—

'Pick up the damn phone, Mom!' she screamed. But all she heard back was a droning ring, again and again and—

'This is Naomi,' her own voice replied on the answering machine. 'I'm probably screening you right now, so—'

With a click, she hung up and started again. Mom's cell. Still no answer. Home phone . . .

'This is Naomi. I'm probably screening you—'

Click. Redial.

Two minutes. Less than two minutes, she swore to herself as she cut off a black Acura and the phone continued to ring. . . . *Dammit, why isn't she picking up!?*

On the GPS screen, the glowing crimson triangle still hadn't moved from her house. *No, don't think the worst—*

Swerving across two lanes of traffic, Naomi jerked the wheel to the left, and her dark green Chevy bucked and bounced over the last few inches of the street's concrete turning lane. The phone beeped and she reacted instinctively.

'Mom?' she asked, picking up.

'Local police are en route,' Scotty said. 'For all you know, this is just—'

'Just *what*!? He's at my house, Scotty – *with my son*!'

'That doesn't mean—'

'*How the hell'd he know where I live!?*'

Ramming the gas, Naomi sank her nails deep into the rubber of the steering wheel. As she craned her neck wildly back and forth, she fought to get a better look past the thin trees. At the far end of the block was a modest, faded yellow rambler with a crooked garage door and . . .

Her mom's car. Still in the driveway. *Oh, no . . .*

'*Who gave him my address!?*' she shouted at Scotty.

'Listen, you need to—'

'I've never been listed! *Someone gave him my damn address!*'

The brakes were still screaming as Naomi threw open her car door and leapt outside.

'Nomi, if he's still in there . . .' Scotty warned.

'Scotty, swear to me you didn't give anyone my address. By accident or on purpose . . . I need to hear it.'

'A-Are you—? I— Of course I didn't!'

There was real pain in his voice. She trusted that pain.

'*Lucas!*' Naomi screamed, pulling her gun and sprinting for the front door. Her feet felt like anvils, her throat like a pinched straw. She tried to breathe. . . .

'*Luuucas!*' She jabbed her key at the bottom lock, but even before it got there . . . the door slowly swung away from her. *God.* It was already open.

She could hear the sirens in the distance.

'Nomi, you need to wait,' Scotty pleaded. 'Don't go in without—'

Darting inside, she felt her heart kicking in her neck. Her eyes scanned the hallway . . . the front closet . . . but all she was really looking for were her son's shoes . . . There.

Lucas's flip-flops.

That means Lucas is still—

Frantically sprinting toward the kitchen, she heard her phone beep in her ear. Another call.

'What're you, a *mental* patient?' her mother asked as Naomi clicked over. 'Who leaves fifteen rambling messages like that?'

'L-Lucas . . . where's—? *Where are you?*' Naomi asked, her gun pointed straight out and her back touching the wall as she prowled around the corner of her dark and clearly empty kitchen.

'The video store – we walked from the park – though I didn't realize that was a reason to call out the entire Customs Service,' her mother shot back.

'Where's Lucas?'

'Right next to me. He wants one of those *Star War* movies – those are okay, right? No nudity or anything?'

Naomi doubled back into the hallway and quickly checked both bedrooms . . . closets . . . bathrooms . . . All empty. Back in the living room, she studied the carpet, the sofa cushions, even the slight sway of the vertical blinds that led to the backyard. Nothing was out of place. The back door was still locked. But something still . . .

'Mom, go to the back of the video store,' Naomi said into the phone. 'There's a bathroom there—'

'Wait, what happened?'

'Just find the bathroom – they'll let you use it if you

ask nice – then lock the door and wait there for me, okay? I don't care who bangs on that door, you don't open it, you don't let Lucas out, you don't check on anything until I'm there. Only me.'

Naomi pulled out her GPS device, clicked back to Scotty on her cell, then began to search for the red triangle.

'Nomi, don't click off like that!' Scotty scolded. 'I thought you were—'

'Shh.' It took a moment to reorient herself. On-screen, the tiny crimson triangle stood completely still. So did Naomi. She was rushing so fast, she never even saw it. According to the screen, the beacon was now coming from behind her.

Naomi twisted around and dashed up the main hallway, rammed her shoulder at the front door, and crashed outside, back into the bright sun.

Outside, her front yard was empty. There was no breeze. And no sound but the shrieking sirens that finally turned onto her block.

'He's gone,' she whispered.

'You sure?' Scotty asked. 'If he came there— No note? No message?'

On-screen, the crimson triangle overlapped almost perfectly with the white, elongated triangle that represented Naomi's location. *Overlapped* . . . Looking straight down, Naomi stepped off the exploding-fireworks-shaped doormat she still hadn't removed since July Fourth and took a peek underneath. On the ground was a tiny and familiar flat oval disk.

'Oh, he definitely left a message,' Naomi said, pinching the transmitter with two fingers. Ellis didn't come here just to leave it under the mat. If her son had been home, Ellis would've— A boil of anger bubbled up the back of her neck. The last time she was this mad was during her repo years. The victim sued for the cost of the hospital bills. And won. Four figures.

'You okay there?' Scotty asked.

Naomi let go of the welcome mat, and as it slapped against the concrete, a swirl of dust cartwheeled out the sides. For a moment, Naomi just knelt there, thinking about her son, and her mom, and everything that might've happened if something might've happened. But it hadn't. And that's what made it so damn easy to focus back on Ellis. And Cal. Especially on Cal. The former agent . . . the one who was at the port last night . . . and the one who could've easily given her family's address to—

'You're plotting their deaths now, aren't you,' Scotty said.

'I want the next flight to Cleveland.'

'Yeah, and I want to eat cream sauce without feeling puffy after.'

Naomi didn't say a word.

'I was joking, Nomi. (Kinda.) Now do you want the bad news or the really bad news?'

'Bad news.'

'You just missed one of the flights to Cleveland; you're on the next one.'

'And the really bad?'

'I got Ellis's full file from the prosecutor, like you asked. They got everything in here: psych profiles, behavior reports, even identifying marks.'

'I thought you said this was really bad?'

'Hear that noise? That's the other shoe falling, Nomi. Because that tattoo on Ellis's hand? You're not gonna believe what it stands for.'

41

'Cain? As in *Cain* Cain?' I ask Roosevelt through my newest disposable cell. As we whip down the highway, I scour the buttons on the dashboard, searching for—

'*Here,*' my father says from the passenger seat. He clicks a switch, and a cannonball of warm air blasts at the fog on our windshield, lifting it away like a raised curtain.

'Now find the heat,' Serena pleads from the backseat as the gray Cleveland sky smothers all light and we plow through the slush and past the blackened snowbanks on I-71.

It's December in Florida, but not like December here. At barely four o'clock, it's nearly dark. Still, we're not completely unprepared. From my job, my dad and I have the two thickest winter coats the donation room had to offer. From Serena's driver's license, we have an untraceable rental car. And from the gas station right outside the Cleveland airport, Serena has a *Cleveland Rocks* sweatshirt, and I – like Roosevelt in Fort Lauderdale – have a brand-new chat'n chuck mobile phone to make sure we're not traced. Everything's in place. But it doesn't stop me from studying every car around us. The next Florida flight to Cleveland left barely an hour after ours. It's not much of a lead.

'I thought you were dropping her at a hotel,' Roosevelt says as he hears Serena's voice.

'If Ellis is following, it's not safe by the airport. Trust

me, we're doing it first thing after the house,' I tell him. 'So you were saying about Ellis's tattoo.'

'Can't you put him on speaker?' Serena asks from the backseat, looking up from a foldout map. Quickly backing down, she adds, 'Sorry. I just—' Her voice drops to a whisper. 'It's not like I can't hear everything he's saying anyway.'

'They can hear me?' Roosevelt asks through the phone.

In the rearview, Serena nods. My dad thinks I don't see him smile.

'Roosevelt, you're on speaker,' I announce with the push of a button as I stuff the phone in a dashboard cup holder. Behind us, I notice a white Jeep with its lights off. 'So the tattoo: It's Cain from Adam and Eve. Okay, so he loves the bad guys.'

'Oh, goodness, son – you're missing it all, aren't ya?' Roosevelt asks, and I swear I hear a swish from his pony-tail. 'Sure, all the images – the dog, the stars, the moon, even the thorns that the man is carrying – they're all ancient symbols of the so-called Mark of Cain. But deciphering that mark is one of the oldest questions of the Bible. Most scholars believe it's something God gave to Cain as punishment for killing Abel: that God marked Cain as a murderer – gave him horns, put a cross on his forehead, made him into some gol-durn half-beast – then sent him wandering in the Land of Nod. But the real question remains: Who is Cain?'

'No . . . uh-uh. No offense to Sunday school, but spare us the lecture,' I shoot back. 'Just tell us why it's important.'

'Cal, this guy tried to kill you. *Both* of you,' Roosevelt says as my father shoots me a look. 'Dontcha wanna hear *why*?'

On the highway, the car plows over a flat sheet of ice. We don't go flying or spinning out of control, but for a full two or three seconds, I turn into the skid and know – as we glide in perfect, soundless silence across the ice – that I'm not in control. Since the moment I found my father, that's my life.

'Just listen to him,' my dad insists, sounding like a dad.

I hold tight to the steering wheel, and the tires again gain traction.

'So back to brother Cain,' Roosevelt says through the speaker. 'God created Adam and Eve – making Cain the first human ever born. First killer. First human villain, correct?'

'Depends what you want to believe: the Bible . . . ' I say, 'or every single carbon-dated archaeological dig of the last hundred years that proves people existed fifty thousand years before Adam and Eve ever supposedly went on their apple rampage.'

'Here – exit *here*,' Serena calls out from the backseat, and I tug the wheel and veer toward the sign for *I-90 East*. Behind us, the Jeep with no lights does the same. I slow down, giving it a chance to pass, but it doesn't.

'The Bible ain't just a bunch of stories about dead people, Cal. It's the greatest and oldest book of human civilization – a book that people through the centuries have given their lives for. But that doesn't mean there aren't problems of translation. It's like Adam and Eve and the apple, right? Like you mentioned, one of the Bible's most famous tales, except for the problem that there was no apple.'

'Says who?' my father asks.

'Look at the text, sir: The word *apple* never appears in the Bible. It ain't there. Eve ate a fruit – probably a fig – but in ancient Greece, when the Old Testament was translated from Hebrew, the scribes put in the word *apple* because at the time, apples were the big symbols of desire and destruction. And those slight editorial changes – over time, they start affecting how we think about the Bible, even though they're not even in the original text.'

'But now, thanks to the wonders of Bible college, you'll reveal the far more interesting alternate history that'll surprise us all,' I say.

'Cal, this ain't about what *you* believe. It's about what *Ellis* believes. And right now, you gotta understand that he's coming at you with what he perceives is the power of *God* on his side.'

We all fall silent. Serena scootches up in her seat and scratches my dad's shoulder. He closes his eyes and takes a deep breath through his nose.

'So to understand the tattoo, we need to understand Cain,' I say as Serena points to the right, signaling for us to get off at the next exit. In the rearview, the Jeep with no lights is barely two car lengths back. I tap on the brakes and slow down to get a better look. Annoyed, the Jeep pulls around us and passes on our right. I get my first good look at the driver: a pissed-off mom with three kids in the back.

'It all goes back to how we view him,' Roosevelt says. 'Cain's the ruthless brother-killer, right? For thousands of years, he's the symbol of our worst sins – the *bad man* who makes us feel better about ourselves. But when you check out the earliest theories – like those geniza fragments they found in Cairo centuries ago – those fragments are as close as we get to the earliest copies of the Bible, and in there, they question the entire premise,' he adds with a brand-new seriousness in his voice. 'Or to put it more bluntly: Instead of thinkin' Cain's the ultimate villain, what if he's the good guy in the tale?'

'Yeah, except for that part in act one where he kills his own brother,' I point out.

'Forget your Sunday school, Cal. Sure, over the years, we all demonized Cain. But the Bible doesn't.'

'That's not true,' I say. 'When Cain asks, *"Am I my brother's keeper?"* – those're hardly the words of a saint.'

'And that's fine. But the story of Cain and Abel isn't just about fratricide. It's about what happens *after* Abel's death. God's reaction. Punishment versus redemption.'

'So now the Mark of Cain is God's way of rewarding Cain?'

'Again, look at the translation. According to most modern Bibles, Cain thinks God's punishment is too much – *"My punishment is greater than I can bear,"* is what the text says – which is why Cain is seen as such a remorseless monster. But when you go back to the original text – like in the geniza fragments – that same passage can just as easily be translated as *"My sin is too great to forgive."* See the difference there? In this version, Cain feels so awful . . . so sorry . . . for what he's done to poor Abel, he tells God he should *never* be forgiven. That's a pretty different view of Cain, no?' Roosevelt asks, letting it all sink in. 'Of course, most religions prefer the vicious Cain. A little threat of evil is always the far better way to fill the seats. But sometimes the monsters aren't who we think they are.'

In the backseat, Serena has long forgotten the map. My dad stares down at the phone. 'So God forgave Cain?' he asks.

'Think about it: What if that's the whole point of the story? The Mark of Cain wasn't a punishment. It was God's *reward*: to show Divine mercy – to teach us that those who repent get forgiveness.'

'So the Mark of Cain could be something good?' Serena asks.

'This is a gift straight from *God*,' Roosevelt replies, his southern accent lingering on the final word. 'So, yeah, I'd wager "good" covers it.'

'C'mon, you're telling me that the whole reason we're running around – the reason my dad got shot—'

'I think he got shot for the address,' Serena interrupts. When I glance in the rearview, she adds, 'From the comic. It's just a feeling, but it's the only thing that makes sense. You said there're other copies of the comic. But the address . . . That's the new piece of information, right? Maybe that's their meeting place. Or their storage place.'

'Or their hiding place,' my dad says without turning back to either of us.

'Whatever it is, they wanted that address on the comic,' Serena points out. 'They thought your dad had it. Maybe . . . I don't know . . . you think that's why Mitchell Siegel got shot eighty years ago, too?'

'Perfect, just perfect,' I continue. 'So what Timothy and Ellis and everyone else – what they're really all after is the long-lost, barely believable Mark of Cain, which is somehow on a Superman comic from some crappy neighborhood in Cleveland?'

'I'm not saying it exists,' Roosevelt's voice goes on as we reach the exit for Martin Luther King Jr. Drive. 'You asked about Ellis's tattoo; I'm telling you what it stands for. And when you look at what the Bible says about the Mark – *"The Lord set a mark upon Cain, that whoever found him should not kill him."* Look at the last part there – *"should not kill him."* The images in Ellis's tattoo, those are God's gifts to Cain: things that're gonna protect him from all the wild beasts in the wilderness.'

'Y'mean like weapons?' my dad asks.

'Or a dog,' Roosevelt says. 'Named Benoni.'

Everyone is silent as I tug the wheel to the right, and

we all sway to the left, curving around the exit. At the red light, it's no different from the Martin Luther King Jr. street at home: Even with the darkness, it's clear we're in a rough neighborhood. Within a few quick turns, nearly all the businesses are either burnt out or boarded up. On each corner, there's some kid in a thick winter coat bouncing in place to find some warmth. Not one of them gets on the passing buses. I work in these neighborhoods every day. I know drug dealers when I see them.

'You still there?' Roosevelt asks.

'You were saying about the dog,' I reply as Serena and my dad glance out their respective windows. Both of them sit up straight. Like they know we're close. 'That from Bible college, too?'

'Nah, that was Google,' Roosevelt says. 'Benoni was apparently Abel's dog, then when Abel got killed, God supposedly gave the dog to Cain as protection.'

'Okay, so Ellis renamed his dog,' I say. 'Big deal.'

'Maybe it ain't just the dog,' Roosevelt says. 'Most people are taught Cain wandered through the Land of Nod for seven generations. But another interpretation says that God's gift – that no one should kill Cain – was literal. That God let him live forever.'

'You mean Ellis thinks he's Cain?' Serena asks.

Next to me, my dad's now mesmerized by our surroundings, staring out the window. 'I think it's the next right,' he blurts. When I look at him, he adds, 'I saw it on the map.'

'It's only been a few hours. I gotta do more research,' Roosevelt says. 'But for a book like the Bible, where nearly every major figure's death is pointed out – Noah lived for X years; Moses lived for Y – the Bible is completely, and almost strangely, silent about the death of Cain.'

'This is it – Kimberly Avenue,' my dad blurts as I turn

onto the narrow block that's lined with small, beaten two-story houses and barely any cars. It's one thing to be in a *bad* neighborhood; it's another to be in an *abandoned* one.

'Do people live here?' Serena asks as the car bangs through one of the street's ice-filled potholes. On both sides of the block, the sidewalks are barely plowed. I check the windows and front porches of every house we pass. It's only four-thirty. There's not a person in sight.

'Roosevelt, can we deal with the rest of the nutty Cain stuff later?' I ask.

'You're missing what I said, Cal. *Ellis thinks he has God on his side.* Take it from the former pastor: The true believers are the ones who'll burn you the worst,' he says. 'Though what all this has to do with an address on a comic book, now you're out of my biblical league.'

'Yeah, that's what I'm worried about,' I say as we reach the middle of the block and pull up to the peeling blue two-story house with the even more peeling red trim. Unreal. The whole house, including the front steps: bright blue and red. Like Superman.

From my backpack, I pull out the old 1938 comic and its protective wax paper.

If found, please return to:
10622 Kimberly Ave. Cleveland

I scan the alleys on both sides of the house (dark but empty), then double-check the numbers on the front porch: 10622. This is it. The address from the coffin.

Before I can even stop, my father's out of the car.

42

'Ring it again,' my dad says impatiently. The words come out in plumes of vapor.

I press the buzzer and put my ear to the frozen metal screen door. I don't hear anything from inside, including the doorbell. I shouldn't be surprised. The way the front porch is slanted and the overhead light is cracked, this place has more problems than just some peeling blue paint.

'*C'mon!* Anyone there!?' My father raps the door with his fist, clearly freezing as he hops up and down. His coat is on Serena, who's rubbing his back as he settles into calm. I keep checking the length of the block, searching for arriving cars. Ellis . . . Naomi . . . neither of them is stupid. Each minute we're standing out here . . .

'Easy, easy – I'm coming,' a man's voice calls from inside.

Serena steps back, almost as if she's checking that we're in the right place. There's no doubt about that. To the left of the door, the front windows that face the porch are filled with sun-faded posters and cards of Superman. A handwritten sign on a sheet of loose-leaf paper says, 'Superman's House!!!'

Serena stares at the sign. My brain flashes to the gun that shot my dad. What the hell does this all have to do with Superman?

The door swings open and an older black man with a

Mr Rogers sweater pokes his head out, careful to keep the cold from seeping in.

'Who *is* it?' a female voice calls out from deeper inside the house.

'Dunno,' the man calls back, eyeing me and my dad. Then he spots Serena. 'I know you?' he asks her.

Like a turtle, Serena shrinks into the shell of her winter coat. 'I – I don't think so.'

'Man, you look familiar,' he adds, and just as quickly shakes it off. Turning back to my dad, he asks, 'Where's your coat? What you want?'

'We . . . er . . . we wanted to see if you . . . y'know . . . we found your address . . . on a comic,' my dad blurts.

The man rolls his eyes. 'Oh, man – white boys in the ghetto – you're fans, ain't ya?'

'Yeah. Huge fans,' I jump in, determined to get some info. 'Why? You get a lot of us?'

'Naw, just here and there. Comes with the house,' he says. 'So. Again. What you want?'

I wait for Serena to maybe jump in and charm, but she's still a turtle in her coat.

'I know this sounds crazy,' I begin, 'but y'ever go somewhere and feel like you were just *meant* to be there?'

'Hoooo, you're *those* kinda fans, ain't ya?'

'We came really far,' I plead.

'How far? Shaker Heights?'

'Florida,' my dad says, bouncing lightly and reminding our host just how cold it is with no coat. 'I was tan when I got here.'

It's just enough of a bad joke to make the man laugh. 'Aw, you're lucky I got a sister in Jacksonville,' he says as he opens the door, shuffling back and revealing the checkerboard pajamas he's wearing under his sweater.

'Shoes over there,' he adds, pointing to a pile of old boots in the corner. 'Wife's request; not mine.'

We nod thankfully, then add our shoes to the pile and hand him our jackets, which he layers on top of an old coatrack. 'If ya want, I can hang the backpack, too,' he offers, taking a double take on me. 'Man, all that white hair – I thought you were old at first. Like me,' he says. 'You get that a lot?'

'Sometimes,' I tell him.

'You should get it more,' he insists. 'White hair's mysterious.'

'He's very mysterious,' Serena blurts, meaning every word.

The man doesn't care. 'Anyhow, your backpack . . .'

'I'm fine holding it,' I say, sliding it onto my back and getting my first good look at the house, which is centered around a main hallway with three side-by-side sofas running along the right-hand wall and an old, thick, projection-style TV on the left, just next to the stairs.

'Introduce yourself, Johnsel!' a woman scolds from the kitchen.

'Sorry,' the older man says, extending a hand. 'Heyden Johnsel.'

'And Vivian,' adds an overweight black woman in a Cleveland Browns apron, entering the hallway with a surprising elegance. She reaches into her shirt and from inside her bra pulls out a tissue and dabs her eyes. 'Not real crying – just onion chopping,' she promises, as if having three strangers in her house is just part of her daily life. But as I look around, I realize it is.

The far wall is covered from floor to ceiling with pictures, drawings, needlepoint, shelves with candles, even a wall calendar with Jesus on it, and in nearly every one, Jesus is pictured as black. It's the same in the administrative offices of the shelters and churches we work with. True believers are always the most likely to take in weary travelers.

'So apparently, back in the twenties, this's the room where the whole family used to gather round the radio,' Johnsel says, pointing to where the TV is and heading toward the worn stairs. 'Though I assume you're really here to see the bedroom, huh? In the attic?'

We all three smile and nod. 'Absolutely,' I say.

'You don't even know what I'm talking about, do you?' Johnsel asks, stopping on the first step.

None of us move.

'D'ya even know where you are? This is the old Siegel house – *sacred ground* – where young Jerry Siegel created Superman.'

'No, that we know,' my dad says, though I can't tell if it's the truth. As always, he's a half-step ahead. And it's the kind of half-step that's getting impossible to ignore. 'We'd love to see the bedroom,' he says.

Johnsel grins and shrugs. 'Hoooo. Fine by me.' He's in his pajamas at four-thirty. He's just thrilled to have an audience.

In a slow spiral, he leads us to the second floor, then around to a shaky set of stairs that lead up to the third. The higher we go, I swear, the narrower the stairway gets – and with each shoeless step, the uncarpeted wooden stairs creak and scream far more than I'm comfortable with.

'Don't worry, it'll hold our weight,' Johnsel promises.

I grab for the banister and realize there isn't one.

'Okay, now, *here's* what people make the fuss about,' Johnsel says as he reaches the third-floor landing and extends his hand palm up like a model on a game show.

I crane my neck to peek over Johnsel's shoulder. I'm not from money. I live in a converted motel room. But even by my standards, the small finished bedroom is a wrecking ball of a room, filled with pile after pile of milk crates, plastic bins, and old furniture. The entire back wall is hidden by mini-skyscrapers of paperback books – all with titles like *Elijah* and *King of Kings*. Up top, huge hunks of the slanted plaster ceiling are cracked and missing, revealing the old wooden slats underneath.

'Hoooo – it's definitely seen better days,' Johnsel admits. 'But like they say, you gotta sorta imagine: This was it . . . the exact spot where a teenage kid was lying awake in bed one rainy summer night and came up with a hero who could fly above all the world's problems. Can ya imagine: one sweaty night to change your whole life?'

I don't have to turn around to know my dad's watching me.

'What about Jerry's father?' Serena interrupts, sounding far more interested than I expected. 'Any idea how he died?'

'I thought it was . . . maybe a heart attack?' Johnsel guesses. I don't bother correcting him. 'I think Jerry was in high school.'

'Is that when he made *this*?' I ask, realizing it's time to show some cards. From my backpack, I pull out the wax-paper protective sleeve that holds *Action Comics* #1. Johnsel takes an excited step toward me. I take a step to the left, stealing a quick peek out the double-square windows that overlook the front yard. They're so thick with dust, I can barely see out.

'That's— Hoooo— Where'd you get an attic copy?' Johnsel asks.

'A what?' I ask.

'Those copies – with the—' He glances down at the typed message on the wax paper. 'And you got one with an address,' he says. 'Hoooo, this's—You know what this's worth?'

My father shakes his head.

'Last I heard, when the movie came out . . . something like 1.2 million,' Johnsel says.

'*Million?*' my dad and Serena ask simultaneously.

I stay silent.

'Cal, maybe we were wrong,' my dad says. 'Maybe it's the comic that they wanted instead of the—' He cuts himself off, watching me carefully.

'You knew,' he adds. 'You knew how much it was worth.'

He's right. I had Roosevelt look it up before we left.

'Why didn't you say something?' my dad asks.

Again, I'm silent.

'What? You thought I'd swipe it from you? You really think I'm that much of an animal?'

For a moment, I close my eyes and try not to picture the fact that my dad knew about the coffin key. Or which block this house was on. Or that we should even come here in the first place.

'Let's just focus on what's important,' I tell my dad, and turn back to Johnsel. I hold up the comic. 'Sorry, you were about to tell us what this is.'

'Already did: It's an attic copy,' Johnsel replies. 'Just like it sounds, one of his personal copies from the attic.' Seeing we're lost, he quickly adds, '*Action Comics Number 1* is the very first appearance of Superman. . . .'

'We gathered that part,' I tell him.

'Then you also know how rare they are. Less than a hundred copies still exist – and of those, most of them are beaten and torn, because back then, who knew to save them? Well, I'll tell you who: the young kid who was so darn thrilled to see his creation in print.'

I stare at the tiny room with the torn-away ceiling and try to imagine the teenage boy sitting up in bed. 'Jerry Siegel.'

'Why not, right? When each comic came out, the publisher used to send a few free copies to all the writers and artists who worked on it. Again, most would give 'em away or do whatever with 'em. Even Joe Shuster – the Superman artist and co-creator – never kept 'em.'

'But Jerry Siegel saved them.'

'He did save them – even preserved them in his own makeshift wax-paper sleeve. But more important – Jerry Siegel *forgot* them. In the attic. Within months, his new Superman idea took off, young Jerry finally got a bigger paycheck, and he eventually moved to New York to get closer to the action.'

'But the comics stayed here,' I surmise.

'With Jerry's mother. The owners before me said they bought it from the Siegel family when his mom died in the early forties. Skip forward a few years later when they eventually start crawling through the attic, and look what's there – tucked away where no one would find them – half a dozen pristine copies of some old Superman comic . . .'

'They didn't even know what they found, did they?' my father asks.

'. . . which they quickly sold at a garage sale for something like a buck or two apiece, thereby scattering these attic editions back into the population—'

'And kicking off the ultimate geek gold rush for Jerry Siegel's so-called personal copies,' I say, running my fingers across the melted edges of the wax paper and rereading the typed address in the bottom corner. I know it's worth $1.2 million. And sure, people kill for much less than that. But that haunting look in Ellis's eyes. All this talk of Cain. There's still no way this is just about a comic.

Across from me, Johnsel rolls up the arms of his sweater and stares out the double-square windows. As if he's looking for someone.

Oh, Lord. If he's stalling us . . .

'I think we should go,' I insist.

'No,' my dad says. 'This comic— The address said to come here.'

'Just what are you boys looking for?' Johnsel asks, confused.

'Mr Johnsel, is this it back here?' a voice calls out behind us.

Following the question, we spin around to see Serena outside the room, standing at the landing at the top of the stairs. She's got a single finger pointed upward.

'That's the one,' Johnsel replies as we join her on the landing and raise our chins up toward the unfinished wooden square that's set into the ceiling. I didn't even see it at first. The entrance to the attic.

Serena keeps staring at it. 'Think there's anything left?' she asks.

'Hoooo – you're dreaming big dreams now,' Johnsel says, laughing.

'That doesn't answer my question,' she teases, smart enough to keep it nice. 'Maybe there's something still up there.'

Again, Johnsel laughs. 'It's been over sixty years – plus all the people that picked through it before we got here. Trust me, there ain't nothin'—'

'When was the last time you were up there?' Serena interrupts.

Johnsel cocks his head, confused. 'When we first moved in. Why would I wanna go again?'

'Wait. Hold on,' I say. 'You haven't been up there since you first moved in? When was that?'

'Not that long. We came in . . .' He thinks for a moment. '1972.'

If I had water in my mouth, I'd do the full spit shot.

'Okay,' my dad says. 'We need a ladder.'

43

'First time flying?' a young woman with a pencil-point chin asked from her seat next to him.

Ellis stared downward at the floor of the airplane, his fingers wedged above his closed tray table. But he didn't answer.

'Sir, you okay?'

Again, Ellis stared at the floor. He was at the window; she was on the aisle.

'You need to throw up?' the woman asked, rifling through the seat pocket. 'There's a bag right—'

'Y'hear that?' Ellis asked.

The woman looked at him, confused. 'You're really gonna throw up, aren't you?'

'You don't hear that sound? Like a high-pitched whimper. Y'know, like a dog?'

At that, the woman raised an eyebrow and lowered her sharp chin. Ellis was still staring at the floor of the plane. 'Ohh . . . you have a puppy down there, don't you?' she asked, motioning downward as if she were pointing through the floor to the cargo hold.

'There it is again!' Ellis insisted.

'Sweetie, I got a mopey cocker spaniel at home. Every time I take her on the plane, I swear I hear her crying for me. And then someone's kind enough to tell me I'm just being nuts.'

For the first time, Ellis turned toward the woman. And grinned. 'I'm just being nuts, aren't I?'

'Totally understandable,' she said, tapping him on the shoulder. 'You're sweet for worrying, though. You really love your pup, huh?'

'She means a great deal to me,' Ellis said. With a deep breath, he stared out the open window at the tiny lights that dotted the landscape.

'We're beginning our descent into Cleveland,' the pilot announced overhead.

'By the way, for your pup,' the woman next to Ellis began. 'Have you tried giving her a sedative? That always calms mine before a big flight.'

'No, I need her alert,' Ellis explained as he reached for his leather diary. 'She's about to have a very busy night.'

44

'I think it's glued shut,' Serena calls down from the top of the ladder.

'Hit it again,' my dad says.

'Not *too* hard,' Johnsel adds.

'Let me just help you,' I say.

That's all she needs. Ramming her palm up toward the ceiling, she slams the square piece of wood that covers the entrance to the attic. It looks thin, like balsa wood. From the thud and the pain on her face, it's not.

'There you go. It moved,' my father says.

'It *didn't* move,' she shoots back.

'I think it did,' I say. 'Now use the flashlight to hit it.'

She looks again, knowing I'm right. To be honest, I should be the one up there, but the hole's so small – she's got the best chance of squeezing through.

'It's good we brought her along, huh?' my dad whispers, but I don't answer.

Serena winds up again with the flashlight Johnsel gave her and grips the ladder for support. On three – one . . . two . . .

The base of the flashlight plows into the wood. There's a loud pop, then a rip as the square piece flips upward like a reverse trapdoor. The only reward is a lungful of dust and a light shower of pebbles and chunks of plaster that rain over all of us. According to Johnsel, the house was built in 1911. Tastes like it.

Waving the dust away, Serena stares up at the square black hole of the attic. It's teeny. Barely bigger than a phone book.

'Careful,' I call out.

She steps up on the top rung of the ladder, raises her arms, and boosts herself easily into the darkness.

'Hoooo – that was anticlimactic,' Johnsel blurts.

Wasting no time, I leap toward the ladder and scale it as fast as I can.

'What're you doing?' my father asks.

'She made it easy. I'll fit,' I tell him as I look up at the black square hole. There's a flicker of white light inside, from the flashlight. 'Serena, anything up there?' I ask.

She doesn't answer.

As I climb closer to the top rung, bits of dust continue to tumble my way.

'You're not gonna fit,' my dad says.

Only one way to find out.

I put my arms straight up.

'Just like Superman,' Johnsel jokes. No one laughs.

I thread my arms through the hole, then my head, as I slowly extend my knees. The darkness descends like a noose.

'You're too big,' my father warns.

He's wrong. The hole swallows everything above my chest. I feel around, palming the dusty floor of the attic. All I need to do is boost myself up. But just as I push off the top rung, something catches my back . . . or, more specifically, my backpack, with the comic inside. Dammit. I'm definitely too big.

'Told you,' my dad calls out as my feet kick wildly from the ceiling.

A bright light blinds me. 'Throw the backpack up here,' Serena says.

'Just drop it – I'll catch it,' my dad promises from below.

The lady or the tiger.

I choose neither.

Thrashing wildly, I'm halfway through. The edge of the hole digs into my stomach. I don't care what it takes. I squirm and shimmy like a worm as splinters and sharp rocks bite at my belly. My backpack tugs like a leash. Above me, Serena grips my left bicep and starts the tug-of-war. I wriggle and plant my elbows. She digs in her feet and jerks harder. The hole pinches my rib cage. The leash stays taut, pulling and yanking me . . . and then . . . then it isn't.

Like a baby shooting from the birth canal, I fly forward as Serena tumbles back on her ass. The flashlight zigzags as she falls. My stomach scrapes across the attic floor, leaving a wide, swerving wake through the dust.

'You okay!?' my dad calls out as he hears the crash. He's tempted to join us himself, but he knows he won't fit.

I'm still catching my breath, which I can see in the beam of light from above. There's no insulation. It's freezing up here. Slowly, my eyes adjust to the darkness, but I don't need to see Serena to know what she's thinking. 'Go ahead – say the line,' I tell her. 'I'm more stubborn than my dad.'

She climbs to her feet, brushes off the dust, and stays hunched to avoid hitting the attic's low, slanted ceiling. But she's not the least bit annoyed. 'You really believe your father's stubborn?'

'C'mon . . . the way he insisted on coming to Cleveland . . . then held his breath like a fifth grader so I couldn't say no to you coming, too?'

'That's not *stubborn*, Cal. Your dad's terrified.'

'He's not alone,' I shoot back. 'If Ellis made that next flight, he'll be here any—'

'He's not terrified of Ellis,' Serena says. 'Your father's terrified of *you*.' She doesn't yell it at me. She's concerned. Almost sad.

Down on my knees, I take a deep breath of sandy air as dozens of small stones stab through my pants. 'Me? You're joking, right?'

She shakes her head, and the beam from the flashlight shakes with her, tracing the inky air. But she never loses sight of what we're here for. Pointing the light across the empty room, she's already on the hunt. 'You need to understand, Cal – in this world, we're not humans having a divine experience. We're divine beings having a human experience.'

'Yeah, I took yoga once, too.'

'See, there it is again: That's what he has to fight.' Above our heads, the rafters crisscross like wooden monkey bars. On our left, the eroded brick chimney rises through the room and out the roof. The floor's so thick with dust, it looks like the moon – and with each step, a cloud of it explodes upward. Serena keeps heading deeper, ducking lower and lower until she's chicken-walking toward the far corner of the attic. But she never slows down. It's amazing, really. No fear.

'Think about it, Cal. In this life, y'ever notice that you face the same challenges again and again? We all do. They're challenges to your *soul*. We repeat them until we face them and master them. Yes, we all have free will, but there're divine patterns out there, and the battle is to see them.'

'Oh, okay,' I say, crouching behind her as she shines the light and draws a horizontal line across the baseboard where the roof and floor meet. There's a few ancient mousetraps and cobwebs and some tiny black droppings, but like the rest of the attic, it's empty. 'So instead of searching for old comic books, we're now searching for God's patterns?'

'The patterns are already there,' she says, squatting like a catcher on a baseball team and turning her sword of light up toward the dark wood rafters. 'From federal agent, to the homeless van . . . why's there such a need in your life to protect people? Why do you think you found your dad lying in that park last night? You think that's all co-incidence? Or better yet: that this is just some dumb search for Superman or the imagined Mark of Cain? You and your dad . . . *This* is your battle, Cal – the one challenge you'll keep repeating until—'

She stops.

'What?' I ask, craning my neck up and following her gaze. 'You find something?'

She points the light up at the rafters, not far from the top of the chimney.

'Serena, what is it?'

She doesn't say a word.

'Serena—'

'There,' she whispers, pointing upward with the flash-light. I follow the flagpole of light up through the shadows of the rafters. Bits of dust sprinkle down like snow in a settling snow globe. But I don't see—

Krrrrrk.

The sound is soft. Like a squeak, or some extra weight on a plank of wood.

She's still silent.

'What?' I ask. 'Is it a mouse?'

Thdddd.

To land that hard . . . That's no mouse.

I jump at the sound. It's up in the rafters.

Above our heads, on our far right, a narrow rain shower of dust cascades from the rafters. Whatever it is . . . we're not alone in h—

Thddd-thdddd-thdddd.

Serena screams. The flashlight falls. And a thick black shadow swoops in, then disappears, leaving tiny waterfalls of dust on our right, then above us, then on our left.

Still hunched over, I grab Serena's wrist and tug her back the way we came. The flashlight twirls behind us like spin the bottle, flickering bursts of light all across the attic. Up in the rafters, there's one last thud. Straight ahead of us.

'Gahhh!' Serena yells, freezing right there.

This time, I see it also – lit by the attic entrance in the floor – two deep-set eyes: one glowing black, the other milky white, where it's been injured. Behind it, a thick fleshy tail dangles down.

I catch my breath and almost laugh. Across from us, perched up on a rafter just past the open hole . . . 'Serena, it's just a possum.'

'I know what it is! *I don't like possums!*'

'Can you please relax? Possums play dead; they don't attack,' I insist, stepping forward to—

'Hsssss!'

'Y'hear that? That's a hiss! It's *hissing*!' she yells, her palms wide open and facing each other as though she's holding the ends of an invisible loaf of bread. She cringes like my aunt when we once found a snake in the toilet.

'That's not a hiss,' I tell her. 'That was—'

'*Hssssss!*' it squeals again, baring tiny triangular teeth and raising its ears and fleshy tail.

'Okay, that part was a hiss,' I admit.

'It thinks we're food!'

'Will you stop, it doesn't—'

There's another sound behind us – *skrrch-skrrch-skrrch*. At first, I almost missed it. But as I turn around and check the rafters, I see what the possum's really after: the small straw-and-leaf nest that sits just above our heads. Two tiny shadows peek out. Aw, crap. 'She wants her babies.'

'Babies!? Where!?' Serena shouts, wriggling wildly as if an army of millipedes were crawling underneath her skin. She tries to run, but she can't. The possum's directly above the hole in the attic floor. 'Nuuuh! Cal, you have to *do* something!'

'Wait, what happened to *facing life's challenges* and your nice big speech?'

'That had nothing to do with giant cannibalistic rats that just escaped from Middle Earth! Look at those mucous eyes! Please, Cal! I'm serious!'

I laugh again, but I hear that tone in her voice. Next to me, her whole body's shaking. Her eyes well with tears. Even Superman has kryptonite. We all have our weaknesses.

'What the hell's wrong up there?' my dad calls from below.

'Zombie possums. They want our brains,' I yell back.

My dad pauses a moment. 'Serena doesn't like possums.'

Next to me, Serena grabs my arm, clutching it against her chest. It's the absolute opposite of her usual guru Zen confidence, and I hate to say it, but there's something strangely reassuring in knowing she can flip out just as easily as the rest of us.

'Do your breathing,' my dad calls out from below.

It doesn't help. She grips my arm even tighter, unable to move toward the possum.

'Serena, it won't attack us,' I promise.

'You don't know that.'

'Yes. I do.' I go back to my old hostage training. Give them calm and they'll find calm. I keep my voice slow and steady. 'Let's just . . . keep . . . going.'

She's still shaking. 'Cal, I can't do this! Uhhh, it's so— Look at it! If it pounces—'

'It's not pouncing, okay? It's just a protective mother.'

'Those're the worst kind!' she says, shutting her eyes and refusing even to look.

I take a small step forward, and the possum raises its rear end like it's about to leap.

'What's it doing!?' Serena asks, her head buried in my shoulder.

'Nothing,' I reply, taking yet another baby step.

Hunched over, we're less than four feet from the hole. The possum hisses again, baring its teeth.

'Cal . . .'

'It's just watching its kids,' I lie as Serena again freezes. I try to tug her forward, but she won't budge. 'Serena, as long as her kids are safe, she won't do anything.'

With her eyes shut, Serena nods but doesn't move.

'Serena,' my dad calls out, 'find your center—'

'Dad, enough already!' I yell.

I can slow my speech and make more reassurances, but instead, I flex the arm that Serena's gripping and take her hand in my own.

'Serena, you take three baby steps and we're outta here.'

Still holding Serena's hand, I take another step. Her

grip goes from vise, to clinging, to— She takes the smallest of mini-steps. It still counts.

'There you go,' I say as we finally move forward.

'You lied about the distance, didn't you?' Serena asks. 'It's more than three steps.'

'Not anymore,' I tell her.

She ducks down quickly, knowing the possum must be close. She's right.

Up above, perched on the edge of the rafter, the possum peers straight down at us. Its pointy nose doesn't move, not a single sniff – and its milky eye looks more yellow thanks to the light shining up from below.

Two hands appear through the hole in the floor. 'Serena,' my dad calls out, 'I'm here.'

We fidget and fumble – my dad guiding her ankles to the ladder, me still holding one of her hands – as we help her squeeze back through the rabbit hole.

She sinks slowly, like she's being sucked down a bright well. There's a metal clink: her foot hitting the ladder. I'm on my knees, reaching down into the hole as she finally opens her eyes and looks up at me.

'When we tell this story,' she warns, 'it ends with me killing the possum with a rock.'

'Of course – your marksmanship alone . . . plus your deft hand and strong will—'

'Don't oversell it, Cal. Now let's get outta here. I need to throw up.'

She lets go of my hand, and as my cheeks lift, I realize that it's the first time in the past twenty-four hours that I'm actually smiling. And that Serena's smiling back at me.

'Y'know, that's the second time you saved me today,' she teases. 'I owe you, Superman.'

'Must be the house,' I tease back. It's nothing more

than sharing a stupid joke. But, man . . . it feels good to share something.

'You're just like him, aren't you?' she calls up at me.

'Who?' I ask, assuming she's talking about my father.

'Andrew. My brother,' she says. 'He was protective, too – and the walls he kept around himself . . . just like with you, they're too tall,' she explains. 'But that's why you brought me, isn't it? To help you lower them.'

I'm about to remind her that we brought her only because we couldn't leave her at the airport.

But I don't.

'Cal, we really should get her to a hotel,' my dad interrupts, helping her down the ladder. 'It's not safe for her to run around like this.'

'You think?' I ask. 'When she's with us, we can at least—'

'What the french *toast*? What'd I tell you 'bout letting people in my roof?' a female voice calls out, making the word *roof* rhyme with *hoof*.

Taking off the backpack and squeezing down through the hole, I spot Mrs Johnsel coming up the stairs.

'Possums are back,' her husband says, calm as ever.

'I *told* you that. You said it was rain.' She then looks up at me. She's not mad, just confused. 'I thought they just wanted to see the bedroom?'

'They got an attic copy,' Johnsel says.

'A whut?'

I hop off the ladder and unzip the backpack. 'We were hoping to find some more details about *this*,' I say, pulling out the wax-paper sleeve with the Superman comic inside.

She studies the translucent cover and the typewritten address. 'You should go to the museum. They got one just like it.' Looking down at the white dust all over the floor, she adds, 'This better not be asbestos.'

'Wait. There's a Superman museum?' I ask.

'*This* should be the museum,' Mrs Johnsel says, bending down and picking up the small bits of plaster and rocks that're scattered across the landing. 'Can you believe the city of Cleveland wouldn't give us a plaque to put out front? Superman was born here! Not even *a plaque*!'

'Um . . . you were saying about the museum,' my father jumps in.

'It's just an exhibit – Maltz Jewish Museum. By the temple over on Richmond,' Mrs Johnsel explains. 'I think you'd like it. They have one of those attic copies. Plus they got all sorts of biblical stuff, too.' She turns casually to her husband. 'We got prayer group before dinner. Don't think of being late.'

45

He parked the rental car around back to stay out of sight.

'You stay here, girl,' Ellis said, giving Benoni a strong stroke along her ears. He kept the car running to make sure she'd be warm, but even with the window cracked, the dog's breath puffed like smoke in the Cleveland air. 'Relax, girl. This won't take long.'

He walked calmly up the snow-covered alley, sticking to the far left side as he marched toward the front steps of the run-down house. There were lights on inside. Someone was definitely home.

In his pocket, he felt for the jet injector and released the cap from the nozzle. The only reason he'd gotten this far was by not leaving witnesses. And as he knew in his heart, this was a war that had lasted over a hundred years. There must be casualties. 'It's cold here,' he whispered into his phone.

'You're still better waiting outside,' the Prophet said on the other line. 'Let Cal do the legwork. He'll have it soon. And when he does—'

'I don't believe in Calvin. I believe in myself,' Ellis insisted, staring at his breath in the night air. 'And I believe Cain's Book was a test. Just as today, it's a test for me.'

'Then it's a test you'll fail. Because if you make a scene and the cops come— The last thing we need is for Cal to run. If he runs – and I'm learning this myself – you *will not* get what you want, do you understand? You should see him right now – born investigator. And the way this is headed, I think we're finally on to something good.'

Ellis slapped the phone shut and looked up at the bright blue-and-red house. The Prophet may've been right about coming to Cleveland, but the Prophet didn't care about the destiny that Ellis's mother laid out for him. The Prophet didn't care about the Leadership and his family's dream. The Prophet just wanted the Book. The birthright. The Judge warned him as much. And for all the Judge's faults, he was right about this: The Prophet wasn't Leadership. And as long as that was true, the Prophet wasn't on their side. In the end, Ellis knew it was no different than with Timothy, Zhao, or even Cal. Only one of them could get what he wanted.

Lumbering up the front steps, he put his foot in each of the shallow snow footprints left by Cal. There were other footprints, too. One of them small. Like a woman's. With two hard raps, Ellis banged on the front door. A handwritten sign in the window said, 'Superman's House!!!'

'Easy . . . easy,' a man called from inside. With a thunk and a twist, the door swung open, and Mr Johnsel studied Ellis for a full five seconds. But Ellis knew that look. All the man saw was the uniform. And the badge. 'Whatsda problem, Officer?'

'No problem at all,' Ellis said, forcing a sickly grin. He should've come here sooner. The last known location of the Book of Lies.

46

'How many?' an older woman with a doughy face asks at the front desk of the museum.

'Three,' I tell her.

She stares, confused, seeing only me. Over my shoulder, the front door to the museum opens and my dad steps inside. It was his idea: waiting in the car to see if anyone followed. But as the door opens, for a moment, I could've sworn he was talking to someone out there. 'All clear,' he announces to me.

The woman's still confused. 'You said *three*?'

'We have— In the bathroom,' I explain, pointing behind me at the ladies' room.

'Welcome to Metropolis,' the doughy woman says with a far too high level of joy as she hands me the tickets. 'Though remember, we're only open till five.'

I look at my watch. Less than fifteen minutes.

'C'mon, Serena!' I call out, heading past the restroom just as the door swings open.

Surprised to see me so close, she jumps back, stuffing something into her purse.

'Who were you talking to?' I ask.

'Pardon?'

'Your phone. Sorry,' I add as I point with my chin, 'it looked like . . . in your purse . . . you were putting back your phone.'

She stares straight at me for barely a second. It's a helluva long second. 'Just checking messages,' she finally replies, calm as ever. Reading my expression, she adds, 'You believe me, right?'

I'm lied to every single day by most of my clients. But as I look at her . . . 'I believe you, Serena.'

'Don't use the phone anymore, okay?' my father barks, so clearly pissed that the woman at the ticket desk looks our way.

'Okay, everybody lose the claws,' I say. 'We're all tired . . . we've got twelve minutes till closing . . . Let's just be—'

'Faster than a speeding bullet!' a baritone voice announces behind us.

'See, now that's just horrible,' Serena says, rolling her eyes as we turn toward the official entrance of the exhibit.

Beneath the tall glass windows and across the long rectangular Jerusalem stone lobby, a six-foot-tall statue of Superman holds a giant Earth over his head. On the Earth, there's a little red flag stuck into Cleveland with a note that says, 'Birthplace of Superman!'

'More powerful than a locomotive!'

And more annoying with each passing second.

I race toward the exhibit. 'Let's just get what we came for.'

From what I can tell, the main exhibit hall of the Maltz Museum is set up like a long rectangle – the back half of it dedicated to Jewish artifacts, the front half to the Superman display, which is split into half a dozen smaller rooms. It doesn't take long to divide them up. I don't like it. But with closing hour quickly approaching, the only way we're finding the attic copy they have here is with some speed. On my far left, my father took the room labeled '*Superman in the '60s*'; on my right, Serena took '*Superman Today*'; and I very purposely staked my claim in the main central exhibit: '*Origins of the Superman.*'

Like any other museum, it has stark white walls lined with Lucite cases of all shapes and sizes, holding everything from old photographs and pencil sketches, to copies of Nietzsche's mention of the Übermensch and Hitler's demand for the master race, to 1940s *Superman* movie posters, action figures, jigsaw puzzles, baseball cards, Colorforms sets, cereal boxes, and every other product that you can possibly put a giant red-and-yellow *S* on. But, amazingly, there's not a single comic book.

In the corner of the wide room, a bright red Superman cape hides the entrance to what looks like a separate part of the exhibit. I'll bite.

As I pull aside the cape and step inside, the darkness tells me it's just a small theater. The curved, blue-carpeted benches look like they can seat ten or so people, and on the far left wall, a flat-screen TV announces:

'*Up in the sky! Look! It's a bird! It's a plane! It's Superman!*'

From the crackling of the recording and the clapping of the crowd, it's an old radio show. But on-screen, it's a black-and-white photo of young Jerry Siegel and artist Joe Shuster. Most people in 1940s photos look like they're somehow older than you. But to see these two . . . these kids dressed in shirts and ties . . . one of them sitting at an old typewriter (I'm guessing Jerry), the other leaning over him with a pencil behind his ear (Joe, the artist) – they can't be outta high school.

'*Yes, it's Superman. Young America's stalwart idol,*' the radio announcer says as a montage of more family photos appears on-screen, along with a caption that says: 'Audio from *Town Hall Tonight* with Fred Allen (1940).'

'*Hey, listen!*' a little boy's voice interrupts. '*A new* Action Comics *just came out, and boy, has it got a swell adventure of Superman in it!*' he says as the radio audience cheers.

On the flat screen, there's another photo, this one of *Action Comics #1* – just like the one in my backpack.

'*Our guest tonight is the man who originated Superman. He's Mr Jerry Siegel. Good evening, Mr Siegel,*' the announcer says.

'*Good evening, Fred,*' a nasal voice replies, and for the first time – even after walking through his house and his bedroom and his attic . . . even after seeing his photo . . . to actually hear his anxious, squeaky voice – Jerry Siegel is suddenly alive, whispering to me from the dead.

'*So you are the man behind Superman, Mr Siegel?*'

'*No, I'm just one of the men, Fred. I write the situations and the dialogue, and the strip is drawn by my collaborator, Joe Shuster.*'

With each question, the announcer revs up his voice, hoping to draw Jerry out. This kid just created Superman! But with each response, Jerry's voice – it's not just that he sounds so wonderfully geeky (though he does) – but to hear his uncomfortable stutter and stammering . . . It's just— This boy— We expect him to be Superman.

But he's just Clark Kent.

'*Well, you seem . . . seem rather young to be the instigator of this highly successful feature, Mr Siegel. How old are you?*'

'*Twenty-five.*'

As Jerry says the words, images from more old comic books fill the screen. Shots of Superman in World War II: his chest out as he literally punches a German U-boat . . . then him walking arm in arm, centered between an army soldier and a navy sailor. The next image is a shot of the planet Krypton, then one of a baby in a blue blanket being placed in a 1940s version of a rocket ship.

'*And how long have you and Mr Shuster been working on your high-voltage Robin Hood?*' the announcer asks as the montage continues.

As the red rocket lifts off, a glass window in the ship shows the baby crying inside, while off to the left of the panel, Mom and Dad appear in profile as they both crane their necks up and calmly wave good-bye to their only child. There's a single tear skiing down the cheek of the mother.

'*We started about eight years ago, but Superman has been in print only the past two years,*' Jerry says.

'*Well, what caused the delay? Cirrhosis of the batteries?*'

'*No, Fred. It took us six years to sell Superman. He was turned down by almost every comic editor in the country.*'

The audience laughs hysterically at that one, while on-screen, the camera slowly pulls in on just the crying baby swaddled in the bright blue blanket. Baby Superman, rocketing to the planet Earth. The camera then shifts left, pulling in on the doomed parents . . . then back to the crying baby . . . then back to the parents. The camera's so close on their profiles, you can see the tiny pink halftone dots that color their faces – and as it pulls even closer – on the mom's nose and eyes and tears—

'It's a bit heavy-handed, no?' a voice asks behind me.

I turn around to find a short, muscular man in a too tight business suit. The name tag on his lapel tells me he's the *Curator*; the way he stands across from me – drifting into my personal space – tells me he's also a real-deal comic book fan. 'It's really hard with these exhibits,' he explains. 'But people forget: At the core of it, Superman is an orphan story.'

'Yeah . . . no . . . I didn't realize that,' I tell him, turning back to the screen.

'Y'okay?' he says in full midwest accent.

'I'm fine.'

'Y'sure? Y'look a little . . . zapped by kryptonite.' He laughs a hiccupy laugh, and for the first time I realize how much more he blinks than the average person.

'So you're the curator?' I ask.

'Welcome to Metropolis!' He beams at me, giving three quick blinks. 'Gareth Gelbwaks.'

'Great, then maybe you can help me with this, Gareth,' I say, going straight for the backpack and pulling out *Action Comics* in the wax paper—

Gareth's eyes go wide, as though I just unveiled the Rosetta Stone. 'Th-That's— Where'd you—?' He swallows hard and blinks half a dozen times. 'Maybe we should go back to my office.'

'That'd be perfect.'

Within seconds, we weave toward the far right exhibit hall, back past the bathrooms, to an oak door marked, PRIVATE − STAFF ONLY.

It's not until he twists the doorknob that I realize I haven't seen Serena or—

There's a rusty squeak as the door swings open, revealing a small conference room, a round meeting table . . . and my father sitting there with his hands in PlastiCuffs.

'Dad, what're you—?' I race forward, already realizing I'm too late.

The door slams behind me, and I finally spot her: the tall Hispanic woman with a cheap haircut and an even cheaper brown dye job.

'Nice to see you again, Cal,' Naomi says, pointing her gun at me. 'Welcome to Metropolis.'

47

'I – I'm sorry,' the curator apologizes to me. 'She said you were armed and wanted. I can't risk the exhibit—'

'Stop talking,' Naomi barks at the curator. Over her shoulder, my dad sits there, devastated. Ex-cons know the consequences best. Next to him, attached to the wall, are two TV monitors: One has a view of the front desk, where we bought tickets; the other alternates among security cameras throughout the exhibit. As the screen blinks, I spot Serena still walking through the exhibit. That's why Naomi didn't grab her. She was in the restroom when we bought the tickets. They have no idea she's with us. It's the only thing going our way.

Turning to me, Naomi approaches with another set of PlastiCuffs, her gun still pointed at my chest. 'Arms out, wrists together,' she insists.

'Before you—'

'*Wrists together!*' she explodes, surprising even me. 'You helped him, didn't you? Did you know he threatened my family?'

'Wha? Your family?'

'Cal, I saw Ellis! *I saw him waiting outside your place!*'

She yells so loud, the curator can't stop blinking. Whatever Ellis did, he clearly lit Naomi's fuse, which means she's not listening until she gets what she wants.

I toss the comic book on the conference table and calmly stick out my wrists. 'Go ahead – put the cuffs on.'

She stops, knowing I'm up to something. 'Cal . . .'

'Put the cuffs on,' I repeat. 'I'm not fighting.'

She steps in close and threads both my hands into the open circles of the PlastiCuffs. But she doesn't pull them tight. 'Tell me what happened on Alligator Alley with Timothy,' she adds.

I glance at my dad, who shakes his head. He still hasn't said anything. So if Naomi's asking, that means they haven't found the body. Good for us. Still, if I tell her Timothy's dead – or even place us at Alligator Alley – there's no way we're not going right back to Miami for questioning. 'I spoke to him that night, but that's the last I—'

She pulls the zipper as the PlastiCuffs bite my wrists. 'Ow! What're you—!?'

'You think I'm taking your word for it, Cal? Especially after what you did with Ellis!?'

'I didn't do anything with Ellis!'

'How'd he find my address!? How'd he find where I live!?'

'Are you—?' I take a breath, knowing that the only way to keep her calm is by leading the way. 'Please, Naomi – if I were really trying to kill you, you really think I'd let you put me in these cuffs?'

For once, she's silent.

'Exactly,' I say. 'And for all we know, Timothy may be fine.' It's an awful bluff, but we're not leaving here without it.

She shakes her head. 'I saw the records. And the video, Cal. I know he helped you take that container from the port.'

'And this is why he took it,' I say, pointing my chin at the comic. 'But Naomi, I promise you . . . I swear to you . . . whatever *did* happen to Timothy, you have to know it was Ellis.'

'I don't have to know anything.'

'Sure you do! You could've stayed in Florida and just called in some local agents here. Instead, you had such a bad feeling about Ellis . . . about everything . . . you came all the way to Cleveland to solve it yourself. We're in the same exact boat, Naomi – and if you just take a moment instead of dragging everyone off by their PlastiCuffs, you'll actually find out what the hell's so important that Ellis wanted this stupid comic book so badly!'

Naomi looks down at the comic, then to my father, then to me.

'Think about it, Naomi: If we really knew what was going on, would we even be here searching for an answer?'

From the table, she picks up the comic and turns to the curator. 'You know what this is?'

'Y-Yeah,' he says.

'You know why it's important?'

'Yeah.'

'Good. Tell me.'

48

'Let me . . . mmm . . .' The curator pauses, his blinking quickening as he watches Naomi pull the comic from its protective wax-paper sleeve. 'Please, don't— Please, can I help you with that? *Please?*' he begs, gingerly prying the comic from her hands and lowering it just as softly to the conference table. 'I'm sorry, but that's . . . mmm—' He stares down at the comic like Indiana Jones examining the Ark.

From his desk, he pulls out a pair of tweezers with wide, flat pincers and uses them to turn the first page. 'No foxing . . . no color loss . . . pristine,' he whispers as he continues turning pages. The blinking gets five times faster. But the way he's frantically flipping forward, he's not reading. It's more like . . . he's looking for something.

His face falls as he reaches the last page.

'What? What's wrong?' Naomi asks, lowering her gun as if that'll calm him down.

'I just thought— Even androids dream, y'know?'

Naomi cocks an eyebrow. 'Are you in the same solar system we are? What's this have to do with my missing partner?'

'Let him explain – it clearly has something to do with the history,' I plead. Turning to the curator, I add, 'You were trying to find something in there, weren't you?'

Gareth nods at me and uses his pointer finger to wipe

a sweat mustache from his top lip. 'They didn't tell you the story, did they?'

'About the comic?'

'No. Not just the comic. To understand this, you need to know . . . mmm . . . do you even know how Superman was created?'

'By the two kids,' Naomi says, pacing behind my dad and still focused on her partner. 'Jerry Siegel and Joe Shuster. We saw the video.'

'I didn't see the video,' my dad says. 'And I didn't do anything wrong here. I was just driving the truck.'

'Let's just— Can we please stay on track?' I plead, strangely unnerved as I stare at my dad, who's gripping his PlastiCuffed hands together to stop them from shaking. Up to this point, he's been strong: plotting and scheming with an almost preternatural confidence. Yet to see him like this, shrinking in his seat with his head down? No one is who they say they are. But of all the faces my father's shown, I feel like I'm finally seeing the real Lloyd Harper.

I'm on the opposite side of the room, my hands also cuffed as I stand next to a tall black filing cabinet that's littered with paper clips. My father won't look up at me. He can't. In the attic, Naomi said my dad was afraid of me. But I'm watching the way he stares down at his cuffs. He's been to prison once. There's no question what he's really afraid of.

'They told us the story at the Siegel house,' I finally say. 'On some rainy summer night, Jerry was lying awake in bed . . .'

'And as he stared out at the crabapple tree, the idea hits him out of nowhere.' The curator nods, already excited as he sways forward and back in his seat. 'Then crack of dawn the next morning, he runs over to his pal Joe's, who starts drawing, drawing, drawing all day, with Jerry making suggestions over his shoulder. By the time the sun goes down, these two poor kids from Cleveland have created Superman, one of the greatest heroes the world will ever know. Beautiful story, right?'

'So what's the problem?' Naomi asks.

'The problem is, it's a beautiful story, but it's not the full story.'

Even my father sits up straight.

'What, so now they *didn't* create Superman?' I ask.

'Oh no, they created him. But Jerry was never a fool. He knew the story of the young seventeen-year-old whiz kids was too good to pass up. So what they never told anyone was that *Action Comics Number 1* – the first appearance of Superman – was actually their *third* attempt.' Reading the confusion on all our faces, the curator explains, 'In late 1932, Jerry Siegel wrote a short sci-fi story called *The Reign of the Super-Man*. It also had a few drawings by Joe Shuster – but what's important is in *this story*, the so-called Superman was actually the *bad guy* – an out-of-control villain who couldn't be stopped. That was their first try.'

'What was the other?' Naomi asks, clearly starting to see the value of pulling apart the past.

'Mmm . . .' The curator nods. 'The other attempt was simply called *The Superman*. But when it got rejected by all the comic publishers, Jerry or Joe – depends who you ask – got so upset, he destroyed all the pages. Ripped them up, never to be seen again.'

'Then how does anyone even know it existed?'

'Jerry spoke about it in later interviews. Then sometime in the 1940s or 50s, a copy of the cover showed up. . . . Wait, I should—' He crosses back to his desk, rifles through a small volcano of files, and pulls out— 'Here . . .

'They found this – just this cover – in some publisher's desk,' Gareth explains. 'To this day, it's the only finished page that exists. One inked page. And that's where the search began.'

He says the words as if it all makes sense. But from the silence in the room, we're all still lost.

'You have ten seconds to relate this to my case,' Naomi threatens.

'Don't you see?' the curator asks. 'Think of the timing: Prior to 1932, young Jerry Siegel spends his time writing silly comic strips for his high school newspaper. Then magically, in 1932, he comes up with three different versions for a so-called Superman. Think for a second: What else happened in the summer of 1932?'

'His father died,' my dad whispers, holding his wound from the same gun.

'Mmm . . . you see it now, don't you?' the curator asks with a grin. His eyes are no longer blinking. 'On June second, 1932, Jerry's father, Mitchell Siegel, was found facedown in the back of his small haberdashery as a puddle of blood seeped toward the door. There were two bullets in his chest, and all the money was gone from his cash register. Now think of the impact on his youngest son, Jerry. It's plain as day – just look at the cover,' he insists, his voice picking up speed. 'When Superman first appeared, he didn't have X-ray vision or all the neat super-powers. In fact, he couldn't even fly. But y'know what power he did have? He was bulletproof. Unable to be shot. And *that's* why Superman was created: He's not some American Messiah or some modern version of Moses or Jesus or whoever else historians like to trot out – Superman is the result of a meek little Clark Kent named Jerry Siegel wishing and praying and aching for his murdered father to be bulletproof so he doesn't have to be alone.'

As he says the words, I close my eyes. When my mom first died, I used to have a recurring dream of squirrels running into my mouth and stealing my teeth. My CASA caseworker at the time whipped up this spectacularly maudlin theory that the dream represented my own power-lessness in preventing my mom's death. I hate neat responses like that. But that doesn't mean they're not right.

Blinking back to reality, I stare down at the table. All I see is . . .

'You see it, don't you? In the picture,' the curator adds. 'His dad died in a robbery at gunpoint. That's the moment that stayed with Jerry forever.'

I try to pretend I don't understand . . . that I've never replayed my parents' fight in the kitchen . . . when I walked in and . . . God, if I hadn't walked in . . . if my mom hadn't turned my way . . . I still see her – those angry eyes – staring right at me as she fell toward the open drawer. I've pictured all the ways to save her . . .

. . . and on the worst days, on birthdays, I've talked to her out loud, and asked her questions, and cried and laughed and sobbed at her imagined responses, especially the ones where she hints that she forgives me. Jerry Siegel had it right. We all live best in our own imaginations.

'Cal, you wanna sit?' my dad asks. 'You look green.'

'I'm great,' I insist, realizing I'm now leaning against the filing cabinet. I go to stand up straight. No. Leaning's just fine. And I'm not the only one.

Across from me, Naomi looks exhausted as she hooks her armpit over the top of a cubicle like a crutch. I was so lost in my own pity parade, I almost forgot. Her son. Her son the orphan. The moment she sees me watching, she stands up straight. I offer a nod of understanding. She turns away, kicking herself for giving even that tiniest piece of her puzzle.

'So this stuff with Jerry's dad's murder – you were saying there was some kinda search?' Naomi asks.

'Yup-yup . . . that's where the weird gets weirder,' the curator says. 'In the weeks after Mitchell Siegel's shooting, there was no police report filed, no investigation opened, no search for any suspects. Even worse, despite the two bullets in the dad's chest, the story that's told throughout the Siegel family is that Mitchell died of a heart attack. Even today, Jerry's widow and daughter say that Jerry told them his dad had a heart attack from the robbery. And even worse than all that, in the fifty years since that day . . . in the thousands – literally thousands – of interviews where they asked Jerry where he got the idea for his bulletproof Superman, he never – *never once* – says it was from his dad. Never even mentions his dad in a single interview!'

'Maybe Jerry just wanted his privacy.'

'I agree,' the curator says. 'But that doesn't mean he didn't need someplace to deal with it. Just look at the original stories: The first character Jerry created after his dad's death wasn't Superman. Instead, Jerry was obsessed with the bad guys, focusing his entire tale around a villain. It was the same in *Action Comics*,' he adds, waving his hand over the pristine comic book. 'Have you even read it? Superman doesn't fight aliens and monsters in here. He goes to Washington, D.C., and fights corruption in government and foreign spies. In fact, when you look at the Cleveland newspaper the day after his dad is killed – if you want to see what Jerry was looking at the day after he lost his father – there's an op-ed saying that we don't need vigilantes anymore, and it's written by a man named Luther, spelled -er instead of -or.'

'Okay, so wait,' Naomi challenges. 'Now we're supposed to believe all the bad guys in comic books are real?'

'No, you're missing it,' the curator says, waving the single photocopy of Jerry Siegel's early Superman endeavor. '*All* the bad guys aren't real. But in Jerry's case, *one* of them might be.'

49

'Okay, let me be as nice as I can about this,' Naomi begins. 'Um . . . did you make all this crap up?'

'This isn't theory. This is history,' the curator insists. 'And it's a search for one of the greatest lost books in the world – a story that eventually gave birth to one of society's most recognized heroes.'

'And also involves kryptonite as a major plot element,' Naomi chides. 'No offense, but I've got bigger worries than solving an eighty-year-old murder.'

'I'm not the only one who believes it. Now I don't know if they hid it in the art or just in the story – but there's a reason those original Superman pages are still missing. And as far as I'm concerned, that's what Jerry put in there.'

'He put his dad's killer?' I ask.

'He had to deal with it somewhere,' the curator repeats.

'So he put his dad's killer in the pages of a comic book?'

'Y'know where he got the name Lois Lane from? Lola Lane, one of Jerry's favorite actresses. Y'know where he got Clark Kent from? His favorite actor, *Clark* Gable, combined with his brother-in-law's name, *Kent* Taylor. All writers steal from their own lives. Why can't the same be true here?'

'But to say he hid some secret message about his own father's death—'

'Why else would he tear up and supposedly destroy that original art?' the curator asks.

'Maybe Joe was embarrassed by the art. You said they were devastated by the rejections.'

'Jerry spent *years* getting rejections on his short stories – he submitted and got rejected by every sci-fi fanzine on the planet. And when it came to Superman, he kept and preserved *every single* rejection letter they got – they reprinted them in *Famous First Edition* years ago. So even if Joe Shuster ripped all the art apart – even if he thought the work was embarrassing or amateurish – you really think a pack rat like Jerry didn't save the pieces? His father had been *murdered* – for all we know, right in front of his eyes – *this* is where all his inspiration came from.'

'Says who?' Naomi challenges. 'A bunch of fanboy psychologists who – no offense – are just a little too obsessed with their favorite superhero?'

The curator stands there a moment, once again blinking, and I wonder if he's about to—

'Y'know how much Jerry and Joe sold the rights to Superman for? One hundred and thirty dollars. A few years after that, they were fired by DC Comics, and their names were removed from all references as creators. Over the next decade, as Superman raked in millions, Joe started going blind, while Jerry became so poor he couldn't afford to eat out for dinner. Eventually, the publisher realized what a PR disaster it would be if they let Superman's creators die of starvation, so they gave Jerry another shot. And in 1960, Jerry wrote a story called *Superman's Return to Krypton*!'

'Oooh, was that in Superman *Number 62* or *63*?' Naomi asks.

'It was in *Number 141,* actually – and don't make fun just because it's a comic book,' he shoots back, more annoyed than ever. 'In the story, Superman travels back in time to his home planet and gets to see his real father, Jor-El. The hardest part for Superman, though, is that he knows that Krypton is about to explode – so these are his last moments with his dad. Even worse, he knows that if he stops the planet from exploding and saves his family, then he will never exist as Superman on Earth. He doesn't care, though. He's so happy living on Krypton – being reunited with his dad – that when the planet starts to rumble and shake, he decides he'd rather die with his father than lose him again,' the curator says as we all listen silently. 'It was Jerry's most constant battle: the life you live versus the life you leave behind.'

It's the first time I see my dad looking directly at me.

'But fate is fate,' the curator continues, 'and at the last moment, the grown Superman gets knocked into a second rocket and is launched away, safe from harm. And the story ends with him returning to Earth, knowing that he can save everyone around him, but he can never save his own father. *This* was the story Jerry Siegel wrote when he was allowed to return to his creation. So don't tell me he wasn't obsessed with the death of his dad.'

My father continues to stare at me. I break away from the look to stare straight at the curator. 'That's what you were looking for before when you were flipping through the comic,' I say, pointing my cuffed hands toward the empty wax-paper sleeve. 'These attic copies of *Action Comics* – what makes them so valuable isn't the comic itself or the typed address outside. . . .'

'Exactly – it's what the most devoted of collectors hope to find hidden *inside*.' The curator nods. 'The remaining, torn-up pieces of Jerry Siegel's most personal story. His greatest tragedy hidden inside his greatest success.'

'So you think that's what Timothy was chasing?' Naomi asks. 'That's the reason he wanted this comic?'

'It's certainly priceless.'

'Maybe,' Naomi says. 'But if *The Superman* – if this story was so important, why would Jerry ever leave those pieces rotting in his attic?'

'Same reason he left ten pristine copies of *Action Comics Number 1* up there. People forget,' the curator replies.

'You're telling me you never hid money from yourself and then forgot where it was?' I ask Naomi.

'This is more important than money,' she shoots back.

'Mmm . . . she's right,' the curator says. 'But that's why he kept it, and sealed it in wax paper, and locked it in the attic. Besides, when Jerry died a few years back, they went through the rest of his belongings. There's no record of that first story. It's gone. These few attic copies are the only hiding spots left.'

'And how many copies are accounted for so far?' I ask.

'Again, the rumor is there were ten copies to start, though that could be wrong. The first one was found in the seventies, right after the first *Superman* movie hit. Then a Baltimore collector found two more, both at garage sales. Another was found in London, and another was bought by some wealthy doctor in China,' he says as I think back to the stethoscope in the coffin. 'So I think seven total, including yours and the one we have here in the *Superman Today* exhibit.'

I look over at the security monitors and spot Serena backtracking through the exhibit hall. We've been gone for fifteen minutes. She's smart enough to not call our names. But she's gonna start panicking soon.

'Here's the other thing that makes no sense,' Naomi

interrupts. 'How would Jerry even know how his father died?'

'Maybe he witnessed it,' my father whispers, staring long and hard at me.

I'm about to turn away. But I don't. Some things need to be faced.

My dad leans forward in his chair, his cuffed hands still shaking. He plants his elbows on his knees, as if he's in midprayer. But the look in his eyes – it's the same frozen look he had when I saved him in Alligator Alley. Back then, I thought it was shock or just relief. It's not.

I'm sorry, he says with nothing more than a glance. After nineteen years.

Naomi stares at me a moment – not judging, just staring, her tall frame looking even taller with my dad seated in front of her. She doesn't offer the reassuring nod. She scratches at her short, choppy hair and turns away. But there's no question we just gave her a piece of our own puzzle. One she didn't have before.

'Okay, so if young Jerry knew what happened, why didn't he go to the cops?' she asks.

'Same reason that for the past eighty years they told that heart attack story to their own family,' the curator says. 'Whatever was going on, there was clearly something Jerry's family didn't want said. And it's a secret still lost to history.'

'Could it have anything to do with Cain?' my dad blurts, his apology long gone.

'Cain?' The curator looks confused. Naomi stays silent, glancing down at the carpet. Whatever she knows, she's not trusting us just yet.

'Maybe Jerry's dad died doing something illegal,' I say.

'Or embarrassing,' my dad adds, following my lead. 'Could he have been cheating on his wife?'

'I don't think so,' the curator replies. 'Mitchell was supposedly a quiet and low-key sort.'

'Like in a mobster low-key way?' I ask. 'Or in a—'

'He was a fed,' Naomi says, looking up at the rest of us.

'Pardon?' I ask.

'Mitchell Siegel. I bet he was a fed.'

'What makes you—?'

'Your Indian pal. Ocala.'

'You spoke to Ocala?' I ask.

'He told me about the gun, which is when my assistant put a name check request on Mitchell Siegel. Tax records, military service, all the typicals. When word came back the files were delayed, I assumed it was because the records were old or buried in some warehouse somewhere, but now – if they're hiding him – it's for a reason.'

Without even touching a button on her phone, she barks into her earpiece: 'Scotty, call the Bureau directly. I need you to get that file on Mitchell Siegel.' Her phone's been on the entire time.

I shoot a look to Naomi. 'If he wasn't a fed, maybe he was an informant,' I suggest. 'Or even a boss.'

'If he was a boss, he could've been making cash,' she agrees.

I turn to the curator. 'Did the Siegels have money?'

'You kidding? Jerry and Joe – they were both so poor, when they worked at Jerry's house, they used to draw on the back side of the wallpaper. Don't forget, when Jerry's dad died, his mom had to feed six kids plus—'

'Is that true?' I interrupt.

'What, the five kids?'

'No. The wallpaper. Did they really draw on the back of wallpaper?'

The curator nods. 'It's as much a part of the lore as the hot rainy night and the crabapple tree. Why? You think that's important?'

My eyes lock with Naomi's. She won't give me a smile, but I see that grin in her eyes.

'You said this is the only attic copy you've seen with the address typed on the outside?' she asks, pointing to the wax-paper covering.

Again, the curator nods.

'Maybe we should take another look at the house,' I say.

My father stands up, suddenly excited.

'No, whoa, whoa – you think this is some kinda team-up?' Naomi shoots back, approaching the table and making sure we again see her gun. 'Timothy's still missing, and you're the last ones he was with. You two are being dropped off for questioning.'

'And then what?' I ask. 'You'll bring us inside and put up with the two hours of paperwork it'll take before they let you leave us there, at which point Ellis will already have beaten you to the source, since I'm guessing he was right behind us and, no offense, ahead of you. This isn't Miami, Naomi. We've already been to the Siegel house. If you plan on being fast – and on actually finding something – you're better off taking us with you.'

She knows the logic's right, but that doesn't mean she's agreeing to it. 'Maybe I should just give you my gun, too,' she offers. 'That way when I'm chauffeuring you around, you can put a hole in my head nice and easy.'

'You really think my goal is to hurt you, Naomi?'

'I was there when you got fired, Cal. There's a reason you're in those cuffs.'

I glance down at my wrists. PlastiCuffs are lightweight

and easy to carry, but as any cop knows, if you wedge something small into the zipper . . . like, say, an unbent paper clip you grabbed from this filing cabinet . . . well . . . With a light tug, I free my left wrist, then my right, then toss the cuffs back to Naomi.

'If I wanted your gun, I'd have that, too,' I tell her.

'You're wrong. I spotted you three minutes ago.'

'I've been free for over ten. Now do you wanna go recheck the attic bedroom or would you rather stay here and leave Ellis to take the prize?'

50

Ellis's back was hurting as he reached the top step of the second-floor landing. He understood the Johnsels' fears. In this neighborhood, there were real consequences for inviting a police officer into your home. But that didn't mean he was staying outside, he reminded himself as he lugged the second body up the stairs. It was actually a blessing for the Johnsels. Being with God was far better than being in that prayer group they were screaming about.

The house was dark now, but Ellis was still smart enough to stay away from the windows. He'd learned that years ago when he and his dad began their life of hiding.

Back then, the rules were clear: With Mom dead, her family would be on the hunt for them. Ellis never questioned why. Looking back, he should've known something was wrong. So much of it didn't make sense: Yes, Mom was dead. But his father never cried. There was no funeral. No grave. So rules were rules: No playing outside, no letting anyone spot you. Ellis used that same approach in school, in life – even as he rose through the ranks on the force. There were benefits to lying low and skills that came with growing up a ghost.

His dad learned – the Johnsels learned – Ellis was good at not being seen.

But that didn't mean he couldn't be found.

There was a low buzz as his phone began to vibrate. Ellis picked up without saying hello.

'Ellis, I know you're there,' the Prophet said on the line. 'Stay where you are. Cal . . . all of us . . . we're on our way.'

51

From the museum, to the parking lot, to the ride back past the burned-out storefronts of Martin Luther King Jr. Drive, I keep peeking in the side mirror, searching every headlight behind us and being careful that Naomi doesn't see what I'm—

'Who're you looking for?' Naomi asks, glaring at me in the passenger seat.

'Just making sure we're alone,' I tell her. It's mostly right.

When we left the museum, the exhibit hall was empty. The good news is, Serena was smart enough to stay out of sight. The even better news is, she had the keys to our rental car in her purse. But the bad news is, as we turn onto Kimberly Avenue, all the cars disappear, leaving nothing but darkness behind us.

'You think Ellis is out there, don't you?' Naomi asks, squinting through the night and fighting hard against the poorly plowed street.

'He's gotta be somewhere,' I say as we pull up to the blue-and-red house with the crabapple tree along the left-hand side.

'They painted it Superman colors?' Naomi asks, offering something close to a laugh.

It's an easy joke, but I know why she's making it. If she warms us up, she's hoping we'll start talking.

'The city won't even give them a plaque,' my dad says, laughing back as he hops out of the backseat. I shoot him a look that tells him to stay quiet. Naomi was kind enough to take off his PlastiCuffs, but after our last encounter with an ICE agent – she's still Timothy's partner.

'How's it look?' Naomi asks as I scan the rest of the block. She knows how I work. We had the same training.

'There're a few cars that weren't here before, but nothing too nice for the neighborhood,' I say, eyeing an old, pale gray Mercury across the street and a silver Ford pickup down the block. Thanks to the snow, I get footprints, too. They're hard to read because of our own previous trampling up the front porch, but at least there're no dog tracks.

Everything's clear. Until Naomi taps a knuckle on the front door, which yawns slightly open at the impact.

My dad steps back. I step forward.

'Mr Johnsel . . . ?' I call out.

No one answers.

'Maybe they're at prayer group,' my dad offers. 'Didn't they say they had prayer group?'

It's a fine explanation, but this isn't the kind of neighborhood where people leave their doors unlocked.

'Mr *Johnsel*!' I call again.

Still no response.

Next to me, Naomi doesn't move. I know how she works. Federal agents need warrants before they can march into a strange house.

'C'mon, I'm a potential suspect wanted for questioning – you can chase me inside,' I tell her, grabbing the doorknob.

'Cal, wait!'

Too late. 'Mr Johnsel, *you there*? Anybody home?' I ask as I step inside.

The main hallway and kitchen are both empty. All the lights in the house are off. That's a good sign. Johnsel and his wife are at least eighty years old. Maybe they did forget to lock the door.

'Mr Johnsel? . . . Mrs Vivian?' my dad adds, halfway up the stairs.

I turn to follow. Naomi's right behind him, her gun clutched in both hands and pointed down by her knees.

We keep calling their names, circling upward past the second floor. A few of the bedroom doors are closed, but again, all the lights are off. Nothing but an empty house. I head for the third floor.

'Dammit!' my dad shouts.

'What? What's wrong?' I call out, racing up the stairs two at a time.

Stumbling onto the third-floor landing, I follow the noise into the open room with the exposed wooden slats along the ceiling and the milk crates and religious books stacked along the walls. The heart of creation. Jerry Siegel's bedroom.

'So this is where he came up with Superman?' Naomi asks.

'Doesn't matter,' my dad says, pointing to the walls. 'It's already picked clean.'

He's right about that. The rest of the house is filled with ancient peeling wallpaper that hasn't been changed in decades, but up here . . . I didn't notice it before . . . all four walls are peeled away, revealing nothing but cracked plaster and some fake pine paneling just between the windows.

'Can we possibly be more stupid?' Naomi asks.

'Don't say that,' I shoot back. 'We had to come and check.'

'But to think that after seventy years, no one would come here and pull the wallpaper themselves—'

'Okay, let's just regroup . . . rethink,' I jump in. 'Maybe there's something we missed.'

'What's to miss? We heard the story fifteen times,' Naomi says. 'Young Jerry lying awake in this room . . . staring out at the stupid crabapple tree and pining for his dead dad. Where else is he gonna hide it? In his sock drawer? Under the floorboards? Maybe he tucked it behind the wood paneling,' she shouts, kicking at the pine panels between the two windows.

'What about the attic?' my dad asks. 'Was there wallpaper up there?'

'No,' I say. 'It's completely—'

'Crabapple,' Naomi blurts.

'Wha?'

We both turn to see Naomi staring out of the room's side-by-side double-paned windows. 'The crabapple tree. You can't see it from here.'

My dad and I race next to her. Sure enough, the never cleaned windows are thick with dust and remnants of cracked paint, but they still give a muddy view of the front lawn as well as the snow-covered street and the equally beat-up houses that sit across the way.

'I don't get it,' my father says.

'*Look!*' Naomi insists, pointing out to the right.

We press our foreheads against the cold, filthy glass, but no matter how hard we push, there's no view of the crabapple tree that sits in the alley on the right side of the house.

Pulling back, I check the far right side of the room, but there's nothing but wall.

'These are the only windows in here,' Naomi points out, still at the front windows.

'So if you can't see the crabapple tree, either the whole Superman creation story is wrong . . .'

'. . . or this wasn't Jerry's room,' Naomi says excitedly. 'Is there another room with windows that overlook—?'

'Right below us,' I say, already rushing toward the stairs.

52

'*There*,' Naomi says, racing toward the small window, then pointing outside at the surprisingly full tree that stood alone in the alleyway on the east side of the house.

'You sure that's a crabapple?' I ask.

She nods. 'You can see the fruit.'

'So then *this*,' I say, turning back to the modest room lined with family photos, old track team trophies, and a *National Geographic* foldout poster of a mountain lion, '*this* is where Superman was really created.'

'They painted over it, but there's definitely wallpaper here,' my dad adds, already tracing the wall with his fingertips. For a moment, I forgot he used to be a painter. 'Here's the seam,' he adds, nicking the 1970s cocoa brown wallpaper with his fingernail.

'So what now?' I ask. 'Peel the whole room down?'

'I peeled wallpaper in my old apartment,' Naomi says. 'Best thing is to wet it with soapy water – it'll come right off.'

Behind us, though, my dad's still running his fingertips from one side of the wall to the other. When he reaches the end, he raises his hand a few inches and goes back the way he came, like an old typewriter. The way his fingers skate along the wall . . . it's as if he's feeling for something.

'What're you doing?' I ask.

'Playing a hunch,' he replies, now on his tiptoes with his hand reaching upward. When it gets too high, he pulls a nearby chair into place, climbing up so he can touch the top of the wall, right where it meets the ceiling. Naomi shoots me a look.

'Lloyd,' I call out to my father.

He's not listening. 'Most people use wallpaper for decoration,' he explains without looking back at us. 'But in older houses, especially if you had access to a lot of it, which I'm guessing they did if they were drawing on it . . .' A few feet from the corner, he stops, his five open fingertips pressing against the top of the wall, sucking it like a starfish. I can see the way the paper gives. He feels something underneath.

'. . . it could also give you one hell of a hiding spot,' he says, shutting his eyes so he can focus on his touch.

With a hard push, he presses his fingertips against the wall. And with one final shove, the paper tears, flopping inward like a fallen playing card and – in a small, decades-old puff of smoke and dust – revealing a softball-size hole that swallows my dad's hand up to his wrist.

'H-How'd you know that was there?' Naomi asks him.

'I told you,' he says, reaching up into the hole like Tom searching for Jerry, 'playing a hunch.'

Naomi gives me a look that says she doesn't buy it, either. But before she can say anything, my dad pulls his hand from the hole. He's crestfallen.

'It's empty,' he tells us.

'You sure?' I ask, waving him off the chair. 'Lemme see.'

Standing on the chair, I reach into the hole and pat around. Filled with dust and old bits of plaster, the space feels like a narrow shelf built into the wall. But whatever was once there is long gone.

'Maybe there's another somewhere else,' my dad says, already skating his fingertips along the wall on our right. Now excited, Naomi starts patting down the wall by the door. But within a minute, it's clear this is the only hole.

'You sure it's empty?' Naomi asks me.

'I'm telling you, it's just dust and sand and whatever old crusty stuff settles in houses after seventy years.' Rummaging in the hole, I sweep out most of the debris, which rains down in a gray cloud, followed by the original flap of wallpaper that was covering the hole. Still attached at the base, the torn flap sticks out at me like a tongue, then sags downward against the wall. But it's not until the flap of wallpaper dangles that I finally see what's printed on the opposite side. It's hand-drawn . . . black-and-white . . . like an old 1930s . . .

Comic book.

Fudge. Me.

'That's it, isn't it?' my dad blurts. 'That's the missing story!'

'What's it say? Are there any more?' Naomi adds.

I tug on the thin flap of wallpaper and slowly peel it away from the wall. There's about a half inch more of art, then the back side of the wallpaper becomes blank with patches of yellow from the old, rancid glue. With a final rip, I hop from the chair. I'm trying to skim the comic – which is only a single panel – but the way my hands are shaking, it's like being eighteen and trying to read a pregnancy test.

'What's it say?!' Naomi insists.

'Hold on!' I shoot back, staring down at the panel.

'*Yowzie?*' my dad reads over my shoulder. But I'm still staring at the book.

Before I can even read the rest, I look at the edges of the panel – from the weight of the small sheet – there's even more art that's stuck together underneath this one. It's hiding other ripped-up pieces.

'Jerry glued them all together,' I blurt. 'H-He— I think I've got a full page of—'

I look up at Naomi, whose back is to the bedroom door. But as she smiles at the news, a pale shadow appears in the open door behind her. Someone's here.

If Ellis—

No. This isn't Ellis.

In a blur, Serena whips around the corner, her yellow blue eyes constricted into two black slits. She's crouched like a baseball player, thanks especially to the fact that she's armed with a broom, which she clutches down by the neck of the bristles, already swinging away.

'*Serena, don't!*' I call out.

But I see the way she's looking at Naomi's gun.

Plowing into the room, Serena aims at Naomi's head and swings the broom like a Major League slugger. The problem is, she's not one. There's a dull thud at the impact. Naomi bends forward, grabbing the back of her head.

'Ow! That— *Ow!*' Naomi shouts. 'You friggin' *nuts*!?'

Lifting her gun, Naomi turns to face Serena. And that's why she doesn't see my father behind her.

Already flying, my dad grabs the hammer-size gold trophy that's sitting on a nearby TV. But the darkness in his eyes . . . even when he killed my— I've never seen him like this.

'Dad?' I call out in a whisper that surprises even me.

Naomi wheels around, off balance as she follows my voice. It's just— Just like before. There I am. The perfect distraction.

Time, once again, slows to a crawl.

My father clutches the golden man at the top of the track meet trophy and swings the heavy marble base toward the back of Naomi's head.

I'm not a child anymore. I run forward. But that doesn't mean I'm fast enough.

Midstep, my father turns toward me. But as our eyes lock— No. My father is long gone. The rage on this man's face . . . I haven't seen him since I was little. I keep forgetting. I don't know this man at all.

Naomi never sees it coming.

When I was nine years old, my father committed the worst accident of his life. But today, as my dad swings the trophy as hard as he can – this is no accident.

Naomi turns, and the base of the trophy is inches from her right temple.

'Naomi!'

The sound is unforgettable.

Like a child's punching bag, Naomi topples sideways, crumpling to the floor as a burst of blood sprays from her head. Her gun slides across the wood floor, under the bed.

'*What're you doing!?*' I shout.

'She put us in cuffs, Cal!' my dad shoots back.

'She also let us out!'

'Not for long!'

'Hold on,' Serena says, confused. 'She wasn't *attacking* you?'

'Why would she—?'

'She had a gun,' Serena insists.

'And handcuffs. And a badge!' I shout back. 'That's what happens when you're a *federal agent*!'

'She was about to shoot Serena!' my dad yells.

'No, she— How can you possibly think that?'

'A federal—? Oh my,' Serena whispers. 'Is she breathing?'

'I think—Yeah,' I say, kneeling down near Naomi. 'She's breathing,'

'You sure she's breathing?' Serena asks, her eyes already filled with tears.

'She's breathing,' I repeat, turning back to Serena. 'Where the hell were you, anyway?'

'Following. From the museum. I saw her force you out, so I thought she was with Ellis or that she was – I don't know – Ellis's partner or something. Then when I got here and saw that you were parked around back and—'

'Wait. *What?*'

'In back. Isn't that her blue Malibu parked behind the house?'

'We parked *up* the block. *Away* from here,' I point out.

'Then whose rental car is that behind the—?' With her mouth gaping open, Serena cuts herself off.

I look at her, then my dad. No one says a word. And the house suddenly doesn't seem as quiet as it was a minute ago.

'We need to get out of here,' I announce as my dad already starts running for the door.

I shove the wallpaper comic in my backpack and, still kneeling, scoop my arm behind Naomi's neck. 'What're you doing?' my dad asks.

'What? I should leave her here?'

'The moment she's up, she'll arrest us!'

'I can't leave her!' I tell him.

My dad is silent. From the look on his face, he has no such problem – and as he darts from the room, I'm once again reminded what a stranger he is to me.

'I – I didn't know who she was. I wouldn't do that,' Serena insists, and as she kneels down across from me, she reaches over Naomi's unconscious body and grips my wrist. Her touch is clammy and unsure, but as she holds on, she clenches my wrist until I finally look up at her. 'Please – I need to tell you this, Cal. This – I'm not like this. I'd never hurt anyone. I was just—'

'Serena, can we not—?'

'I just wanted to protect you,' she blurts, her voice stronger than ever.

I freeze at the words – the same words I say to every client every day. But for once— I know she's talking about my dad, too, but— It's been a long time since someone was protecting *me*.

'Did I say something wrong?' she asks, reading my expression.

I shake my head, staring down at her hand on my wrist.

'*Cal, move!*' my dad calls from the stairs.

Without another word, Serena helps me lift Naomi fireman style over my shoulder. Naomi's heavier than she looks, and she looks pretty heavy. I hear the comic getting crushed in my backpack. 'Cal, we need to go.'

Serena's right about that. But as I burst out onto the second-floor landing, I notice that the back bedroom door on my left is now open. It was closed before. For a split second, I peer inside and spot two bodies lying on the bed, their necks bent awkwardly. Mr and Mrs Johnsel. Both dead.

'Oh, God,' Serena whimpers, the tears coming fast. But if Ellis is still in the house—

'*Go!*' I shout, shoving the hips of Naomi's unconscious body into Serena's back. 'Hurry!'

The wooden stairs rumble and squeal as we circle down at full speed. Carrying Naomi, I'm off balance, but not by much. As for Serena, she's the one who needs the missing handrails, looking like she's about to pass out. She's too nice for this.

Ahead of us, my dad had a good head start, but as we reach the main floor, he's just standing there on the last step, still holding the trophy and staring at something in the living room.

'*Move!*' I yell.

But I quickly see why he doesn't.

'I'd like the Book of Lies now,' Ellis announces in full police uniform as he taps the tip of his air gun against his open palm. 'And Cal . . . I haven't forgotten what you did to my dog.'

53

'I don't even know what a Book of Lies is,' I tell him.

'I know you found it,' Ellis says, calm as ever. He blocks the way out and pushes his copper hair back from his forehead. 'In the wallpaper. The rest of the Map.'

'That's not what you . . . what'd you call it again? A Book of Lies?'

'Now you're stalling. People stall when they're scared, Cal. Scared little boys whose mothers get taken away,' he says. 'My father cut me with that same blade.'

I look at my father, then over to Ellis. 'You know nothing about me.'

'Right. Next time try saying that without your voice cracking,' Ellis says. 'Life is a monster, Calvin. Especially when it doesn't turn out the way you hoped. But that doesn't mean you can hide from it.'

This time I don't say a word.

'Exactly,' Ellis adds. 'The Prophet said you'd understand that one.'

In front of me, Serena freezes at the word. Next to her, my dad does the same. The Prophet. Who the hell's he talking about?

'Ellis, listen to me, when you lost your mom—'

'Don't try sympathy! I'm not one of your homeless pets!'

'No, you're just one of those normal guys who spends

time with someone named *the Prophet*. Does that sound like a rational thought to you?' I say.

'How do you think I knew you were coming back here?' Ellis asks.

This time, I'm the one who freezes. No one – not even Roosevelt – knew we were making this second visit to the house. Besides myself, Naomi, and her assistant, the only people who knew were—

I stare again at Serena. Then my father.

I see her only from behind as Serena wipes her eyes with the back of her hand, her whole body shivering. She sways back and forth, barely able to stand. On her right, my dad barely moves at all. He breathes like a bull – slowly and deeply through gritted teeth – puffing faster and faster with each breath. He's starting to fume. The way he studies Ellis – chin down, stabbing him with an angry glare – my father's not the least bit scared. Everyone has their breaking point. And the way his grip tightens around the top of the trophy—

'*You're done!*' my dad detonates, leaping forward before I even realize he's moving.

Stumbling backward, Ellis is clearly unprepared. My father's not fast, but at six foot two, he plows forward like a falling tree. With one hand, he grips Ellis's shoulder; with the other, he swings the trophy as if it's the hammer of Thor.

The impact is frightening. Ellis's jaw is rocked sideways with a gob of flying red spit as the marble base of the trophy slams into the side of his mouth. I was wrong before. When my dad hit Naomi, he was holding back. He's not holding back anymore.

Ellis tries lifting his gun, but my dad's momentum, his size – he's just smothering. Pressing his forearm like a billy club across Ellis's neck, my father sends Ellis crashing backward into the wall as the shelves of needlepoints and religious candles tumble from their nests. But Ellis was a cop. He knows how to fight back.

Gripping my dad by his lapels, Ellis spins to the right, twirling my father as though they're ballroom dancing and slamming him backward into the wall. On impact, another shelf of needlepoints and candles tumbles and bounces across the floor.

I go to put Naomi down, but there's no need. My father's doing just fine.

Ellis thinks he has the upper hand, but within seconds his eyes go wide, and I realize my dad just kneed him in the nuts. This isn't a burst of raw rage. This is a prison fight. And with Ellis in his police uniform – I swear my dad's smiling. It's already over.

For the past two days, I've known my father was hiding something. But as I watch him now – his lip curled in a snarl – I finally see what he was really trying to contain.

'We're finished,' he whispers to Ellis.

With a final ballroom spin, my father flings Ellis to the right, not even realizing as he sends him whipping backward toward the double-hung window in the hall.

'The glass!' I call out.

He doesn't hear. Or care.

For a moment, the large glass pane crackles like ice in warm water, and with the full impact of Ellis's back, shards of glass explode outward like fireworks, sucking Ellis into the wide black hole created by his own weight. As he crashes out the window and disappears, a nasty winter wind leaps inside and swirls through the hall. We hear a thud outside.

Still holding Naomi over my shoulder, I rush to the

window, which overlooks the concrete driveway on the west side of the house. Like a bloody snow angel, Ellis is flat on his back, the right side of his face covered with cuts and scrapes. He's gasping – the wind knocked out of him – but already struggling to his feet. On my far left, at the end of the driveway, Benoni is bucking wildly in the backseat of Ellis's rental car, her barks muffled by the windows.

Behind me, Serena is bawling, her arms curled around herself.

'Y-You still have the comic strip?' my father asks, putting a hand on my shoulder.

I spin around and look him straight in the eye. My father looks exhausted, his mouth open, his breathing heavy again. For a moment, I wonder if it's all an act, but the way he's cupping his waist . . . I look down and see blood soaking through his shirt. His bullet wound has reopened. Outside, Ellis is almost up, reaching for his gun. We're in no shape for a second round.

'C'mon,' I tell him, motioning us to the front door. 'We need to go.'

54

'Hi, Clydene – I'm looking for Special Agent Guggenheim,' Scotty said into his headset.

'And who may I say is calling?' Clydene asked.

'Agent Naomi Molina from ICE would like to talk with him.'

'And is Agent Molina on the phone right now?'

Scotty rolled his eyes and rolled back slightly in his wheelchair. The FBI was always such a pain in the ass. 'I have her waiting on hold,' he said.

'Then can you put her on, so that way Agent Guggenheim won't be waiting when *he* gets on?'

Rolling forward and leaning both elbows on the desk of his small cubicle, Scotty reached for a small red egg of Silly Putty and cracked it open. It didn't have the smell he loved when he was a kid, but as he tweezed it from the egg and squeezed it in his fist, it was still the best stress relief around.

'Clydene, you show me your boss, I'll show you mine,' Scotty said.

'That's fine,' Clydene agreed, 'as long as this is a real call from your actual boss and not just you calling for the third time today, pretending to have her when you actually don't.' She paused for a long breath. 'We're all in this together, Scotty, but Guggenheim's still the number three guy here. He doesn't talk to assistants.'

Scotty kneaded the Silly Putty with his middle finger. For the past ten minutes, he'd been dialing Naomi on the other line. She still wasn't picking up. But as he'd learned when he'd first started – when he'd first met Timothy – some things had to be done without the boss.

'Clydene, I'm gonna say this slowly so you understand it,' Scotty began. But before he could finish, he looked up and noticed the two tall shadows that were now standing over his cubicle.

With a pivot of his wheelchair, he stared up at two men in cheap navy suits and matching Rolex Submariner watches. Definitely Bureau agents.

'Did you send anyone over here?' Scotty asked into the phone.

'What're you talking about?' Clydene replied.

The agents didn't say a word.

'Lemme call you back,' Scotty said as he hung up the phone, never taking his eyes off his two new visitors.

'I take it you're Scotty,' the taller one said as he flashed his credentials. 'Agent Randy Aldridge. FBI Counterintelligence Division. You mind me asking your clearance levels?'

'Why would—?'

'I checked the signature on that name check request you put in earlier. You always forge your supervisor's signature?' Aldridge asked. 'Now if I don't get your levels, I'll be asking you for your wrists instead,' he said, patting at his handcuffs.

Scotty studied them both. This was why he hated the Bureau. 'Top secret with SCI access,' he replied confidently. 'So you might as well cozy up and acknowledge that you wanna know as much about our case as we wanna know about whatever it is that made you leave your office and come all the way down here.'

The two agents exchanged a glance. The FBI was definitely a pain in the ass.

'There's a reason your request didn't bring back any records,' said the shorter agent, a blond man with close eyes and flat ears. 'Even these days, the Bureau has to be careful when it comes to Mikhel Segalovich.'

'Who's Mikhel Segalovich?'

'That's his real name,' Agent Aldridge said. 'At Ellis Island, he went by Sigalowitz. But here in the U.S., he was known as Mitchell Siegel.'

55

'—ou okay?' a man's voice echoed. 'Can you hear me? . . . You okay?'

Blinking back to consciousness, Naomi was groggy, lost. That stench of ammonia. Smelling salts, she realized as she stared up at the young African-American man standing over her.

From his white uniform, plus the bright overhead lights . . .

'Do you know your name?' the male nurse asked.

'Wh-Where is this?' Naomi asked. She tried turning to the side, but her head . . . It wouldn't move. She touched her neck. There was a huge plastic collar. *Am I paralyzed?*

'You're at Huron Hospital, ma'am. Your friends brought you into our emergency room. Can you move your toes?' the nurse asked. 'Do you know your name?'

'Get this offa me!' Naomi shouted, tugging at the Velcro along the collar.

'Ma'am, don't!' The nurse grabbed Naomi's arms, then undid the plastic collar and checked the back of her neck. 'Can you move your toes?'

Naomi kicked both feet out and tried to sit up, but she was far too dizzy to make it. She touched the back right side of her throbbing skull but felt only the thick gauze pad that was wrapped around her head.

'My purse, my gun . . .' Naomi blurted as she felt herself up. 'They took my gun!'

The nurse stepped back, wary.

'Relax – nuhhh – I'm a federal agent,' Naomi said, gripping the metal rail on the gurney and finally sitting up straight. 'I need a phone. Have you seen my—?' From her pants pocket, she pulled out her phone and earpiece.

'Lord, didn't you gimme any painkillers?' she asked as the throbbing got worse.

'You were unconscious,' the nurse began, though before he could finish, Naomi was done dialing, focused now on her earpiece.

'C'mon, Scotty, pick up,' she muttered as it rang in her ear.

'You have a laceration and contusion, ma'am. You need staples to close that up.'

'Fine. Put 'em in.' But all Naomi really cared about was the endless ringing of the phone in her ear. Something was wrong. 'Where the hell are you, Scotty?'

56

'You left your dad and Serena upstairs?' Roosevelt scolds through my phone. 'By themselves?'

'What was I supposed to do? Bring them along all three of us marching arm in arm and completely matching the *two white men with a light-skinned black woman* APB that I'm sure is now out for us?' I lower my voice as I reach the supermarket's checkout lane and dump my only items – vinegar and fabric softener – onto the old conveyor belt that rumbles as it rolls.

Behind the counter, an Arab teenager with a cowboy hat belt buckle doesn't bother to look up at me. In this neighborhood, I understand why. The market is called Star's Grocery, but with the metal bars across the front windows and the armed-with-a-shotgun African-American man sitting high up in the crow's-nest seat that overlooks the front of the store, it's clear how poor the area is. It's why I picked it. Neighborhoods like this hate calling the cops.

'Cal, this is the time to be smart,' Roosevelt says in my ear. 'Whatever your dad has going with Serena, when you leave them alone like this, it's all going on behind your back – and that's never good for you.'

'It's not like that with them. Besides, Serena – she wouldn't do that.'

'*She wouldn't do that?* Oh, *fudge* me! Don't tell me you're falling in like with this girl!'

'*What?* No. I barely know her. I've barely seen her.'

'And you barely recognize your own blind spot for helpless women.'

'She's not *helpless*. She was trying to help *me*.'

'And there it is again – I hear it in your voice, Cal. And I know it's warming your cocoa to finally have someone looking out for you, but stop picking out her corsage for the prom and instead focus on the fact that she's the one who hit Naomi in the head.'

'You should've seen Serena, though. She felt horrible. She was crying. It was even her idea to drop Naomi at the hospital.'

'And that's a wonderful thing to do – especially as a way to snake into your *save everyone* heart. But take some notes here, Cal. I don't care how calming or pretty Serena is – I don't care if you shared a little Zen moment with the rabid possum – the only reason she's around is because of your *dad*. So if you don't believe him, you shouldn't believe her. You can't just take the Bonnie away from Clyde.'

There's a loud jingle as the register spouts open, and the cashier hands me my change. 'Sorry, no bags,' he says as I pick up my two items and head for the door.

'Trust me, Serena's not the problem,' I tell Roosevelt as I glance around the empty streets of East Cleveland, duck my chin into my jacket, and head out into the cold. It's nearly nine p.m. One mission down; one to go.

'I notice you don't have the same kind words about your dad,' Roosevelt points out. 'And then there's Ellis – and whoever the hell he's talking to.'

'The Prophet.'

'That's a stupid name,' Roosevelt says.

'That's the name he gave.'

'Whatever he calls himself, he's clearly helping Ellis – and considering how everything's gone, you need to find out how this Prophet somehow knows, at all times, where the three of you are.'

'He doesn't know it now.'

'Or for all you know, he – or she – *does*,' Roosevelt warns.

I freeze midstep, and a chunk of ice slides into my sneaker, nibbling through my sock. 'What're you saying?'

'The whole reason you're all running around is to track what's in this old lost comic, right? Jerry Siegel hid something in there, and everyone's racing to find it. Timothy teamed with Ellis to find it. Ellis teamed with the Prophet to find it. And then . . . by whatever grace of God . . . in the wallpaper, you found it.'

'So?'

'So now, maybe this Prophet doesn't need Ellis anymore. Maybe he's feeling secure about his position and doesn't want Ellis screwing it up, or even worse, having Ellis take it all for himself – so he knocks Ellis out the window, which conveniently uncorks the pressure cooker but still leaves all the pawns on the board, just in case he needs to play them later.'

Across the street, there's an old Plymouth in a snowed-in parking spot. The driver guns the engine, but the wheels spin hopelessly. I know exactly how he feels. 'So you're saying *my dad's* the Prophet?'

'Your dad . . . Serena – maybe it's both of them. But ask yourself: How did this all start, Cal? Because you saw your father that night in the park, right? Then when you got the hold notice taken off his shipment, you started realizing that as much as he tried to act clueless, he always seemed to have this uncanny sense for what was really going on. Then he convinces you to go off to Cleveland, promising to track down whoever hired him. But whatever happened to that search? Has he spent a single minute on it? No. And the reason you can't find who hired your dad . . . well, maybe it's simply because *no one* hired your dad. Or his girlfriend.'

The wheels of the Plymouth continue their futile spin. The driver just needs a push. Up the block, there's half a dozen people waiting at a bus stop, all of them watching. Not one of them gets up to help.

'I know you want the happy ending, Cal – and I know what you're really chasing up there with your father – but don't forget, in the original Pinocchio story, Jiminy Cricket gets stomped and left for dead. By Pinocchio.'

'Thanks for that. But I'm not my father's conscience,' I insist.

'You sure about that?'

I stare at the stranded Plymouth, tempted to help. But there's a reason I didn't bring my dad or Serena or even our rental car. When I close my eyes, I picture the Johnsels' lifeless bodies spread awkwardly across their mattress. The only thing keeping me from joining them is staying out of sight. Lowering my head, I walk past the Plymouth. Destination is the Burger King that's dead ahead. I don't need food. But they have something far more valuable. 'Can we please get back to the research?' I plead. 'What'd you find out about this Book of Lies?'

Through the phone, I hear Roosevelt turning pages. 'I know this'll sound a little hoo-ha, but . . . I think it's a murder weapon.'

'The book is?' I laugh as my frozen breath fills the air. 'Must've been a hell of a paper cut.'

'I'm serious, Cal. Scholars have spent centuries theorizing

that Cain killed Abel with a rock or a club or even the jawbone of an ass. But one of the oldest theories is that Cain used, of all things, a book.'

'And I suppose no one cares about the fact that Cain's tirade supposedly took place thousands of years before the Chinese or the Egyptians got their hands on a single piece of papyrus?' I ask as I peer over my shoulder. A local bus hisses to a stop at the bus bench, carting all the people away. Even the Plymouth is gone. Good sign. I cut as fast as I can into the Burger King parking lot.

'Sure, today, when we hear the word *book*, we think *bound paper between two covers*. But let your brain stretch a little, Cal. If someone carved a message on the blade of a sword . . . or along the length of an ancient wooden staff . . . or on a sacred tablet . . . Couldn't those be *books*?'

I stop just outside the Burger King, stealing a peek through the glass. It's cold out here. And colder every minute. 'Just tell me what the book theory says.'

'According to the story, knowing that the great flood is coming, God instructs Adam to create a book – in Jewish legend, they're said to be *carved pillars*; in Babylonia, they use the word *tablets* – but God tells Adam to fill it with all earthly knowledge, and that Adam should give this birthright to his most favored son. When Adam chooses Abel, well . . . Cain grabs it in a fit of jealousy and turns it into the world's first murder weapon. But as I've always said, the real story is what happens next. As penance for the crime, even the Bible says that God gave Cain a *Mark* – and from what I can tell here – I think this *Mark* and the *Book* are actually the same thing.'

'Says who?' I ask as I watch two teenagers placing their order at the counter. There's a man with a red scarf standing behind them. I can't see his face.

'Again, it's all translation. The word *Mark* in Mark of Cain comes from the Hebrew word *Ot*. And when I was looking at some of these other theories, *Ot* can just as easily be translated as an *omen*. A *sign*. A *remembrance*.'

'So God gave Cain a remembrance – the actual murder weapon – to remind him of what he'd done.'

'That's the idea. And when you trace the word *Ot* in the Bible, the next time it's used is to refer to Moses's rod that turns into a snake in front of Pharaoh – an everyday item that suddenly becomes a deadly weapon.'

'I don't know,' I say, still studying the man with the red scarf. 'Old tablets . . . weapons of Cain . . . I'm really supposed to believe this all happened, much less *somehow survived* to modern days?'

'You can roll your eyes all you want, but nearly all we know of ancient Greece comes from the clay and stone artifacts that survived.'

'But if this tablet or book or animal skin or whatever it is – assuming it *was* filled with all the world's earthly knowledge – why would having it be such a punishment?'

'See, that's where Ellis was finally helpful,' Roosevelt says as the man with the red scarf turns my way. He's no older than the teenagers. Just a kid. Nothing to worry about. 'When Cain grew jealous of Abel and killed him for it, God gave Cain a very different *book* to carry.'

'A Book of Lies.'

'That's what Ellis called it. Penance, punishment . . . a remembrance for Cain,' Roosevelt says as I cross around to the side of the Burger King and check the seating area. 'Look at it this way, Cal – whether this *book* is filled with lies or all the world's knowledge – don't underestimate the power that people attribute to a sacred object.'

In the seating area of the Burger King, an employee

wipes down one of the tables. The teenagers share a booth in the corner. No one else is there. 'You really believe all this is real?' I ask as I pull open the door and head for the bathroom in back.

'You really believe it's all fake?'

I stop at the door to the men's room, still picturing the way Ellis stroked his tattoo and stared so obsessively at his pointy-eared dog.

'Cal, the only thing more frightening than a disbeliever is a true believer.'

Entering the bathroom, I know Roosevelt's right. But that's what brought me here.

A quick glance around tells me I'm alone. Perfect.

Ducking into the single open stall, I ignore the usual mess of graffitied insults that decorate the walls, step up on the toilet, and reach for the grid of white ceiling tiles that're directly overhead. With a push, I shove open the nearest square grid and pat inside the ceiling. Nothing. I lift another tile and try again. Still nothing. I don't panic. This is the third restaurant I've tried. Sooner or later, one'll be here.

Studying the rest of the ceiling, I spot a tile with a few smudges. Fingerprints. Bingo. With my fingers spread apart like a waiter balancing a tray, I lift up the white tile and slide it aside. Patting around inside, I feel nothing . . . nothing . . . *kuuunk*.

My hand slides around the grip even as my finger hugs the trigger.

'Finally find one?' Roosevelt asks.

From the ceiling, I pull out a polished .380-caliber pistol. No serial numbers. No question, illegal. Cain grabbed a book. My father grabbed a trophy. I need something for myself.

It's hardly a perk of my job, but it's the same in every crap neighborhood in America: Show me the local fast-food joint, and I'll show you where the kids are hiding their guns.

I tuck the pistol in the back of my waistband, then zip my jacket and dive back into East Cleveland's ferocious cold. It's a two-minute walk back to our motel – a two-story dump that doesn't even have a name, just a sign out front that's painted red, white, blue, green, black, and more red. U.S. and Palestinian colors, with the word *Vacancy* along the bottom.

'You got the supermarket stuff?' Roosevelt asks.

In my jacket pocket, I feel for the vinegar and fabric softener. 'All set,' I tell him.

'So you're gonna do the rest by yourself, yes?'

I circle up the outdoor stairs and follow the signs for room 216.

'Cal, please tell me you're doing the rest by yourself,' Roosevelt pleads.

'Listen, I should run,' I say, stopping at the door.

'You're not even listening, are you? Dammit, yo momma's so fat—'

'Don't start,' I warn as I twist my key and use my shoulder to shove open the motel door.

'Didja get it?' Serena calls out, leaping my way.

'Cal, you're a big boy,' Roosevelt warns in my ear. 'You do what you want. But *please*: I know what happened at the Siegel house, but don't feel the need to protect her just because she protected you.'

I slap the phone shut.

Serena's already holding my hand, dragging me inside. I take my jacket off slowly. They know about the supermarket. They don't need to know about the gun.

'You get it or not?' my father calls out from the narrow bed. He's no longer holding his side. The bleeding's stopped.

'Of course I got it,' I say as I toss my two supermarket purchases onto the empty bed. My dad knows it from his painting days. Vinegar and fabric softener. The best way to unstick wallpaper glue.

From my backpack, I take out the swatch of wallpaper we found in Jerry Siegel's old bedroom. Four panels glued on top of one another. Ellis called it the rest of a map. Looks like torn-up pages from an old comic book to me. But whatever Jerry Siegel hid by gluing them together, it's time to finally peel it apart.

57

August 3, 1900
Brussels, Belgium

Mikhel Segalovich was vomiting. It was coming fast now, a hefty heave that emptied his stomach of the stale bread he'd fished from the trash. From his lips, strands of drool twirled in the wind, dangling down to the cobblestone of the narrow alley, but even as he wiped it away, he never once let go of the leather hold-all at his side.

It'd been nearly four months since he left his hometown in Lithuania. Four months without his wife. His parents. His children – two daughters. He knew bad times were ahead when he was drafted into the Russian army. It was always bad for Jews in the army, which was why so many tried to bribe their way out. Mikhel's father had tried the same – selling his gold, his wife's rings, even the family Bible. For all Lithuanians, there was mandatory army service for at least five years. But the Jews were taken for ten, twenty, sometimes as long as twenty-five years. Mikhel's father begged and pleaded to keep his boy safe. But the Segalovichs were poor. And the poor went into the army.

In the beginning, Mikhel committed himself to hard work. Maybe he'd make cavalry or even sergeant. But he learned quickly. A Jewish sergeant giving orders to Russians? Never. Even in the cavalry – they weren't giving sabers and pistols to a poor uneducated Jew. No, the Jews were beaten and practiced on. Low infantrymen to sweep stables and live in feces. That's all Mikhel would ever be.

Until Sweden.

Back then, they called the trips *scientific expeditions*. It was how the Russians discovered the Bering Strait, as well as the mammoth fossils in Siberia. Mikhel heard the rumors . . . the search for an imperial treasure . . . the ancient carving known as the *Book of God*. But when Mikhel heard that *he* was chosen, that he and a dozen other Jews from different units were being allowed to leave the Russian Empire for this *expedition*, he knew what his group really was. A suicide squad.

They didn't expect the group to survive. Didn't expect them, in that winter, to even make it to Sweden. Most of them didn't. But the youngest, Mikhel, did.

He wasn't a hero. Indeed, he was simply the kid in charge of the horses and dogs. So when they finally found the cave – the makeshift tomb left behind by the monks – Mikhel was told to keep watch outside.

He did his job. He stood, in his unlined Russian riding boots, knee-deep in the snow. He waited in the icy silence, wondering what was happening inside. And then Mikhel heard the screams.

'*Hopen problemen, eh?*' a Belgian teenager teased, laughing as he ran past Mikhel vomiting in the alleyway. 'Heaps of problems, eh?'

Ignoring the child, Mikhel spat violently at the ground, clearing the last bits of vomit from his lips. Tucked between two modern houses, he knew this wasn't a perfect hiding spot, but it *was* the one with the best view of Avenue Louise.

Still clutching the handle of his leather hold-all, Mikhel studied each and every lime and sycamore tree that lined the main avenue. He eyed the two motorcars rumbling through the square. He even checked the windows of the blue-grained stone house across the street. He knew he had been followed. They had to be close. So from here on in, for Mikhel, it was simply a question of timing.

According to the pocketwatch they gave him, it was exactly half-past ten in the morning. He didn't hear the warning sounds, but if he wanted to pull this off . . . no question, he had to have some faith.

Bursting from the alleyway, he darted straight toward the pushcarts and milk wagons that filled the square. Sure enough, the *kling-ting* of the electric tram tickled the air. On his right, the tram's bright red carriage hummed and stuttered along the tracks that ran up Avenue Louise. Just as they had promised.

At this hour, the passengers were few. The suspicious would have no place to hide. Cutting behind a fruit wagon with a large striped umbrella, Mikhel, for the fourth time, checked over his shoulder. All clear.

'Huelp nodij met uw kossers?' a porter in a crisp linen smock asked as the tram pulled up to the platform. 'Help with your luggage?'

Mikhel shook his head, refusing eye contact. No. He hadn't brought it this far to let the hold-all out of sight.

He took a final scan of the platform. Except for the porter, he was the only one there. He still waited until the last minute to hop aboard.

'Welkom, meneer. Eerste of tweede klas?' asked a ticket collector with a thick mustache.

Mikhel didn't understand.

'Eerste of tweede klas?' the collector repeated again, this time motioning to the back of the tram, which was divided into two sections. One with cushions. One without. 'First or second class?'

Mikhel had spent his whole life knowing the answer to that one. 'Second class,' he whispered, handing over threepence.

The change was a halfpenny, and the collector paused a moment, hoping that Mikhel would let him keep it.

Mikhel opened his palm. The collector shot him a look. Mikhel didn't care. To get from Sweden to here . . . He had nothing left. Nothing but the items in the hold-all.

Walking to the back of the mostly empty tram, Mikhel followed the directions they'd sent along with the pocket-watch. He took a seat in the second to last row and held tight to the leather case in his lap.

At the next stop, he waited for them to appear. An old woman with a silk shawl boarded. She sat up front.

For nearly an hour, it stayed the same. Local Belgians coming on, getting off, as the tram grumbled past groves of chestnut trees and into the suburban countryside.

At their next stop – nearly at Waterloo – the old woman with the shawl got up and left the tram. As they started moving again, Mikhel looked around. He was the only passenger left.

'*Kak dela?*' a voice asked behind him in perfect Russian. 'How are you?'

Mikhel jumped, nearly dropping the hold-all. Sitting behind him – *how the hell'd they get behind him?* – were two men in gray and black wool coats and matching dark hats.

'*Vy gavareeteh pa anglisky?*' Mikhel asked as he turned anxiously in his seat. 'Do you speak English?'

'*Odin jazyk nedostatočno,*' replied the one with the thick glasses. 'One language is never enough.'

Mikhel nodded. Their Russian was flawless. The Americans were not as uneducated as the empire always said.

Looking toward the front of the tram, Mikhel saw that the collector was now seated and facing front. Neither he nor the tram driver bothered looking back.

'They're with you, too, aren't they?' Mikhel asked in Russian.

Thick Glasses stayed silent.

Mikhel shifted in his seat. Not uneducated at all.

'Sounds like you had quite an adventure,' Thick Glasses began. 'And to be the only one to walk away from it – you must be quite an expert fighter, huh?'

Staring out at the blur of sycamore trees, Mikhel could still feel the burn of Swedish snow in his boots. The dogs had reacted first, barking and pressing against their restraints. Outside the cave, Mikhel didn't move. He panicked, just standing there, frozen as the snow, as the fighting began.

At first the screaming was all in Russian. But there was French . . . German, too. And then, above all else, a foreign tongue – one he still didn't recognize.

Mikhel wanted to help. He wanted to rush in the cave and save them. But when the gunshots started . . . The snow was so cold in his boots. All he had to do was move. But all he did was stand there. Stand there until the screaming stopped.

'I got lucky,' he whispered to Thick Glasses.

'I didn't think you Jews believed in luck,' the man in the gray coat shot back with an extra dollop of sarcasm.

Mikhel's eyes narrowed at the man's small nose and burning blue eyes. Clearly, they had anti-Semites in America, too.

'I still don't know who they were,' Mikhel said. 'The ones who killed my unit.'

The two men in hats exchanged a glance. The one with the small nose shook his head. But Thick Glasses ignored him.

'They're known as the Thule Society,' he began. 'The group you encountered was what's known as Thule Leadership. That's their symbol,' he added, pointing to the small brand – the knife and the quarter-moon – burnt into the front flap of the leather hold-all.

'And that language they were speaking . . . What was it?' Mikhel asked.

Again, there was a pause. 'It's an incantation.'

'Y'mean like *religion*?'

'No, Mikhel. Like magic.'

Mikhel sat with this a moment. Back in Sweden, when the shooting and the screaming and the fighting had stopped, Mikhel had released one of the dogs, which sprinted straight for the mouth of the cave. But Mikhel didn't go in himself until the dog returned safely.

It was then, slowly, that he finally made his way inside. He saw the carvings along the cave walls . . . the odd symbols and stick figures. The deeper he went, the more bodies he found. Not everyone was dead. At least three or four were still breathing, still crawling to get out. But all the blood . . . from the fight . . . There was so much shooting. They weren't breathing for long.

For the second time at the cave, Mikhel wanted to run. He tried to run and leave. But again, he couldn't. Instead, he stood there, seized by the carnage as he re-created the scene inside. It was there – at the far end of the cave, where Abram and Mendel lay facedown – where the ambush happened. Where his friends fought back. And where he spotted, way in the back, the small flickers of flame from a knocked-over torch.

As the cave's only light source, it was impossible to miss. But as he got closer . . . the smell . . . It wasn't wood that was burning. No, it was like burnt tires, but sweeter. Like leather.

Like a tanned leather hold-all being licked by flames.

Mikhel still didn't know what possessed him to pull it out.

'But you brought the totems?' Thick Glasses asked.

'Only if you brought my paperwork,' Mikhel replied, still clutching the hold-all as he pretended to stare out at the sycamore trees.

It was cold outside. But not as cold as Sweden.

From the inside pocket of his coat, Thick Glasses handed over a folded pale envelope that was closed with a string tie. Mikhel opened it and examined the contents. The Secret Service were men of their word.

'The ship is called the *Statendam*. It leaves from Rotterdam,' Thick Glasses explained.

'Where?'

'In the Netherlands. Don't fret – we'll have a broad carriage take you. The ship will get you to New York. From there, we've selected a place called Cleveland, Ohio.'

'You'll like it,' the other man said with a grin. 'Best Jewish city in America.'

'What about my family?'

'All the paperwork is inside. Your wife, daughters . . . They'll join you soon. New lives for all,' Thick Glasses promised.

'And in return?' Mikhel asked.

'If we need you, we know you're there,' Thick Glasses said. 'In today's world, we need a few Russians we can count on.' Once again staring at the leather hold-all, he added, 'Now about the totems . . .'

No question, the Americans were smart. Mikhel put the case on the floor and slid it backward under the seat.

The tram began to slow down as it pulled into the next station.

'Agent Westman, this is your stop,' the tram driver called from the front.

But neither agent moved, both still rummaging through the items in the hold-all.

'Mikhel, I see four items here,' Thick Glasses said, looking up.

'That's correct,' Mikhel replied.

'Your message said there were five,' the other man insisted. 'Five totems.'

Mikhel stared at him calmly, taking in the man's burning blue eyes. The tram bucked to a stop. 'No,' he said. 'There were only four.'

No question, the Americans were smart. But that didn't mean Mikhel Segalovich was stupid.

'Sirs, you need to leave,' the tram driver insisted. 'Your transport is waiting.'

The two men stood from their seats and headed for the front.

'Have a good life, *Mitchell*,' Thick Glasses called out as he carried the hold-all. Reading the confusion on Mikhel's face, he added, 'Only way to start a new life is with a new name. An American name. Mitchell Siegel.'

'Mitchell Siegel,' Mikhel repeated, saying it aloud. 'It sounds . . . silly.'

'You'll get used to it,' Thick Glasses replied in English as he stepped off the tram. 'Good-bye, Mitchell. See you in the land of opportunity.'

Today
Miami, Florida

'I don't get it,' Scotty said, looking up at the two agents. 'Mitchell . . . Mikhel . . . whatever his name was – he kept one of these . . .'

'Totems. A sacred family object.'

'. . . he kept one of the totems for himself?'

'It took years for the Thules to figure it out – especially with the second name change at Ellis Island,' the FBI agent named Aldridge explained. 'Their Leadership is patient, though. In their eyes, they'd already waited centuries, so what was a few more decades? And once they realized Mitchell was alive – and that we were hiding him – according to the files, we lost a half dozen agents as they tightened their noose.'

'You seem pretty interested in all this for just an assistant, though,' the other agent added. 'I'm surprised Agent Molina had you making these calls instead of calling herself.'

'It's been a crazy day,' Scotty replied as his cell phone vibrated in his pocket. He knew it was Naomi. But he wasn't picking up just yet. 'Who were these Thule guys, anyway?' he asked the agents.

Agent Aldridge shook his head. 'It's not the *who they were* that you have to worry about. It's who the Thules *became*.'

58

'Try it now.'

'I thought it needed to soak,' I tell my dad.

'Try it now,' he repeats as all three of us hunch like Macbeth's witches, our foreheads almost touching, over the plastic motel ice bucket that sits on the round Formica table. Inside the bucket, a single comic book panel stares back at us, floating for nearly forty minutes in the soapy, pungent mixture of warm water, vinegar, and fabric softener. The panel is an unpublished work by the creators of Superman, which makes it irreplaceable. But if Ellis is right, it's what's glued behind it that makes it priceless.

'Any luck?' my father asks as I dip both hands into the bucket and try to peel away the layers of wallpaper. It's like trying to unpeel two stuck stamps. The liquid makes it slippery – it gives just slightly – but it's not there yet.

'Don't rip it,' my father warns.

'I'm *not*. I was – ' I shoot him a look. 'You're the one who said, *Try it now*.'

'Let's all just find a moment,' Serena pleads, doing her usual push for quiet and calm. 'If Jerry Siegel really had Cain's book – this Book of Lies – let's just worry about finding it, yes?'

She points her nose at the ice bucket, where I stare down at the submerged panel.

No question, that's what the newspaper boy's arm is covering. The Book of Lies. But I'm not believing anything until I've seen the rest of the panels.

'Try it now,' my father says for the third time.

With my hand in the bucket, I rub the corner of the wallpaper between my thumb and pointer finger. It's mushy now, sliding away from the panel underneath. With a pinch, I peel back the top layer slowly, like a stubborn Band-Aid.

The wallpaper tears slightly, but not much. I pinch the opposite corner and start peeling the other way. The longer the wallpaper sits in the water, the more the glue dissolves and the easier it becomes.

'Can you see anything?' my father asks, almost butting foreheads with me.

Actually, I can.

And just like that – with a final tug of the Band-Aid – it's done.

The top panel – with the newspaper boy running from the bullets – is completely free, revealing a second panel underneath.

A gunshot.

'It's just like the curator said,' my father points out as we all stare into the ice bucket. 'In this first Superman story – Jerry Siegel put his dad's real killer in it.'

'Can you feel how many more panels there are?' Serena asks.

I'm already peeling away the next layer, which shows the newspaper boy running toward a building. I have to squint to read it, but— 'There's an address. . . .'

'184 King Street. Is that where Mitchell Siegel was shot?' my father asks. 'We need a map.'

'I can try on my phone,' Serena offers.

'I threw your phone away,' my dad says.

'What?'

'In the house – when you hit Naomi – Cal screamed your name,' my dad explains. 'The moment Naomi wakes up, she'll be looking for you. I tossed it on the way over here. Sorry – we'll buy you a new one when all this is done.'

I nod in agreement. For once, he's got it right.

Turning back to the panels, I peel the final one away. If we're lucky, we'll get a face or a name. If Jerry really did put his father's killer in here, we need to know who we're up against – and how they got this Book of Lies.

But as the final panel of wallpaper gives way, all we're left with is . . .

'*That's it?* A man in some cave?' my dad asks as I slap the final piece of wet wallpaper against the table. 'That's no murderer.'

'Maybe that's a clue,' I point out.

'It's not the newspaper boy anymore. This guy's older. Could that be part of it?' Serena asks.

'Maybe that's where it started,' I add, already re-arranging the panels. 'The Cain book is supposedly ancient, right? Maybe they found it in a cave or something. Maybe that 184 King Street building is where the killer tried to hide. Something like – Something like *this*.'

'How does that make sense?' Serena asks. 'It doesn't even read right.'

'It's *not* right,' my dad insists. 'If all we're supposed to get is the address and some random cave, then why include the close-up of the gun and the dodging bullet panels? What'd the curator say? When this story got rejected, Siegel or Shuster supposedly tore the whole thing to shreds. But of those shreds, these four panels, for some reason, got saved. That isn't happening without a good reason.'

'Maybe it's like the KKK thing,' Serena suggests. Reading our confusion, she reaches for a pamphlet on Superman history that she pulled from the museum gift shop. 'In here. It's . . . *here*,' she says, flipping to the page. 'In the late 1940s, as a way to destabilize the Ku Klux Klan and make them think they were being infiltrated, the *Superman* radio show was covertly given the secret passwords that the Klan used to call and organize meetings. They were aired as part of the broadcast. Regular listeners had no idea. But the Klan knew. From there, they started infighting, looking for the snitch. The show hid it right in front of everyone.'

'Meaning what?' I ask. 'Jerry Siegel hid it in front of everyone, too?'

We all look down at the panels. There are worse ideas.

'What about the first letters of the captions,' Serena says. 'L . . . U . . . T . . . H . . . E . . . If there was an R, it'd spell Luther. Lex Luther.'

'I think *Luthor* has an o, not an e,' I point out. 'But if you rearrange the letters: Let Uh . . . Tel Uh . . .'

'It doesn't spell anything,' my dad says.

'Maybe it's the whole text. *Luckily he sees a torch*,' I read from the first line.

For the next ten minutes, we rearrange the letters, coming up with such insights as 'A Churches Likely Toes,' 'A Checklist Holey Ruse,' and 'Holy Accuser Heels Kit.' From the map we got at the car rental place, the search for 184 King Street is just as fruitful. There's a King *Avenue*. But in all of Cleveland . . . all of Cuyahoga County . . . there's not a single *King Street*.

'Maybe we still have the order of the panels wrong. Maybe the one with the torch is last, not first,' Serena says as she rearranges them. 'Instead of the man *reaching* for the flame, maybe he's tossing something into it.'

'So now they *burned* the book? Then why save any of this?' I ask.

Once again, Serena and I look down at the panels. My father hasn't taken his eyes off them. And once again, like clockwork, he's fourteen steps ahead of us.

'It's not a word puzzle. It's a visual one,' he says.

'What?'

'Comics are a visual medium. All the panels – they're pictures, right? Now look at the pictures . . . see what they have in common.'

I stare but see nothing. 'What're you—? You spotted something, didn't you?'

'A moon,' Serena blurts.

'Exactly. A moon,' my father says. 'There's a moon in each one.'

On the table, I see the moon in the Yowzie panel but nowhere else.

'Like Ellis's tattoo,' my dad says, now excited. 'He had a crescent moon in his tattoo.' But as I continue to stare . . .

'You still don't see it, do you, Calvin? It's in every panel – and not just in the sky,' my dad says, finally pointing it out. 'Look at the base of the flame . . . the barrel of the gun.'

'Hocus-pocus,' Serena whispers to herself. 'How'd you even see that?'

I'm tempted to ask the same, but I know the answer. My father was a painter. To match that restaurant lettering . . . he always had the perfect eye.

'So you think the moon's the key?' Serena asks.

'Not the key,' he says. 'More like the *X*. As in *marks the spot*.'

One by one, he peels each of the wet panels from the table.

'What're you doing?' I challenge.

'Just watch,' he says as he overlaps the moon in the Yowzie panel with the moon in the King Street one. Thanks to the wetness of the wallpaper, we can practically see through them.

'And that does a big fat nothing,' I point out.

Undeterred, he peels the sopping wet gunshot panel from the table and overlaps that moon with the other ones.

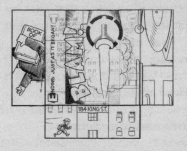

Like before, it's just a mess of overlapped art.

'So now what?' Serena asks.

It's the only question that matters, but my dad's not answering, his eyes dancing from the overlapped art to the final panel, then back to the overlapped art.

'Yowzie,' he blurts.

'What? Is *Yowzie* good?' Serena asks.

'I don't believe it,' he adds as his voice picks up speed. He's not scared anymore. He's excited. 'Those sneaky sons of bitches – when you match up the moons . . . It's like you said – just like they did with the KKK.'

He peels the final wet panel – the one with the man

and the torch – from the table, then lowers it toward the others, overlapping its moon with the rest. 'Hidden in front of everyone.'

I study the panels again but still come up empty.

'You really don't see it?' he asks.

I stare again. It's still a mess. 'Lloyd, tell me what the hell I'm looking at. Is it something in the middle or—'

'Not the middle. On the outside. Wait, lemme . . .' From his front pocket, my dad pulls out a cocktail napkin – looks like it's from a bar – and covers the center panel. On the napkin is the handwritten note '*GATH 601174-7.*' The container number from the original shipment. But that's not what he cares about. '*Here,*' my father says as he presses the napkin into place. 'How 'bout now?'

His fingers race as he traces the outer edges of each panel. 'We just— We had it wrong. It's not a Book of Lies at all. It's a Book of— Book of—'

'Truth,' Serena and I mutter simultaneously as we study the outer panels and read clockwise.

'Book of Truth,' I repeat. 'That's great, but— I don't— What's that even mean?'

'It means here's how the panels are supposed to be,' he says, still excited.

'I thought it was supposed to have who killed Jerry's dad,' Serena points out.

'Maybe it's not,' I say. 'Maybe it's something else.'

'Do we even know what a Book of Truth is?' Serena asks.

'I think . . . that's what some people call the Bible, isn't it?' my dad says, rotating the napkin and still fiddling with the letters that show up in the overlap.

'T-H-U-L-E,' my father spells out, pressing his finger on the H as it seeps through the wet napkin. 'Who's Thule?' he asks, his voice much slower, as though he's confused. 'Or maybe Theul or . . . Uleth?'

'Maybe that's the killer's name,' Serena points out.

'Maybe it's someone Jerry knew,' my dad adds.

'Or maybe the curator had it wrong,' I say.

But as all three of us sit there, crowded around the table and lost amid what feels like another dead end, my father freezes.

'I don't think the curator had it wrong,' he announces. His voice is still flying, but as he motions to the art, his mouth falls open and he shakes his head. Forget excitement. He's back to fear. 'Oh, God. This is— Serena, this is bad.'

Like before, he's staring down at the panels. But with all our sitting around, the water has now soaked through the napkin that covers them. Like before, he's the only one who sees it.

'What? What're you looking at?' she asks.

'Their symbol . . . it's their symbol. . . .'

'Whose symbol?' I ask, scanning each of the outer panels. 'The KKK?'

'Worse.'

'Who's worse?'

My father points back to the moon, but it's not until he slaps his palm against the art – like he's swatting a fly – that the water fully seeps through the napkin and I finally see what he's talking about. It's not just the letters on the flaps. It's the picture that's created when you line up the images underneath.

A flush of blood buzzes my ears. A sharp burn ignites inside my chest, as if there's someone curled inside my rib cage trying to kick his way out.

The curator had it only partly right. Jerry Siegel didn't know the exact person who killed his dad. But that didn't mean he didn't know who the killer worked for. Or who we're now up against.

Even in 1932, there was no mistaking a swastika

59

I'm not a Nazi, Ellis had told himself when he first read the diary. Yes, his grandfather's and great-grandfather's names both had been found on the officer list kept by the ITS, the International Tracing Service, which kept some of the most meticulous records of the atrocities. His grandfather even served briefly at the Wolf's Lair in East Prussia. But their allegiance was never to Hitler. Their allegiance was to Thule. Always Thule.

That's what made them Leadership.

Of course, the swastika confused the issue. Today, it was nothing more than the Nazis' symbol of death. But the swastika existed long before the Nazis, dating back over three thousand years, when it was a symbol of life, good luck, the sun, and even the spinning thunderbolts of Thor's ancient hammer to fight evil spirits.

Most important, as Ellis learned from the diaries, it wasn't Adolf Hitler who chose the swastika. Indeed, it was used years earlier, selected by the elite Germans – his great-grandfather among them – who made up the Thule Society.

From its earliest days, the elders of Thule chose their membership carefully from German aristocracy. Yes, they began as occultists, which usually brings to mind crazies in long cloaks. But the original Thule members – the Leadership – knew there was nothing crazy about the quest for the secrets and origins of the universe.

Thule, after all, meant 'the mystic center' and 'God's order.' And in ancient times, Ultima Thule – *the farthest land* – was rumored to be a secret island, well-known as the true home of a long-lost and supremely powerful German race. The Leadership was committed to bringing that power back.

It was their research into early archaeology that led to the discovery of so many of the ancient totems. But their true goal was always the all-important one: the priceless find that the Coptic monks had carried all the way from Egypt. It was the Leadership's mastery of runic symbols that let them decipher the messages the monks had left behind – and sent them to the rock art site in Sweden, to the cave covered with the carved lines and circles. The Leadership weren't the only ones. The Russians and Americans were on the trail, too. At the turn of the century, this was the time when so many of the totems were tracked by governments and hidden in their museums. But at the cave – in April 1900 – the Thules were unquestionably first.

Back then, lesser men would've focused on the scenes of the animals and warriors that were carved on the walls. The Thules knew better. When they saw the ancient carving of the man with the raised arms – the rune known as 'the Son of God' – they knew what they'd found.

From God to Adam. From Adam to Cain. The treasured birthright that brought murder into the world. That kept men invulnerable, invincible. And that would lead them to the true ancient origins of the first Aryan race.

Ellis knew it wasn't far.

Keeping his head down as he walked through the sliding doors, Ellis headed for the reception desk, where a Hispanic woman clicked at a computer. His lower back was still on fire – he hadn't been smart in his encounter with Cal's father, hadn't expected the fury inside him. But as he reminded himself from last night, the trickster was full of surprises.

Fortunately, so was Ellis.

'I'm looking for a patient,' he said to the receptionist. 'She came in within the last hour or so. Naomi Molina.'

'Gimme one second,' the receptionist replied.

Ellis could still remember standing in the lawyer's office, how his feet felt like tree roots sinking into the earth when he first read his great-grandfather's theory. So much of it made sense. Indeed, murder is what makes us human. But the Book that Cain carried wasn't given as punishment. It was a reward. For repenting.

A gift from God.

The Russians wanted it as simple religious proof. The Americans chased it, thinking it was a weapon. But based on the runes, the Thules knew what the Coptic monks had really unearthed in Egypt – and how they survived their trip from half a world away. Cain's *Book* contained more than just a way to live. God had given him far more than that.

Maybe the monks were afraid of the power. The Leadership had no such problems. And apparently, in a lightning bolt of good fortune, neither did Mitchell Siegel.

It took years for the Leadership to recover from the massacre with the Russians. But as with a broken bone, injury and healing made it stronger. By 1917, the Thules widened their net, attracting over 250 followers. By 1918, they incorporated the ancient and powerful swastika into their coat of arms. And in 1919, they attracted the eye of a young failed painter named Adolf Hitler. A man who desperately wanted to be somebody. And who wasn't afraid of power.

Was it any surprise that *Mein Kampf* was dedicated to Thule member Dietrich Eckart? Or that Hitler credited Thule elder Dr Friedrich Krohn with designing the swastika flag that the Nazis adopted?

Under Hitler, many Thules – Heinrich Himmler and Rudolf Hess among them – were absorbed into the highest positions of the Nazi Party. But even as their political power grew, the Leadership never lost sight of what had been stolen. Or how it might be found.

In 1930, they made their first contact with a dissatisfied member of the United States' new Bureau of Investigation. By 1932, they had Mikhel Segalovich's new name and address. And today, over a century later, Ellis was finally ready to finish what his family had begun.

'You related to Ms. Molina?' the Hispanic woman asked, flipping through her clipboard.

'She's my wife,' Ellis replied.

'Exam room E. Third curtain on the right.'

It'd been well over an hour since Cal and his dad had run from the house. Ellis knew they were long gone. But Naomi was a different story. Ellis had seen the blood running down the side of her face. A wound like that needed a hospital. And if Ellis was right, finding Naomi would also help him find the Prophet. Indeed, maybe she *was* the Prophet.

It was simple math. When Cal and Naomi left the museum, there were only four people who knew that the group was headed back to the Siegel house: Cal knew. Naomi knew. Plus Lloyd and the woman. Serena. Four people. And since the Prophet knew, the Prophet had to be one of them.

All along, Ellis assumed it was the trickster: Cal's father. But when he saw the group on the stairs – when he saw

Naomi being carried by Cal . . . and her earpiece dangling downward . . . Her phone. The earpiece.

There it was.

Her earpiece.

Such a simple way for someone to overhear.

Naturally, Ellis didn't want to jump to conclusions. But if Naomi *was* reporting in – whether to stay safe or just get information – Ellis's math was wrong. There weren't just four people who knew that Cal was headed back to the Siegel house. There were five. And if that was the case, well . . . Ellis had to know: Who the hell *was* Naomi speaking to when she was talking into that earpiece?

'It's me!' a familiar female voice shouted angrily from the corner of the emergency room. 'Where the hell you been, Scotty?'

Following the sound, Ellis turned to his right and stared at the closed blue curtain that was now just a few feet in front of him. Scotty. The only other person who heard everything was Scotty. Scotty heard what was happening. Scotty knew what was coming. Scotty knew it all in advance. Like an oracle. Or a seer. Or a prophet.

'*Scotty, can you hear me? Where you been!?*' Naomi yelled.

Ellis nodded to himself.

That was a damn good question for Scotty.

60

'It's always Nazis, isn't it?' Naomi asked into her earpiece, lying flat on the gurney and trying hard not to move.

'Ma'am, can you please put down the phone?' the young nurse pleaded as he tugged on the forceps and threaded another stitch through the cut on Naomi's temple.

'I told you: federal business,' Naomi said.

'They're not Nazis,' Scotty clarified through the phone. 'Back then, they called themselves the Thule Society.'

'But you said they helped bring Hitler to power— *Ahh, that stings!*'

'Put the phone down,' the nurse again insisted as Naomi made a face.

'I don't know,' Scotty said. 'I think the Thules were after a power that wasn't necessarily political.'

'You mean this Cain book? What'd the FBI guys call it?'

'A totem,' Scotty said. 'And if it weren't so important, why spend over a century searching for it?'

Naomi closed her eyes as the nurse hooked the curved needle through her skin. 'So you think Ellis is part of these Thules as well?' she asked.

'According to the FBI, the Thules haven't been active since World War II. But that doesn't mean Ellis isn't trying to bring the band back together – especially if he thinks there's some kinda magic power that'll come from it.'

'Is that what the Bureau guys said? They used the words *magic power?*'

'To be honest, I don't think they know what to make of it. This was Germany at the height of occultism. Himmler and the Nazi leaders kept a list of *breeding cemeteries* because they were convinced that babies who were conceived in graveyards would inherit the attributes and spirits of all the German heroes buried there. Even Hitler supposedly carried around a magical mandrake root to help ward off evil. These Thules were eating a whole lot of crazy. And speaking of which: Any idea where Cal and his father ran off to?'

'Trust me, we'll get there,' Naomi said as the nurse tugged hard on his final knot. Naomi felt that one, even with the anesthetic. 'You still haven't answered my question, Scotty. What'd the FBI boys say was in Cain's so-called book?'

'Again, depends what ghost story you want to believe. One theory says that Cain carried a book that contained the location of where Abel's body is supposedly buried. Another says Adam gave his children a book with all the herbs they should never eat. There's even a theory at York Minster in northern England in one of the largest pieces of medieval stained glass in the world, where the top panel shows God holding a so-called Book of Creation. In the book it says: *Ego sum alpha et omega.* That the beginning and end of the world will come via the beginning and end of the Greek alphabet.'

'Okay, good as new,' the nurse announced.

Naomi barely noticed, still focused on Scotty. 'And the FBI boys told you all that?'

'Well . . . let's be honest . . . those requests I sent in were in *your* name. They were really just helping *you.*'

'That's fine,' she said, sitting up straight and letting her legs dangle off the gurney. 'What about Timothy? Any word yet?'

'Listen, I didn't wanna be the one to say it, but—'

'They found the body, didn't they?'

'They found a leg. Fish and Wildlife guys just called it in. It's gruesome, Naomi.'

This time, Naomi was silent.

'You okay?' Scotty asked.

'I need to call his family. I don't want them seeing this on the news. God, his poor twins. . . .'

'Suarez's already on it. First call he made. Then he called me. You've officially got your murder investigation.'

For a moment, Naomi just sat there as the nurse tied the final knot in the stitches and put some ointment on the wound. 'Scotty, put a lookout in NCIC for Cal—'

'Already done. NCIC . . . IBIS . . . I listed him as a threat to the homeland just to make sure the other agencies take a long look at his photograph.'

'I also need you to run both Cal's dad and this woman he was with. Cal called her *Serena*. Check the airline records. If she's a novice, maybe she flew under her real name.'

'So you think one of them might be this Prophet?' Scotty asked.

'Where'd you even hear that name – *the Prophet*? That from the FBI?'

'No, from you – through your earpiece when you were unconscious. Anyway, you think it's one of them?'

'I have no idea. But I'm telling you right now – to do that to Timothy – to his twins . . . I don't want these lowlifes anymore. I want *chunks* of them.'

'I assume that means Cal, too. I assume you got the bug on him?'

'Of course,' Naomi replied, reaching for the tracking device in her front pants pocket. 'I slipped it in his jacket back at the—' She patted her front pocket, then her back. The tracking device was gone. But if Cal had that . . . If he'd found the bug . . . 'Oh, don't tell me he—' Cutting herself off, she pulled the earpiece from her ear and unscrewed the small rubber tip by the microphone. No listening device there.

'Ma'am, just give me one more minute to close this,' the nurse pleaded, fighting to cover the wound with a bandage.

Undeterred and already frantic, Naomi reached for her phone.

'Nomi, what's wrong?' Scotty's voice echoed distantly from the earpiece that now sat on the gurney.

With her thumb wedged against the back of her phone, she slid open the compartment, revealing the battery, the serial number – and the small round listening device that she'd planted on Cal back at the museum.

'Sonuvabastard!' she shouted, hopping off the gurney and holding the small disk to her lips. 'I know you can hear me, Cal! I know you heard it all, you sack of turd! His *leg*!? You're letting his twins bury a leg!? Every part they find, Cal – I don't care if they have to slice open every gator's stomach – you're gonna feel the pain of every part they find!'

'Ma'am, if you don't sit down . . .' the nurse warned.

'Are you done stitching me up?' Naomi shot back as she tossed the listening device into the red biohazard trash can.

'Y-Yes.'

'Good. Thank you. Bye,' Naomi said, whipping the blue curtain sideways and storming out, the bandage barely held in place. The hallway was busy – doctors, nurses, and pushcarts buzzing in every direction – but Naomi stopped.

'Nomi!' Scotty's tiny voice squeaked from the earpiece in her hand. 'Nomi, what happened!?'

'Scotty, stop talking,' she scolded, sliding the earpiece back in place and staring out at the emergency room lobby. A tall doctor was talking to the receptionist. An Arab family was huddled in prayer. An older black woman was either sleeping or unconscious with a half-knit quilt in her lap. 'Scotty, y'know that itch in the back of your brain when you feel like you're being watched?'

'I'm sure it's nothing. Just get moving,' he said.

'I know, but the—'

'It's nothing. I understand you were close with Timothy, but don't let it make you imagine stuff,' Scotty insisted as Naomi took one last scan of the lobby. 'The only thing you have to worry about now is finding Cal and— Serena Amend.'

'Excuse me?'

'That's her name. On the flight that Cal and his dad took to Cleveland, a woman named Serena Amend sat in seat twenty-five C.'

'Thank you,' she said, stepping out into the night and realizing there was no way she'd find a cab in this neighborhood. 'Scrub her through the system, then send that name to every Cleveland rental car company. There's a LoJack tracker in their car. Those companies hate it when their stuff gets lost.'

'It's nearly ten at night. This is gonna take some time.'

'Scotty, I've got fifteen stitches running down my right temple, I feel fishing line tug through my skin every time I move my eyebrow, and I'm now wondering what I'm going to say if they ask me to speak at Timothy's funeral. Now you find me that LoJack signal, and I'll find us Cal, and this Prophet, and whatever it is those Nazis wanted in Jerry Siegel's old comic strip. Oh, and I need a cab to get to my car.'

'Don't worry, boss. Whatever you want, I'm already on it.'

61

'*His leg!? You're letting his twins bury a leg!? Every part they find, Cal – I don't care if they have to slice open every gator's stomach – you're gonna feel the pain of every part they find!*' Naomi's voice ripped through the small round speaker of the tracking device.

'Still wanna go to the cops?' my dad asks, patting me on the shoulder. 'This is *exactly* what I said would happen.'

'We need to get rid of the device,' I say as I shut the black box and pull the batteries from the back.

'You think she can trace it?' my dad asks.

'You willing to take a chance?' Before anyone can answer, I toss the tracking device into the bathroom sink and run it under water. It'll only get worse when they find the Johnsels' bodies. But even without them, Naomi's done listening to reason. The only way we're not taking this fall is if we hand her the truth, and right now there's only one way to get it.

'What about the dialogue?' Serena asks, still studying the comic book panels. 'Maybe Jerry hid something in that, too.'

'Yowzie?' my father reads from the panel. 'Yeah, that really sounds like you cracked the nuclear codes.'

'I'm serious,' Serena says. 'You heard Naomi: Mitchell Siegel supposedly kept this Cain book, or totem, or whatever the so-called murder weapon is, for himself. We know who killed him, we know what they wanted – and since they obviously didn't get it, the only question is: Where'd Mitchell hide it?'

'That doesn't mean the answer's here,' my father says, shaking his head and pointing to the wet comic panels.

'You kidding?' Serena blasts back with an anger that surprises even my dad. 'Ellis is clearly one of these Thule guys! He doesn't care who killed Mitchell Siegel. He just wants the prize. And *this*,' she adds, motioning to the four panels, 'he called it a *map*, for God's sake! Why're you being so dense?'

'I'm. Not,' my father says with the coldest of glares. 'I'm just saying, Jerry Siegel wasn't some NSA cryptanalyst. He was a high school kid who lost his dad. So no offense to the rash of movies and books, but not everything has to come in some secret code. Especially when it's staring right at us.' He jabs a thick finger against the last panel: with the boy dodging bullets on the way to the building.

184 King Street.

'I thought you said no such street existed,' I point out, taking a seat at the table and looking for myself.

'Not on our rental car map, but let's not forget, this was eighty years ago – the Cleveland suburbs were just being built. For all we know, this was one of the main thoroughfares.'

Now I'm the one shaking my head. 'No way is it that easy.'

'I agree,' Serena says, leaning over my shoulder and putting her hand on my back.

My father shoots her the kind of look that comes with divorce papers.

'What?' Serena asks, still not pulling away. She has no idea what he's mad about. But I do.

In a huff, my father grabs his coat from the bed and storms for the door.

'What'd I do? Where're you going?' she calls out.

'Front desk had a sign for free Internet,' my dad explains. 'There's gotta be old Cleveland maps online.'

Before we can argue, my phone rings. Caller ID tells me who it is. I need this call. But I don't take my eyes off my father.

'Want me to come?' Serena asks him.

'Stay with him,' my dad shoots back. 'You're apparently getting good at it.'

As the door slams, I flip open my phone and lean my elbows against the round table. The way we've been running, exhaustion is finally setting in.

'Tell me that message wasn't bullcrap,' Roosevelt says, his voice galloping through my phone. 'The Book of *Truth?* For real?'

Who is it? Serena asks with a glance.

Roosevelt, I mouth back as she takes the seat next to me and leans in to share the ear of my phone.

I could push back and chase her away. Roosevelt would tell me to do exactly that.

I tilt the phone slightly, and we both listen in.

'Cal, what you found . . . all the theories . . .' Roosevelt says. 'We had it so wrong. Don't you see? If this's really a Book of Truth . . . this wasn't penance for Cain . . . no . . . it *truly was* God's reward.'

'Y'mean all those secrets of earthly knowledge you were talking about?'

'Forget earthly knowledge. This secret . . . look at the name: the Book of—' He's so excited, he can barely get the words out. 'It's a Book of *Truth*, Cal. In Hebrew, "truth" is *emet*, one of the most mystical words in the language. Writing that word was how the Golem was brought to life – it's how—'

'It's ten o'clock, Roosevelt. I don't care. Just tell me what's inside.'

He takes a deep breath, fighting to calm down. I keep forgetting. As much as I'm trying to save my rear, Roosevelt's the one coming face-to-face with his faith.

'Remember when we talked about the Mark of Cain?' he finally asks. 'How I said some people thought Cain was immortal and that God let him live forever? Well, what if that's what's actually in the book?'

'The truth about his immortality?'

'No. The secret to it,' Roosevelt says, his voice more serious than ever. 'In the Bible, Cain never died. What if the Book of Truth was his instruction manual?'

Twelve hours ago, I would've laughed out loud. But as I look down at the comic book panel with the hidden ancient Nazi group symbol, and the young boy clutching a book and running for his life . . .

'Does 184 King Street mean anything to you?' I ask.

'As an address?'

'As anything: 184 King Street . . . 184 kings on a street . . . Anything Cain-like come to mind?'

'I'll look it up, but even without it . . . Cal, if this is really the Book of Truth . . . I think you're close, Cal! I can feel it!'

'I'll be sure to tell Ellis that the next time he sends the hound of hell at us.'

'Forget Ellis. You're now— I know you think I'm nuts, but this is what you're meant for, Cal. We all have higher callings. All of us. It's no different than Jerry Siegel. We think Superman was his calling, but in reality it was watching over his father, protecting this gift . . . this book. It's the same with you, Cal. Same calling. Protect the gift.'

'Roosevelt, I appreciate the faith, but we're not getting anything unless you start figuring out King Street.'

'That's fine. I'm on it. But take strength from this, Cal. You're close. Close to something far bigger than most people will ever see.'

As he hangs up the phone, I try my best to ride his excitement, but after a full day of running and dodging and fighting, my shoulders plummet. Next to me, Serena does the opposite. I'm still leaning on the motel's round table. She hops up, on a rocket of newfound adrenaline.

'He's right, Calvin. You see that, don't you?'

'I don't know – for me, religion's always been more of an acquired taste.'

'This isn't religion. This is how life works – the hunches you have that tell you to not walk down a certain alleyway . . . or to stay with you and your dad instead of cowering in a hotel . . . that feeling in your belly that tells you someone you love is in danger – we have to have a certain trust in the universe.'

'I hear you. And for once, I really am trying to believe it. But the universe screwed me a big one.'

'But now it's trying to make amends. These are the

divine patterns I told you about. You still think it's a co-incidence you found your dad in that park? Or that I got on that plane? There are no accidents! Ooooh, I feel *fantastic!*' she insists, reaching both arms straight up, fingers fully extended, in some yoga/praise-the-Maker pose.

It'd be so easy to make fun, but as I watch her . . . 'Serena, I'm trying to be sulky and pessimistic here.'

'You can't,' she insists, her arms still in the air as she rises up, eyes wide, on her tiptoes. 'I'm happy. Love and hate can't occupy the same space.'

I laugh at that one. 'Obviously, you haven't seen me with my father.'

'I've seen. I've watched how you struggle, Calvin. But I can also tell you're trying to decide. Love or hate. Eventually, we all need to choose.'

When I look away, she steps toward me and reaches out, gripping my shoulder. She's trying to be reassuring, to shake me awake. But in the euphoria of the moment, she pulls me forward and I'm suddenly a half-step too close. It's an odd few seconds, crossing into her personal space.

I'm about to step back, but as I look down at her, I find myself planted right where I am. Serena would credit my stasis to listening to your soul or finding divine patterns.

But there's something to be said about plain old euphoria.

We both slowly lean in.

'N-No . . . we're not supposed to,' she says, pulling back. 'I swear, I – I – I—' She looks down and away. The way her head shakes back and forth, she feels awful. Like she overstepped some unmarked boundary.

But all I'm really focused on is that her hand is still on my shoulder. It skates down my arm, like a skier, until her fingertips rest on my forearm. But she never lets go.

I stare right at her. I'm smarter than this. I am. I should know better. And I do. But that doesn't mean I'm stopping.

We move even closer and her lips press against mine. The warmth burns in such a good way.

There's a whispering voice outside. Then it goes silent.

'—why call it free Internet if it's not even . . . *free*?' my dad says as the motel door bursts open.

Serena and I jump backward, like two high school kids being caught. We're not nearly fast enough.

My dad stands at the door, frozen.

'We're not— This isn't—' I wave my hands, unable to get the words out.

'Lloyd, w-we have a theory on the Book,' Serena says, sounding truly concerned.

My father still hasn't moved. He stands in the open door, staring at us as the wind and bits of snow dive into the room.

'Dad . . .'

'I'm perfect,' he says flatly. The door slams shut behind him. His eyes are still on us, but his focus has shifted, as if he's looking at something that's moved farther away.

On the plane ride here, Serena swore they weren't together. Otherwise I wouldn't have kissed her, I tell myself, trying hard to believe it.

My dad takes a deep breath through his nose. His big Adam's apple moves just slightly. 'I have good news about the address,' he blurts.

'Lloyd, I just want you to know . . .' Serena begins.

'Stop. It's fine. I promise you. It's fine,' he repeats, revealing an *I'm okay* grin and approaching the comic strip. He puts a hand on my back and adds a strong, single pat as we turn back to the table. 'Now, you wanna hear where we can find 184 King Street or not?'

Bouncing on the balls of her feet, Serena's so excited that I barely notice as she slides up next to me.

My dad smiles even wider.

But every time I turn away, I swear I feel him painting a bull's-eye on the back of my head.

62

'It's too early. They're not even open,' Serena says, stuffing her hands in her winter coat (mine, not my dad's) and running to keep up as we rush through the bottom floor of the parking garage.

'It's not too early,' my dad insists, leading the way. From the moment we woke up this morning, he hasn't said a word about last night. I should be thankful. I'm not. We got four Band-Aids to close his wound, and he hasn't mentioned anything about that, either. As all three of us know, some things can't be fixed by a Band-Aid.

'C'mon, Calvin – *keep up!*' he hisses, ignoring all the signs for PATIENT ENTRANCE and PHYSICIAN PARKING. Instead, he heads in the opposite direction of the arrows, cuts between two cars, and takes us outside, where the sun is just up, revealing a baby blue sky, half a dozen American flags, and a red-and-white sign that says, 'Happy Holidays to Our Vets!'

The parking garage connects to Cleveland's largest Veterans Administration hospital. For us, it's the best and closest place to keep our rental car out of sight. But we're still not completely safe.

As we reach the end of the block, I glance over my shoulder. The only one there is Serena.

'What?' she asks, following my gaze and looking over her own shoulder. 'What're you doing?'

'Trusting in the universe,' I say as I study the parking garage and check each level. Then I check again.

'No one's there,' my dad insists.

I check the garage a third time. Maybe it's just nerves, but ever since we left the motel—

'If Naomi were here, we'd already be in handcuffs,' my dad points out.

He's right. But Serena wasn't wrong yesterday. The human body can sense when danger's nearby. It knows it. Just like I know when I'm being followed.

'Let's just get inside,' Serena says, grabbing my hand and tugging me forward. 'Do we know which building it is?' she asks my dad.

As we turn the corner, my dad doesn't answer. He doesn't have to. There's only one building in sight: the spare 1960s-ugly structure that's home to Ohio's oldest and largest historical society.

'You sure they have it?' Serena asks as we dart across the street and head for the building's wide glass doors.

'According to their online catalog, it's in here,' my father says.

A small sign out front tells us the building doesn't open for another hour. But inside, a young janitor with a mop bucket and music earbuds proves otherwise.

It takes two taps on the glass to get his attention.

'We open at nine!' he calls back.

'No. You don't,' I tell him, pulling out the federal ID Timothy gave me and slapping it against the glass. As with the guard at the port, that's all the janitor needs.

With the turn of a key and a low *thunk*, the door opens, bathing us with warm air as we hop inside. I stare over my shoulder as we kick flecks of wet snow onto the wide welcome mat. The streets are empty. No one's there. But it's not until I turn around that I finally see exactly where we've run to.

The wide beige room has a World War II biplane hanging from the ceiling. Across the floor, there're at least a dozen antique cars, including, according to a sign, a 1898 Winton Phaeton on loan from the Smithsonian. On the left, I see brochures and a donation box for the Crawford Auto-Aviation Museum.

'I thought this was a library,' my father says.

'We all share the building. Library's down the hall, just past the gift shop,' the janitor explains as we take off. 'By the way,' he calls out behind us, 'welcome to the Western Reserve Historical Society!'

Two minutes later, the long narrow hall descends and winds around to a set of turnstiles that dumps us into a tall, breathtaking reading room filled with shelf after shelf stacked with volumes of old books.

'Did Jacobs leave that door open again?' a lean thirty-something with an argyle sweater asks on our left. He's handsome, with crisp brown eyes, a pointy goatee, and (this could be a winner) a gold cross hanging from his neck. According to his name tag, he's 'Michael Johnson – Librarian.' 'Sorry – we don't open till nine,' he says.

I flash the ID, stepping close enough so he can read it. 'How'd you like to help your government?'

63

'They're wrong,' Naomi said into her earpiece as she eased the steering wheel to the right and struggled to leave the three-lane roundabout that was filled with early morning traffic.

'Nomi, I know you had a head injury, but listen to me: Satellites aren't wrong,' Scotty replied in her ear. 'People are wrong. Rental car companies are wrong. But LoJack tracking systems hidden in some secret spot below a rental car? Never wrong.'

With a long honk of her horn, Naomi tried shoving her way past a silver minivan, but the van wouldn't budge. *'You think I don't know the hell of morning carpool!?'* Naomi screamed through her closed window. Ignoring her, the driver of the minivan pretended to scratch her head while giving Naomi the finger.

'I hope your kid has disciplinary problems!' Naomi shouted back, now making her second lap around the roundabout.

'Nomi, you need to calm down.'

'This *is* calm,' she said as the VA hospital once again appeared in front of her. 'I'm just saying: Why would Cal be here? They had full access to a hospital when they dropped me off last night.'

'Maybe something happened. Maybe one of them got hurt.'

'Yeah, but a VA hospital? Cal . . . Cal's father . . . neither of them was military. Something's not right.'

'Just head for the parking garage around back. Based on the records and their LoJack signal, you're looking for a white Pontiac parked near the southeast corner stairwell.'

Eventually exiting the roundabout at East Boulevard, Naomi passed the VA hospital on her left and followed the signs for the parking garage around back. But just as she made the turn, she noticed, out of her passenger-side window, the wide set of short sandstone and taller red-brick buildings that overlooked the hospital's parking garage . . . exactly at the southeast corner.

'Scotty, you looking at a map?'

'With a little blinking LoJack logo on it.'

'Fine. Tell me what those buildings are across the street from the VA.'

'Looks like . . . one's an auto museum, there's an Ohio historical society, plus a pretty big library.'

The car bucked and bumped as Naomi climbed over the speed bumps in the VA's parking garage. 'What kinda library?' she asked, peering in her rearview.

'You see something?' Scotty asked.

'Not yet. But it makes a damn lot more sense than a VA hospital.'

Half a block back, as Ellis drove past the hospital, he studied the taillights on Naomi's car, then tapped his own brakes to make sure he stayed far enough away. To be safe, he kept a strong hand on Benoni in the passenger seat, scratching her neck just to ensure she kept her head down. Yesterday, he lost so much by listening to the Prophet . . . by not trusting himself. The bloody red spot in his right eye – the result of a broken blood vessel from the fall through the window – was a reminder of that. But as he'd realized when Naomi ran out of the hospital last night, there was no need for him to attack, or threaten, or do anything else to scare her away.

To be moving this early, Cal had cracked the Map. The Book was close. And since Naomi was so much faster than the Judge – as long as she was doing her job, as long as she had their LoJack signal, Ellis was about to get a whole lot closer.

64

According to their Web site, even when it was founded back in 1867, the Western Reserve Historical Society has never been just an Ohio library. It's a storehouse and research center dedicated to documenting and preserving over twenty million items – from the very first area phone books, to old wills, telegrams, birth certificates, even naturalization papers – that trace the earliest days of the state. They also have a hell of a map collection.

Not that it's doing us any good.

'We're missing something,' my dad insists. 'We have to be missing something.'

'What's to miss?' asks the librarian with the pointy goatee, motioning at the wide mahogany reference table that's now lost under the sea of maps, atlases, and original city plats. 'I even pulled the guides from when Ohio was still owned by Connecticut. Trust me on this: King Avenue, King Court, Kings Highway, even King's Cross back during the late 1800s. But near as I can tell, we've never had a King Street.'

'And this map here,' I say, leaning both elbows on the table and scanning a small yellowed foldout entitled *Official Vest Pocket Street Guide of Cleveland*. 'This is from 1932, right?'

'Thirty-one or thirty-two,' the librarian says, nodding as Serena reads over my shoulder. She knows what I'm looking for: This is exactly what Jerry Siegel's hometown looked like when his father was shot. But according to the map, still no 184 King Street.

'Maybe it's not an address,' Serena says.

'What else would it be?' my father asks.

'I don't know. Maybe it's someone's name. Martin Luther King. Larry King. A famous King.'

'King James,' the librarian blurts.

'Y'mean like the Bible?' I ask.

'Actually, I was talking about LeBron,' the librarian laughs. We all stare at him blankly. 'Y'know, in basketball? The Cavs?' We still stare. 'You're not from Ohio, are you?' he asks.

'Wait . . . go back to the Bible,' my father says. 'There's a section called Kings, right? Maybe the numbers . . .'

'184 King Street,' Serena says, quickly hopping aboard. 'Kings, chapter 18, verse 4.'

'Or chapter 1, verse 84,' my father says, his voice already quickening. He searches around, glancing at the rows of books. 'You got a Bible handy?' he asks the librarian.

The librarian grins. 'You kidding? We got three thousand of 'em.'

As Pointy Goatee goes to fish one from the reference desk, there's a metal *kuh-kuunk* behind us. I jump at the sound. Through the turnstile, a young, petite woman with a round face unzips her long, dirty-white winter coat and reveals stylish pink reading glasses around her neck.

'Jacobs left the door open again?' she asks in a southern accent that's well past annoyed.

'They're with me,' Pointy Goatee calls out, approaching the woman and giving her a quick kiss. 'My wife,' he explains, turning our way as she hands him one of the two coffees she's carrying.

My dad and Serena force hello smiles. I don't. It's nearly nine a.m. If Naomi's doing her job, our faces are minutes away from showing up on the local morning news. We've already been here too long.

'Take a breath,' Serena says, still standing behind me and scratching my shoulder. My father works hard pretending not to notice.

'Okay, so 1 Kings, chapter 18, verse 4,' the librarian announces as he puts his reading glasses to use. '*Obadiah took a hundred prophets, and hid them fifty in a cave, and fed them with bread and water*. That sound like anything familiar?'

I look at my father. He's looking at Serena. The word *Prophet*, plus a *cave*, where Mitchell Siegel supposedly found the Book of Truth. There's no ignoring the coincidence. But even with that, it still means nothing.

'I don't think that's it,' my father says, trying hard to keep it calm. But he's right. Just another dead end.

'What y'all working on, anyway?' Pink Glasses asks as she approaches the table, warming her hands around her cup of coffee.

'184 King Street. Mean anything important to you?' her husband asks.

'I know King *Avenue*,' she says.

'Nope. King Street.'

She shakes her head. 'It's funny, though – almost sounds like the vault.'

We all turn toward her. 'What vault?' I ask.

'Our vault – for our rare book collection,' she begins.

'Y'know, I never thought of those,' her husband interrupts. 'That's not a bad—'

'Just let her say it!' my father insists. I shoot him a look to cool down.

'It's not—These days, we're on the Library of Congress system,' she explains, 'but in the early 1900s, back before Dewey decimal was widely accepted, we used to file rare book collections under the names of big donors.'

'This was way before everyone wanted their name on a brass plaque,' her husband points out.

'Exactly. So when the Silver family donated all their correspondence with President Garfield, they got a whole section in the rare book room with call numbers *1.0.0* Silv . . . *1.0.1* Silv . . . *1.0.2* Silv. Paula and Mark Cook got *1.0.0* Cook. And I think – I could be wrong – but I think the Kingston family, when they donated the glass windows at the front of the building, got a section starting with *1.0.0* King.'

'So there very well could be a *1.8.4* King as a call number in your collection,' my father says.

'Only way to find is to seek,' her husband replies, pushing back from the table, heading behind the reference desk, and flicking on a computer terminal marked 'Internal Catalog.' On our right, the turnstile again *kuh-kuunk*s as the first library visitor – a bald man with Buddy Holly glasses – arrives.

'Morning, June. Morning, Mike,' he calls out, headed to the magazine section. Serena shoots me a look. Time is, most definitely, not on our side.

'Is there any way we can speed this up?' I ask.

Behind the desk, the husband is clicking at the keyboard and humming the theme to *Jeopardy!*

'Junebug, how is it possible to always be right?' he announces as a wide smile takes his face. 'There most definitely is a King collection. And when you put in *1.8.4* as the call number . . .' He studies the screen. 'Oh, that's curious . . .'

'*What?*' I blurt as the turnstile delivers yet another visitor.

'Back then, they used to keep such meticulous records for the rare books. Anyway, it was filed with the Kingston family because they had a spectacular Russian book collection. But when you look at the actual path of ownership . . .' He turns to us, and his gold cross sways from his neck. 'According to these records, *1.8.4* King was a book donated by someone named Jerry Siegel.'

65

'Where'sthevault? Isthebooktherenow? Canwegoseeit?' my dad, Serena, and I all ask simultaneously.

The husband and wife librarians look at each other. 'Pretty important case you're working on, huh?' the husband asks.

'Y'all are law enforcement?' the wife adds, suddenly excited. 'Ooh, is this gonna be on the news?'

'Can we just see the book?' I plead.

'Sure, let me just—' The husband reads from the screen. 'It's a big one, too. Nearly six hundred pages.'

'What is it, *Moby-Dick*?' my father asks.

'No – but back to your Scripture – it *is* a Bible. A Hebrew one. Published 1875 by M. R. Romma. Says here "Russian." Poor condition. This book took a hell of a beating.'

'His father's Bible,' I whisper to myself.

'You think this is *it*?' Serena asks, referring to Cain's murder weapon.

'If it is – and he thought people were after it – maybe he donated it here to keep it safe,' I say as Serena nods.

'I'm confused,' says the wife librarian. 'Why would someone be after a Bible?'

'We're not exactly sure yet,' my father interrupts, doing his best to downplay. We've already got enough competition.

'Oh, and this is great,' the husband adds. 'Says here the donor claimed the book was bound in . . . ready for this? . . . human skin.'

'Barf,' Serena says.

'I've heard of that,' his wife adds. 'There was a seminar on it at the ALA last year. Back in the seventeenth century, they used to bind private anatomy books with skin,' she explains. 'People are more twisted than people think.'

'Regardless, according to this, our reference team back then said that if it was anything, it was sheepskin or just cheap leather. They probably put it in Special Collections just to keep him happy.' Turning to us, he adds, 'Everyone thinks their old books came straight from Gutenberg's press. But if you tell 'em otherwise, they won't donate the next year.'

Serena again tosses them a polite grin. But as my dad and I exchange glances, it's clear what he's thinking. According to the legends, Cain killed Abel with a book. According to the FBI, Jerry's father had it. Whatever's inside this skin book, it can't be just a Russian Bible.

There's a noise on our left. The turnstile again hiccups, and a new library visitor passes by us at the reference desk, heading for the microfiche room. None of us says a word until he leaves.

'We'd like to see the book now,' my dad insists.

'Yeah . . . no . . . that's the pickle, isn't it?' the husband replies, scanning the screen. 'From what I can tell, it's no longer part of our collection.'

'Someone checked it out?' Serena asks.

'Kinda.'

'What's *kinda*?' I ask.

The librarian pauses, rechecking the screen. I lean my

chest against the tall reference desk, squinting to read. He's got the cursor on a text box that says:

DEACCESSIONED
7/27/98

'Deaccessioned?' my father asks. To my surprise, he's back behind the reference desk, reading over the shoulder of the librarian. He's swaying in place, even more nervous than the night I first found him. It's not just from the computer. He's now got a full view of the security monitors and cameras that overlook the various entrances to the building. He can see who's coming.

'It means you gave it away, doesn't it?' Serena asks, just as anxious.

'That's part of running a library,' the husband explains, taking off his glasses. 'Even with our offsite storage, there's only so many copies of *Harry Potter* we need.'

'This isn't *Harry Potter* – it's a Russian Bible from the turn of the century,' my dad says. 'How many of those can you possibly have?'

'Around here? You know how big the Jewish population used to be in this area? When those generations die, where do you think the kids give all their books? I told you, we've got thousands of Bibles. So if we had this old Russian one and then someone brought in a brand-new one, or even a few similar ones . . . Every year we have to pare down the collection. And it sounds like this copy was already in terrible condition.'

'So you destroyed it?' Serena asks in clear panic.

'Destroyed? We're a historical society – no, never destroy,' he explains. 'Old books get donated: to hospitals, churches, we used to do this big event with one of the local nursing homes.'

'Is there any record where this one went?' I ask.

He pauses to think about it, his fingertips flicking his goatee. 'Y'know, that's a fair question. Sometimes these older entries – especially the ones that used to be in the card catalog . . .' His fingers tap at the keyboard, and a new window opens on-screen.

He leans in to read it. 'Ahh, yeah – that makes sense for a book like this, and that's just when it opened.'

'Please just tell us where the book is now,' my father demands, still eyeing the views from the security cameras.

'You have to understand, most places won't accept old Bibles. But there's one place that goes through them like holy water.' With a kick of his foot, the librarian rolls backward in his chair and let's us see the destination for ourselves.

O.S.P.

'I don't get it,' I say.

'Trust me, you don't want to,' the librarian warns. 'But your Jerry Siegel book? From what it says here, in 1998, it became the official property of the Ohio State Penitentiary.'

'It's in a prison?' Serena asks.

I wait for my father's reaction, but he's far too busy staring at the security monitors – and the familiar brown-haired woman who's just appeared on-screen. Naomi's here. Right outside the building.

66

Watching from the far corner of the parking garage, even Ellis had to admit he was impressed. From the moment Naomi spotted Cal's rental car, she didn't waste a second – popping its locks, sliding inside, and picking through the interior with the speed of a veteran thief.

From what she was saying to Scotty, it was the small, foldout rental car map that gave them away. There was a tiny black dot – from the point of a pen – on the library across the street. The Historical Society. No question, Cal's destination.

Naomi went racing down the nearby stairwell, not once checking behind her, so it was easy for Ellis to follow. That was the problem with being desperate. It always made you sloppy.

And now, as Ellis reached the bottom steps and the cold spun like a tornado up the stairwell, Naomi was halfway across the street. Approaching the Historical Society building, she paused and looked up. Cameras, Ellis realized.

Naomi didn't care. With a tug of the glass doors, she disappeared inside. Ellis waited a moment, then stepped out casually across the snow-lined street. No reason to run, he reasoned as he pulled out the jet injector. Everyone was finally in the same place. Both Cal and Naomi . . . he still owed them for what they did to Benoni.

Climbing the few front steps, Ellis kept his head down as he passed the camera, then gave his own sharp tug to the front glass door, which swung open and revealed a burst of heated air, dozens of antique cars, and—

The punch hit Ellis in the throat, nearly taking his head off. He stumbled back, falling to one knee. The next shot came from a kick, cracking him in the knuckles and sending his jet injector crashing to the marble floor, the vial of hemlock spilling everywhere.

'*You think I'm a schmuck!?*' Naomi exploded, her arm cocked back as she rushed forward and again swung down in full fury.

Ellis could taste the sour-sweet blood bubble at the back of his throat. He was still down on one knee. But this time he was ready.

And so was Naomi.

They each hit hard. With a thunderclap, a single shot rang out, booming and vibrating through the marble hallways.

Then it was over.

67

'Was that a gunshot?' Pointy Goatee asked.

'Call the police,' his wife snapped.

'It was a gunshot, wasn't it?'

'Just call them! Now!'

There was a loud scream in the distance, echoing down the long hallway.

'*Now!*' she insisted as her husband darted to the phone at the reference desk.

'Was that an explosion?' asked one of the library visitors, sticking his head out of the microfiche room.

'We're calling the police right—'

'—all okay! It's under control!' a voice yelled from the hallway. 'Everything's okay!'

In mid-dial, Pointy Goatee stared past the turnstiles as a set of footsteps grew increasingly louder. But it wasn't until he saw the badge that he finally took a breath.

'Police! Relax! You're all safe!' Ellis announced authoritatively, striding through the turnstile and making sure they got a good look at his uniform. 'Sir, you can put down the phone, please. I'm here. There's nothing to worry about.'

The librarian slid the phone back to its cradle, staring at the blood that ran down from Ellis's nose.

'Thank you,' Ellis said, wiping it away with the back of

his thumb as he scanned the library. 'Now perhaps you can help with one last thing: I'm wondering if you've seen my friends.'

68

There was no pain. No burning. She didn't feel anything. Not at first.

Indeed, as Naomi lay flat on her back, the blood puddle swelling below her, she simply stared up at the bottom of the World War II biplane that was hanging from the ceiling. She was seeing double now. Two. Two biplanes. Lucas . . . her son . . . Lucas would like those.

On her far right, down the hallway, there was screaming and panicking. Then another gunshot.

Naomi didn't hear it. The world was muffled – her vision narrowed – like sitting in the bottom of a well and looking up, up, up. Wow. Two biplanes. Lucas would like those.

And then . . .

Ow.

On the back of her shoulder. A mosquito bite.

No, not a mosquito bite. It was burning.

'—omi! Nomi, you okay!?' a frantic voice screamed in her ear.

'S-Scotty? Where—? Why're you yelling at me?'

'I heard a gunshot! You okay!?'

'I'm fine,' she stuttered, trying to raise her head and finally seeing the puddle below her. 'I got— Is that my blood?'

'I think you were shot. *Don't move*, Nomi! I think Ellis shot you.'

'I broke his nose,' she said as the pain in her shoulder sent an electrical fire down her arm. 'He pulled— He had another gun. A real one.'

'Don't move! Ambulance is on the way.'

'No, that's not . . . aaahh . . . *he shot me!*' she said, gripping her shoulder as tears of pain flooded her eyes. The wound was wet and mushy, pulsing with its own beat. 'That's two hospital visits in twelve hours. How cliché,' she added, her voice wilting. 'I – I broke his nose.'

'Nomi, don't pass out on me.'

She shook her head wildly, refusing to fade. 'He's still . . . Ellis is up the hallway . . . and Cal . . . if he heard the gunshot . . . Cal's going for his car. The LoJack. Check his car.'

'Already did,' Scotty promised. 'He's still there.'

'Look again,' Naomi grunted, lying on her back and using her heel to shove herself across the floor. A wide streak of blood trailed along from the puddle. But at the wall, she fought hard to sit up straight. Straight. Better to get her head up. And to get a look through the glass doors.

Outside, across the street, Cal's white rental car flew from the mouth of the parking garage, its tires screaming as it fishtailed to the right and disappeared up the block.

'Knew he'd go for his car,' Naomi whispered, gritting her teeth and fighting to keep her head up.

'Nomi, Cal's moving! They're definitely moving!'

'G-Good,' she muttered. 'Call in state, federal . . . tell 'em you want helicopters, fighter jets . . . bring damn tanks if they have them. Then call my son. Tell him I'll be okay.'

69

Cal's white rental car was moving quickly – not too quickly, no reason to stand out – as it dashed down the final empty stretches of Martin Luther King Jr. Drive and headed toward the entrance ramp for I-90 that was up ahead.

Thankfully, there still weren't any nearby sirens or much traffic. In fact, as the car blew past the empty bus stops in the Siegels' old neighborhood, it became abundantly clear that it was one of the only cars on the street.

It wasn't hard to figure out why.

'This is not good.'

Already racing up the on-ramp, the white Pontiac followed the corkscrew and climbed toward the inter-state . . .

. . . where a barricade of half a dozen police cars, motorcycles, and unmarked federal vehicles were blocking the way and at least a dozen state troopers and other agents were ducked down with their guns drawn.

'Freeze or we *will* shoot you!' one of them barked through a megaphone.

The rental car screeched to a stop just as a silver-and-blue police helicopter rose straight up, appearing from nowhere.

'Out of the vehicle! You're under arrest!' a speaker in the helicopter blasted from the sky as the ground agents swarmed the rental car, guns still drawn. Within seconds,

they tore open all four doors, searching for Cal and his father.

But the only person inside was the light-skinned black woman sitting behind the steering wheel.

'I'm sorry. I give up,' Serena said as she held up her hands in surrender.

'*Out!*' yelled one of the state troopers, yanking her from the car.

'Whattya mean, they're gone?' a female voice squawked through a nearby walkie-talkie. 'Christ on a crutch, don't you see what he—? *Get someone back to that parking garage! Now!*'

'Is that Naomi? Is she okay?' Serena asked, meaning every word.

'Let me be honest with you,' the state trooper said as he clamped handcuffs around Serena's wrists. 'You've got far bigger things you need to be worrying about.'

70

It was easy for us to swipe the librarian's keys. It was even easier to find the librarian's car (parked right in front, best spot at the library, and hopefully won't be missed until the end of the day) and zip away in the opposite direction from Serena. The early bird gets the worm, but the smart bird is the one who knows the value of a good distraction. Still, as I grab yet another glance in the rearview, only the fool bird would think we were home free.

'Will you relax? They have no idea where we are,' my father tweet-tweets from the passenger seat as we follow I-80 out of the city. We've been driving for nearly forty minutes, and it's scary how fast billboards and morning traffic have given way to farmland and pristine forests. From the passing signs, we're deep in Cuyahoga Valley National Park, which is dotted with pine trees and layered in fine white snow imported directly from a Christmas card.

'We shouldn't have left Serena like that,' I tell him.

'I thought you didn't trust her.'

'That's not—' I cut myself off. 'I trust her.'

'Why? Because you kissed her, or because she offered to run interference with Naomi?'

I again look in the rearview. There's no one in sight. 'You're still mad about the kiss, aren't you?'

My father laughs to himself, staring straight out the front window. 'I was never in this for a kiss, Calvin.'

It's a beautiful response. Plus it deflects from Serena and the kiss and all the other heavy baggage we've been trying to hide in our respective overheads. In fact, when you add in the huge frozen lake and the snow-misted trees on our left, it's damn near the perfect father-son moment.

'Lloyd, are you the Prophet?' I blurt.

'Pardon?'

'It's not an attack. I just need to— Everywhere we've been – everything that's happened – you're never surprised. When we found the coffin, you went right for the comic. When we got here, you knew how to find the Siegel house. When we got to the Siegel house, you knew how to find that hole in the wallpaper.'

'And that makes me the enemy?'

I bite my lower lip and take one of Serena's deep, cleansing breaths. It doesn't help. 'I heard you talking, Lloyd. You were whispering outside the museum . . . then again back at the motel room. Every time we go somewhere, you disappear for a few minutes, and then right after that – ka-pow – Ellis somehow magically knows where we are.'

'I'd never do that to you.'

'Then who were you talking to?'

'Calvin, I don't even have a phone.'

'Cal. I'm Cal. And that wasn't the question. Who. Were. You. Talking. To?'

He doesn't answer.

'Aw, jeez, I knew this was—'

'Your mom,' he says softly. 'I was talking to— I was talking to Mom.'

'W-Wha?'

'Sometimes – I don't know – when things get hard . . .' He stops and turns to me. 'You don't talk to her sometimes?'

My thumbnail picks at the cruise control buttons on the steering wheel. I see him looking at me, but this time I'm the one staring straight ahead. Beads of sweat rise up, filling my brow. 'Sometimes,' I whisper. 'Usually on her birthday. And sometimes on mine.'

'See, no – don't save it for birthdays. She's there, Calvin. I believe it. You talk, and she's there. She'll always be there for you.'

The car rumbles across a tall bridge that overlooks one of the most breathtaking and deepest valleys I've ever seen, with just the tops of the pine trees peeking through the snow. I usually hate heights. The falls are too long.

'How is she?' I finally ask.

'I don't—?'

'Mom. You speak to her, right? How is she?'

My father thinks about this one. He turns away, pretending to stare out his passenger window. But I see his watery eyes – and his smile – in the reflection. 'She's better.'

For a moment, we just sit there, listening to the *dmm dmm dmm* as the car's tires churn across the long bridge.

'Y'know, I pushed her,' my dad eventually says, still staring out his window. 'On that final night – the lawyers said I just tapped her . . . that she slipped on the mayo – but I pushed her. I remember pushing her. Hard.'

I nod, more to myself. 'I know. I saw it,' I tell him. Below us, there's a frozen waterfall – long, captured shards of ice frozen in midfall. Like they'll never hit bottom. 'Still didn't mean you had to run away.'

'Sure it did.'

I pause at this, for the first time wondering if he might be right. 'Even still . . . if I hadn't walked in – if she hadn't turned to me – I'm the only reason she didn't see it coming.'

The *dmm dmm dmm* flattens and disappears as we leave the bridge. The world has never been more silent.

'Calvin, she forgives you,' my dad insists.

They're just words – stupid, empty words – but the tears quickly well in my eyes.

'I – I know,' I say, wiping them away. 'She forgives you, too.'

He tightens his jaw, unable to face me. His reflection in the passenger window nods a thank-you. He's fighting to hold it together.

'So you really talk to her that much?' I ask.

'Cal, when Jerry Siegel died in 1996, half his ashes were put in a copper urn, and the rest were put in a hollowed-out set of fake books with all of Jerry's creations on the spine – Superman, Clark Kent, Lois Lane – which his wife is saving for whenever Cleveland decides to take that synagogue's exhibit and build a proper Superman museum. That way he can be with his fans forever.'

'Who told you that?'

'It was in the pamphlet Serena got from the exhibit. The point is, as death gets closer – it's no different than this Book of Truth – what's so wrong with wanting someone you love to live forever?'

Following the curves in the road, I tug the wheel to the right, sending both my dad and myself leaning to the left. For the first time since we've been together, I've got no reason to argue.

Within ten minutes, we're out of the park as the powdered pine trees are once again replaced by fast-food signs, empty rest stops, and far too many billboards for local massage parlors. The neighborhood's sinking quickly.

My dad doesn't care. He's still lost in thought and wiping his eyes. But even that fades as we leave the exit and the local two-lane road eventually reveals our destination: a four-story slablike brick building filled with hundreds of narrow, vertically slit windows.

Of course there's no welcome sign. They don't welcome anyone at the Ohio State Penitentiary. But that doesn't mean they can keep us out.

71

'If you really missed us that bad, you coulda just sent us a card,' the young nurse said to Naomi as he cut away the dead gray skin from the bullet wound in her shoulder.

'That's funny,' Naomi replied, using her free hand to dial a number on her phone. 'You should be on *M★A★S★H*.'

'What's *M★A★S★H*?' the nurse asked.

Naomi looked up, staring at him. 'Oh, God – you're not even twenty, are you?'

The sharp ring of Naomi's phone interrupted the exchange.

'Scotty?' she answered.

'Nope. Becky,' replied a woman with a cigarette-scarred voice. 'Becky Alter.'

'I don't know any Becky Alters.'

'From C3.'

'I don't know what that is, either. *Ow!*' she hissed, pulling away from the nurse's dabbing Q-tips.

'Sorry,' the nurse whispered. 'It needs to be cleaned.'

'It can wait two minutes,' Naomi shot back, shooing the nurse out of the small curtained exam room. 'Go Google *M★A★S★H*. It'll make you smarter.'

'C3 – Cyber Crimes Center,' Becky explained. 'I do computer forensics here at ICE. I was at your birthday party.'

'Of course, of course,' Naomi said, eyeing her wet, open

wound, which was now burning from whatever cleaning ointment the nurse had put on it. Naomi was nauseated just looking at it and took a seat on the gurney to steady her stomach. 'You have dark hair.'

'I'm blond,' Becky said. 'Don't fret. I just came for free cake,' she added with all the sensitivity of someone who does computer forensics. 'Leastways . . . I just finished picking through those files you asked for.'

'I asked for files?'

'The ones Scotty sent – through HUD – Service Point homeless records for a Calvin Harper: all the people he picked up during the last year.'

'No – of course,' she said, remembering the database entries from Cal's laptop. 'What took so long?'

'Long? Scotty just sent them last night. This is *fast*,' Becky pointed out. 'So not to panic you, but there's one record here I think you need to see. You sitting down?'

Naomi stood from the gurney. 'Yeah.'

'Good. Because I think I figured out the real name of your so-called Prophet.'

72

'You can feel it, can't you, Benoni?' Ellis asked, gripping the steering wheel and, thanks to the info from the librarians, turning into the wide, paved parking lot at the Ohio State Penitentiary. With the push of a button, he rolled down the passenger window and let Benoni stick her head out. There was still snow on the ground – the cold was brutal – but Benoni didn't hesitate. Extending her neck, the dog sniffed the air as Ellis circled through the lot.

'*Rrrkk! Rrrkk!*' Benoni barked as they approached an old black SUV.

Ellis hit the brakes and kicked his door open. By now, Benoni was well accustomed to Cal's scent.

Sure enough, as Ellis stepped toward the parked SUV and peered in at the backseat, he saw the blue backpack. Cal's backpack. Of course he had to leave it behind. No packages or weapons inside. 'You knew it, didn't you, girl?'

Benoni barked again, and Ellis returned to his car. But just as he reached for the door handle, he spotted the reflection of his face and uniform in the driver's-side window. His nose was definitely broken. He didn't care. Not when he was this close. He reached up and smoothed his hair.

'It makes sense, doesn't it?' Ellis asked as he slowly slid back into the front seat and parked right next to Cal's SUV. Of course the Book was here – at a prison. It was the world's first murder weapon. 'How could it *not* make its way to such violence?'

Benoni barked again, and Ellis, to his own surprise, felt a swell of tears in his eyes. 'Same here – I couldn't do it without you, girl,' he said, adding a loving pat to Benoni. He meant every word. Like that Plato quote in his great-grandfather's diary: 'A dog has the soul of a philosopher.' Ellis knew it was true. It was all coming true. And once he had the Book—

Benoni let loose with another bark. This one was louder. Angry. She smelled someone.

Reaching for his gun, Ellis spun toward the window. It was already too late. The door to his car flew open and a sharp golden knife stabbed Ellis – *chhhk . . . chhhk* – once in the chest, then deep into his stomach. It happened so fast, Ellis didn't even feel the pain. All he saw was the blood seeping through his uniform . . . and the knife still stuck in his belly.

The car door slammed shut just as fast, locking Ellis in with the now wildly barking and clawing Benoni.

'Hggh . . . hggh . . . hggh,' Ellis panted, slowly sinking in his seat and finally getting his first good look at his attacker.

'Oh, c'mon now,' the Prophet said. 'How'd you think it was gonna end?'

73

Outside the chain-link fence that surrounds the prison, I glance over my shoulder, checking the thin path that leads back to the parking lot. As my father appears from around the corner, he's moving slower than ever.

'What the hell took so long?' I hiss, careful to keep my voice down.

'It's hard to pee in the cold,' he says, hustling to catch up but never making eye contact. It's not until he gets close that I see what he's looking at. Over my shoulder, I spin back and spot that nearly every one of the building's narrow slit windows has someone staring down at us. The librarian at the Historical Society mentioned this was a supermax, which means inmates aren't sharing cells and playing harmonica behind the standard prison bars. Supermax means solitary confinement – all alone in a concrete box – twenty-three hours a day.

The idea originated in the nineteenth century with the Philadelphia Quakers, who thought isolation would lead to a prisoner's quiet contemplation. Instead, it leads to at least a few prisoners every year smearing feces on their teeth and insisting that heaven is attacking them. But from the look on my father's face, it's not the inmates who scare him. He was locked up for eight years. The terror in his heart is from the thought of going back.

'If you want, you can wait in the car,' I tell him.

'No.' He shakes his head, staring straight ahead. 'I'm fine.'

'Listen, Lloyd . . .'

'Let's just get it and go,' he insists, twisting the handle and opening the chain-link fence. As we step through, there's another closed fence just a few feet in front of us. In law enforcement, they call it a 'sally port' – the front door doesn't open until the back door is closed. For us, it means that for at least the next minute, we're trapped.

I think back to the fact that Naomi had to've put a lookout for us in the system. The only question now is, how hard are the guards here looking?

'Can I help you?' a soft male voice asks through the intercom.

'We're here from the Western Reserve Historical Society. To see the librarian,' I call back. 'We have an appointment.'

We don't. But that doesn't mean it won't work.

'Hold on for me, sir,' the man says, leaving us in silence. My father's standing barely a foot behind me. I can't see him, but I hear the speed of his breathing. The inmates in the windows are still peering down at us. From the angle we're at, we can't see their faces. They're just shadowy, opaque ghosts haunting from above.

'Come on up – I'm calling her now,' the voice announces as the metal gate clicks and we follow the walkway toward the front door of the building.

My father looks directly upward and takes one last look at the prisoners. Ghosts don't go away that easy.

Inside the building, a thick-necked guard with a triangular face and delicate, spindly fingers stares down from a podium. 'ID, please,' he says as we're blinded by the sea-foam green walls and matching sea-foam tile floor of the waiting area. I'm assuming the colors were picked because they somehow soothe the savage beast. But as my dad fidgets with his wallet, fighting for his ID, it's clearly not doing its job.

'We're from the Historical Society,' I tell the guard as I hand over the two IDs we used to get on the plane. 'We do the society's book donations, and—'

'I'm sorry, can I help you?' a woman in a flat midwest accent calls out. She's got boyish Buster Brown hair, a long knit skirt, and the strongest, most painful handshake I've ever received. 'Ann Maura Spencer, prison librarian,' she adds as I spot the bright orange Chuck Taylor sneakers peeking out below her skirt. 'They said you were from the Historical Society?'

'We do book donations,' I clarify. 'And since we donate so many titles here—'

'Which we appreciate so much,' Ann Maura says.

'And we'd love to keep doing it,' I tell her. 'That's why we set up the appointment.' I stare straight at her, smiling like she should understand.

'I – I'm sorry,' she offers. 'What appointment are we talking about?'

'To visit the library. Y'know, to see where all our books are going – to make sure your facilities can deal with and distribute them so we can keep—' I cut myself off. 'No one told you we were coming, did they?'

'Oh, I bet you spoke to Elliot. In the morning, was it?'

'It was definitely early,' I say.

'That's Elliot. He's kinda—' She forces a laugh. 'He kinda flounders with details.'

We all laugh together.

'Listen, we didn't mean to catch you unprepared,' I say.

'Why don't we come back next week when you're all ready for us?'

'No, don't be silly – we're ready – of course we're ready,' she promises. Even the world's toughest prison knows better than to disappoint one of its biggest donors.

I look at my dad, then back to Ann Maura. 'You sure?'

'Positively.' Turning to the guard, she adds, 'Kellis, can I get two passes, please?'

Up on his podium, the guard who's still holding our IDs is now staring down at them. There's a small laptop in front of him. Here's where the fire starts to singe some skin. For most prison visitors, he'd do a LEADS check, putting us in the Law Enforcement Automated Data System to discover exactly who we are. But I know for a fact that most prisons don't have the time to run it on every single delivery that comes through the door. Best of all, he's heard our conversation. He knows we're not here to see inmates. We're here to see books.

So why isn't he handing back our IDs?

The guard hits a button on his laptop, and I feel drops of sweat rolling down my stomach. He squints at his screen, and I swear it takes every muscle in my face to hold my grin.

'Here you go,' the guard says, passing us our IDs as he stuffs them into two visitor passes with small cutout holes for our ID photos. 'And thanks for the donations. The inmates really appreciate them.'

'I assume you left all your weapons at home?' Ann Maura laughs, pointing us toward an X-ray machine and a walk-through metal detector.

'Always do,' I tease, forcing another laugh and tossing my car keys onto the conveyor.

We're moving quickly now – even my father's excitedly keeping up – which is why I can't help but hesitate. Last time things went this well was when Naomi ambushed us at the museum. I look back at the guard, who tosses me a friendly nod. In front of us, we bypass the elevators and the standard visitors entrance. Instead, we walk through a narrow doorway and stop at a thick steel door that could easily do the job at a bank vault.

'Step in,' Ann Maura says.

There's a soft pneumatic hiss behind us, and I realize we're in another sally port. From out of the wall, a matching steel door slides sideways, all set to seal us in this small, five-foot-long, bright white space.

My father motions to our left, and I spot the mirrored wall. Two-way glass. The key question is, who's watching?

Behind us, the back door slides shut, clicking with the cold *thunk* of a meat locker. The sound echoes like the first clods of dirt hitting a fresh coffin.

This isn't like the chain-link fence outside. With that back door shut, we're officially in prison. Next to me, my father is as green as the fluorescent lighting.

'Say *cheese*,' Ann Maura says, tapping a finger against the two-way glass. 'Just hold up your badges for the control center.'

As we do, my dad can barely lift his ID. I'm worried he's about to pass out.

'I know . . . it can be a bit intimidating,' Ann Maura adds as she presses her palm into a hand scanner and waves her own ID. 'What's odd is how easily you get used to it.'

There's another pneumatic hiss as the metal door in front of us slowly, slowly slides sideways, disappearing into the wall and revealing a long concrete hallway that runs down to our right. I've never been so happy to see sea-foam green in my life.

'And here's our little island of literary freedom,' Ann Maura sings, stopping at room number H-277. The sign on the door says, 'OSP Library.' 'Now what can I show you first?'

'Whatever you like,' I reply.

My father's not nearly as patient. He steps into the room, already eyeing the bookshelves. 'Where do you keep your Bibles?'

74

'Oh, believe me, we can always use Bibles,' Ann Maura says as we follow her through the prison library, which is centered around a large uncluttered worktable, with tall bookshelves lining all four walls and a small glass office in the far corner. Like the hallways, the room is a cheery, maddening sea-foam green, but as I look back to my dad, he can't take his eyes off the library's oddest pieces of decor: a collection of soda cans, bedsprings, peanut-butter jars, an empty spool of thread, a tiny cassette-tape motor, a set of chocolate Tootsie Roll Pop lollipops, a moon-shaped horn that soldiers used to carry gunpowder in, a rusted cigarette case, a zebra-print animal skin, and even rabbit ears from an old TV, all of which are glued directly to the wall and run like a junkyard border above the tops of the bookcases.

'What're those?' my father asks.

She laughs. 'The guards call it their trophy case – y'know, all the things they've confiscated over the years. See that cassette-tape motor? A prisoner ripped that out of a Walkman to make his own homemade tattoo gun. And those Tootsie Pops? They replaced the lollipops with tiny bags of heroin, then melted new candy around the bag so we wouldn't find the prize inside. I'm telling you, you wouldn't believe how viciously crafty these folks get.'

My dad nods. 'I can only imagine.'

'Aren't you worried about keeping the items on the wall?' I ask. 'Won't the prisoners grab them?'

'Oh, no – we don't allow prisoners in here,' Ann Maura says, which explains why there are no cameras in the room. 'With our population – no – we deliver the books directly to their cells.'

On my left, there's a large industrial sink with two tall piles of paperbacks: one labeled 'Clean,' the other 'Unclean.'

'Some of the prisoners are a little . . . rough with our collection,' Ann Maura adds.

I look back at the piles. I don't even want to think about it.

'So do you have enough Bibles for your entire population?' my dad asks as she approaches the reference desk on the right.

'Actually, standard Bibles are handled by Religious Services,' she explains as she realigns the stapler and the three-hole punch so they sit perfectly parallel on the reference desk. Librarians can't help themselves. 'We do foreign languages, other religions, things like that. In fact, if you have a few extra Korans, we've been getting lots of requests for those.'

'What about Russian?' I ask. 'How's your stock on those?'

'Y'know, it's funny – I'm not sure if we have Russian.' At the card catalog that sits next to the reference desk, she kneels down on one knee and tugs open one of the lower drawers. 'I know, I know – we need computers – card catalogs are dead – but I'd rather use our budget to acquire more books,' she explains. 'The prisoners really are grateful.'

As her fingers flip through the card catalog, my dad can barely stand still. Once we find this book—

'Nope. Not here,' she announces.

'Sorry?' I ask.

'Chinese, Ukrainian, even Arabic,' she says, flipping forward through the cards, then back. 'But no Bibles in Russian.'

'You sure?' my father asks. 'At the Historical Society, someone said—' He cuts himself off. 'A few years back, I could swear we sent an old Russian one your way.'

'Really?' she asks. 'You don't happen to remember the original call number, do you?'

'*1.8.4 King*,' we both say simultaneously.

Still on one knee, Ann Maura looks up at both of us.

'It's fine if you can't find it. It was sort of a curiosity – we just wanted to know where it went,' I offer.

'Of course,' she says. 'Might as well take a look, right?' She closes one drawer and opens another that has a circular red sticker in the corner. Her fingers pick through the cards . . . and just as quickly come to a stop. 'Here we go,' she announces.

'You have it?'

'We did. It arrived in 1998.'

'That's the one!' my dad blurts. 'Where's it now?'

'Ah, that's the thing. According to this, well . . . I hate to say it, but looks like we pulped it.'

'You *what*?' my father asks.

'You threw it away?' I add. 'Why?'

'Doesn't say. Sometimes a book gets worn apart – other times, an inmate rips their favorite section out, and the whole copy becomes unsalvageable. You have to understand, our clientele can be pretty selfish sometimes.'

'So it's gone,' my dad says.

'Definitely gone,' Ann Maura says as she slides the card drawer shut. 'I'm confused, though. Was there something special about that particular copy?'

'It was just – It was first donated to us by one of our board members, and we thought it might be nice to maybe track it down for him,' I say. 'Sorta reunite him with his 1875 family Bible.'

'Hold on,' Ann Maura says. 'Did you say 1875 or *1975*?'

'1875.'

'So it's an *old* book, not a new one.' Before I can even respond, she's got that faraway look, like she's checking the card catalog in her mind. 'And it's Russian,' she mutters. 'Oh, how funny – I didn't even think about that.'

I'm about to interrupt, but she's already gone, dashing to the glassed-in office in the corner of the room. On the wall, she's got framed head shots of the governor and lieutenant governor of Ohio, as well as a few other frames below those two. Staring down with her back to us, she grabs one of the lower frames from the wall.

'When you first said it, I thought we were looking for a modern Bible,' she calls out as she heads back toward us, carrying the frame, 'which is the only reason I didn't think of *this*. It was a gift from my predecessor – just to keep me on my toes.'

She flips the frame around, revealing a crinkled sheet of paper that's yellowed like parchment and split into two columns: On the right is Hebrew writing, on the left is . . .

'That's Russian,' my father says excitedly, rushing forward.

But what's most noticeable is the crescent-moon-shaped hole that's cut out from the center of the page and is about the size of a banana.

'Don't you see? That's the reason it got pulped,' Ann Maura explains, pointing to the hole in the page. 'Somewhere along the way, one of our prisoners must've sliced through the pages to smuggle something inside.'

Or Mitchell Siegel did it years earlier, I say with a look toward my dad.

But to my surprise, he's not studying the framed page. Instead, he crosses behind the librarian and stares up at the trophy room items that're glued to the far left wall above the bookcases – or, more specifically, at the moon-shaped horn that's—

I squint hard and give it another look. The moon-shaped horn. That's not— That's not for gunpowder. That's an animal horn.

I glance down at the cutout in the Bible. A perfect animal horn shape.

Oh, God.

When Jerry Siegel's Bible got transferred to the prison . . . they confiscated what was hidden inside, then put it up as a trophy for—

There's a choking sound behind me, like someone fighting for air.

I spin around just in time to see my father's hands gripping the librarian's neck from behind. His face is red from squeezing, and a thick vein swells across his forehead. She thrashes and kicks but doesn't have a chance. Before I can even react, she drops to the floor like a cut puppet, her head sagging down and her orange sneakers pointing in toward each other.

'Wh-What're you—? *Are you insane!?*' I demand.

'It's okay. She's just unconscious,' my father insists, his eyes wide as he rushes to grab a nearby chair.

'Stop! *Right now!* Stop!'

'She's fine, Calvin. I know what I'm doing.'

'You could've killed her!'

'She's fine,' he repeats, his voice at full gallop as he runs with the chair.

I check the librarian's chest. She's passed out but definitely breathing.

'Lloyd, she was just—! *Listen to me! Why aren't you listening?*'

'This is it – I finally got it. You see it, don't you, Calvin? Cain's murder weapon . . . the Book of Truth – it's not a book!' he says, shoving the chair against the bookcase and climbing up toward the horn. 'You can see the carvings – it's written on the animal horn! This is it!'

'Lloyd, you can't do this.'

But he already is. Standing on the chair, he stretches above the bookcase, up toward the trophies, where he grips the animal horn and tries to rip it from the wall. It doesn't budge. He tries again with both hands. It's glued on better than he thought.

'Dammit, get down!' I shout.

Undeterred, he yanks the nearest hardcover from the top shelf of the bookcase and flips it around so the spine is facing the wall. Turning it into a makeshift guillotine, he slices the book downward, slamming it into the horn and trying to cleave it from the trophy wall.

'Lloyd, I'm talking to you!'

'He's not listening, Calvin,' a voice announces from behind me.

I spin back to the front door of the library, and my heart falls from my body. 'Th-That's not possible.'

'Sure it is,' the Prophet says as he slowly steps forward. 'All I needed was a little help from your dad.'

75

'I'm lost. Back up,' Naomi barked into her phone, scooching up on the gurney as she stared down at the polished floor. 'What does this have to do with the Prophet? And where the hell's Scotty? He explains stuff better than you.'

'Okay, forget the Prophet. Go back to Cal,' Becky says. 'What's Cal's job? He picks up homeless people, correct? So to make sure he's not taking these people and selling them to tattoo parlors for practice skin, Cal is required – by law – to put the name of every person he picks up into his laptop, which connects to the state database that keeps track of such things. You with me so far?'

'Keep going.'

'The point is, Naomi – on that first night Cal found his father, he keyed in his dad's Social Security number and entered him into the database.'

'So?'

'So Cal's dad's name came right up.'

'Again . . . so?'

'And again . . . so Cal's database isn't NCIC – he doesn't have a full list of everyone on the planet. The only people in there are people who were *put* in there.'

'And for the third time . . . why is that so damn important?'

'Naomi, you have to understand: On most nights, when

Cal enters a client's Social Security number, it's not just so the government can play big brother and I Spy from the Sky. It's so Cal can pull up the homeless person's records and see who he's dealing with. Does this person have a history of drugs? Of mental illness? When was the last time they were helped? Or is this someone just leeching off the system, who goes to a different place every night? Cal covers the entire Fort Lauderdale area – he needs this information to do his job.'

'But you're saying Cal's dad was already in his system.'

'There you go. If it were any other night, Cal would've scanned the file, looking for details about whoever they found. But when his father's name popped up . . .'

'. . . Cal went bursting from the van, anxious to start dealing with his daddy issues.'

'And thus he misses one key detail about his father's background.'

'So which is it?' Naomi asked. 'Drugs? Mental illness? You should've seen Lloyd attack me with that trophy. He's a sociopath, isn't he?'

'Not according to his Service Point file. In fact, the last time he got picked up . . . Dad's got some real issues.'

'Define *issues*.'

'He's suicidal,' Becky said as Naomi hopped off the gurney. 'His case notes say he was a mess, too. Found him on Fort Lauderdale beach four months ago after he swallowed fifty tabs of trazodone and fell in a pile of fire ants that were – no joke – eating him alive.'

'Okay, and that makes me officially feel bad,' Naomi agreed. 'But I'm confused. You said Dad was picked up four months ago – that that's when he was put in the system. But if Cal picked him up . . . even with the fire ants, didn't he recognize his own father?'

'See, that's where I was stuck, too. Until I finally started thinking that maybe Cal wasn't the one who found him that first night.'

'Wait, I don't get it,' Naomi shot back. 'You just said Dad was found on the beach in Fort Lauderdale. That's Cal's route, right? But if Cal wasn't the one who picked Dad up, who else is driving around in a homeless van except for—?'

This time, Becky didn't say a word.

Naomi grabbed a nearby IV pole just to help her stand.

'Fudge. Me,' she whispered to herself.

76

I understand pain. I've lived with pain my entire life. But pain is nothing compared to betrayal. And betrayal is nothing compared to knowing that the javelin in your back was rammed there by the one person in your life you actually trusted.

His ponytail swings like a hypnotist's watch as he calmly enters the room. I have no idea how he got in here or how he even—

'Cal, you need to listen to these words,' Roosevelt says, his hands out and his palms up. 'I need you to hear this, okay? I'm sorry this had to happen. I mean that. This was never supposed to be about you.'

'Y-You're the Prophet,' I blurt.

'You're not listening, are you?'

'In the park – when we stumbled onto my dad – that was no stumble, was it?' I stutter. 'You *knew* he'd be there, didn't you? Just like you knew I'd come running to— How could—? *You're supposed to be my brother!*'

'I still am. Don't you see?' he asks. 'Months ago, when I started setting up the shipment . . . when I got word that the man in the coffin – the doctor in China – was dying – I could've asked you from the start. But I was trying to protect you.'

'That's how you protect me? By using my dad as some

emotional carrot and then . . . with Ellis . . . You sent that psycho to kill me!'

'No. That's not— Cal, if there wasn't that hold notice, I never would've involved you. Never. In fact, I didn't find your dad until *after* the doctor died. But as I was putting together the shipment – to see your dad on the street that night – how could I ignore a sign like that?'

'That wasn't a sign! It was my *father*!'

'And I did nothing but right by him. I saved his life! But with that shipment coming – you know what it's worth and how easily those things get stopped. I didn't know if I'd need you, Cal. Your dad was just— I needed insurance.'

'Oh, then that's a far more forgivable story. So now my dad was just your lucky rabbit's foot? What'd you do, throw him some cash as a delivery boy and then you'd at least have a surefire way to get my help just in case something went wrong?'

'Something *did* go wrong!'

'*That doesn't justify it, Roosevelt!* I mean, okay, so you were nervous about your shipment, that doesn't mean you – you – you—' A pinprick of vomit knifes the back of my throat, then slides back down to my belly. 'Y-You shot him. In the stomach. You shot my dad, knowing it would pull my heartstrings and—'

'He shot himself,' Roosevelt says. 'He took my gun – the gun I searched so long for, that I spent so much of my family's resources to find – and shot himself. He was worried you wouldn't help him otherwise, isn't that right, Lloyd?'

I look back at my father, who's standing on the chair, staring down at us. He's still got one hand gripped around the animal horn. Never letting go of the prize.

'I saved your father's life, Cal,' Roosevelt insists for the second time. 'Tell him, Lloyd. Tell him how I found you, all those ants crawling through your nose and in your ears.'

My father doesn't answer.

'He *was* a sign, Cal. God sent him. Lloyd didn't want to see ya, but I knew it – everything for a purpose, right?' Roosevelt adds. 'He was sent to me to be saved. And I did. I set him right – cleaned him up, found him a counselor, even gave him some cash to restart his life. All he had to do was make his delivery. Instead, he got greedy, didn't you, Lloyd?'

'It wasn't greed,' my father calls out.

'Then what was it?' Roosevelt shoots back. 'Love for your son? Is that your new story? No, no, no. I like that. It's a nice confession. You saw him, and when your paternal side was reawakened, you decided to go for Father of the Year.' Roosevelt shakes his head and readjusts his ponytail. 'There's only one problem, Lloyd. Why didn't you ever tell Cal the truth? Oh, that's right – priceless religious artifacts aren't half as good when you have to share them.'

'How can you—!? You sent Ellis to kill me!' my father shouts.

'And me!' I explode. 'You knew Ellis was a butcher! And you sent him after us!'

'No. Your father lies. He always lies,' Roosevelt insists. 'I never sent Ellis to kill you. I was just trying to get back what was mine.'

'You still helped him!' I yell.

'Only after Alligator Alley. Remember, Lloyd? When you stopped calling in? When you wouldn't answer your phone at the warehouse? Or at the airport? You're lucky our delivery guy in Hong Kong – poor Zhao, Lord rest his soul – had told me Ellis was sniffing around. He's the one who said Ellis made a better offer, even gave me his contact info. When Lloyd went AWOL, what was I supposed to do?'

'Are you really that deluded?' I blurt. 'When you sent Ellis to Cleveland—'

'Ellis was always the enemy – always on a tight leash – tell me you don't see that. But Ellis was on his mission whether I was there or not. At least this way . . . I was keeping him under control.'

'There was no *control*! He killed the Johnsels! Those deaths are on your hands!'

'I told Ellis to stay out of the house. I was fighting for you there, Cal. Trying so hard to keep you safe. *I was*. I *fought* him to stay out of there.'

'But he didn't. He tried to kill us, Roosevelt. *You* tried to kill us!'

The problem is, no preacher likes to hear his own flaws named. Refusing to face me, Roosevelt stays locked on my father.

'You're a sinner, Lloyd. All you had to do was hand over the comic book. Instead, you ran to Cleveland, hoping to steal God's treasure for yourself. But here's your chance. I have your penance. Hand it back now, and you'll get everything I promised.'

Without a word, my father turns back to the animal horn, slamming it again with the spine of the book. It connects with a loud *duumm*. Even he freezes. This is still a prison. The librarian's out cold, but we don't have much time.

'Now you're offering deals?' I ask as my father again guillotines with the book, unleashing another loud *duumm*. Roosevelt doesn't even look up.

'You have any idea how I got in here?' Roosevelt challenges. 'All I had to do was say we were together. So simple, right? If you've learned nothing else, can you even comprehend the power of God's will?'

It's a perfect bluff. And as he slides his hand into his jacket pocket, I tell myself there's no way they'd let him bring in a weapon. But I also see that smug twinkle in his eyes. I used to call it southern charm. I was wrong. He's no different from Ellis. Just another zealot who'd give everything to get his old life back.

'I know that look, Cal. You're judging me,' he says as he fidgets with whatever's in his pocket. No way it's a gun. No way. He circles sideways, toward my dad, with the prowl of a mountain cat. But all he's really doing is trying to keep the reference desk between us. The last thing he needs is to give me a clear path. 'You wanted it, too, Cal. You chased it as hard as I did. There's nothing wrong with wanting forgiveness from the past.'

'Oh, so that's your big grand plan? Go back to the church and offer the weapon in exchange for a brand-new pulpit? Or are you dreaming the big dreams now?' For once, Roosevelt doesn't answer. 'That's it, isn't it? Now that you've seen the prize, you can save far more than just your old parish, can't you?'

'Didn't you listen at all when we spoke? Cain created *murder* with this weapon. Ellis and his Nazis – Lord knows what they were trying to create with it. But now – as a Book of Truth – "*What you intended for evil, God intended for good*"! Don't you see, Cal? That's why you were chosen – and why I kept helping you. You took us further than anyone's ever gotten,' he says, still making it sound like we're a team. 'B-B-But this isn't just about you or me or any one person,' he insists, his eyes dancing wildly.

I search his face, looking for my friend. But somewhere – this deep in his fervor – he's long gone. As he bounces on his heels, Roosevelt's voice flies faster than ever. 'And this isn't about them kicking me out, or my old little church, either. Can you see the bigger theological picture? All the naysayers of God – all the doubters and smug skeptics who love looking down at us – this ends the argument, Cal. Forget relying on faith – this is *proof* God didn't punish Cain. *Real* proof. Do you understand the power in that? Everyone . . . everyone . . . everyone thinks we need monsters, but we don't. We need forgiveness. And understanding. Just like we give every day in the van. Just like you were searching for when you first came to me. When Cain repented, God rewarded him. He granted that forgiveness. *That's* the religion the world needs to see – that we can make sure they see. How can you and your father not want to share that with everyone else?'

A swell of rage rises like mercury through my body. I circle around to his side of the reference desk. From above, there's another *duumm* from my dad. 'The only reason I wanted this thing was to prove I didn't kill Timothy!' I shout.

'C'mon, Cal – chasing ancient artifacts . . . coming here – it doesn't prove your innocence. It never did,' Roosevelt says. 'Don't you see? Even if all the guards in the building come running, no one will ever believe the disgraced agent and his pathetic murderer father. It's over,' he insists. 'It's always been over. You lost.'

I shake my head, tensing to jump. 'Not if I give them . . . *you.*'

I fly at him like a bullet. He goes for whatever's in his pocket. Maybe it *is* a gun. I don't care.

77

I slam my shoulder into his chest, and Roosevelt flies backward toward the bookcase. On impact, I hear the air forced from his lungs. The way his head snaps back, one of the shelves clipped him in the back of the neck.

But he laughs, fighting to stand up straight.

'Really, Cal – the two of us – two brothers fighting? Isn't that a bit on the nose?'

I've got two decades of pent-up fury. My fists are made of thunder.

'You're not . . . my brother!' I shout, burying a punch in his face. The bookcase again catches him from behind. But at his age and size, he's already starting to wobble.

'Okay, your teacher, then. I did teach you everything,' he says almost proudly, his left eye already swelling shut.

I shake my head and hit him again. And again. The skin on my knuckles cracks open as his nose pops.

'You didn't teach me how to fight,' I growl.

'Sure . . . ptthh . . .' He spits a wad of blood to the floor, tottering sideways. He's holding on to the edge of the reference desk just to stay on his feet. 'Sure I did. You just didn't like fighting dirty.'

There's a noise from above, a loud crack, like a snapped bone. A few shelves down, my father pulls the animal horn free from the wall.

'I got it!' he calls out.

I look away for barely a second. That's all Roosevelt needs.

From the edge of the reference desk, he grabs a stapler, flips it open like a butterfly knife, and swings straight at my face.

I try my best to turn away. I'm not nearly fast enough.

Cunk.

The staple sinks its teeth into my cheek, biting hard as my jaw lurches sideways.

'*Naaaahhhh!*' I scream through clenched teeth.

Already stumbling backward, I'm completely off balance as Roosevelt plows toward me. He's big like a truck and knows how to use it to his advantage.

Winding up with the stapler, he swings at my face again. And again. And again. I raise my arm – still sore from Benoni – to block each shot, but all it does is send the staples into my forearm, which burns from each metal bee sting.

But it's not until I spot him glancing over my shoulder that I see what he's really aiming for: the empty mop bucket that sits next to the sink – and is now right behind me.

The backs of my legs hit it at full speed. I've already got too much momentum. Like an overloaded lever, I tumble backward, my head hitting the hard green industrial tile with a brutal thud. For a moment, the world goes black with bright, burning stars.

As I blink them away, Roosevelt pounces, ever the mountain cat, landing on my chest and using his full weight to pin my arms back with his knees. With his big paws, he holds my throat with one hand, then pins the stapler against my Adam's apple. He learned this one talking to Ellis. He's aiming for my jugular. And as hard as he's pressing down, he's gonna take a deep chunk of it.

'Lloyd, I see you!' Roosevelt calls out.

Back by the bookcase, my father leaps down from the chair and freezes with the carved horn in his hand.

'I need to know what you're doing, Lloyd,' Roosevelt says in full southern drawl. 'You got a real big decision to make.'

I wait for my father to panic. From where he's standing across the room, I can only see him out of the corner of my eye. But he's not swaying or stuttering or scratching at his beard. Worst of all, he's not even looking at me.

'Dad, whatever he offers, he's a liar!' I shout, barely able to get out the words.

Roosevelt presses the stapler even harder. 'Your boy has a point, Lloyd. But do you really wanna go back to your old life? That old trailer? Or better yet, a second visit to prison? I can tell you right now, they're not gonna have your fancy Michael Kors shirts there.'

My father stares at Roosevelt, never once breaking eye contact. My dad doesn't hesitate.

'I found it. I want a finder's fee,' my father insists, gripping the horn.

'Money won't be an issue,' Roosevelt promises. 'Now what about your son?'

'You don't have to hurt him.'

'That's not really one of the options, Lloyd. Try again.'

'I can stall him. I'll stall him. If I don't, then you don't send me my cash.'

Roosevelt doesn't smile. His eyes narrow.

'Thank you, Lloyd,' he says calmly. 'I just need the weapon first,' he adds, extending his free hand. No question, this part's a test.

But my dad again reacts quickly, passing with flying colors. Heading toward us, he holds the ancient brown animal horn from the bottom tip, like an ice-cream cone.

The top of the cone – the wider side of the horn – is covered by a tan piece of leather that's pulled taut as a drum. The closer he gets, the more clearly I can see that half the horn's carvings have cracked off or faded away.

I fight hard to break free, but Roosevelt's weight is too much. He presses the stapler against my jugular, and I can barely breathe. The far edges of my vision go blurry and the burning stars slowly return.

No . . . please don't pass out.

I turn to my right, searching for my father. He's just a few steps away, but he still won't look at me.

Dad . . . please, I beg, though nothing comes out.

I can see the end. It doesn't come with a fistfight, or macho banter, or even a quiet prayer. It comes with a desperate pastor from Tennessee flattening my windpipe.

Roosevelt grins, pressing even harder.

I take a final breath, ready to see my mom.

And my father loosens his grip on the bottom tip of the ice-cream cone, letting the horn slide down in his palm until he's holding it from the wide side. Like a weapon.

My dad cocks his arm back and stabs the jagged horn at Roosevelt's neck.

My father spent eight years in prison. He knows exactly where to strike.

The problem is, Roosevelt spent his years getting attacked by street drunks. He knows exactly how to defend himself.

In one fluid movement, as my father lurches forward with Cain's birthright, Roosevelt grips my dad's wrist and twists. Hard. Air returns to my lungs, blood to my brain, and my head starts to clear.

I hear the snap of muscle and bone. But it's not nearly as bad as watching my dad hunch forward as Roosevelt sends my father's wrist – and the jagged pointed horn – stabbing back toward the wound in my dad's stomach.

Skrrrp.

My father's eyes go wide as it rips his stitches and pierces deep into his belly. A small spray of blood soaks his shirt. He tries to yell, but all he musters is a toneless gasp.

'Dad!'

A shrill bell rings, screaming through the room. From the floors above us, we hear the metal *ch-chunk* of hundreds of prison doors slamming shut simultaneously. Lunchtime's over.

Without a word, Roosevelt climbs off my chest, approaches my dad, and effortlessly tugs the blood-covered horn from my father's stomach. I'm still catching my breath as my dad falls forward, crumpling to the floor. He's not breathing . . . not moving . . .

'That wound needs pressure,' Roosevelt says coolly, wiping the horn on my father's back, then heading for the door. He shoots me a look to make sure I get the point.

I can still catch him, but only if I leave my dad. And after what my father did to me . . . no question, it's a simple choice.

I look at my dad, then back to Roosevelt, then down at my dad.

But there's no choice at all.

I flip my father over. His eyes are open and rolled back in his head.

'That's why you found it, Cal,' Roosevelt calls out, already at the door. 'The purest soul gets the prize.'

With a sharp tug, he pulls open the library door. But instead of a hallway, all he sees are metal bars and the two prison guards who block his exit. That sound we heard before . . . the metal *ch-chunk* . . . The protective gate that rolled down from the ceiling doesn't budge as he grabs it.

'That's him! He stabbed me!' Ellis barks, hunched over and holding a thick gauze to his chest as he steps between the guards and points at Roosevelt.

Two enormously pissed guards reach through the bars, grip Roosevelt's shoulders, and tug him forward, smashing his face into the metal gate and holding him there as if they're about to physically pull him through the four-inch space between the bars.

It takes me a moment to process, until one of the guards steps aside, and I spot Ellis still wearing his Michigan State Police uniform.

'This what he stole?' one of the guards asks, snatching the animal horn from Roosevelt's hands.

'That's it,' Ellis says without even the smallest of grins as he holds open a clear plastic evidence bag and the guard drops Cain's birthright inside.

'*N-No!*' Roosevelt screams. 'H-He's a killer! He killed two people in Cleveland!'

'Didn't I tell you he'd say that?' Ellis asks, already out of sight.

'That's not—! *He's lying!*' Roosevelt explodes, spit flying from his mouth. '*He's not a real cop!*'

'Ann Maura's down! Plus we got a bleeder!' another guard shouts, staring through the gates at me and my dad. 'Tell Henkel we need medical *now!*'

Down on my knees, I give my dad a few breaths and start CPR. He coughs, breathing quickly, but the bleeding in his belly won't stop. The red puddle on his shirt swells and expands, starting to bleed onto the floor. I grab a rag from the sink and start applying pressure. We need paramedics.

'*Ahuuh . . . ahhuh . . .*' my father coughs, unable to lift his head as he turns my way. His voice is less than a whisper. 'I – I didn't mean to— I tried to do better, Cal.'

I nod, refusing to look down at him.

'I mean it, Cal. And when I – *ahuuh* – w-when I . . . in the car . . . what I said about Mom. N-None of that changes.'

His voice cracks and fades with each syllable. His face is pale, all the color running from the hole in his belly. He knows what's coming. His last wound was superficial. This one is deep.

'D-Didja hear me?' he whispers. 'With Mom . . . please . . . none of that changes.'

He's begging now, his eyes flooded with tears.

I shake my head, feeling my own bubble in my throat. 'Of course it changes, Dad. Of course it damn well changes.'

'*He's stealing it!*' Roosevelt rails, spit still flying through the bars. '*Tell them, Cal! You need to tell them!*' he shouts as he finally looks over his shoulder to face me.

I'm already racing at him.

My fists. Still made of thunder.

Roosevelt turns just as I swing, but he never sees the punch coming.

78

Four days later
Orchard Lake, Michigan

Few things excited Ellis. It wasn't that he wasn't capable of the emotion. But life delivers far less disappointment when your expectations are low.

Still, as he pulled up to the circular driveway of the tasteful, snow-capped Georgian Colonial – as he parked the car and reached over to the passenger seat to pick up the worn leather case that used to house his jet injector – Ellis's heart, his ears, everything was buzzing.

'Let's go, Benoni,' he said as the dog leaped out of the car, and Ellis strode after her. He could swear the Michigan wind was whistling just for him.

Tonight, no question, was worth the excitement.

Sure, Ellis could've come sooner. But the wounds in his chest and stomach . . . to get them cleaned and stitched . . . No. This was his arrival. The completion of his mother's wish. He needed to be strong.

Ignoring the front door of the house, Ellis followed the Judge's instructions and took the slate path to the guest-house around back. The Judge was still a public man. And this – to unlock the birthright – tonight had to be private.

'This way, Benoni,' he called out, keeping the dog from running into the woods.

'Boy, what a beauty,' a croaky bullfrog of a voice called

out as the door to the guesthouse opened. Leaning down to welcome Benoni, Judge Felix Wojtowicz looked older – much older – than when Ellis first came to visit a year ago.

'Okay to give her a treat?' the Judge asked, wiping his wispy white hair to the side as he welcomed Ellis into the bungalow, which held a modest home office, a leather sofa, and a mirrored bar in the corner. 'I saved her some steak. It's filet.'

Ellis couldn't help but grin. The Judge was sucking up now.

'She loves filet,' Ellis said as Wojtowicz knelt down to let Benoni eat from his hand.

'I saw the story in yesterday's paper,' the Judge added. 'You know, they had your picture in there. From the prison videocamera. I understand Cal's using that as support for his own defense. It'll work.'

'I'm aware. But he still lost what mattered, and I don't just mean his friend,' Ellis said, delicately setting the leather case on the bar's glass countertop. He took a final deep breath as he unzipped the case and carefully, so carefully, peeled through the thick wad of bubble wrap and acid-free tissue paper to reveal the precious prize inside.

'My great-grandfather died for this,' Ellis said as he held the gray-and-ivory-striated animal horn in his open palms and turned toward the Judge. 'You better know how to read it.'

The Judge studied the object, nodding over and over. Goats, cows, sheep – most horns were composed of keratin, the structural protein that toenails and hooves and claws are made of. In ancient times, horns were some of the strongest objects around, making them ideal writing implements. And weapons. In fact, in the right dry resting place – like a cave – an animal horn could survive for centuries.

'Heaven above,' the Judge said as tears pooled in his eyes. 'You actually found it. Praise you, Ellis. Praise you.'

Hands shaking, the Judge reached for the leather case, then had Ellis place the horn back into the wad of bubble wrap and tissue paper. 'The markings . . . the crossed sickles: This is it,' the Judge said, looking at Ellis. 'This is it!' His hands still shaking, he carefully carried the ancient carved horn toward the back room of the bungalow. 'I need my magnifier.'

But as he followed the Judge into the back bedroom, the only thing Ellis saw were two older men – they looked like twins, both in their late sixties – dressed in herringbone overcoats.

Motherf—

Ellis just stood there, arms plainly at his side, as the first silenced shot was fired.

The Judge was smiling and holding the birthright as the bullet pierced Ellis's neck.

Ftt.

Benoni! Benoni, attack! Ellis screamed, crumpling awkwardly onto his side as he hit the floor. But his words were lost in the bubbling froth of blood from his shattered voice box.

Ftt. Ftt. Ftt. Ftt. Ftt.

Five hushed gunshots. All of them in Ellis's chest.

As Ellis lay there on his back, the last thing he saw was the Judge standing over him, staring down. He suddenly didn't look so old anymore.

'Just remember, Ellis. No one likes a bully.'

Within seconds, the Judge, the room, the world went blurry.

'*Heil, Thule,*' one of the other men called out.

'Yes— *Heil* – of course,' the Judge said. 'Now get me my gloves. Time to open the Book of Truth.'

79

Fort Lauderdale, Florida

'It's a trap, Cal! *It's always a trap!*' Alberto screams.

I nod, tugging Alberto to his feet, wrapping an arm around his waist, and trying to steady him as we leave the alley and walk past the Thai restaurant's front brick patio. He's wearing the same ratty clothes he had on last week, though he's added a REHAB IS FOR QUITTERS bumper sticker that he's taped around his ankle.

'I clipped my toenails into that soup!' Alberto shouts, pointing to a blond patron's bowl.

'H-He's joking,' the restaurant manager swears as he follows behind us. But the way the blonde scowls at her waiter, who then scowls at me, it's clear no one believes it.

'Alberto . . .'

'Don't fight with me, Cal! Where you been, anyway? This sonuvabitch thinks he owns the whole block!'

'I hear you. I'll take care of it. But no more yelling, okay?'

'Cal, he—!'

I cup my hand, pressing it into the small of Alberto's back. I don't press hard. I don't need to. He gets the picture. I'm here for him.

'Alberto, when you talk . . . I'm listening. You understand? I'm listening.'

His bloodshot, hound-dog eyes study me a moment,

but not for long. I wait for him to say something – to say anything – but he just clutches his old RC Cola can with the plastic wrap on top, then turns to the curb, where I've parked the used maroon van I borrowed from another shelter.

'Where's Roosevelt?' he blurts.

'In jail.'

He thinks on this a moment. 'I heard.' Then, in a reassuring voice, 'You don't need him.'

Without another word, he hops in through the open side door of the van. 'You got coffee for me?' he asks, fishing around on the front seats.

'Hey, listen – before you go,' a voice calls out behind me.

I turn back to find the restaurant manager – a sweaty Asian in a shiny hipster suit – making his way toward me.

'Thanks again for your help,' the manager says. 'I wouldn't've called, but the customers started complaining.'

He extends a handshake, all set to slip me a fifty. 'Just to say thanks for getting here so fast,' he says.

I look down at my old black T-shirt, faded sweats, and Vans sneakers. Nothing's changed.

Except me.

I step toward the manager and wrap an arm around him with newfound ease.

'Listen, I'm not allowed to take cash like that, but can I ask a favor?' I say, motioning over his shoulder. 'Would you mind if I donated this to your wait-staff? You can add it to their tips – especially this guy serving the blonde,' I say, pointing to the table with the angry woman who's now returning her soup. 'He's gonna need a bit of help tonight.'

The manager smiles, his thin eyebrows rising. 'That's

nice. Fair deal,' he says, offering another handshake. This time a real one.

I cross around the back of the van, climb behind the wheel, and manually roll down the window, where I take a deep breath of Florida's salty beach air. But as I twist the ignition key and turn on the lights, I finally see the man blocking my way, standing in front of the van, his hands in his pockets and his shoulders as slumped as usual.

'Lloyd, what're you doing here?' I call out.

'I was just— I thought I'd . . .' My father's voice trails off. 'I don't really know,' he finally admits. 'I spoke to Serena.'

'I don't want to talk about Serena.' I pump the gas and jerk the van forward, hoping he'll move out of the way. All he does is rush around to my open side window, gripping it like a child holding on to the counter of an ice-cream truck.

'Did you get my messages?' he pleads, refusing to let go.

I hit the brakes but stare straight ahead, through the front windshield. Even without eye contact, I can see his beard's gone and his grizzly hair's combed. He got a better lawyer than last time, which explains the deal he got for testifying against Roosevelt. And a better doctor, which explains why he's out of the hospital. 'Yes, Lloyd. I got all fifteen of them.'

'You didn't call me back.'

It'd be so easy to explode and shout in his face.

'No. I didn't call you back.'

He watches me, still gripping the ice-cream counter. 'You're not going to, are you?'

'I told you – I need some time.'

'But that's just what you're saying, hoping I'll go away.'

For the first time, I look down at him from the driver's seat. 'What'd you really expect? Tossing a ball back and forth like *Field of Dreams*? Everything you said – everything we did – it was all poison. You lied and tricked me. On purpose. And, oh yeah, almost got me framed for murder, not to mention almost killed, all for your own selfish reasons.'

'That's not true. All we wanted was help with the shipment. And once we— In Alligator Alley, when you saved me—'

'Then what? You came to your senses and realized that the love of your long-lost son conquers all? Save it for the TV movie, Lloyd. I don't care that you cut ties with Roosevelt – you still knew I was on the phone with him every free minute. Even in the car, you never once said, "*Hey, Cal, your best friend is going all Judas on you.*" Why didn't you say something then?'

My father looks down, unable to face me.

'Lemme guess,' I add. 'You were worried if you told the truth, I'd walk away forever. Well, guess what? You get the same result either way. Karma is kinda a bitch like that.'

He nods to himself, still holding the ice-cream counter, still staring down. 'You'll understand when you—'

'When I what? When I have kids? Is that the parental chestnut you're reaching for? That I'd understand what you did if I had a son?'

'No, Calvin,' he says, finally looking up at me. 'You'd understand if you *lost* a son.'

I tighten my jaw and try to look away. But the words undo me, tugging on a bow – maybe it's a knot – that's buried far deeper inside me than the pain and rage of my current anger.

'I'm sorry for what I did, Calvin. I really am. It's just . . . in life, you can either be a hammer or a nail. And for far too long . . . I guess I got tired of being a nail.'

'But don't you see? You made me the nail instead. So no matter how much you want to justify it—'

'I don't want to justify it,' he interrupts. 'I admit: I wanted a better life. It was just . . . to see you . . . to *really* see you . . .' He looks away, then back, then away, pretending to stare at all the passing cars that whip up and down the beachfront strip. 'I just want to be forgiven.'

Outside the window, my father's grassy green eyes are even more terrified than that night in the park. He swallows hard and his big Adam's apple tightens like a fist.

'That heart of yours made of rocks?' Alberto calls out from the backseat. 'Give your ol' man a little somethin'!'

I can't help but laugh.

My dad leaps at the opening. 'Just hear me out on this, Calvin: A few weeks back, in the newspaper, there was this columnist who said, "Wouldn't it be great if we could live life backwards?" You start out dead and get that out of the way – then you wake up in old age and feel better every day. With each passing year, your illnesses disappear, and you get more hair, more handsome, more virile – and best of all, you keep getting younger, finally ending life as a fantastic orgasm,' he says with his zigzag smile. 'Okay, the column was just a joke, but imagine it a moment: What if all our mistakes – all the bad choices and painful regrets – would just undo themselves and fade into nothingness? Wouldn't that make this so much easier?'

I stare straight ahead. 'That isn't how life is, Lloyd.'

Up the block, a police car wails, fighting through the dinnertime traffic along the beach. As it gets closer, my father is bathed in the siren's glowing blue lights, which smooth away his wrinkles and flatter his sun-beaten skin. For those few seconds, as it passes, my father is young again. Just like on the night he pushed my mom.

'I forgive you, Lloyd.' I take a long, deep breath. 'I just don't want to see you.'

Still gripping the base of the window, my father simply stands there. There are some prisons with no bars.

But that doesn't mean you can't dig your way out.

'I'll always be your father, Cal.'

'I'm aware of that.'

'How 'bout this Friday, then?' he asks. 'We can go to dinner.'

The police car is long gone. But I still hear it in the distance.

'Maybe.'

Pumping the gas, I pull out toward the traffic. For the first few steps, my father holds on to the window, trying to limp along with the van. He doesn't get far.

'You like Indian food? We can grab Indian,' he calls out, excited.

'I *hate* Indian,' I call back, leaving him behind.

I peer out the window. He looks older again. Too old to run. But even in the darkness, even as he stops, I see his zigzag smile.

It matches my own.

As we zip up the block, I check the rearview to get a final look, but all I see is Alberto, his nose pressed to his RC Cola can with the plastic wrap on top.

'Let me ask you, Alberto – you really think it helps, talking to your dad's ashes like that?'

Alberto looks up, confused. 'Ashes? What you talkin' about?'

'In the can. Those aren't your dad's ashes?'

'Cal, I may be a drunk, but I ain't wacky.'

'But that night – you said—'

'Damn, boy – we was in a crowded van full of junkies and baseheads. I go tellin' 'em where I keep my piggy, and it'll be gone by lockdown.'

His *piggy*? 'Hold on. That's your *bank*?'

Flashing a gray-toothed smile, Alberto shakes the RC Cola can, and I hear bits of change *cling-cling* against the insulation of crumpled dollar bills. 'You keep it in yo' socks, they steal it,' Alberto says, beaming. 'It's like your story, Cal – that coffin you was chasin': Once people think there's a body inside . . . ain't no better hiding spot in the whole damn world.'

He's right about that. But in our case, with the coffin, there *was* a body in—

My heart lurches, leaping up to my throat.

Double crap.

I need an airline ticket.

80

Orchard Lake, Michigan

Judge Felix Wojtowicz wasn't a fool. Electrified from the moment he saw it, he knew the power of history. And ritual. And even the ceremonial value of a blood rite.

He knew – thanks to his own family's diaries – that the blood sacrament was what delayed his brethren at the Cave of Treasures all those years ago. So with Ellis's body at his feet, already wrapped in plastic, he knew he wouldn't make the same mistakes here.

Most of all, the Judge knew the stories from times past.

He knew that dating back to 3500 BC, Mesopotamian women used to wear cylinder seals – carved stone cylinders no bigger than the cork of a wine bottle, but with a hole through them, like pieces of ziti – around their necks to ward off nightmares and evil spirits.

He knew that early archaeologists mistakenly thought the seals were jewelry. But the true secret of the seals was what was carved on them. Indeed, when the seals were rolled in blood – like a roller stamp – they'd reveal pictures and stories.

And he knew that the best of these pictures even had their own narratives.

Like a book.

For decades, the archaeological community had overlooked so much. In 1899, *The New York Times* reported on the British Museum's unearthed cylinder seals that dated to 4000 BC in Babylonia. So many of them, when rolled in wet clay, revealed what the *Times* called 'biblical incidents,' including vivid carvings of the 'Genesis stories of the creation, of the fall of man, the flood, and others.'

Archaeologists at the time didn't know what to make of it.

But the Thules did.

Just as they understood that long before Babylonian times, man hid ancient secrets by carving them onto everyday objects – like the horns of goats or rams. Or sheep. Abel *was* a herder of sheep.

'I'm confused,' the sixty-year-old named Kenneth asked, carrying a wide cookie sheet of wet modeling clay to the glass bar. 'All the carvings on the weapon – they're faded and cracked away. Look at it, it's practically smooth. There's gonna be nothing to see.'

The Judge laughed to himself.

Again, he wasn't a fool. He knew – even anticipated (especially with a beast like Ellis) – that would be the case.

If this really was the weapon that murdered Abel – if the ivory-and-gray animal horn was indeed the true Mark of Cain – a Book of Truth – carved with God's greatest secrets and passed to Adam, to Abel, and eventually as a sign to Cain – surely the carvings would have faded over time.

But the Coptic monks who first unearthed it in the late sixteenth century? They weren't stupid, either.

Which was why they kept a backup copy.

The Judge stuffed his hands into a pair of white cotton gloves, then held the animal horn in one hand and picked up a brand-new X-Acto knife in the other. Just touching it, gripping it – Lord, to finally have it after all these

centuries – this wasn't just a find. It was a reawakening
for the whole movement. Thule revived!

Like a surgeon, he edged the knife underneath the lip
of the tanned flap of leather that covered the wide end of
the horn.

'You knew all this time, didn't you?' Kenneth asked as
his partner looked on behind him. 'You *knew* the monks
hid something inside.'

'I couldn't possibly know,' the Judge admitted. 'But I
had faith.'

With a sharp slice of the knife, the leather gave way,
opening with a silent burp and delivering a rancid stench
that wafted from the innards of the horn and smelled like
vinegar and foul eggs. It stung the Judge's nose and made
his eyes water. But he didn't look away.

Without a word, Judge Felix Wojtowicz peered inside.
His eyes narrowed, searching – then grew wide again.

'What? What's it say?' Kenneth asked.

The Judge didn't answer.

Panicking, he turned the horn over and shook it to
double-check. Nothing but a cloud of fine dust rained out.

'I-It can't be,' he stammered. 'Someone . . . they . . .
someone already took it.'

81

October 17, 1931
Cleveland, Ohio

'You okay with this, yes?' Mitchell Siegel asked in his heavily accented English.

His youngest son, Jerome, sat on the radiator, his foot anxiously tapping the floor, his eyes locked on the thick, oversize Bible that rested like a cinder block in his lap. He was a restless, gangly kid with a weak, pointy jaw, a bush-top of thick black hair, and oversize glasses that came off only at bedtime, during showers, and for yearbook photos.

'I can't, Pop. This is yours.'

'And now yours,' Mitchell insisted, his big voice bellowing from his big body.

Jerry was tempted to argue, but the truth was, he didn't want his father to take the book back.

'You keep it, then, yes?'

Jerry nodded, brushing his fingertips along the fine, tan leather. Smooth as skin. 'Can I just ask you . . . the object inside—'

'The totem,' his father said.

'The totem inside,' Jerry repeated, his foot still tapping as his knee rocked the book like a seesaw. 'Do you even know what it is?'

Mitchell's eyes went dark. 'You think that matter!? All

that matter is men gave lives for it. Men died for it, Jerome!'
Mitchell cut himself off, thinking back to how his own
father used to raise his voice. He took a heavy breath
through his nose. 'Is your gift now, Jerome. Yours to
protect.'

Shifting his weight on the radiator, Jerry glanced over
his shoulder and stared out the second-story window,
where his two older brothers played skully in the street.
'Why didn't you give it to Harry or Leo – or even Minerva?'
Jerry said, referring to his older sister. 'I mean, I'm the
smallest.'

Standing over his youngest son, Mitchell knew Jerry
was right. Of his six children, Jerry *was* the smallest. And
weakest. And least popular. When his siblings came home
from school and raced out to play games in the street,
Jerry regularly stayed inside, scribbling stories and drawing
daydreams.

Just as Mitchell used to back in Lithuania when he was
the same age.

'You argue with your father? Show respect!' his dad
insisted, seizing Jerry's shoulder in his meaty mitt.

Still staring outside, Jerry nodded, knowing better than
to fight.

For an instant, his father's grip softened and Jerry
thought his dad was about to say something else.

But he never did.

In a slow, heavy shuffle – Jerry always thought he was
hiding a limp – Mitchell Siegel headed for the door.

'Oh, say, Pop – can I ask one last thing?'

His father turned, framed by the threshold.

'What you said about those men – the ones in the cave,
with the cloaks and the blood and the—'

'What's your question, Jerome?'

Jerry looked at his father. 'They tried to kill you, didn't they?'

Mitchell didn't say anything.

'What if they try again?' Jerry asked, his foot tapping faster than ever.

'They won't,' Mitchell promised. 'They can't. There is no way they know where I am.'

Jerry nodded as though he understood. 'But still . . . when you were there . . . do you really think they were trying to create some kind of monster?'

'Jerome, this was long time ago. Nothing to worry about today.'

'I'm not worried. I—' Jerry put aside the book. His eyebrows furrowed. 'It's just, well . . . if someone really could do magic or summon something or build whatever Aryan creature those men were building . . .' He tilted his head slightly, and the streaming outdoor sun made him look like a little boy. 'I don't know, Pop. Couldn't it also be done for good instead?'

82

The word *Superman* comes from
Nietzsche's Übermensch and George Bernard
Shaw's *Man and Superman*.
But it was Hitler, stating he wanted a nation of 'supermen,'
that gave the term its popularity.
– Maltz Museum brochure

Today
Marina del Rey, California

'You look scared.'

'I'm not scared,' I tell Serena as I grip the steering wheel of our rental car, which is parked at the end of the wide cul-de-sac. 'I'm just nervous.'

'About this – or you still thinking about your father?'

I pause for a second too long. 'About this.'

In the passenger seat, Serena tucks her legs into an Indian-style position, never taking her eyes off me. 'If it makes you feel better about it, Cal, your dad—'

'Please don't give me a Buddha quote right now. Can't I just worry I'm being too easy on him?'

'Maybe you are,' she admits. 'But just remember—'

'I said no Buddha.'

'No Buddha. Just listen: When baby Superman gets rocketed to the planet Earth and his real parents die on Krypton, he lands here and gets two new flawless parents who treat him perfect as can be.'

'So?'

'So that's just a comic book. Real life has much more complicated endings. And beginnings.'

'And that's it? Now I'm supposed to feel better? Or just forgive him? Or not second-guess myself for potentially inviting him back into my life?'

She turns to me, her yellow blue eyes trying to absorb whatever pain and regret she thinks I'm feeling. She's not my girlfriend. I know she's not. But there's no denying the fact that throughout this whole mess, she's the one clear reminder, even with all the hokey self-help quotes, that not everything carries freight with it.

'Cal, the soul would have no rainbow if the eyes had no tears.'

I stare at her. She stares back, unblinking.

'That was Buddha, wasn't it?' I ask.

'Native American. Minquass tribe.'

I nod, still gripping the steering wheel. I fight for my clients every day, and I always will. It's nice to finally feel someone fighting for me. 'Have I thanked you for coming here?'

'Over nine times. You still nervous?'

I stare over her shoulder at our destination: the three-story, beige-and-white apartment building with the odd flock of pelicans nesting on top.

'Terrified,' I tell her.

'That's why you need to go. Without me. You're the one who needs to know, Cal.'

She's right about that.

As I nudge open the car door and step outside, the California sun salutes me. I hear the squawks of pelicans and a boat horn in the distance. We're not far from the marina.

'Take your time. I'll pick you up in an hour,' Serena calls out, already pulling away. She's worried if she waits around, I might back out. She's right.

Behind me, I hear the car take off and disappear.

Following the concrete path and counting door numbers, I make my way to the back of the older, three-story apartment building, where, just past a set of open jalousie windows, there's a coral-colored door with four different locks. I hear an old Dean Martin song playing inside. Just below the doorbell is the name:

SIEGEL

I study it for a minute, collecting my—

'I see you out there,' an elderly woman's voice announces. 'You here for the air-conditioning?'

It'd be simple to say yes. Or to flash my wallet in front of the eyehole and pretend I'm still a fed. She's gotta be nearly ninety. She wouldn't know the difference.

But I would. And this woman – and her family – deserves better.

'I'm – if you can – I was hoping to ask you about your husband,' I tell her.

The door stays shut. 'If you're one of those comic book people, I don't do interviews. I don't talk about Superman. I've told my stories,' she tells me.

'Ma'am, I don't care about Superman. I'm here about your husband. Jerry.'

'Then you care about Superman. You think you're the first yahoo to try that line?'

'Ma'am—'

'I've been putting up with people like you since 1948,' she yells through the door.

'I know who murdered Jerry's father.'

'Nice try. I've heard that one, too. Lemme guess: You wanna write a book. Everyone loves a mystery.'

'I know it wasn't a mystery. And I know Jerry saw it happen.'

There's a long pause. The pelicans continue to squawk.

'I found these,' I add, pulling the four panels of the old comic strip – with the old Thule symbol – from my pocket and holding it up to the peephole.

There's another long pause.

Tnnk. Tnnk. Cuunk. Tnnk. The locks come undone.

I'm expecting a frail Miami Beach Golden Girl. Instead, I get an elderly woman with teased reddish brown hair, lively dark eyes, and the most stunning cheekbones I've ever seen. According to the brochure from the museum, this woman posed for Jerry and Joe, making her the physical model for Lois Lane. Of course she's beautiful.

'Why don't you come inside, Mr . .'

'Cal Harper,' I say, extending a hand.

'Joanne,' she says, inviting me in without shaking back. 'Where'd you find the art?'

'In Jerry's Cleveland house. In his room,' I say, watching as she stares at the comic panels in my hand. 'You didn't know they were there, did you?'

She doesn't answer. Instead, she leads me into her living room, which is decorated in light pastels and sea-foam green. Just like the prison. There's a bookcase on our left, but the rest of the walls are filled – absolutely stacked – with picture frame after picture frame of family photos. Pictures of her and Jerry, her and her daughter, her and her grandchildren. There's not a single one of Superman.

Over by a white Formica credenza, she reaches for the double cassette player and lowers the Dean Martin volume – but doesn't turn it off. She doesn't like being alone. Me neither.

She takes a seat on her wicker-and-peach sofa, crossing her ankles like a true lady. 'Tell me what you want from us, Mr Harper.'

'No. No no no. I don't want anything.'

'Then why're you here?'

'I'm just— It's hard to explain.'

She raises a thin eyebrow. 'Every single day of my Jerry's life, someone wanted something: the lawyers, the reporters, the so-called fans, and don't even start me on the publisher. Before the whole mess went public, when Jerry was in his sixties, y'know he was reduced to sorting mail? The man creates a billion-dollar legend, and he spent his twilight years dropping packages on people's desks and fighting to get paid for it. Even when they finally wrote the check and tried to make right, everyone eventually wanted something from him, Mr Harper. So you might as well tell me: Are you doing this for the cash or just for the story?'

'I know this sounds odd, Mrs Siegel. But I think . . . I think I'm doing this for my father, if that makes any sense.'

'It doesn't make any sense at all.'

'I know, but I was right before, wasn't I? Jerry did witness his dad's murder.'

At first, she's silent, staring off at the family photos that fill the wall. 'You need to understand, in the comic book, Superman was the hero, and Clark Kent was the act. But in real life . . . Clark Kent . . . that was Jerry.

The awkwardness, the fears, even the slight stammer –
he was the little guy that the bully would kick sand at on
the beach. But that would all disappear when he was
talking about his stories. Then he was a dynamo – excited,
energized – able to hold his own with anyone. It was like
he had this well of strength inside him that would over-
flow once you got him in his element. But only when he
was in his element. Did you ever meet anyone like that?'

I can't help but nod, seeing my own reflection in a
nearby picture frame. 'Every single day.'

'Y'know Hitler banned Superman? Mussolini also. Jerry
was flying then. But when he lost the rights to Superman
– when they took his name off it – Jerry the dynamo disappeared, too. But even then, even at his lowest, when the
electric company said they were shutting our power off,
he was still strong inside. Jerry took that beating in front
of everyone. And that – I can't explain it – but I know
that strength came from his dad.'

'That him?' I ask, pointing to a gray-tone photo of a
young, mustached man in a Russian army uniform. His
body is small and thin, barely filling his buttoned tunic.
In the photo, he's posed in front of a railing, as though
he's holding it to stand.

'That's Mitchell,' she says.

'So Jerry spoke of him often?'

'No. He just . . . he spoke of him *differently*.'

'But never in public.'

'See, that's the misconception. Sure, Jerry gave thousands of interviews, but just because he never mentioned
his father, people want to see it as a flaw or a controversy
– or say that Jerry didn't want to be pitied as the little boy
who lost his parent. But that's not why Jerry was so quiet
about his dad.'

'You think he was protecting him,' I say.

'He was protecting *something*,' she acknowledges.

'And you know what it is.'

'I never said that, Mr Harper.'

I shake my head, turning toward the bookcase on my left. The shelves are packed with mostly romance novels and a few random hardbacks, but along the top shelf, there's a set of tall leather books with the words *Superman, Clark Kent,* and *Lois Lane* across their respective spines. 'I know about the ashes, Mrs Siegel.'

For the first time since I've been here, Joanne Siegel's high cheeks fall.

To be fair, it was my father who mentioned the story: of Jerry Siegel splitting his ashes between a copper urn and a set of hollowed-out fake books that his wife was saving for when Cleveland finally builds a true Superman museum. But it wasn't until Alberto said the magic words that the truth finally hit me. Once people think there are ashes in something, it becomes the one hiding spot no one'll ever open.

Shazam.

'You're going to take it away now, aren't you?' she asks.

'I promised you, ma'am, I don't want anything.'

I walk toward the shelf. Joanne stays silent.

'Can you at least tell me what it is?' she finally asks.

Glancing over my shoulder, I stare back at Jerry Siegel's widow. Of course he never told her. The contents inside had already cost his father his life. If his wife knew the truth . . . if they ever came after her . . . No way would Superman ever put Lois in danger.

'You really don't know?' I ask.

'I have an idea. But not for sure.'

I pull out the fake books and realize there's one more

book attached to the set: a green one that says *The Spectre* on the spine. 'The Spectre?'

'Jerry's other great creation: A murdered man gets sent back by God to take vengeance on evil sinners,' Joanne explains.

'Sounds pretty biblical.'

'All the best stories are,' she says. 'Jerry always said that. Don't you see? Comic books aren't just a ragbag of words and pictures. The Superman story exists in every culture on this planet. We all need our heroes. And our villains. So how could it not be like the Bible? Jerry apologized for it, but I don't. There's nothing wrong with wanting someone to save us – or admitting we can't do it all ourselves.'

'Yeah . . . my pastor used to say that.'

'Your pastor's right. Jerry never learned that part. Always thought he could fight the world himself – or at the very least outsmart it,' she says, focusing back on the hollow books that supposedly hold half of her husband's ashes.

With her nodded permission, I lower them from the shelf, and it's clear that all the volumes are glued together as one. Sure enough, there's a small latch in back. With a flick, it opens and the spines of the books pop forward half an inch, like a barely opened drawer.

'You're nervous,' Joanne Siegel says behind me.

But all I hear is Roosevelt's voice buzzing in my head with theories of God's most precious gift passing from Adam to Cain, from Mitchell Siegel to his son, and at the cherry-top of this surreal sundae, somehow, from my father to me. According to Roosevelt, when Cain repented, God gave him a mark, a sign, this Book of Truth that contained the secrets of immortality.

I don't believe in magic. Or immortal gifts from God. But I do believe that there are some sons who will do anything to carry out their father's final wishes. And protect their family.

I edge my fingertip into the crack and pull on the spines of the books, revealing a deep, tissue-lined compartment that holds two sheets of paper stuck together. I finger-tweeze them out, feeling how sticky they are. Of course. Jerry's favorite. Wax paper.

Like the holder for the original comic book, the paper's been melted and sealed around the edges, preserving what-ever's inside. I try my best to peer through it – there's definitely writing of some kind – but it's all mottled and brown, impossible to read. This isn't another comic book. From the crumbled bits of sand and stone collected at the bottom, it's something far older than that.

After tearing the corner of the wax paper, I poke my finger in and slide it like a letter opener down the right-hand side. My hands should be trembling. But they're not. Whatever's inside, I just want the answer.

A thin stream of sand pours down in a fine waterfall as my letter opener finger slides along the bottom edge of the wax seal. Inside is an ancient sheet of – it's not paper. The way it's yellowed and dried . . . as if it's written on some kind of animal skin. But it's not until I fold back the protective wax cover that I get my first good look.

My eyes narrow, then widen. Dean Martin continues his serenade.

Oh my wow.

It . . . it exists: the one and only chapter of the Book of Truth.

Behind me, Joanne says something. I don't hear it.

The only sound in the world is the slow-motion *poomp-puuum* of my own heartbeat.

Bits of the dried animal skin crack off as I touch it.

It's not some cryptic message in Hebrew. Or Greek. Or some lost ancient tongue I can't understand.

The Book of Truth is written in the one language the whole world speaks.

It's a picture.

And it's glorious.

At first it looks like an etching, but the way it's framed at the corners – like a stamp . . . or a seal. The horn . . . this is the carving that was on the horn. Someone pressed it in ink and rolled it like a rubber stamp. Right onto the skin.

I study the lines, which are rough, almost primitive. The pale brown color . . . it's dried blood. Ancient blood. But what makes my eyes well with tears is the picture itself: It's rudimentary, with poor, crude dimensions – but there's no mistaking the image of a young child sitting on his parent's lap – his father's lap – as the man whispers something in his ear.

A story.

A father telling his child a story.

My brain turns into the skid, searching for traction. At first I assume it's Adam, whispering to Abel . . . to Cain . . . it's gotta be one of his sons. My eyes scan it again, inspecting each ragged line for clues. The way the father leans in close . . . the way the boy dips his head downward, like he's relishing every detail. I think of Bible stories from when I was young – of Noah and his quest to save God's creatures. I think of Jerry Siegel, alone in his bedroom, staring at his ceiling. And of course, I think of my father and all the secrets and stories

I missed. So much harm comes into this world when the wrong thing is said. But that's nothing compared to the pain from what goes unsaid.

The image blurs from my tears, but with an eyeblink, they're gone. And I see father and son and story. Clear as can be.

Roosevelt . . . Roosevelt was right. It *is* a birthright – a mark – a sign – the ultimate remembrance – a 'book' that Adam created to pass all earthly knowledge. The instructions are right there:

Tell your story.

That's the secret of immortality. The one true way to live forever.

'So it's one of Mitchell's old sketches, right? Something he did for Jerry maybe back in Lithuania?' Joanne calls out behind me.

I blink more tears from my eyes and feel the smile that's overtaken my face, and all I can think about is Ellis and the Thules. Their theories were so wrong. But when they called it magic . . .

They were absolutely right.

'Yeah, it's just one of Mitchell's old sketches,' I say, sliding the brittle parchment back into its protective cover, which I tuck back into its hollow hiding spot behind Jerry's greatest creations.

'Jerry always hoped it would go into a Superman museum – y'know, let his dad live on and all. But Cleveland barely seems to acknowledge that Jerry and Joe even existed. I mean, those boys created *Superman*, for God's sake. But you know how it is . . . some dreams linger for years.'

'And some last forever,' I tell her, returning the fake books to the shelf.

'So that's it? You just came to see the sketch? No Superman questions? No were-you-really-the-model-for-Lois-Lane?'

'I got what I needed, ma'am, thank you,' I tell her. 'By the way, these are for you,' I add as I hand her the four original comic strips that we pulled from Jerry's wall.

She fans out all four panels on the glass table in front of her, then stares at them with the kind of look that elderly women save for their wedding photos.

'I can't pay you for these,' she says, her voice quivering.

'Your husband already did,' I say, heading for the door. I know they're worth a ton. I don't care. Everything eventually has to make its way home again.

'Wait!'

She thanks me with a sweet peck on the cheek. I got a kiss from Lois Lane. Then Joanne Siegel waves goodbye, and the door closes behind me.

I head down the breezeway, the father and son image still fixed in my mind.

'What's with the happy face?' a familiar voice calls out.

I turn just in time to see Naomi sitting on the bottom step of the open stairwell. There's a bandage still on her arm.

'You're kidding, right?' I ask. 'C'mon, Rambo, war's over.'

'I can't help myself. We always get our man.'

'Naomi, my deal with your bosses – to nail Roosevelt, to ID Ellis – we're done. Finished. So don't take this the wrong way, but coming this far? Sometimes you just gotta let things go.'

'Says the man who couldn't stop chasing his dad.'

It's a slight push, but I see that smirk in her eyes.

'Look, Cal, I just wanted to say . . . no hard feelings, okay?'

I know her better than that. 'You flew all this way just to say *thanks*?'

'I didn't say *thanks*. I said *no hard feelings*.'

'Naomi, tell me why you're really here.'

She bites at her bottom lip, then finally looks up, standing from the steps. 'You flew across the country with barely seven hours' notice. The animal horn is still missing. I was worried you were coming here to meet up with Ellis.'

'How do you know I wasn't?'

She motions to her phone. 'I just got the call. They found Ellis's body. In Michigan.'

I nod but don't reply.

'And that weird gun he had that I wrecked at the library? With the hemlock? They matched it to what was in Timothy's blood. Oh, and we also found a twenty-thousand-dollar payment in Timothy's bank account. From a fake name they think was Ellis.'

She kicks at the concrete. We all have our own secret identities.

'Y'know, I still think your father – I don't care what kinda rosy picture you painted in his plea deal – I still think he got into this for the wrong reason.'

I don't argue with her. But she doesn't understand.

'Don't think I don't understand,' she adds. 'My son? He was an orphan, too.'

'Naomi, please spare me the rah-rah.'

'I'm just saying, if his parents came back, I wouldn't blame him for wanting to find out who they really are. It's not a weakness, Cal. I mean, most people don't *really* want to know their parents. They just want to know themselves.'

'That doesn't make me feel better.'

'It will when you think about it,' she promises. 'I'm a mother. We're not wrong.'

I can't help but grin. I head up the covered walkway toward the car. But Naomi doesn't follow.

'So whatever happened with the Book of Lies . . . or Truth . . . or whatever you named it?' she calls out. 'Y'ever figure out what the story was with those old comic strips from Jerry's wall?'

I spin around and see her staring at Joanne Siegel's closed door.

'No. Not really,' I tell her.

She stays locked on the door.

'Yeah . . . me either,' she finally says, following in back of me and leaving Joanne Siegel behind.

I nod a thank-you. She pretends she doesn't notice.

As we reach the end of the breezeway, the sun bakes us from overhead.

'Just tell me one last thing,' she adds. 'You really traveled three thousand miles just to see Jerry Siegel's widow?'

'Yeah. I did.' I turn to Naomi. 'Though I thought you didn't know who I was meeting with?'

This time, she's the one who's silent. But the smile on her face says it all.

'By the way, about your son . . .' I start. 'Y'ever tell him what you do?'

'With what? With work?'

'With anything. Does he know what your job is? What you fight for?'

'He knows I have a gun. That's enough to impress him.'

I shake my head. 'No. You need to tell him. Tell him your stories.'

For a moment, she makes a face, loading up the quick comeback.

But it never comes.

'I will,' she says, brushing her dyed brown hair from her face.

We both cross the small grass patch that leads to the cul-de-sac. 'So how do you explain to your boss that the animal horn is still out there, and you're coming home empty-handed?' I ask.

'Empty-handed? I got a nibble on Ellis's old phone records. There's a judge in Michigan I'm gonna go say hello to,' she says. 'And you know judges just hate wearing those PlastiCuffs,' she adds, already starting to wave goodbye. 'Just remember, though, Cal: You only lose what you cling to.'

'That's nice. That Native American?'

'Buddhist,' she calls back, ducking into her white rental car.

Her tires howl, she takes off, and I'm left standing in the empty cul-de-sac as the wind shoves my white hair back, revealing my face.

Serena won't be here for at least a half hour. I'm alone. All alone. And for once, I think that's how it's supposed to be.

On my far right, between two other apartment buildings, I spot the edge of a dock and a few bobbing boats.

Before I even realize it, I'm walking toward it.

Jerry's father had it so damn right. There's the life you live and the life you leave behind. But what you share with someone else – especially someone you love – that's not just how you bury your past. It's how you write your future.

Following the nearby path and a few pelicans, I head toward the lapping splash of water at the marina in the distance. Even between the buildings, the sun shines like gold from overhead.

With a final, deep breath, I crane my neck back and stare straight up at the heavenly blue sky.

'I know it's been a while, Mom. But have I got a story for you . . .'

AUTHOR'S NOTE

Over the past two years, I've spent far more time than I ever anticipated thinking I could solve the murder of who killed Mitchell Siegel. From the original death certificate, to the built-in lore that comes with any family's stories, to tracking down the old owners of the funeral home that held his body in 1932, I took up this quest in the hopes of unearthing real answers about why the world actually got Superman. And to this day, I am convinced that the only reason young Jerry Siegel dreamed of a bulletproof man is because of the robbery that took his father.

But to be clear, this book is a work of fiction. Yes, Mitchell Siegel was in the Russian army, and there is no explanation for how (at such a young age and with no money) he got out of the army and was able to come to America, but that does not mean that he was a government asset or that he found the murder weapon that Cain used to kill Abel.

But.

The details of Jerry's life – the unsolved, uninvestigated death of his father, the fact that half the family was told it was a heart attack and the other half a shooting, the two Superman stories that preceded *Action Comics* (one whose art is seen in these pages, of a robber pointing a gun at an innocent man), that all of this happened right after Mitchell died, *plus* the fact that in thousands of interviews, Jerry never once – not once – ever mentioned his father *at all* – these observations are not just me playing fanboy psychologist (okay, maybe it partly is). The death certificate says Mitchell Siegel had a heart attack during a robbery. The robbery was never investigated. No autopsy was done. And at least one of the coroners I spoke to pointed out that a small .22-caliber gun (favored in 1932 during the Depression) would not leave an entry mark in someone's chest (easily making anyone there mistake it for a heart attack). We'll never know. But in that moment, young Jerry did create the ultimate orphan story. And in 1932, the newspaper did run an editorial about vigilantes – written by someone named Luther – the day after his father's death. There are parts of this story that cannot be argued away.

Jerry Siegel knew the benefits of thinking big, which is why he hid his ashes inside a set of fake books in the hopes that his memory would live on forever (that's true, too). And in a place like America, which was founded on our own legends and myths, I believe it's vital that we know where those myths come from, even if it means admitting our own vulnerabilities. That's how we truly honor our heroes.

For me, Superman's greatest contribution has never been the superhero part; it's the Clark Kent part – the idea that any of us, in all our ordinariness, can change the world.

As for Cain and the Thule Society, it is true that in 1936, the head of the Nazi SS went to explore the first rock art site in Sweden, in one of many quests to find the origins of the Aryan race. What they unearthed was a carving of a man with raised arms, which they believed was 'the Son of God.' The explorations continued for years, many led by Thule leaders. What else did they find? C'mon, I gotta have something to put at www.BradMeltzer.com.

Finally, and perhaps most important, in the past few months, a small group of us have been working to raise money to save the bright blue Siegel house that is now falling apart on Kimberly Avenue in Cleveland. The city ignored it for decades. Not anymore. By the time you read this, the house should finally have its plaque. Wanna see what else we can do? Visit www.Ordinary-PeopleChangeTheWorld.com.

Brad Meltzer
Fort Lauderdale, Florida, 2008

BRAD MELTZER

THE BOOK OF FATE

In six minutes, one of us would be dead.
None of us knew it was coming . . .

So says Wes Holloway, a once cocky and ambitious presidential aide, about the day that changed his life forever. On that Fourth of July, Wes put the chief executive's oldest friend into the presidential limousine. By the time the trip came to an end, Wes was permanently disfigured, and Ron Boyle was dead, the victim of a crazed assassin.

Eight years later, Boyle is spotted, alive and well. Trying to figure out what really happened takes Wes back to a decade-old presidential crossword puzzle, mysterious facts buried in Masonic history, and a code invented by Thomas Jefferson two hundred years ago.

But what Wes doesn't realize is that The Book of Fate holds everyone's secrets. Especially the ones worth dying for . . .

Out now

HODDER